THE WILL

JOE EDD MORRIS

Black Rose Writing | Texas

ISBN: 978-1-68513-344-3
PUBLISHED BY BLACK ROSE WRITING
www.blackrosewriting.com

Printed in the United States of America
Suggested Retail Price (SRP) $21.95

The Will is printed in Garamond Premier Pro

Map artwork courtesy of Jan Cobb

*As a planet-friendly publisher, Black Rose Writing does its best to eliminate unnecessary waste to reduce paper usage and energy costs, while never compromising the reading experience. As a result, the final word count vs. page count may not meet common expectations.

To Bill Rutledge

In memory of my father, William Edward "Bill" Morris

characters spring from the earth itself. This is a book you won't put down. A story you will remember for many years to come. What a novel. What a writer."

–Steve Yarbrough

"A Powerful Redemptive Epic: One of Joe Edd Morris's great gifts as a writer is to immerse the reader fully into time and place. For his redemptive epic *The Will*, Morris covers much ground in 1950s Mexico, but in the process carries the reader across the country's tangled history, one riddled with disappointment and tempered by hope. In the journey of Jo Shelby's journey to regain his rightful legacy, we discover how the quiet determination of those long oppressed can address injustices. The novel demonstrates how the peasant classes in both Mexico and the American South have had to pick their way nimbly and cleverly across minefields of corruption to find the way forward. Led by Jo Shelby's charming pigheadedness, a younger generation of Mexicans, including the misunderstood Juan, the resourceful Carmen, and the young lawyer Edgardo, demonstrate a willingness to adapt and fight as powerful forces seek to continue to control the land about them.

All that said, *The Will* is a riveting and fun read. The love triangle among Jo Shelby, Carmen, and Jo Shelby's longtime sweetheart Athen gives that novel an emotional gravity that can be poignant and amusing, sometimes simultaneously both. And the efforts for restoration of both Senora Moncada's hacienda and Jo Shelby's land lead to some memorable confrontations, especially a climax worthy of the best Westerns.

Ultimately, the novel cuts a swath that returns an old legacy and begins a new one. It resides in the shadows of Zapata in Mexico and lurches toward the plight of the Southern black man. It is a sweeping romance in terms of its depiction of time, place, and love. But ultimately, The Will is most true to its title, in that while Jo Shelby must track down the physical will to prove his legacy, he and the compadres in the novel must summon the deepest reserves of their own wills to begin to right so many wrongs. Morris's style manages to be charmingly plainspoken in its eloquence, a wonderful narrative voice true to the tradition of Twain."

—Michael Hartnett, Best-selling author of
The Blue Rat *and* **The Blue Gowanus**

THE

WILL

River
Mississippi
Rome
Parchman
Greenville
Louisiana
ALABAMA
MISSISSIPPI
New Orleans
GULF
OF
MEXICO
Vera Cruz

TEXAS
MEXICO
Piedras Negras
Eagle Pass
Laredo
Brownsville
Monterrey
Matamoros
Saltillo
Matehuala
San Luis Potosí
Querétaro
Ciudad de México
Cuernavaca
Taxco
Hacienda Michapa

GENEOLOGY

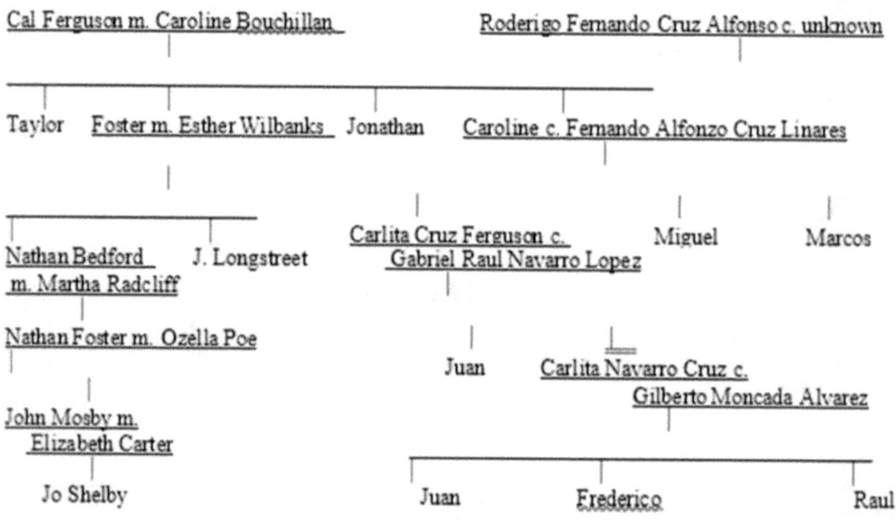

Cal Ferguson m. Caroline Bouchillan
Roderigo Fernando Cruz Alfonso c. unknown
Taylor
Foster m. Esther Wilbanks
Jonathan
Caroline c. Fernando Alfonzo Cruz Linares
Nathan Bedford
m. Martha Radcliff
J. Longstreet
Carlita Cruz Ferguson c.
Gabriel Raul Navarro Lopez
Miguel
Marcos
Nathan Foster m. Ozella Poe
Juan
Carlita Navarro Cruz c.
Gilberto Moncada Alvarez
John Mosby m.
Elizabeth Carter
Jo Shelby
Juan
Frederico
Raul

"The will is the strong blind man who carries on his shoulders the lame
who can see."
-Arnold Schopenhauer

Part I

I

Carlota, he whispered, the word coming from his mouth like a sigh, a supplication.

What did you say? she said standing beside him, her eyes scanning the same patchwork of erratic trails and anemic coffee and tobacco and sugar cane plots and makeshift tawdry structures set in among them and white-blossomed orange trees of golden fruit rising occasionally from the scruffy and disheveled irregularity of it all like fresh flowers in an old untended graveyard.

They had taken a bus from Vera Cruz and told the driver to let them off at Paraje Nuevo where a lady in the Bureau de Turismo had told them they might find the American confederado village, or what was left of it. But all they saw when they got there was a small cluster of houses and tiendas with a railroad running through them then a snow-bearded Mexican perched on the stoop of a tienda next to the railroad pointed a shaky finger in the direction they were looking and said, Allí. Pero, no mas.

Carlota, he answered her, louder, above the chirruping birds on a utility wire overhead and cacophony of local traffic moving behind them. That was the name of the Empress. My great-great-great-granddaddy and grandmama and their children had a place here ... somewhere. He thought where their house might have been, his eyes attracted to a grove of mango trees where a brook ran through, to a fenced structure within its dim shade that was not house and not hut and not jacale and not anything in between but something sure enough cobbled up from the tattered leftovers of somebody else's.

Silence. For a long moment neither spoke.

Then she stepped closer to him, cautiously, as one might the bereaved standing before an open casket, and held his hand. But, Jo Shelby, there's nothing here but Mexican farms and dirt trails.

Once there wadn't. Once there were houses and shops and hotels. There were governors and senators and generals. There was even cotton. That was almost a hundred years ago. Juaristas and bandidos and free-booters undid it all in a night. Gone. He snapped his finger. Snuffed out like a candle. Stores and houses robbed. Men shot dead on their doorstep. Suit cases and trunks and what was in them strewn all over the streets. Folks scrambling to get out. From what my great-grandmama Caroline wrote in her last letter it's a miracle she and the colonel and their families got out alive. It's a miracle I got any kin at all alive down here.

It's a miracle you've got yourself, she said, her voice as solemn, slipping into the seriousness of his mood.

The Confederates came that way, he said, raising his arm toward the cloudless sky and pointing west as if he hadn't heard her. Over those mountains from Mexico City where they'd met with the emperor, Maximillian, and he gave em this land. Within a year it was gone and they went back the way they came, at least the old colonel and his family did. His hand was still raised as he spoke, as if in benediction, then he brought it down. That's where we're headed. He placed an arm around her shoulder and pulled her closer to him then let his arm drop. Let's go. It's too sad here.

There was no bus from Paraje Nuevo to Mexico City so they hitched a ride with a local farmer into nearby Córdoba, a small city painted in pinks and blues with a spacious zócalo sided with arcades and a large church with a chiming clock. Red and green and white banners draped from the eaves of the buildings and lampposts and streamers of the same color radiated outward from the square's center. The next bus for Mexico City left in an hour, leaving them time for a snack. From a street vender Jo Shelby bought some steamed corn on a stick and cacahuates and Cokes and they sat on a shaded bench in the plaza and ate.

This is a nice place, she said. What are the decorations for? Vera Cruz had them, too.

It's for their independence celebration, or one of them.

They've got more than one?

Yep. They been at it a while.

Guess that's why I left home the way I did. I was in a bigger hurry for mine.

Hurry's not a word down here.

They ate.

Wonder what their thinkin right now, your mama and daddy and brothers, he said, breaking the silence. Takin off the way you did.

Jake and Josh don't care. They're too busy drinking and carousing. As for mama and daddy, there's not much more for them to think. I spelled it out in a three-page letter I left. I told you that.

He nodded as his eyes leveled out over the stick of corn his teeth were digging into then he drew it away from his mouth to speak. You didn't say what you said.

I just told them I was tired of them running my life, making my decisions for me. I was tired of pretending to be somebody I wasn't. I was tired of smiling when I felt like crying and saying yes when I meant no. I was tired of cotillion and debutante balls and pedigree and pecking order and all that. I was tired of the Delta. When you challenged them over the title to the land, stood up in court the way you did and they did everything they could to get me to testify against you, turn me against a friend; that was the last straw. Teaching jobs are a dime a dozen. I can always come back to one. I told them I still loved them but getting away seemed more important at the time. Besides, I thought it would be fun, she grinned. But I didn't write that.

He grinned back satisfactorily over his corn and said nothing, her use of the word friend lingering on in his rumination.

A warm Gulf breeze blew up the slopes of the Sierra Madre Oriental and stirred the air around them. She'd worn her hair in a ponytail but taken it down and the wind lifted the dark tresses from around her face so her emerald green eyes burned brightly in the midday sunlight. He thought how much more beautiful she looked natural, without the made-up sorority face and stylish clothes and Delta plantation glamour she'd run off and left behind. How much more the Athen of old, when they were growing up together. On the same land but in separate worlds. Her father, the master; his, the hired hand. That wasn't how it had always been. Somewhere a half-century along the way a will got lost. Or suppressed or stolen or hijacked. That's why he was in Mexico and she was with him, though her reasons were less certain. When he was in prison on a twenty-year sentence, she'd gone on with her life, her parents happy he was out of it until he showed up on their doorstep six years later free and reinstated in life. He left for Mexico and gave her a second chance to wait for him and when he came back she was wearing the same Greek letters around her neck again. They worked through all that and fought her mama and daddy and brothers and the rest of the Delta it seemed only to have her run off again because he was taking her family to court over land she would inherit some day. He thought they had that worked out then she said they didn't. He needed to grow up and get the land out of his system because she had it out of hers with a teaching career waiting on her and only time would tell if they were meant to be. Then she showed up at the court trial and not only didn't testify against him but for him and several days later stepped up into the bus at Indianola and plopped down beside him and said she was getting her heart in the right place. None of it would make sense to anybody on the outside and only a little seeping through to him on the inside but he was glad she was with him. Then he thought of what lay ahead, not what but who, and how much simpler the trip would have been without her. There were times a man just had to take what came and adjust his life accordingly. Time would tell. It always did. What day is it? he said.

Wednesday, September 7, she said. I'll tell you the year in case you forgot, she said and winked teasingly at him.

There was a time I did, he said unsmiling, his thoughts spiraling back to the six years in prison for the crime he didn't commit and his release, almost to the day the year before, nineteen hundred and fifty-four, when he read his great-grandmama's letters and struck out for Mexico with forty dollars in his pocket and an old Navy Colt that wouldn't shoot looking for his long-lost confederado kin, the only family he had left in the world. He thought of all he'd been through, the Mexican prison the gun had landed him in on that long trip and the kind man who got him out and the man's beautiful daughter in Mexico City who got the gun out of hock for him and there his thinking stopped. Because there was where he needed to go next.

Why did you need to know the day? I thought you said time didn't matter down here.

Just seems like we oughtta be further along, he said.

They continued eating, in silence, one she seemed uneasy with, like an intuition gnawing at her, something women have that men don't.

A penny for your thoughts, she said.

Still thinking about Carlota, he said, what the place is called now.

Paraje Nuevo?

Yeah.

What's it mean?

New Place. Which reminds me. I need to start teaching you a little Spanish, in case we get separated.

I'm not planning on that happening.

We're in Mexico now. No such thing as plannin down here. Everything's day to day. Mañana and no problema.

Now, I know those words.

You might wear em out.

Nothing was said for a while and they continued eating.

Which independence day is it? she said.

September sixteen. It's the big one, like our Fourth of July. They were having it when I was down here. Goes on for days, before and after. He told her the story, as much as he could remember that had been passed on to him from his first journey, of the dictators, the country's plight for freedom, the back-and-forth seesaw of power in the name of freedom, but not freedom, how the people still had no real voice. He could have told her more, but he'd leave that to his great-aunt, Senora Moncada. She'd lived it. When he finished, Athen had stopped eating, her eyes rapt, scanning his face for more of the country's history.

The bus departed a few minutes late and was crowded, but they were able to find a seat at the back. The vehicle was a sight better and cleaner than ones he'd ridden, the people more nicely dressed, more intelligent looking, a suggestion this part of the country was faring better than the stretch he'd seen the year before when he'd traveled south from Monterrey.

The trip to Mexico City took five hours, the lady at the ticket booth had told them. Athen had insisted on paying for her ticket, as she had most everything else along the way. She'd sold her sports car and gathered what savings she had from the same Mississippi bank where, if her father hadn't cut her off completely, her inheritance, the land, was in hock. That was another problem he'd have to deal with if he found the old colonel's will saying it belonged to his family to begin with. He remembered something about a Roman general who'd crossed a river and when he did there was no going back. He couldn't remember the name of the river, but the general's name was Caesar and he figured Athen was head to toe with him. He thought, too, of his last venture into the country, of the loneliness of that solitary journey and how often he manufactured her presence in his thoughts and dreams and how her sitting beside him now almost made that agony an afterthought as the bus left the city and began its climb into the high sierras. He wondered, too, how long the feeling would last, if she might backtrack and try to re-cross that river and find that teaching job after she met Carmen. When she saw Carmen she was gonna shit. He might, too.

The road ascended the dramatic rise of the Oriental, leveling occasionally in valleys and plains where they saw fields of coffee growing in the mountainshade and tobacco drying on racks and vast emerald cane fields surrounding sugar mills, the ragged banana and papaya and pineapple patches of the coastal plain long behind them. In Fortin de las Flores they passed gardens of gardenias and camellias and orchids and azaleas, nurseries and Indian women with small baskets selling flowers, venders at stalls selling fruit and local honey. In a wide valley where the mountains seemed to have fallen away she let out a gasp. What is that?

That's Pico de Orizaba, the tallest mountain in Mexico. There's more up ahead, prettier'n it.

I don't think they could be more beautiful, she said, her eyes fixed on the snow-capped cone, alone against the brilliant blue sky, its symmetrical russet sides sloping onto the green-quilted plain as if a god had reached down and pinched the earth's skin, pulled it to that perfect tented shape.

The trip was long and he had tried to sleep but with every turn in the road a different sight slid into view and she would punch him and marvel in awe as though scenes from a fantasy had suddenly sprung to life.

I can't get over these mountains, she said.

It ain't the Delta, he said. You ever even seen a mountain before?

Just The Smokies. Daddy and mama would take us vacationing there. But The Smokies are just bumps on the earth compared to these.

What was that you were going to Atlanta to teach?

English.

You'd make a good un. Got a way with words. I'd never seen a mountain till I came here. First time I saw em I thought they were clouds trapped on the land.

You don't do so bad yourself, she said.

How's that?

With words.

Maybe. If I could just get em in the right order. He thought about what he'd said and the order he needed to get his thoughts in as the bus entered Mexico City and the Avenida Zargoza and the lights and scenes of the city in the early dusk began sliding by.

So this is Mexico City? she said.

Sí, he said. Ciudad de México. But they just call it México, like the country. It's bout as big.

She scooted up on the edge of the seat to get a better view of the passing sights, the rows of shops and lights, the garish glitter, the streams of competing traffic, the brilliant energy.

Where will we stay? she said, as if suddenly overwhelmed by the vastness of the place, their minuteness within it.

In front of them a small child had turned around, his dark eyes examining the sombrero propped on Jo Shelby's knee and he probed his thoughts for an answer as simple as the innocence he saw in the child's eyes.

Remember the gun I told you about?

Yes. More than once.

It belonged to my great-great-great-granddaddy Cal, the colonel, and somehow ended up in the family trunk along with my grandmama's letters. That's one I hadn't been able to figure out.

What's that?

Why he'd take his family to Mexico with General Shelby and his bunch, knowing he'd have to fight his way all the way to Mexico City, and leave a perfectly good firearm behind.

There's probably a reason.

There's a reason for everything, he said. In this case he must've just given it to Foster, the son who stayed behind, because he figured Foster was going to need it more against Yankees than he was against Mexicans. That's the only reason I can come up with.

So? What does all this have to do with where we stay?

He thought a moment.

The child reached a tiny hand over the back of the seat and began toying with the blue cord around the hat's crest.

Well … . He cleared his throat. The man in the Mexican prison who helped get me out, Ramon …

Yes?

His daughter … he's got this daughter, see … she lives here, in Mexico City … and I wired her money, a hundred dollars, to get the gun out of hock before the time ran out and it got put up for sale. The dealer agreed to hold it six months.

You never told me about her. She turned and faced him, her eyes narrowed, the city flowing around them suddenly insignificant to her.

The child let go the cord and spun back around.

Well I … I never really thought to, he said, knowing he was lying. Knowing she knew he knew it, too.

I see. That was all she said, her voice, like her eyes, shifting quickly from surprise to irritation.

So I need to …

So you need to get the gun back and we're going to stay with her.

Yessum. That bout sums it up.

She said nothing, turned her face momentarily toward the window then back.

What's her name?

Carmen.

Is she special to you?

Not like you. We're just friends.

But she's special.

I didn't say that. The gun is what's special and she's got it. That's all. I would've come back for it regardless.

She faced the window again and said nothing but he saw her reflected image in the glass, the glowering hurt trying to decide where to look, what to say next. But she did neither, just sat there and stared silently at the passing crowds and lights and signs, the anonymous blur of the city.

Just friends, he thought, as the bus weaved in and out of traffic and around the glorietas with their lit-up statues and geometrical displays of flowers. Just friends, as the trees and globed lights lining the wide avenues they'd walked down flicked by. Just friends, as a sidewalk restaurant where they'd had coffee came into view and further down the street from it, a cinema where they watched Gary Cooper and Grace Kelly in High Noon and the man sang Oh don't forsake me o my darlin and it all came back. He'd spent last Christmas with her on his return trip home. They'd held hands across candlelit tables and strolled the Paseo arm-in-arm. They'd sat drinking wine shoulder-to-shoulder on her couch and shared deep parts of themselves. On the last night before heading north her moist dark eyes and a haze of alcohol drew him close and they kissed, then again ... and again. But no hand moved further. They did not sleep together. A mutual respect and something, someone, moved between them. They were just friends. Or was that a lie, too? Had he stayed longer, might he have stayed for good? Where he'd left off, was that where he was expected to pick back up?

The bus drove on.

The depot was the same he'd been before and much busier. They stepped down from the bus and waited while the driver climbed on top and handed the luggage down to a porter.

Here, you take this, Jo Shelby said, handing Athen his valise. It looks more like a woman's sewin satchel than a suitcase.

Then why did you buy it?

Cause that was all Pinkus had and I was short on time, he said, picking up her duffel bag, one her brother had brought back from the army and she had pulled from the attic. Follow me.

They entered a large open high-ceilinged area with rows of wooden benches. They found one that was empty and sat down, placed their luggage before them on the floor. The place was as noisy as he remembered, the low roar of people scurrying about, loudspeakers barking arrivals and departures, venders calling out their wares. The large clock over the sallygate to the buses said almost six.

He pulled a tattered map from his valise and opened it on his knees. This is where we are here, he said, pointing to an X previously made. She placed a hand on his shoulder, as if she'd forgotten her earlier anger, and leaned over to see. And this is where we need to go. He pushed his finger upward, crossing grids of streets and fine print, kept it moving until it stopped at a short street just off a major thoroughfare in the far north of the city. The small print said Av. Toltecas.

That looks like it's out of the city limits, she said, her finger tracing a dark dotted line stitching the outer edge of the map.

It's a ways.

I guess you have the address, she said.

Not written down. It's 521 Toltecas.

She removed her arm from his shoulder and pulled away from him. Oh, so you have it memorized, she said, her voice clipped.

I didn't work at it.

She opened her mouth to say something then shut it. A few seconds went by and she tried again. Does she even know you're coming?

She knows I'm comin, just not when.

Don't you think you should call her and let her know we're coming instead of just dropping in out of the night? Do you have her phone number? She'd twisted sideways on the bench with her hands on her hips, driving the words at him like she would when they were kids growing up on the plantation and her status, not her age, gave her permission to boss.

Nope. She doesn't have one.

She didn't look convinced.

She's got a job, he said, but it takes every centavo to keep herself fed and clothed and a roof over her head.

Athen glanced up at the clock. It's after six. If we're going, we need to go. By that map, it looks like it might be several miles. We can take a taxi.

He flinched and snapped around like he'd been stung from behind. I'm not gettin in a taxi. Damn near got killed in one last time I was down here. They make bats outta hell look like canaries in a cage. We can walk. It's not that far. I walked it before.

I'm sure you did, she said cooly, but you didn't have a suitcase and a duffel bag.

We can take a bus, he said.

Night fell fast, the darkness complete when the bus stopped and they got off.

We're on the side of a mountain, Athen said as she stepped into the street and looked back at the city below, its cupped glitter in the dark folds of mountains like an inverted bowl of starlit night. The air was cooler there and they took a moment to get out their jackets and put them on as the roar of the bus faded, its gears groaning against the incline.

The city's over seven thousand feet high, he said. We're up maybe another thousand from that. It's surrounded by old volcanoes. He trailed a finger along the jagged purple horizon above them where the sky and first stars began, then aimed it lower at the city and its millions of competing pulsing lights. Down there?

Yes?

That was one huge lake once. The Spanish, when they conquered the Aztecs, drained it and built the city. It's sinking in places.

You seem to know a lot about it, she said, her eyes showing awe, her voice something else. The intuition again.

Everybody down here knows this stuff.

They began walking.

The Avenido Toltecas was in a quiet part of the city and poorly lit. A handful of streetlamps cast dim cones of light along its dark corridor and random puddles of water left from the last rain reflected the same. But there was light enough for her to see its state of disrepair and dilapidation, the rundown condition of cinder-block apartments fronting it, indiscriminant trash and garbage scattered along the curbs and sidewalk, the utter disarray of it all. And the smell.

She lives here? Athen said.

Yep, then he told her the history of the area, of the large villa hidden in the dark at the end of the street, how a rich oilman bought it, built the apartments and now his widow just collects the rent. She don't do diddly but collect the money, he said. That's why it looks so bad. He wanted to say that was why Carmen could afford it and go into her financial situation and the plight of working women in Mexico but decided that would be knowing and showing too much.

Near the end of the street he stopped in front of a red door. The numbers 521 were painted in black at the top and a red bougainvillea arched across the eave. Either side the door quartered squares of yellow light shone palely through two small windows. The broken pane of one he recalled had been replaced and he pondered the hands that might have fixed it, if hers or another's and if another's if they were there, too.

This is it, he said. Hesitantly. Nervously. He'd retraced all he could remember he'd told each of them. The only lie he'd told Athen was not thinking to tell her about Carmen. He couldn't think of a one he'd told Carmen. He shouldn't have to say a lot, just introduce them and hope Carmen offered wine and it wore down whatever shock still shook their thinking then let em talk till that wore off and they were tired and ready to go to bed and sleep. He'd been thinking, too, about that, where he and Athen were going to sleep. They'd made love once by a lake on the land beneath a star-spangled sky and a chip of moon but after all the legal upheaval back home between him and her parents and her in the middle, neither seemed inspired to go that far again. They stayed with a college friend of Athen's in New Orleans, slept on a bench in the Brownsville depot and on the beach in Vera Cruz. Carmen only had her bed and a couch in the small living room. He'd let Athen have the couch and he'd sleep on the floor. That was the best arrangement he could configure. There was another. By the time they were through with him, the street might be safer.

He stepped up onto the small stoop and removed his hat. Athen remained behind on the sidewalk. He paused a moment before knocking, as if he expected the door to open of its own.

A light bulb over the door came on, no sound preceding it. Then came the sound, a soft, low voice: De quién es?

Soy yo, Jo Shelby.

The door flew open simultaneous with the shriek and in the split-second Jo Shelby forgot where he was and who was behind him. The last time he'd seen Carmen it was her eyes he remembered most and they were what he saw first as she exploded through the doorframe and he automatically gave himself to her outstretched arms.

Jo Shelby, she shouted. Mama mía, Dios mío. Qué gusto de verte, words of surprise flying excitedly from her mouth as they hugged and kissed then she saw Athen behind him in the glare of porch light and said, Oh, and released him and stepped back, drew a hand quickly to her hushed mouth.

He spun unsteadily as if thrown off balance, a needle quivering between two poles. He looked at Athen standing motionless in the bright spray of light, her mouth ajar and extended a shaky hand toward her. Carmen, permiteme presentar mi amiga, se llama Athen.

Complying uncertainly with the signal, Athen stepped from the sidewalk up onto the stoop. What did you say? she leaned over and whispered.

Carmen meet Athen.

It sounded like a lot more than that, she whispered again as she stepped in front of him to accept Carmen's extended hand.

It's nice to meet you, Athen said, bowing slightly.

Mucho gusto, Carmen said, reciprocating the courtesy.

He watched their faces as they shook hands, the strained smiles, how their eyes locked momentarily then slid away. He'd come to get the gun. That was all he'd been telling himself. He was not prepared for the other. The way Carmen made him feel.

Bueno, Carmen said, taking a deep breath and bringing her hands prayerfully together. She was in stocking feet and still wearing what looked to be her work clothes, a light blue blouse and beige skirt. Her hair was in a bun and large hoop earrings hung along her cheeks. Por favor, entre. Athen, Bienvenida a mi casa.

Athen looked at Jo Shelby. What did she say?

Please forgive me, Carmen said, smiling nervously. I forget. I must speak English. I said to you, Athen, please come in and welcome to my home.

Thank you, Athen said, forcing a smile. I'm not as far along with my Spanish as Jo Shelby.

Carmen held the door as Jo Shelby picked up the luggage and they stepped inside. The old wooden floor was cleanly swept with a waxed sheen he noticed as he set the bags down then looked around and recalled the tidy compactness of the small place, its simple handed-down furniture, its clean domestic smell. Where he'd spent the last Christmas on his journey home. Where he almost spent more than time. Where he could've settled down for good.

Please sit down, Carmen said, gesturing toward the small living room, part of an open floor plan that included a kitchen and dining area. Down a short hall was a bedroom and bath.

Athen lowered herself tentatively onto an armless upholstered chair and sat flat-footed, her hands balled in her lap. Carmen sat diagonal her in a matching chair, her legs crossed above the knee. The only place for Jo Shelby was across from them on the lumpy brocaded couch. There was a lamp on in the kitchen and one by the couch, the room mostly in shadows. A magazine lay open on a coffee table separating them and beside the magazine a glass of red wine probably just touched when she was interrupted. A pair of black high-heels lay tipped over on the floor beneath the low table.

Forgive me, Carmen said, eyeing the shoes. She rose and retrieved them. There was much walking today in my job and I was resting my feet when you arrived.

Don't bother, Athen said. I'm sure we look rag-tag in our blue jeans and T-shirts and tennis shoes.

No, please, Carmen said. She sat back down and began, first one, then the other, slipping her tapered feet into the shoes.

Jo Shelby angled his eyes at the ceiling and tried not to look. She wasn't just a specimen of beauty from the neck up but had the body and legs of the model she once was. He'd seen the look on Athen's face when she saw Carmen and he didn't want to see it again.

They sat.

Carmen erect, her hands composed in her lap like a socialite.

Athen stiffly, looking at a picture of a mountain on the wall above the couch.

Jo Shelby eyeing the glass of wine and feeling like the convicted before a jury of two, the verdict already in before he could present his case, before he could even say 'your honor,' that last word resonating through his thoughts.

In that frozen eye-averted silence they sat, the only sound water dripping in the kitchen sink. Then Carmen raised her hands and brought them together in a soft clap: Quierías ... please excuse ... would you like wine?

That'd be nice, Jo Shelby said, too quickly.

Athen smiled weakly, gave an approving nod. She was still sitting ramrod straight in the chair.

Carmen got up and walked to the small kitchen behind them.

Jo Shelby looked at the ceiling again. He could feel Athen looking at him. He'd drop his eyes momentarily and she'd blink, not automatic but one she wrung from the normal sequence, like it was a message she was sending him, one he didn't want to understand and he'd raise his eyes again. He couldn't tell if she was mad or sad or dumbstruck or some of all. Something else, too, in both their faces his eyes couldn't decipher, probably because they couldn't either. What they should feel.

A cork popped in the kitchen then a thin musical splash against glass, the sounds louder than they should be. He thought about that, too, the kind of silence he was in. One that brought out the things in the room he hadn't noticed before. The diamond designs on the curtains. The embossed pattern of the couch. A small crucifix hanging from the lampshade beside him. A picture within the picture hanging on the wall opposite him. His eyes roamed the room, touching everything, everything but Athen. The kind of silence that made her too loud to look at.

Carmen returned carrying goblets of red wine and white napkins. She served Athen first then Jo Shelby. Through her moves he saw the history of her country and its way of life. He thought of restaurants where he'd eaten and recalled no service that compared, none as courteous and flawless in its delivery. He thought of a land of servants without complaints because waiting on others was all they had known. He and Athen had dropped from nowhere into her quiet evening, her quiet time of rest at the end of a long day of work. She'd poured a glass of wine and kicked off her shoes and was reading a magazine, her thoughts probably on some faraway dream a picture brought to mind when she heard the knock on the door. Observing her now, moving unhurried with the gentle touch and calm voice of a child's nurse, he thought the hospitality an attention he did not deserve, the gall, his bringing Athen *there*.

He was holding his glass, his thoughts on a cautious toast, but Carmen preempted him. A amigos, un antiguo y una nueva. To friends, one old and one new, she said, lifting her glass and glancing first at Jo Shelby, then Athen.

They rose and chimed glasses, then sat and drank.

He pondered Carmen's toast, what the Spanish said the English didn't and what both together left out. He was the old friend and Athen the new and of the three, only he had two old friends.

Tell me about you, Athen said abruptly, leaning toward Carmen, the words jarring the temporarily settled moment.

They were words Jo Shelby had often heard his mother say when she met someone for the first time or a stranger came to visit. Tell me about you. He'd never heard a man say them, just women, as if women were the only ones who cared or were interested. Tell me about you. That's what the words said, but the sound and the look on her face conveyed something else. They said tell me about you because Jo Shelby has told me nothing. Because I didn't even know you existed until a handful of hours ago. Because I want to know if what he hasn't told me is a reason I ought to be on the next bus out of here. That was what the sound and the look said. He thought Carmen might feel caught off guard and stammer and stutter yet ...

Slowly, she brought the glass to her lips, took a sip then, with equal unhurried and circumspect intent, lowered it to her lap where she balanced it between her fingertips. There is not much to tell about me, she said. But if you wish.

I do, Athen said firmly but politely, the sound and the look unchanged.

Very well. Let me think. Where to begin?

Anywhere you want, Athen said, turning up her glass and taking a long swallow.

She began with the convent in San Luis Potosi where her parents had sent her at an early age. She told of the strict rules of the convent, of her small cell-like room, large enough for only a table and bed, the only adornment, a small religious picture on its bare walls. She told of being marched to classes and marched to prayers and mass and marched to meals. She told of food withheld as punishment when she broke rules, of going to bed hungry, of endless nights crying herself to sleep. My father finally took me out against my mother's pleas, she said, and enrolled me in La Ciudad Universitaria, the City University, where he was a professor.

As she spoke, Jo Shelby watched the mood, like a cloud, lift from Athen's face.

Your mother wanted you to stay? Athen said sympathetically.

Yes. She was a strict Catholic. She wanted me brought up to be a "good Christian girl." My father, too, was Catholic but not as devout. He saw how sick it was making me. In those days there were political problems, political pressure. My parents were for the little people, not the hacendados, who owned most of the land, over ninety percent.

Hacendados? Athen said. I'm sorry. You'll have to interpret for me again.

The wealthy land owners. The word is from hacienda. Like, perhaps, your plantation.

Athen's brows arced in quick understanding and she nodded.

My father had spoken against the government, Carmen continued. My parents lives were in danger, here, in México City. So they moved to Monterrey, far to the north. My father was able to get a job at Universidad de Nuevo León. Later he was incarcerated, in Matamoros, because of his political opinions.

Yes, Athen said. Jo Shelby told me. He was the man who helped arrange his release from prison.

This is true. But there is something I did not tell you, Carmen said, the reason I did not go to Monterrey with my parents. Sometime before, there had been threats to my family, from beneath President Alemán and his administration. My grandfather, a banker and powerful man, was murdered in Monterrey because of his stand against the wealthy hacendados. I was very close to my grandfather. I could not return to the city where he was killed in the main plaza, in cold blood, in broad daylight and the killers never arrested. So, I stayed here, in México City. I dropped out of school and got a job as a model. I took night courses in stenography and bookkeeping and, of course, English. I have a job as a secretary at a factory, one of your American garment industries. It is a good job. I make about one hundred sixty-five dollars, American dollars, per month.

That's all? Athen said.

Yes. But that is good money for a woman in Mexico. Because I speak two languages, I make more than most. She raised her glass, her fingers spiraled gracefully around it, and drank again. So that is about me. Of course, already I know some things, Athen, about you.

He'd never watched a tennis match up close but Jo Shelby imagined it little different than what his eyes and ears were tracking, stopping suddenly on the last shot, his thoughts scrambling to remember what he'd told her.

Oh? Athen said.

Yes, Carmen smiled. Jo Shelby, he spoke to me of you. You grew up together on the hacienda, on the plantation?

Yes, Athen said, her eyes widening, her face expanding.

Helpless he felt sitting across from them looking on, a story-teller isolated from his own story. He hoped she got it right.

He said you were very lovely and pretty, Carmen said. Es verdad.

Es verdad? Athen looked quizzically at Jo Shelby.

Means it's true, he said.

Thank you, Athen said, looking back at Carmen, a soft blush rising in her cheeks.

He said you were a senior in college, Carmen continued, that you were a good student and made good grades.

I've graduated, Athen said. She cast a thin smile at Jo Shelby and he returned a nervous grin.

He said the two of you rode horses. You went fishing and swimming. Let me see, oh yes, that you picked, something, some berry—

Dewberries, Jo Shelby said from his spectator spot, awe-struck at her near perfect memory, at Athen's awe-struck face listening to the near perfect memory.

Yes, Carmen said. And cotton, I believe. Then ... She paused, her mouth screwed to one side as if stuck with the next sentence.

Then? Athen said.

Then, Jo Shelby thought, everything hanging on that one word. He could feel it coming. In the words, the rhythm in her voice, the cadence, he'd sensed where she was going. It was like listening to a story and feeling the plot narrow, then the *then,* the trap-door ending.

Then he told me you live in a very big white house with a swimming pool and a tennis court, she said, turning her glass in her hands as she spoke. You have two brothers who have families. Your mother belongs to many clubs. Your father is a hacendado, a man with much land, land I believe Jo Shelby said once belonged to his family.

She believed, he thought. She knew good and damn well. Nothin was left to belief when he told that story. He looked over at Athen, her astonished face gone suddenly blank. She would not ask him later why Carmen knew all these things, or why he told her. She'd still be too caught up with why his Mexican amiga never forgot them, kept them tattooed right there on the front of her brain, where they sizzled like brands hot from the fire. She still hadn't pulled the final *then*. It was coming though. The glass turning in her hand had stopped.

Then he went to prison for a crime he did not commit and ...

She raised her glass again to her lips, as if to gain nurturance for the next thought, or strength to utter it or delay it because she didn't yet possess it, her face masking the reason for the pause, her eyes closing on it, her painted nails bright red against the darker wine, the wine darker going down, then she lowered the crystal goblet and balanced it in her hands once more over her lap, sat there in that rigid poise signifying completion, her lips pressed tight. She'd gone from Athen to the land to him then never finished the sentence, like a stone skipping three times over water before sinking. He'd never been in a war or seen a battle but the way she said it was like a first shot fired, first blood drawn.

He thought back. All he'd done was listen when Carmen told him the Aztec legend of Popocatépetl and the Sleeping Lady and when she finished all he'd said was she told it good. That was all. From that, and that alone, she'd figured the rest on her own, read between the lines and in his eyes, translating from the vacancies the pieces of the story left out, that there was a sore spot deep down in the history of his family and Athen's.

Athen tried not to look any particular way but he saw how the words cut through and opened her up inside, letting out the questions he would hear later. Did you tell her my father was partially responsible, that he raised no hand in your defense? Did you tell her my father denied me visitation? Did you tell her I tried? She'd probably ask, too, if he told her she was off to college, the University of Mississippi, Ole Miss, party school of the South, drinking and dancing and living it up while he was picking cotton beneath the barrel of a gun and at night falling into something that couldn't be called sleep the way it came down on him like a hammer? Then she'd have one final question: Would you tell her all that is behind us now, forgotten and forgiven, that I came here with you because I believe in what you are doing, because I love you?

And I waited for him, Athen said, completing the truncated sentence still dangling in the long silence, her eyes unblinking, steady on Carmen.

Women, he thought. Hostile fire returned, the shot neither true nor straight. She'd damn near married a frat rat not once but twice, both times he was away. If that's what she called waiting for him, the meaning had taken several strange turns on its way in search of its true self. She was there with him, and the senorita, too, and how all that was going to wash out time indeed would tell. He had a thought that would slow the clock down but Carmen was, once again, a step ahead.

Jo Shelby, your teeth. Qué bueno. I did not notice.

He curled his lips back in an exaggerated smile revealing the new additions to his mouth. Yep. Gottem back. Dentist back home did it. If I die down here, knock em out to pay for shipping me home. On the back of both of em, he thumped the porcelain of one with a finger, then the other, there's gold plating, couple of hundred dollars worth. Come to think of it, might have to knock em out anyway if we run low on money. He looked at Athen and winked but she didn't wink back.

I worried about your teeth, Carmen said.

Yeah. You and everybody else. He glanced again at Athen, her face still blank as dough. She'd worked her way back into the conversation only to get worked out again.

The story was not funny, Carmen said, but I laugh when I think about … about … She lifted a hand to her mouth to smother a chuckle.

Yeah? he said.

When I think how you almost captured a hacienda gerente and his mozos sin ayuda, with your one hand—

Single-handed, he said.

Yes, single-handed, and with a gun that would not shoot, the hand over her mouth again, this time giving up laughter. I am sorry but that is very funny.

The gun. In his struggle to put one sentence before the other, he'd forgotten about the gun. It was the reason he came before he arrived but might not be the reason he came by the time he left, that reason swaying in the balance like the rest of the high-wire evening unspooling itself blindly into the night.

I'm guessin you got the hundred dollars I sent you, he said to Carmen.

Oh, Sí, claro, she said, smiling confidingly, as if he should have known.

And the gun, he said, still facing Carmen but his eyes cutting on Athen.

Sí, sí. No es un problema. Yo lo tengo. I have it.

Thank God, he whispered. He looked down and said it again, into the glass he was holding, into the dark swirl working the edges of his thinking, smoothening them so he barely heard her leave the room and return. When he raised his eyes she stood over him. She was holding a multicolored cloth bolsa of Indian design, its top folded over.

Solamente, para ti, she said.

She spoke in Spanish again, her speech moving more and more in that direction as the evening wore on, in the language only she and he understood. Solamente, para ti. He wondered if she meant only for him because he owned the object at hand or only for him would she have gone to such lengths. The look in her eyes, as she bent over to hand him the weighted bag, said the latter. The way her hands slid along his as she made the transferal said it again. The look in Athen's eyes watching the transaction hammered it home.

He cradled the bolsa in his lap as though it was the packaging of some precious and fragile commodity then unfolded the top and slipped a hand inside and retrieved the revolver in its leather flap-holster. He carefully unhooked the flap from the finnel and gripped the wooden handle encased in brass and slipped the pistol free of its scabbard, the revolving cylinder and long barrel and brass frame with the name COLT engraved beneath the cylinder gleaming mutely in the imprecise periphery of pooled lamplight. He half-cocked the hammer and spun the cylinder, making sure the mechanisms were as he had left them then he uncocked the hammer and held the pistol closer to the light.

So, that's the gun, Athen said, ironically, drawing a sharp look from him.

Well, it aint no cannon.

I didn't mean it like that, she said ironically. It looks so real is what I meant, like it really could shoot and kill.

With the right ammunition it could, he said. It's a Navy Colt 36 caliber lever action, works like this.

The two women pulled their chairs closer and leaned their heads over the coffee table.

If you had a mini-ball, it would go here, he said pointing to one of the empty chambers. Next would go the powder then the lever would pack it all in so when you looked down that cylinder hole it'd look like a little white doughnut ready to fire.

So, all you need are some mini-balls and powder then it could really do something, Athen said, her words again attracting a look of rebuke from him.

It's already done more without firing a shot than a hundred that could, he said, sliding the gun back into the holster, fastening the holster snap and returning the composite to the bag.

They had both heard the stories, or fragments of them, but there was greater safety in his talking as opposed to the two across from him cranking up again, so he told them once more how the gun that got him thrown into prison in Matamoros became the bargaining chip that got him out, then later helped him bluff his way into the hacienda of the only kin he'd tracked a thousand miles to find only to get jumped from behind at its very steps before the aging kin, the Señora Moncada, shouted from an overhead window and saved his life. He could have stopped there, but they were listening intently so he told how the Señora retrieved the gun from Ricardo, her administrador, the one who'd beaten him within an inch of his life and damn near hanged him and how he, Jo Shelby, within twenty-four hours hocked the firearm to a gun dealer in Cuernavaca for money to get home.

And now I got it back, he said, and patted gently the bolsa still cradled in his lap, as though it were some animate object of affection that might stir to his touch.

I will return it to its safe place, Carmen said.

Yeah. But just for tonight.

Oh? Solo para la noche? No más? Pero, ya llegaste. Her lips puckered into an exaggerated pout.

Athen sat, said nothing.

Jo Shelby skirted the temptation to respond in Spanish and spoke back to her in English. He apologized they had just arrived and were having to leave then told her about the letter he'd received from Señora Moncada, her cry for help, problems she was having with back taxes, government officials trying to foreclose on her house and land, what was left of the once great La Hacienda Tierra del Puente. He told, too, of the other reason he could stay no longer, of the search for his great-great-great-grandfather's will, that a legal clock back home was ticking and he had only a short window of time in which to find the one document that could prove that the great hacienda in the north belonged to him, and if not to him, at least his Mexican kin.

When he finished Carmen looked at Athen, then at Jo Shelby, then back to Athen, puzzled eyes swinging back and forth between the two before resting on Jo Shelby.

But it was Athen who spoke: Carmen, I see how you might be confused. Jo Shelby does not want to take anything away from my father or my family. He only wants what is right. If he is right, and can prove it, he will redistribute the land to its rightful heirs, including some of the Negroes who have lived on the plantation for years and never owned land. I admire him for that. That is one of the reasons I came with him. Not to do anything against my father, who is but one man, but to do what is right by so many others in my country.

And the other reasons? Carmen said.

There's just one.

Yes?

Because I love him.

There was a long silence.

Admiration, that is one thing, said Carmen, her face downfallen. But love, love is something much different. I think, maybe, it is for the love, and only the love, that you came. She smiled faintly and there was a tone of resignation in her voice but her eyes were bright as a new thought as she rose, took the bolsa from Jo Shelby and left the room.

Jo Shelby sat slumped against the couch, his arms draped across its back as though he'd been blown into that defenseless posture by a sudden explosion of bright light. He knew why he was going to Mexico and Athen knew why he was going to Mexico, but her intent had come to him only in the bits and pieces one choses to feed another. She'd mentioned getting away, like she might be running from something, a sidekick along for the trip, the fun she'd mentioned. Except what she had revealed to him in the note she'd left her parents, there'd been no discussion about the land, its legal status or family loyalties. He recalled, too, something she'd said when she jumped on the bus: *I couldn't let you go traipsing off to Mexico by yourself where some senorita might grab you, now could I?* But there had been no declarations of fondness or affection. The entire trip nothing had been said about the land or the law or love, as if all were bombs set to go off at the slightest mention.

You hadn't told me any of this, he said.

You knew I loved you.

You hadn't said it.

You hadn't either.

He unhooked his arms from the back of the couch and leaned forward, his hands folded between his knees.

It was the other I didn't know, about the land, how you felt, he said.

It hadn't come up, Athen said.

Why'd you wait til now?

It just seemed the right time.

No contesting that, he thought, as he heard Carmen's footsteps returning. Athens had done what he'd been afraid to do. Cut the tension to its nitty gritty core and uncomplicate his life so they could move on. He thought.

Carmen took her seat. She sat with her knees pressed together, her back erect, legs driven straight into the floor, as if perched to proclaim something profound, something of great importance. *Hay poder en los números*, she said.

Then he rethought and looked at Athen. She didn't have the foggiest but he didn't like what he'd just heard and she could read it on his face.

What did you say? Athen said, turning to Carmen, this time requesting the translation from her.

I said there is strength in numbers. I should go with you and help.

Jo Shelby came to the edge of the couch and Athen's posture snapped straight and stiff, both appearing possessed of speech, but neither capable.

Carmen continued: This is a very difficult thing you wish to do, finding a legal document a hundred years old. As before when I helped you—she looked at Jo Shelby—you will need to know the many places to go. Your Spanish, Jo Shelby, it is good. But, for this problem, you will need an interpreter. Es verdad. The Señora and her hacienda, I have not met this person and know only vaguely of the place, near Cuernavaca, but she will need more than just two persons. These are big problems. I have friends. This is the first week of September. Our national holiday is one week away. People do not work then. Many in Mexico now can take vacations from their jobs. I will go with you, my friends and I.

Naw, now, he said. Ain't no need for you to—

No! Es final! She brought her hands together, pressed them against her chest. These are big problems. We are friends, Jo Shelby. And now, Athen, my new friend. In Mexico, friends, son para vida, are for life.

Lord God in heaven, he thought. What had he done to deserve this? Was it punishment or reward, a horrible deed or act of heroism? Where in his journey of justice had he slipped off the rails. All he wanted to do was help an old woman and find the ancient will of an old man, a will that would help many people. Then Lord God in heaven you produce two women, poof them like magic, one popping up on a bus at the last minute and the other popping up to join the ride. Adam had it pretty good. He only had one to deal with and, Lord, you give me two. Pray tell, how am I going to manage this. Though one would surely help, I don't need an answer right now, but if you're will be done and if you're in a mood to move a little faster, I'm gonna need one directly. I'd say before mañana. I'd say before we wake up. Cause that's when the proverbial shit is gonna start hittin the fan.

Athen sat speechless, her face an open window of disbelief and resignation.

Surely, you are hungry, Carmen said, sensing the tone of the room might change if a steady voice moved it along. For this, Athen's first night in México, we take her to dinner, show her my city. Yes?

Whatever appetite Jo Shelby had, had been ambushed, knocked cold and tied up somewhere deep in his innards. We been travelin all day, he said. If Athen feels up to it.

Athen gave a nod, one that could have meant anything—agreement, disagreement, indifference.

That a yes or a no? he said.

Athen looked at her wristwatch. It's late, past nine o'clock. Restaurants are probably closed. I'm not that hungry anyway.

Oh, no, Carmen said. In México the evening is just beginning. If a restaurant is closed now, that is because it has not yet opened. Once you smell the food, you will be hungry. So, we go. Yes? I know a good place. Her smile invaded the hushed politeness like a contagion.

Jo Shelby sat, waited.

Yes, Athen said. That would be nice.

He knew the bus route into the centro as though by heart, the names of the plazas and radiating streets, the lit-up statues and buildings, names Carmen was calling out now to Athen sitting tightly beside her oohing and aahing, smitten by the same Mexican charm that had claimed him. *Hay poder en numeros.* Not if you're on the other side and the numbers begin adding up against you, he thought.

They were going down Lazaro Cardenas, the names of the side avenidas flicking by—Dominiques, Gonzáles, Mosqueta—then the bus came to a large intersection and stopped and Carmen motioned them off.

This is the Paseo de Reforma, she said, pointing to a wide boulevard of globed streetlamps and flood-lit statues and leafy trees festooned with lights, string upon string of colored lights draping the broad thoroughfare, tiered as far as the eye could follow them up the glittering and bejeweled neck of night. Magnifico, no, she said, tugging on Athen's arm for a response, oblivious to Jo Shelby standing behind them.

I went once with my parents to New York and saw Times Square, Athen said. But this ... she paused as if to catch her breath ... this is absolutely gorgeous. She looked at Carmen. Yes, magnifico. It is magnifico.

Carmen smiled proudly. The colored lights across the street are for our independence, she said. They will be gone in a month.

Athen made a panoramic wave of her hand. This doesn't need colored lights, it doesn't need any help.

Muchas gracias, Carmen said. That is a very nice thing you say about my city.

Jo Shelby imagined a fifth wheel as he continued standing behind them, wondering if perhaps he should have stayed on the bus and left these two suddenly blooming bosom-buddies to figure each other out on their own. He didn't even look like he belonged. Carmen had freshened up but remained in her business attire. Athen, not one to be outclassed, had changed into a blouse and skirt and heels and combed out her hair, put on makeup.

He'd put on a white shirt and khaki slacks, spit-combed his hair into place. He could have worn a tuxedo and still looked an improbable fit with either, much less both.

We walk, if you like, Carmen said. The restaurant is in the Zona Rosa, not far from here. She slipped an arm through Athen's and turned and did the same with Jo Shelby, almost yanking him beside her. Off they went, arm in arm and stride for stride down the moon-globed and glitzy Paseo.

The air was light and cool and smelled of the city, of dark foreign people and car exhaust and vendor food steaming off the makeshift ovens along the curbs but something else overriding all that, a freshness of clouds and mountains, smells that never came to a person on land flat with the ocean. He wore his jacket and the girls' sweaters were draped around their shoulders. Close together they walked, Carmen's arms interlocked with theirs, her head tucked slightly forward, pulling them along the wide sidewalks, stopping them at street corners then shepherding them across, herding them through the gathering night crowd, it might seem to a passerby, like a babysitter with two small children. Occasionally, she'd stop to observe a display window or tell the story of a building, comment on one of the many statues along the way. But mostly she walked, plowing through the throngs like a woman of vision, commandeering each step. Captain Carmen in charge of the night, he thought then considered the other option. He on the inside and two heeled beauties of the night on the outside. He wondering what to do with his hands, wondering which way to go. He wasn't sure where the complicated evening was headed but thank the Lord he was not in charge, a comfort he added to the lingering wine and elevated night air.

Los Suspiros was the name of the restaurant and it was on a quiet side street of the otherwise noisy Zona Rosa, the center of the city's *vida nocturna*. The interior was simple, a single large room, candle-lit tables generously spaced, some beneath open windows overlooking a garden. Soft yellow light from low-hanging lamps. Quiet guitar music as background and somewhere behind that, outside perhaps in the garden, the sounds of a fountain splashing. Romantic. He would have preferred something livelier, with distractions, a mariachi band, dancing, a place too loud for talk. Too loud for truth.

The maître d' guided them to a table in a corner and pulled chairs out for the two ladies. Jo Shelby seated himself. Carmen was on one side, Athen the other, his back to the intersecting walls. *Entre la espada y la pared.* Ramon, Carmen's father, had said that to him in the Mexican prison when he was negotiating with the commandante for his gun and release. It meant he was between a rock and a hard place and he figured the metaphor as appropriate now as then.

The maître d' handed each a large menu, bowed slightly and left.

This is charming, Athen said. Very cozy. Do you come here often?

No, Carmen said. It is a restaurant very much liked by my parents. The few times they come to México, they come here to eat. Sometimes I come with them, sometimes not. The food is good and not very expensive."

Los Suspiros, Athen said. What does it mean?

Carmen cast an appraising glance at Jo Shelby, a do-I-dare-say glint in her eyes. It means ... let me see ... how do you say in English? Breaths of disappointment. Sighs, I believe. Yes that is it, the sighs.

I see, Athen said looking down, removing her silverware from her napkin.

Jo Shelby stared at his menu.

A camarero came and they ordered drinks, margaritas for everyone Carmen suggested.

But sin hielo, Jo Shelby said. I made that mistake once, not gonna make it again.

Por qué no? she said.

Por qué la agua.

What are you talking about? Athen said.

I don't want us gettin sick, he said. The ice they use aint purified.

That is no problem, Carmen said. No ice.

Standing patiently and looking on with some consternation, the waiter, a tall and slender young man with dark hair slicked back to a slight curl above his neck, hurriedly wrote down the order and went away.

They looked over the menus. Athen couldn't read hers and Jo Shelby translated then left her alone to ponder her decision.

For a while the waiter did not return and everything seemed to grow suddenly quiet. There was the soft guitar music and the fountain splashing outside, but little else by way of sounds. The waiters spoke to one another in whispers. People at nearby tables spoke in soft murmurs. There were no sounds of dishes rattling and silverware clinking from a kitchen, as though it was sealed off. Los Suspiros, Jo Shelby thought, the atmosphere designed to reduce sound. As if to say you had to work things out by sight and touch, by feel and smell as he observed his companions' hands toying with their menu and dinnerware, arranging and rearranging their napkins. He moved his foot and it touched another, Athen's he thought. He waited. No touch returned. He waited longer. Something grazed his ankle. Was it Athen or Carmen? He tucked his feet beneath his chair, out of harms way. He needed to speak with each of them separately. He couldn't think of a time he'd be alone with Carmen but the way she was steering things so far he figured she'd come up with one. He'd be alone with Athen when they went to bed. Surely Carmen would leave them in the front room alone. After that they'd all be three peas in a pod off to Cuernavaca.

He didn't have to make a choice, he told himself. Though he was glad to have her with him, it was not he who chose for Athen to come along. He did not choose to spend the night at Carmen's. It just worked out that way. She had the gun. He did not chose a restaurant named Los Suspiros, set up and geared down for romance. He'd certainly had his share of disappointments, probably sighed enough for everybody at the table plus some at the next. Carmen didn't say it, but sighs could mean longings. He didn't have to choose but the word was bearing down upon him like an intruder breathing down his neck sooner or later he'd have to turn around and face. But not until he did what he'd come to do and gotten what he'd come to get.

The waiter finally returned. Jo Shelby ordered first for Athen, pechuga con hongo then a plate of enchiladas rancheros for himself. Carmen had considered the grilled chicken breast he had ordered for Athen, but settled on a guacamole salad. She had had a long day and was not that hungry, she said.

They wore down the evening drinking and eating and talking, the conversation taking on the quality of streams that meander but do not touch. Jo Shelby said little and listened, his life already an open book to them, one that didn't need re-reading. Athen asked questions about Mexico, more about Carmen's mother and father, her face, Jo Shelby observed, genuinely open, receptive as she listened. Carmen in turn asked more of Athen's past, her parents and family, her life in the Delta and was it really as flat as Jo Shelby had described to her.

It's so flat, Athen said, there's not even a bump in the road.

Laughter among them, the first of the evening. But beneath the polite inquisitions, the gentle probes of curiosity, deeper emotions moved and Jo Shelby understood why Carmen had chosen the restaurant. Why, with her long rapid strides, she had seemed in a hurry to get there, as if for some rendezvous with concocted revelation, as if getting there was part of a larger plan. *She dances around men, throws flowers to them, seduces them. They fight over her. She flits about causing trouble, kind of like a gypsy moth.* Miss Floy, his adopted mother back home, had said that of the Carmen of opera when he first mentioned the name. *Nome, this Carmen's not like that,* he'd said back to her. Now he understood more than he wanted or desired the events unfolding, how Carmen, with a little push here, little nudge there, was orchestrating, channeling the movements of the evening. And Athen, it seemed, oblivious to it all, so enthralled she was by the charm, the mystique of the city and its people.

He'd lost count, the number of margaritas carrying the flow of conversation, the spirit of the alcohol percolating through their voices, giving rise to glibness, to stories. To jeopardy. Athen told of the time she and Jo Shelby were being harassed by her brothers in a prominent Delta restaurant, the awful things they were saying. She described their drunken heads bobbing obnoxiously over their table then the stupefied shock in their eyes when Jo Shelby whisked out the steak knife and fork impaling their ties to the table. Can you believe, right there in the middle of the cream of Delta society, she said.

A round of laughter.

Carmen's turn was next. It was around Christmas, she thought. Returning from dinner, she and Jo Shelby entered a farmacia filled with people. In Spanish he requested an item, only he mispronounced the word and the clerk brought him, instead, sanitary napkins. You should have seen his face, Carmen said with a throaty laugh. It was red as a matador's cape.

Jo Shelby crossed his cutlery on his plate and fixed his eyes on Carmen.

Athen smiled wryly, the mention of Christmas, that time frame, surely not lost on her. She straightened herself in her chair, flicked the corners of her mouth with her napkin and pushed back her plate, movements, he knew, signaled she wasn't through, and worse, might even be just beginning. She folded her hands in space the plate had occupied then leaned across the used dish of scraps, her face near the candle, her eyes cat-like with the ellipsoidal yellow flame dual-dancing on her pupils. Speaking matter-of-factly, and without humor, she flashed vignettes across the table, clips of times of just her and Jo Shelby. Of riding horses and sliding down haystacks, of passing notes in church and swimming in the creek that ran through the property. Leaving no room for interruption she flipped the calendar forward, told of their reading together the letters written by his great-great-great-grandmother, his leaving for Mexico on his first trip the next day and her farewell to him, wondering if she'd ever see him again.

And you did, Carmen said, more subdued, sensing the mood turning.

Yes, I did at that, Athen said.

The two women sat, regarding each other with detached scrutiny.

Jo Shelby sat, a thought triggered by something Athen had said. You know where wills are kept in México? he said to Carmen.

Cómo?

Wills. Los Testamentos.

Ah, sí. I am not sure. When my grandfather was murdered in Monterrey, I think my father had to go to a notario publico.

Notary public?

Sí. But it is not like a notary public in your country.

How's that? he said

In México, a notario publico is an attorney appointed by the Presidente or governor of the state. You mentioned before this testamento. It is very important to you.

Yes. The judge in my country said if I could find that will … it's a long story.

Long? Carmen said. We have the night.

He told her the story, parts of which he had told before, how his great-great-great-granddaddy, Colonel Calvin T Ferguson, and his wife and two sons and daughter followed General J O Shelby into Mexico at the collapse of the Confederacy, but one son, Nathan, remained behind to take care of the plantation only he was a midnight gambler and lost the land and the house, everything, kit-n-kibuttal, in a poker or dice game, nobody knew for sure, except it wasn't his to lose because that was in 1875 and the Colonel didn't die until 1882. So there was a defect on the title, he said, something wrong with it and the first Patrick who bought it from the yankee who won it in the gamble—he glanced sheepishly at Athen—knew there was something wrong with it and so did the man who inherited it.

That's my daddy, Athen said. She'd been tapping a finger impatiently on the table as if counting down to the moment she could chime in.

So, Jo Shelby continued, when I took this to court, and I won't go into all that, the judge said the ownership was taken with the knowledge, or the possible knowledge, of a defect, a cloud on the title. In other words I convinced him with my story only the story aint over.

Por qué? Carmen said.

Por qué I only half won. In order to get rid of this cloud I got to come up with the will, the old colonel's will. The judge is letting the case run …

Run? Carmen said.

He's leaving it open, in other words, he's not closing the book on it just yet. It's all complicated, but I got about a year-and-a-half to two years to come up with the will.

Carmen took a sip from her margarita. That was not such a long story.

It's a lot longer than I told it, he said.

My daddy likes to own things, Athen said in an absent voice, one that seemed to be thinking of something else.

So what I've got to do next is go to the publico notario in Cuernavaca, he said.

I am not that sure about these things but I think, yes, Carmen said. That is in the state of Morelos, so he is probably appointed by the governor.

Did they have them that far back, publico notarios? he said.

I do not know, Carmen said. We can find out in Cuernavaca when we get there.

On *we*, Athen began tapping her finger again.

On the other hand, he might not have gone to a publico notario, Jo Shelby said. He might have just written it out on a sheet of paper and put it somewhere.

That was long ago, Carmen said. You may be looking for una aguja en una paca de paja, a needle in a haystack.

Yeah. That's what my attorney back home said.

Then you have much work to do, Carmen said. Perhaps the night should not be so long. We need to arise early in the morning to catch the first buses.

Athen's finger stopped tapping. What are you going to do about your job?

I will stop somewhere and call my boss. I have much time accumulated for vacation. Then there are the holidays. He will understand. I am a hard worker. He likes me.

I'll bet he does, Jo Shelby thought as he raised a hand and motioned to the camarero.

The waiter came quickly, as though he sensed some urgency pervading the air. Si señor?

La cuenta, Jo Shelby said.

Si señor. Un momento, the camarero said and he went away again.

Athen and Carmen finished their drinks. There was half of a drink left in his glass but he decided he'd had enough alcohol. The evening was not over. They had to make their way back to Carmen's. A lot of dust had been kicked up and he was going to need a clear head before it settled.

The camarero returned with the bill. Carmen and Jo Shelby made simultaneous grabs but he came up with the slender sheet.

You are my guests, Carmen said.

We are friends, Jo Shelby said. Remember.

All the more reason I should have the bill, Carmen said.

Why don't we just split it, Athen said, the words rending the air prophetically.

The camarero stood, his head moving back and forth with the dialogue, as if he'd been observing the table throughout the evening and wondered how the trio was to be divided.

That's a good idea, Jo Shelby said.

Carmen shook her head disapprovingly.

Vamos a repartir, Jo Shelby looked up and said to the camarero, para dos. He pointed two fingers at him and Athen then one at Carmen. Y a uno.

Pero ... Carmen attempted.

Es final, Jo Shelby said.

Foggy with drink, slower and without conversation, they made their way back to Carmen's apartment, the half moon a silver buttock pasted onto the sky, the image that came to him when he exited the bus, the only clarity he gleaned from the night.

Carmen brought out several blankets and an extra pillow and gave the predictable sleeping arrangements. The pillow was for Athen; he could use a smaller one from the couch if he wished. There were fresh towels and bath cloths in the baño. With those terse instructions she gave them both a hug and expressed pleasure at their presence in her casa, that she was looking forward to their trip to Cuernavaca together then turned and departed down the short hall to her bedroom and when she was gone the room turned suddenly quiet.

Jo Shelby was still standing, his hat still in his hand.

Athen was sitting in one of the chairs, a tired, sullen look on her face, one that could have been angry or drunk, or both.

Christmas? she said.

He could scratch drunk. We wadn't engaged or nothing, he said, rotating his hat in his hands. You dated while I was in prison, was wearing a frat rat's letters when I got out.

That's not the point. I told you about him. You never told me about her, especially that you stayed with her. I feel like an unwanted tag-a-long. She sat stiffly, her face long, her knees touching, her body pulled in tightly like she was cold. I might never have gotten on that bus if—

If I recall, that was why you got on that bus, cause you couldn't let me go traipsing off to Mexico by myself and let some senorita grab me. And none hadn't. All I did was sleep here. That was all.

How long?

A few nights.

How many's a few?

The hat spun faster in his hands. Couple of weeks.

Her eyebrows suddenly shot up. Her lips compressed and her eyes narrowed, the slits showing small black bullets newly shucked into the chambers for firing. She got up and went to her duffle bag that lay against the outer wall where he had laid it when they entered. She unzipped it and pulled out pajamas and a small pouch and went to the bathroom.

He made a pallet on the floor with the blankets Carmen had left and grabbed a small pillow from the couch. He thought of making up her couch for her, having it ready when she returned then decided against it. She would just say he was kissing her ass, the image of the moon coming back to him. He undressed and put on a pair of used flannel pajamas he'd purchased before the trip and slipped between the blankets, pulled them up to his chin.

She was wearing long blue silk pajamas when she reentered the room and hung the clothes she'd worn that evening over a chair in the small dining area opposite the living room. The bullets were gone from her eyes when she reentered the room, but so was her make up which made her face look cold and hard. She said nothing as she made up the couch. He lay watching her, trying to think of something to say, but the place in his mind where he was trying to think was an empty hole where a bomb had gone off.

She finished preparing her bed, then turned to him. Ready for me to turn off the light?

I guess so.

Good night, then.

Good night.

That was all. Because of the circumstances of the trip there had been no opportunity for passion. Until Athen had said it when the evening was young, neither had said they loved the other, as though the word was something they might trip over if dropped in the path of conversation. But there had been warmth and closeness. There had been feelings. She'd clung to his arm on buses, laid her head on his shoulder. They'd hugged and kissed occasionally, and always each night before going to bed. Women.

A storm came up that night, lightening falling all around them, sharp cracks, like china thrown and smashed, one after another, bright flashes, as if he and Athen were smack in the middle of the heavens where it was all being birthed. He tried counting the seconds, but there was no time to count. The storm seemed in the room with them, simultaneous light and thunder a mile high, the room without shadow in the bright nuclear bursts. He expected her to call for him, maybe reach out and touch him. He was only a few feet from her. In one of the daylight flashes he glimpsed her lying on her back, her eyes open, hands folded across her chest like an effigy on a catafalque. She might really look like that if her eyes hadn't been open. But they were. And they showed no fear. That was what he saw in the split-second before the long streak of lightning played out. When it struck again her eyes were closed.

They were already up and dressed when Carmen emerged bright-eyed and dressed like something out of a Spanish western. She wore dark tight-fitting pants, pearl buttons snapped high on her waist and a white blouse with a high collar flipped up around her neck and long leather boots that came below her knees. Her hair was unpinned and framed her face handsomely and on her head was the same wide-brimmed straw sombrero she'd worn on other occasions with him, only with a red instead of a yellow ribbon. All she needed was spurs and a whip. He and Athen wore the clothes they'd arrived in, blue jeans and T-shirts, and he wondered if Carmen might have changed her mind and made other plans for the day. How come you're dressed like that? he said.

We are going to a hacienda, no?

Yeah.

So, I dress for the hacienda.

She was dressed a far cut above where they were going, but he said no more.

They ate a hurried breakfast of toast and orange juice, conversation lean as the meal. Athen was still cool to him, moved around him as if she touched him she'd catch a disease. As if she spoke to him her breath might suck up his germs. He offered to carry her duffle bag to the end of the street where they caught a city bus to the main depot, but she declined. He didn't offer to carry Carmen's suitcase.

At the main terminal they caught a bus with few passengers and by seven o'clock were on their way. Athen sat by Carmen. He sat in the seat behind them. This was the way it was going to be, he thought, adding a question mark then taking it away as he pondered the new alignment in his life, the *poder en los numeros* he saw stacking up against him. This was probably the way it was going to be because this was probably the way women dealt with men. Probabilities. They found strength in numbers. It was going to be a long day.

They rode on in the strained silence, past the rag-tag fringes of the city, the tawdry strips of gasolineras and tiendas and cafes and make-shift stalls with thatched roofs where lean sombreroed men and full-bodied women wearing scarves filled stands with vegetables and fruit and ceramics and flowers and men and women old enough to be grandparents bicycling against the traffic toward the city, the grim desperation on their faces suggesting they were not going to work but in search of it, then the road rose and ascended the sierras into clouds and cooler air. For a while they climbed through mist and light rain then declined sharply so the clouds were above them, a dark gray cottony ceiling where, in patches, bursts of sunlight shot through and shafts of gold fired below a long valley with green fields of unusual geometry and rising among them, like the outcroppings of a lost world, crater-shaped moss-covered formations, and looming above all that high serrated mountains and ridges and Athen broke the silence.

That's the most gorgeous sight I have ever seen in my life. She looked at him when she said it, not Carmen, a ray of hope into the dark unpromising day. As if God designed such scenes for that purpose, to draw people closer.

What are the craters? she said, still looking back at him.

They're old volcanic cones, volcanoes that never got to be volcanoes, he said. They heated up and smoldered some but never caught fire. Least that's what I was told.

Carmen turned and nodded. Yes, and some are still smoldering.

The bus trundled on, hugging the sides of the mountain, veering near precipices as the road wound its way down from the higher elevation then leveled out onto the safer tabled land between the mountains and into bright sunlight and Athen saw the sight to the east before he could point it out to her.

Would you look at that? she said pointing to distant snow-capped peaks. They look like magnificent white tents painted on the sky.

They are Popocatépetl and Ixtaccíhuatl, Carmen said. We just call them Popo and The Sleeping Lady. There is an ancient Aztec legend about them. But perhaps you are not interested.

No, no. I am. Please, tell me.

Carmen glanced back at Jo Shelby, as if to get his permission. Perhaps I should let Jo Shelby tell the story.

Naw now, he said. Carmen can tell it best.

Very well, Carmen said confidently. Long ago, as the story has come down to my people, there were two Aztec lovers. They were from different families. One was very wealthy and one not wealthy at all.

Jo Shelby began to squirm in his seat and removed his hat. This wasn't the beginning he'd heard when first told the story by her and he wondered where she was going with it, what version she might stamp on it.

Carmen stopped and looked back at him. Está bien, Jo Shelby?

Yeah, I'm okay, he lied. Just getting a little warm in here.

We can open a window, Carmen said.

Naw. Continua, por favor.

She continued. These two families lived close together. They did not dislike each other, but they did not like each other. They just ... what is the word ... soportado ...

Tolerated, Jo Shelby said. She was sure as hell telling it different now.

Sí, yes, they tolerated each other. But their children, their son and their daughter, they liked each other very much. The families did not like this, their son and daughter being lovers.

Jo Shelby rose and unlatched the window above Athen and lowered it.

So, you want the window open, Carmen said.

He nodded, but shot her a hard look.

There was a war, Carmen said, undeterred. The man was sent off to the war and he became a prisoner of war. The lady was told this by her parents, that her lover died in a prison far, far away. The lady was so distressed, she went up to the mountain and laid down and let herself die. But the man, he did not die in the prison, he came back and when he discovered what his lover had done he went to the mountain to grieve over her and he let himself die. Look carefully, and you can see them, frozen in their deaths. You can see her stretched across the sky, her head, her breasts, then her legs and feet and not far away, as though leaning in toward her, contemplating her, her lover, Popo.

Yes, Athen said. I can see them. What a sad story.

Aint it though, Jo Shelby said ironically, the sarcasm aimed at Carmen. The first time she'd told the legend to him both families were wealthy and of nobility. The male lover went to war and was killed in the war. That was it. Nothing about a prison.

The bus rode on, passing livestock and poultry and people on burros and ponies pulling carts. They approached the outskirts of Cuernavaca and its odd collection of private enterprise, most of the signs in English—Coca Cola, Bardahl, Esso—sights of bare-bones commerce, living hand to mouth. Soon they were gliding down a shaded boulevard of trees heavy with colorful blooms, elegant houses behind stone walls covered with bright bougainvilleas, gardens of tropical flowers.

I've never been to Europe, Athen said. But this is what I think it would look like. Beautiful and old world.

It's old all right, he said. He was leaning in closer to them now, his head right behind theirs. There'd been a warming of relations, it seemed, and he felt drawn closer.

Over four hundred years ago Cortez chose it as his capital, Carmen joined in. It is called the city of eternal spring. In the past many generals retired here. Now Americans live in their homes. They come here and cannot leave.

Where are we going? Athen said.

To see a lady who helped me when I was down here last year, he said. She owns a hotel. She's one of those Americans Carmen mentioned. Some of her family lived and died down here. She'll probably die here, too. She'd know about American wills in Mexico.

They passed the imposing Jardin Borda Hotel and Cathedral and other places of interest Athen asked about and Carmen, before Jo Shelby could respond, answered. At the centro bus station they gathered their baggage from the driver and Jo Shelby led the way through the sally port into the street. Again he offered to carry Athen's duffle bag and again she declined. Again Carmen looked on with a calculating eye and detached circumspection, a look that said this is not my fight but I've got a stake in it and will stick around to see what's left when it's over.

Through narrow tilted cobble-stoned streets and twisting paseos and arcaded passages they wound their way, along hedges of crimson flowers and ancient stone walls draped with bougainvillea, by private gardens filled with sweet-smelling flowers, beneath the fragrant yellow and red blossoms of mango and tulip trees, walking at times on covered sidewalks teeming with people and crossing plazas where small bands played or a lone musician strummed a guitar and sang in sad nasality a story of his country and everywhere, draping from the rooftops and facades of buildings, streaming outward from the plazas, like the spokes of a magnificent wheel, the colors of that country, the colors of celebration and Athen oohing and aahing every step of the way until they stood before an old massive building with a sign across the top that said Hotel Bella Vista.

This is it, Jo Shelby said.

They stepped through the columned entrance and set their baggage against a wall of the small lobby. There were a couple of wicker chairs around a coffee table laden with magazines and several potted ferns but nothing else in a place where one might expect more. The desk clerk recognized Jo Shelby and spoke to him with a flare of familiarity.

Ah, señor, Cómo estas?

Bien. Y tu?

Bien. Quieres ver la señora King?

Sí. está aquí?

Sí, momentito. Voy a hablarla.

While he inquired about Mrs King and the desk clerk climbed nearby stairs to call for her, Athen and Carmen were peering into the adjacent restaurant and reviewing an open menu tacked to a wooden stand in its entrance. It was later in the morning, only a few patrons sitting randomly in the spacious open-air room that opened onto a patio along the back.

We should eat here, Athen turned and called back to him. Carmen says it's a good menu.

She actually spoke to him, he thought. Carmen says, he thought. They're becoming buddies again, he didn't want to think. It's expensive, he said.

We can afford one good meal, Athen said.

We ate that one last night, he said.

Carmen stood innocently looking on but her mind, he knew, was brewing something. He wondered why she didn't just slam him on the floor of her apartment Christmas when she had the chance and do things to him that would've nailed his heart to the place. But then maybe that wasn't her way. Maybe she was waiting for him to make the first move but he couldn't because she had a dignity he was afraid to touch. Maybe she knew he'd be back for the gun and there'd be more time, just as he thought, too, only time wasn't always what you thought it was going to be. Sometimes it would stretch out before you like a straight Delta line running forever into the sky and at others it would just disappear, that same sky meeting you head on, nothing in between. That was the time he was feeling, a fuse burning toward him, eating up the space between him and that open sky. He figured it was the same time Carmen felt and she was going to make the most of it.

Jo Shelby Ferguson, Cómo estás? Blanche King's words echoed operatically from above as she bounded with a flourish down the lobby stairs, her slippers slapping hurriedly against the concrete steps. She wore a flowing pink robe that billowed around long silk pajamas of like color and moved the air aristocratically before her with a cigarette between her fingers. She hadn't changed a bit.

Bien, he said. Mighty good to see you. He removed his broad-brimmed sombrero and bowed slightly. It had been a year since he'd seen her and she'd be eighty-two now but time had cost her nothing. She looked as stout and healthy. She had the same masculine bearing, deep raspy voice. The bun of rusty-gray hair looked as though it hadn't been touched. The same pair of glasses hung from the same plaited cord around her neck. Her rigorous movements, mannerisms, all seemed to project a confidence and energy carried over from other years, that old people had to do that, he thought, take as much of their youth with them to fight off death, making up some of it along the way.

Likewise, she said, clearing the last step with a bounce that propelled her toward him. How in the world are you? She extended a hand then withdrew it and hugged him instead. She pushed herself back but kept her hands on his shoulders. She had not yet seen his two companions. So, what brings you back to México? Ah, do not tell me, she smiled and winked teasingly. It is the señorita—

—Señora Moncada, he broke in. By the way, I'd like you to meet two of my friends. Athen and Carmen had heard the commotion from the restaurant and were standing nearby. Mrs King, this is Athen. She's my friend from Mississippi.

Athen, so very nice to meet you, Mrs King said.

My pleasure, Athen said, as she extended a hand and smiled and they shook.

And this is Carmen, he said. She's a friend from Mexico City. He'd at least had time to run that much through his brain, the difference between possessive pronoun and indefinite article.

Mucho gusto, Carmen, Mrs King said, alternating appraising looks between the two ladies, a pointed forefinger ticking towards one then the other. What a lucky young man to be traveling with such charming and beautiful companions.

Yes ma'am, it's luck all right, he said, his lips compressed so the smile appeared involuntary.

Shall we go to the terrace for coffee and some time to catch up? she said.

Yes ma'am, that'd be nice, he said.

The girls nodded approvingly.

They followed her exaggerated strides over the slate tile through the restaurant and to the terrace, her robe ballooning around tables she passed, its hem fluttering over cups and saucers that shook lightly at its touch, as though in deference to the passing ownership.

The terrace was a large open dining area decorated with huge clay pots of laurel and palm trees and smaller containers of jacaranda and oleander. It was bordered on its outer perimeter by a hibiscus hedge. Down a back wall alternating vines of purple and red bougainvillea interlaced and trailed. An ordered arrangement of wrought-iron tables and matching chairs, neatly set with white napkins and crystal goblets and shining flatware, added a touch of elegance as if to say, reserved for the rich. The area was typically closed for breakfast, Mrs King had previously told him, in order to keep the patrons corralled inside for faster serving, but he'd reached the conclusion it was because she wanted the privacy for herself and her guests.

Mrs King chose her favorite table near the edge of the terrace and indicated places for each to sit. Jo Shelby pulled chairs out for Athen and Carmen next to Mrs King then seated himself across from her and removed his hat. They were in a higher part of the city and could see, beyond the descending red tile roofs, the distant ridges of eastern sierras and Popocatépetl and the Sleeping Lady, their snowy peaks laying against the cloudless sky like figures sculptured from marble.

This is just lovely, Athen said, unable to pull her eyes from the panorama.

And your name is Athen, Mrs King said, crushing her cigarette in an ashtray then raising a hand and twirling a finger for a waiter.

Yes ma'am, Athen said, reluctantly pulling her eyes from the view.

And you are Carmen, she said.

Yes, Carmen said. With her leather boots and straw sombrero, she cut the most imposing image of the three.

Very good, just wanted to make sure I've got your names straight. At eighty-two one's memory does tend to slip a little.

The slippage in his own memory worried him. He'd told her about both but couldn't remember what or how much. She knew good and damn well what their names were. Saying them over again was just a contrivance to jostle a memory gear so it bucked and slipped into place. Eventually it would and he hoped when it did she was circumspect enough to let it idle quietly and not shift down to her mouth.

A waiter quickly appeared and Mrs King called out orders for coffee and the waiter departed with equal urgent attentiveness.

So, let me get this straight, Mrs King said, looking at Jo Shelby.

Jo Shelby cringed.

Athen came with you from Mississippi and the two of you met Carmen in Mexico City.

Yessum.

She was doing it again, working the memory, kept looking at him waiting for him to help her out but in his mind she'd summed it up enough. Anything else might have started another story and he was having enough trouble just living out the one he was in, that thought leading him gratefully to the next.

I'm looking for a will, he said.

My, my, Mrs King said. The last time you were down here you were looking for a hacienda and your next of kin.

I found those.

Yes. You stopped and told me on your way home. I did not think I would ever see you again. She swung a calculating look to Athen, then Carmen.

Now I need to find this will, he said. He began to rehash his family history and she cut him off with a flippant wave of her hand.

Yes, yes, I know all that. My memory's not that weak. I know all about the great La Hacienda Tierra del Puente and don Fernando Edgardo Cruse Linares. We talked about him, you and I, right here on this very terrace where he would come with his bride, your great-great aunt, Caroline I believe was her name ...

Yessum, he confirmed.

... until she passed away, God rest her soul. Then he would come alone, sit at the far table there, in the corner near the hibiscus hedge and order two glasses, one for himself and the other for his dearly departed. He might drink several glasses of wine, but the other remained untouched.

Qué romántico, Carmen said.

How touching, Athen said, not to be left out.

It is true, Mrs King said. But those were other days.

The waiter arrived with a white porcelain pot of coffee, white vapors of steam rising from its spout. With great care and formality he moved around the table and served each cup. When he was through he stood at a soldier's attention beside Mrs King and said, Algo más?

No gracious, Felipe. Éste suficiente, she said and he bowed graciously and departed.

There's more you don't know, Jo Shelby said.

Obviously, there is. You told me about one of your great-grandfathers losing your family's land in a poker game and I guess I'm waiting for you to tell me this will has something to do with that.

Yessum, it does, he said and was about to nervously embark on that story when Athen put her cup down and interrupted.

Mrs King, it might be better if I told this part.

Mrs King nodded. By all means.

Proceeding matter-of-factly, Athen told of recent events back home, the suit Jo Shelby had filed against her father, the trial and the judge's ruling. From their childhood years to the present, she traced her history with Jo Shelby, only what was essential for the clarity of perception. She omitted details personal and private but told of her father's lack of support for Jo Shelby when he went to prison and the reason why, because his only daughter was dating someone beneath her, the son of hired hand. She told of her family's obsession with land and wealth and her estrangement from them for all the above and through the telling showed no emotion and none when she concluded except a sharp glance at Carmen across from her: And that's the main reason we're here.

Jo Shelby looked at her and gave an approving nod.

Carmen sat erect, her face one of cool calculation, what had been won or lost, added or subtracted, divided or multiplied.

For a while nothing was said. Everyone sipped their coffee as though it was a source of relief, an excuse not to talk then Mrs King broke the silence. I will say, Jo Shelby, whether told by you or someone else, your stories never cease to fascinate. Famous writers have stayed at this hotel and if any of them ever heard what I've heard and wrote it, you'd be famous.

I just came to help out an old lady and find a will, he said.

If I'm the old lady, I don't need help.

No'me. Señora Moncada at La Hacienda Tierra del Puente or what's left of it. She wrote she needed help. The government's tryin to take the place from her.

I see, said Mrs King. And you think she might be able to help you with the will.

Maybe. I was hoping you could.

How's that?

Like I told you before, my great-great-great-granddaddy came to Mexico with his family to live. He brought his wife Caroline and two sons, Taylor and Jonathan, and a daughter, Caroline, the one who married don Fernando. One son Foster stayed behind to take care of the plantation. My granddaddy wouldn't have died without leaving a will. He wouldn't have just handed the land lock-stock-and-barrel over to Foster to be lost in a crapshoot, particularly when he was still alive in Mexico with two sons and a daughter when the crapshoot took place. You're an American. I figured you'd know something about American wills in Mexico.

Actually, I'm British, but down here that makes little difference. I know some things. My husband passed away here and left this hotel to me along with enough money to live comfortably the rest of my life.

He had a will, then.

Yes. Wills work here much the same as they do in the United States.

You have to go to a notario publico, Jo Shelby said, glancing at Carmen.

Yes. But if land or property is involved, it is registered with the state in a government office, El Registro de la Propiedad You have to go there to change the title, el título de propiedad it is called, to those who inherit.

The land involved in this one's back home.

Athen and Carmen looked like spectators at a tennis match watching an invisible ball.

I'm not sure how that would work, she said. In that case, he might have written a will and not registered it with the state. You might have to speak with an attorney. I do know, though, from other friends and acquaintances, stories I've heard, that American wills were written in Mexico and made valid here long before the turn of the century, which would mean the eighteen seventies, if that helps you.

Yessum. It helps a lot, he said. Where do they keep em, the wills?

I have a copy of my husband's. There is also a copy here in Curenavaca in the Registro de Notario.

That kind of like the Registro Civil?

Yes. Except the Registro Civil keeps records of births and deaths, marriages. You are familiar with it.

Yessum. They're the ones who did all the research and told me I had family still alive here.

Perhaps the Registro de Notario will have the will you seek. Perhaps you'll walk in and ask for it and they will quickly furnish you a copy.

Perhaps so. That would be nice.

Because if they don't, you'll be looking for a needle in a haystack.

Yessum. I heard that before. More'n once.

Lets hope the Registro has it and you can proceed on to the hacienda to help the señora. But, she raised a finger, only if you promise to return with your charming friends to see me.

Yessum. We'll definitely do that.

Athen and Carmen nodded. They had been sitting and listening with nothing to add to the discussion.

There was a brief silence. Mrs King turned around as if to assess the business in her restaurant then turned back around and faced Jo Shelby. Would you like to see a copy of my husband's will? It's upstairs in my apartment.

Yes ma'am. By all means.

Very well, come with me. Athen and Carmen, make yourselves at home. Order something to eat if you like. It's on the house.

Both smiled and thanked her.

Jo Shelby followed her through the restaurant and lobby and up the stairs, down a familiar corridor to French doors through which he had passed before but there she stopped.

Jo Shelby, please forgive me, she said in a low serious voice. I did not tell you the truth. The will is not here. It is in a lock box at the bank. I just wanted to speak with you privately.

He said nothing and nodded.

Perhaps this old woman is being meddlesome, but what in God's good name is going on with these two women you brought?

He's prob'ly the only one who knows that.

And you don't?

No'me. Not even sure they do.

You mentioned them when you were here. Told me you were going home to Athen. Now you show up with both in my hotel.

He shrugged. It wadn't planned.

How did Carmen get back into the picture? Now I'm really sounding like a nagging mama.

She had the gun. I didn't invite her along. She invited herself.

The gun. Oh yes, that gun. I *do* remember the gun. The one you were going to pawn but didn't, then had to for money to get home.

Yessum. I wired her the money to get the gun back.

You and that gun. You remember my telling you it was like the ark of the Israelites in the hands of the Philistines, all the trouble it caused them, that you'd do well finding another home for it.

Yessum.

And look what it's done now.

It saved my life once. I've grown attached to it. I'm rock hard sure it belonged to my great-granddaddy Cal and he's the reason I'm down here.

If it can get you out of this, you ought to treat it like the Ark of the Covenant and build a temple for it. Do you have it with you?

Yessum. Not sure what's goin to get me out of this though, the women. Maybe time and luck.

They were still standing at the French doors, the sounds of the restaurant below echoing upward through the stairwell. Mrs King smiled and draped a motherly arm around his shoulder. Jo Shelby Ferguson, would you like a little advice from a surrogate mama?

What's surrogate?

Substitute. I know I cannot take your mother's place but this is what I think she would say, that is if you're interested.

Yessum. Go on.

I'd go after the will you came for and let those two women work out their own destiny. Pretty soon, one of them will give up.

That's what I'm afraid of. It might be the wrong one.

I don't think so. Trust Mama King. Keep your eyes on your goal and the rest will work out. Now, we need to get back to our guests. I'll just tell them I had forgotten and the will wasn't here.

When they returned to the table, Athen and Carmen were engaged in conversation.

You two seem to be getting along fine without us, Mrs King said. Sorry it took so long. I must have put that will in the lock box at the bank. She looked at her watch. It's almost eleven, she said. I've got an idea. Why don't you three be my guests and stay for lunch.

Much obliged Jo Shelby said, but we really need to be getting along. I want to go by the Registro de Notario and reach the hacienda before dark. The señora's not expectin us and I don't want to surprise her at night. Last time I did that I was beaten, my front teeth kicked out and I was almost hanged.

The Registro de Notario is not far, on Humboldt near the Registro Civil, Mrs King said. The hacienda is just beyond La Joya, less than an hour by bus from here. You've got plenty of time before dark. Besides, you've got to eat.

The bus only goes as far as La Joya, Jo Shelby said. Then we have to hike the rest of the way. That'll take a while.

You could get a taxi in La Joya, Mrs King said.

He frowned. No gracias.

Let's stay and eat, Jo Shelby, Athen said, before he could generate another excuse.

I agree, Carmen said. Señora King is right. La Joya is less than an hour from here.

He cast a hopeless look at Mrs King who was smiling.

When will we eat? Athen said, an antsy rush in the words.

Around noon, Mrs King said.

Good. That'll give me time to do some shopping. Are there any shops nearby?

Absolutely, some of the city's best just outside, all around the plaza.

Thought you brought enough clothes with you, Jo Shelby said.

I did.

So, why're you buyin more? That's just more to tote around.

Because I didn't bring any riding clothes that's why. And I'm the one doing my own toting. Care to join me, Carmen?

Oh, Sí, Carmen said, snapping her head as though stunned by the invitation.

See you back at noon, Athen said cockily over her shoulder as she and Carmen exited through the terrace doorway and disappeared in the shadows of the restaurant.

Jo Shelby looked at Mrs King and rolled his eyes.

She smothered a laugh with her hand. Las aparencias engañan, she said. Things are not as they appear. Just remember your goal, she said. Keep your eyes on it. You'll come back some day and hug my neck for that advice, Jo Shelby Ferguson.

He smiled and lifted a cup in salute to her. Think I'll go check on that will while the ladies are shoppin.

The Registro de Notario was easy to find. It was only a few doors down from the Registro Civil where he'd spent much of his time the previous trip looking up the records of his lost kin. The building was much smaller and not as imposing as the Registro Civil and he figured that was because the birth and death and marriage rate in the country was so much higher than the will rate. Most of them had nothing to leave.

Inside, the layout was similar to the Registro Civil and Circuit Clerk's office back home. Similar, he guessed, to any government building that kept records. There was always a long counter for people to line up and beyond that rows of desks for the clerks and secretaries to keep up with all the volumes of folks' legal affairs stacked ceiling-to-floor around the walls. The volumes were always made the same and of the same color, light pea-green cloth clovers with brown leather spines and he wondered who started that trend and if the colors possessed any significance.

He went through a short foyer and stepped up to the counter. A lady left her desk and approached the counter to greet him and asked if she could help him.

Estoy buscando para un testamento, he said.

You wish to inquire about a will, she said. I speak English.

That's good, he said. Yessum, I'm looking for a will.

And this is a will made and notarized here in México, in the state of Morelos?

That's what I'm tryin to find out. You see, it's a long story, if you got time to listen.

Sí, senor. I have the time. She moved an upturned palm across the counter. You can see no one is here. We are not busy.

He told the story he had told so many times before and when he finished she pressed her hands to her cheeks and said, Mama mía, that was many years ago.

Yessum, before this century. You got wills back that far?

Sí, we have wills much further back in time. But this was an American. We have very few American wills and most of those are more recent, of this century.

But you can check and see, caint you?

Sí, señor.

Señor Ferguson. Jo Shelby Ferguson.

Sí, Señor Ferguson. And this person's name?

His name was Colonel Calvin T Ferguson, T for Tyson.

She picked up a pencil and began writing on a pad on the counter, then stopped writing and looked up. United States of America?

No'me. That's not what he would've put. He would've written Confederate States of America.

Cómo?

Confederate States of America. He was an American but he was a southern American, not a yankee one.

Oh, Señor Ferguson. I understand. A cloud passed over her face, one that traveled forehead to chin and drew the lines in her face downward. This may prove more difficult.

How's that?

In those years your government, pardon me, maybe not your government but the United States Government ...

Naw, now. I'm an American. That's my government. It just wadn't my great-granddaddy's at the time.

I understand, Señor Ferguson. But that is the problem. The United States government did not accept any transactions of Mexicans with Confederados. Confederados were considered outlaws, bandidos. Your government was very much against Emperor Maximilian and anyone connected with him.

But Col Ferguson died nearly ten years after all that, he said. Maximilian was assassinated and Jaurez took over and things settled down, least that's what I've been told.

Señor Ferguson, your Mexican history is much better than my knowledge of American history. I do not think we have this will but perhaps I should just check and see if there is any record by that name, Colonel Calvin T Ferguson. That is correct, yes?

Yessum. T for Tyson.

Yes, of course. Do you have any identification, Señor Ferguson?

Yessum. He pulled out his wallet, opened it and tweasered out his driver's license and laid it on the counter.

This identifies you, Señor Ferguson. But I need also something showing your relationship with the testator.

For this, he was prepared. He opened his shirt and pulled out papers he had retrieved from his valise back at the hotel and laid them on the counter, documents he had been provided by the Registro on his previous trip.

The señora immediately recognized their authority but another frown shadowed her face. Señor Ferguson, these are official documents but they do not show your relationship to the testator, Colonel Calvin T Ferguson. I do not see—

Just a second, he said, interrupting her. Look up at the top, he moved his finger up the page, where it says Caroline Ferguson casada Fernando Alfonso Cruse Linares.

Sí, Sí.

And right above that, her father's name in small print.

Aha! Claro! Calvin T Ferguson, yes, it is there. But I do not see your name.

He retrieved another piece of paper from inside his shirt, one much smaller, the print in white against a black background, and laid it on the counter beside the other papers. This here's my birth certificate.

Yes, I understand. It says your father was John Mosby Ferguson and your mother was Elizabeth Carter Ferguson.

Yes ma'am. Next he pulled out the letters dated from eighteen hundred sixty-six, laid them on the counter and drew the clerk's attention to the signature on both, Caroline Bouchillan Ferguson. She's the wife of the colonel in question, he said. It says so in the letters if you care to read em. These letters were passed down in my family and saved by my mama. They also tell the colonel came to Mexico with his wife and two sons and a daughter and the date on them is important because the colonel didn't die until eighteen hundred eighty-two. That date's not as important to you as it is me, he added parenthetically. He's buried in a church graveyard in La Joya, right down the road. The date's on the tombstone and I got a camera and can go take a picture, get it developed and bring it back to you. And one more thing—

Señor Ferguson, she said, holding up her hand and stopping him. This is a story very incredible, but I believe you. You do not need to say more.

I'm much obliged.

Technically, I need more identification but for this story, what you have is sufficient. Momentito.

She turned and left the room through a door at the rear and he began picking up his documents and returning them inside his shirt and buttoning it.

She was gone a while and his legs grew tired. He looked around for a place to sit, like the bench at the Registro Civil, but there was nothing. He figured it didn't take as long to retrieve the artifacts of the dead. Either that or his earlier conclusion was being confirmed. Not many people came here. Only the rich. And you could count the rich in Mexico without leaving the hundreds.

After almost half an hour the lady returned, no smile on her face.

Señor Ferguson, my apologies for taking so long, but I looked in several different volumes. I wanted to be certain.

I can tell by lookin at you.

Sí, the news, it is not good. We have no will that was notarized with the same Calvin T Ferguson, T for Tyson. But Señor Ferguson, as you know, that does not mean there is no will. It just means there is no notarized will. Many times the family keeps the will and the will is passed down just as your letters. Your papers, she looked absently at the counter. Por favor, may I see your papers again?

He unbuttoned his shirt once more and retrieved the papers and handed them to her. She sifted through the disheveled sheaves until she identified one from the Registro Civil. She laid the document on the counter for him to see then ran her finger down the page. Here, Señor Ferguson, this person, she said, pointing at the name of Carlita Navarro Cruz Moncada, may have some knowledge of this will.

He picked up the documents, squared them on the counter and slipped them once again inside his shirt. Yessum, that's where I'm goin next. Muchas gracias, he said tipping his hat.

De nada, she said.

He was almost through the foyer when she called out, Buena suerte.

He stopped and turned. Muchas gracias. I'll take all the luck I can get, and he tipped his hat again at the lady.

He arrived back at the hotel and the maitre d' informed him Mrs King was waiting for him on the terrace. She had changed into a bright colored pink blouse and turquoise slacks and wore heavy pieces of turquoise jewelry that made the pink an afterthought. She was by herself, which meant Athen and Carmen were still shopping.

Any luck, she said to him as he pulled out a chair and sat down.

Nada. The lady said it was never notarized, that it was probably kept by the family, somewhere.

Somewhere could be anywhere, she said. If I recall, you said the old colonel had other children, two sons beside the daughter and the one son who stayed behind to tend the plantation.

Yessum. Taylor and Jonathan. Foster's the one who stayed home.

Did they have families?

Foster did. Not sure about the other sons. All Señora Moncada knew were their names. They all lived on a hacienda near Michapa. It bordered La Hacienda Tierra del Puente, which is how my great-great-grandmother Caroline married into that family. She and the don's oldest son, Fernando, fell in love.

Seems I've heard a similar story.

One that aint as old. Anyhow, the Señora said the hacienda where they lived was in ruins, that it was destroyed by Zapata, only the walls still standing.

Those sons were young when the family migrated to México.

That's right. Prob'ly late teens, early twenties.

Zapata went on his tear around nineteen hundred ten. So they would have been alive then.

That makes sense.

Perhaps they were killed in that rampage. They and any families they might have had. Zapata was ruthless.

Perhaps. There's not a trace of em now. I checked all that out last time I was down here.

You checked at the Registro Civil, where they record births and deaths?

Yessum. But because they were Americans and the Mexican government back then, Jaurez and his gang, were goin after Americans who were Confederados, the family wouldn't have registered it. They wouldn't have darkened the door. Great-aunt Caroline was the only one who got in the books because she had a Mexican last name.

She reached for a pack of Camels on the table and thumped out a cigarette on her knuckle. You really think you'll find that will?

Yessum.

But what if you don't, she said, striking a match and lighting the cigarette.

That's a what if I don't even consider.

You're a stubborn young man, Jo Shelby Ferguson. Her cheeks sucked in on her first drag and she blew an authoritative stream of smoke into the air.

My mama called it single-minded. You called it keeping my eyes on my goal. It's all one and the same to me. Got something to do with will power.

Mrs King smiled. Whatever it is, it has worked well for you in life.

She glanced at the cigarette. I'm sorry, would you like one?

No'me. Better not. Athen doesn't like me smokin.

Sounds like one of those two women is changing you.

Both are workin at it, that's for sure.

Speaking of the angels, Mrs King said, nodding toward the restaurant.

They were a spectacle to be behold coming through the tables of diners, both decked out in straw sombreros and high-waisted tight pants and leather knee-high boots. They could have been a pair of bandidas in a showdown walk. Heads rotated left and right as they made their way onto the terrace.

Well I'll be damn, Jo Shelby said.

Mrs King chuckled and coughed on her smoke. You've got your work cut out for you.

Yessum. But if you recall, I'm single-minded, got the will power.

They were on their way to the bus station, headed down the street called No Reelección, when Carmen stopped.

I need to contact my friends to help at the hacienda, she said. There is a telephone at a farmacia near here. It may take some time. Our telephone system is not like yours.

Do they all live here? Athen said.

They all live in the state of Morelos. So they are not far away. There are not many telephones in Cuernavaca and I may have to wait in line.

Do you have to pay?

Yes, a small fee. Wait for me at the Plaza de Armes. It is not large. I will look for you.

Jo Shelby and Athen nodded and kept walking.

Why is a street called No Reelection? she said.

Down here the same folks keep gettin reelected. That's why their revolution is taking a while. So I guess the street's a reminder it aint over.

Men get reelected back home.

Yeah, but it aint the same.

He could tell she wanted to ask another question but nothing more was said.

They kept walking.

La Plaza de Armes was the heart of the city's centro. At one end was El Palacio de Cortez, the oldest colonial structure in the hemisphere, and at the other, El Palacio de Gobenador. Linking those two imperial structures was a promenade of statues and fountains and gardens, shaded walkways and benches. Along the plaza's perimeter waiters scrambled with orders at sidewalk cafes and street vendors, weaving in and out of the waiters' paths, hawked their wares table to table and local traffic circled, the drivers looking for a place to park or gawking at the women, las chicas, and some just looking, their world that empty until they came to the plaza. A stranger upon entering the city would have no trouble finding La Plaza de Armes. La Plaza de Armes would find them, draw them to its festive energy.

The Café del Vulcan was located across the plaza and the only one of several with an open-air second story. The maitre d' greeted Jo Shelby and Athen at the arched entrance and led them up a tiled stairway to a table on the upper level where they would have a clear, elevated view of the plaza; where they could see Carmen when she arrived and she could see them.

It was the first time they had been alone since the evening and conversation for both was still a minefield. Athen was being cordial but distant, guarded, probably still hurt, he guessed. He wondered if she knew he felt the same. She looked striking in her new attire. He thought Carmen was the one turning heads as they walked down the street. Now Carmen was gone and dark feral eyes were tracking Athen like a prey.

He ordered a round of margaritas and she did not protest. Their detached, nervous eyes roamed the restaurant where artifacts of the culture—sombreros and panchos and guitars and serapes and basketry—hung on the walls and large ceiling fans wheeled overhead adding a cooler edge to the already chilly breeze flapping the awnings and blowing napkins off tables. There was distant mariachi music, coming from somewhere. By the intermittent static, probably somebody's radio at the bar.

I'm sorry things turned out the way they did, he said, swallowing his words with his drink. I didn't intend it. All I wanted to do was get the gun and move on.

She held her glass with both hands close to her lips and studied him over its rim and for a while said nothing, just stared at him with narrow green calculating eyes, her teeth clenched behind her lips, then said: I believe you. I'm not upset about that. It's your not telling me about her, staying with her, I'm upset about.

He'd been down this road before. She'd had another life before his was reborn. No telling with how many. He could run that dog again but it wouldn't hunt before and probably wouldn't again so his thinking took another approach. If she'd been important, he said. I'd have told you.

She took a sip from her drink then set it down. Her face seemed to relax, her eyes, too, as they opened wider.

She was just keeping the gun, he said.

The green eyes narrowed again. Jo Shelby Ferguson, this is about more than a gun and you know it. You've blamed and praised that gun for just about everything that's happened to you, like it was some kind of talisman.

What's a talisman?

Something with magical powers.

He thought about that a moment, the possibility ... probability.

You haven't answered me, she said.

I didn't hear a question.

She leaned across the table, her eyes bearing down on him. This is about more than the gun.

Damn, woman. I stayed with her two weeks and slept on the couch because I didn't have money to do otherwise.

Their voices were rising and heads were turning.

Don't raise your voice, she said. People are looking.

They were already looking, he thought, but at her, get up like a bandida escaped from the silver screen. He didn't have to worry about anybody looking at him as long as he was with the two of them. He was just a comma between two exclamation points, maybe not even a comma but a space. All I can say is I wish to hell the gun was what you said so I could twirl it in my fingers like a gunfighter and make a wish and, poof, you'd see the truth.

What is the truth?

With respect to what?

To us?

With all I been through the past six years it's hard for me to say. The words are there. They been there, all those six years and before that. I have to admit they faded a time or two, but that was when I was back home and you left, took off back to school and wouldn't return my phone calls or answer my letters. I've said them before and they got roughed up, but I never let go of em, never cast em off. So, what I'm about to say doesn't come easy.

The waiter came to the table to check on their drinks and Jo Shelby politely waved him away. He was about to continue and glimpsed Carmen across the plaza. She was standing on a corner, her head turning left and right, scanning in search of them. There's Carmen, he said. He began waving his arms but the afternoon sun was in her eyes and she couldn't see.

Finish what you were going to say, Athen said.

I will, but we need to let Carmen know where we are first.

We need to know where we are first, she muttered under her breath, across her drink as she gulped it down.

Carmen stood a moment canvassing the area, a bewildered look on her face, then began walking down the street bordering the plaza. In front of the Café Universal, two men seated at a table near the street, called out to her.

She won't look this way, he said. Two men said something to her and she's talking to them.

Carmen spoke briefly to the men then continued walking.

Jo Shelby, Athen said, her voice a smothered scream.

He swung his attention back to her. Her face was suddenly pale. She looked stricken. Are you okay? he said. You choke on your drink?

Look! she said, nodding in the direction of the cafe where Carmen had stopped.

What? he said.

That café. Those two men.

Carmen slid from his view and he trained his eyes on the two men. They wore broad-brimmed sombreros similar to his; like they were trying to look Mexican but they weren't. They looked American. The clothes looked American, blue jeans and khaki shirts and cowboy boots and large fancy sunglasses. The sombrero brims were raked low and shaded their faces but they looked ...

There was a moment of brief confused silence.

Well I'll be damn, he whispered.

II

It was a word he knew and had heard before but in a different language. In his tongue it had to do with planting but in theirs it meant to create or to make, a word so essential that without it their language, any language, would collapse into a fragmented incoherent babble. In the time of his forefathers it was a word that meant wealth and ownership and privilege; it was a word that meant poverty and inequality and disenfranchisement. It was a word that gave to few and took from most. A word hailed as the savior of the country, the one entity above all others that created work and livelihood for its people; yet a word defamed as the villain of that same history, the residue of dominion and viceroyalty. It was a word that had made the country, pulled its vast and sprawling diversity together, then caused it to be unmade and made over, much as its cousin word, plantation, had in his own country, which was the reason he was there. The word was *hacienda*.

At one time La Hacienda Tierra del Puente was one of the largest ranches in Mexico. The main section stretched south from the Desierto del Carmen along the southwest spurs of the Sierra del Ajusco to the village of Michapa, then northeast up the slopes of Sierra de Miacatlán to the high plateau and ancient Aztec fortress of Xochialco. There a narrow section crossed the Valle de Cuernavaca and another took up, including most of the Valle del Rio Yautepec, a rich agriculture region that was once a fiefdom of Cortez, and a third bordered the Rio Cuautla south to the slopes of the

Sierra de Tetillas. He guessed that was one of the reasons it was called Tierra del Puente, land of the bridge, the way its big pieces all linked together.

The hacendado of this small country within a country was Roderigo Fernando Cruz but the man responsible for its expansive grandeur was Porfirio Díaz, the mestizo president who rewarded his friends with unjustified extravagance and once referred to Mexico's poor as the sleeping tiger of its history, an animal that should not be awakened. At don Roderigo's death the hacienda passed to his eldest son, Fernando Alfonso Cruz Linares, who, by no fault or defect or incompetence of his own, lost most of it. Not because he did not possess intelligence or courage or political savvy, which he did. Not because he did not have the money to hire and maintain and equip a small standing army of his own, which he had. Not because he was wanton and reckless, which he was not. But because most of La Hacienda Tierra del Puente lay in the State of Morelos and in the heart of the state of Morelos was a small Indian village, Anenecuilco, which means place where the waters swirl, and the heart of Anenecuilco was the Charro of Charros, the finest of horsemen, an angry and dashing young man hell bent on returning lands seized by the haciendas to the people and the name of the charo was Emiliano Zapata.

Jo Shelby had heard all this from señora Moncada, who told him how don Fernando, reasoning a breakup of the great hacienda might soften the blow of the revolution he saw coming, before his death apportioned the land among his two sons, Miguel and Marcos, and daughter, Carlita, the señora's mother. But Zapata was no government subject to reason or political influence. He was an enraged and vengeful revolutionary, born with a mark in the form of a hand on his chest. Throughout Morelos, from the Rio Amacuzac in the south to Cuernavaca in the north, zapatistas overran the haciendas.

All that remained of the main casa of La Hacienda Tierra del Puente near Michapa, Miguel's inheritance, was the neglected shell of a once magnificent casa, ruined and charred walls, floors of rubble, vacant doors and windows. The same fate befell Marcos' hacienda to the south near the Sierra de Tetillas. Only her parent's hacienda in the north was spared. Possibly because her father was good to his workers, treated them fairly, the señora said, and Zapata knew this. Or because her mother was a very attractive woman, known throughout Mexico for her beauty and Zapata muy enamorado, very much the lover, spared her. Or perhaps in his blind rage to destroy the hated haciendas around them, Chinameca and Mapatzlan and Atlihuayán, and move on the cities of Cuernavaca and Cuatula, he passed over her parents, for they had done nothing to antagonize him. Just when the thunder of the hooves had passed and her family thought they could breathe again, the señora told him, then came the campaign of 1916 by General Gonzalez to exterminate the zapatistas who controlled Morelos. In some ways Gonzalez was even worse than Zapata, laying waste to the countryside, looting haciendas and wrecking the sugar industry. Zapata struck back with even worse savagery, the aftermath predictable devastation. Through all of that, whatever the reason, to God she gave daily thanks for her house and land; that she had survived.

Those were his thoughts as the ancient overgrown road on which they had been walking came to a place where the land, like the crest of a wave frozen in time, swelled then fell and fanned outward and there before them, amid a green panorama of sugar cane, hued darker in the orange and pink dusk light, rose a structure of gray stone walls centered by an arched entranceway and cornered by watchtowers and above that the canted red-tiled roof of a mansion, a composite in partial silhouette against a blazing sun firing its last spokes of light through reefs of burning clouds and the sight, like a cinematic back drop for the last scene of a movie, or the first, stopped them speechless in their tracks.

In brighter sunlight they would have seen the gouges along the walls where the adobe had eroded and crumbled, the century-old sun-dried clay and straw brick where the stucco had chipped and fallen, the missing tiles on the roofs of the towers and mansion, the overall rundown neglected appearance of the place. But there in the twilight shadows it looked as new and grand as the first day of its hundred years and in those moments his mind imagined all he'd been told before of its lustrous and magnificent history, of the baptisms and weddings and celebrations held there, the galas and great fiestas, the famous people who came. The Emperor Maximilian and his empress Carlota waltzing beneath high-hanging crystal chandeliers. President Diaz sitting on the veranda with don Fernando and his great-great-aunt, the three of them discussing the problems of the country, its future, where they all might be when the sleeping tiger awoke which snapped him back to reality and made Jo Shelby think of the sleeping tiger stirring in his own country.

There it is, he said.

Athen and Carmen said nothing except what he detected in their sighs, their sudden long and deep breaths.

It looks like something in a movie, Athen finally said.

It'd be one helluva movie, he said. If it could fit in one.

Carmen remained silent, as if she, too, had seen what he had seen, her country's grand and chequered history in miniature, what was left of it, boiled down to the last hacienda.

They crossed the threshold beneath the archway and the señora saw them from the long covered porch where she sat rocking, a scene that would fit any part of the world, along with the next, a woman up in years trying to make her legs run but all she could manage, her upper torso pumping up and down on her hips and legs, was a fast unsteady walk powered by old eyes suddenly fired by a miracle.

Jo Shelby, Jo Shelby, she called, her arms outstretched before her small frail frame, wisps of iron-gray hair trailing along her temples in the slight breeze her tottering movement generated, not unlike a windup doll except for the full force of feeling in her face and animated hazel eyes and trembling mouth hanging open and the loud breathless, Gracias a dio, gracias a dio, Jo Shelby, Tu estás aquí, you are here, after she'd slammed into him.

He put his arms around her, embraced her gently lest he snap a bone in the brittle, birdlike frame pressing against him.

She held him a long moment then stepped back, her hands still grasping his shoulders, in no hurry to let go. You got my letter after all, she said.

Yessum. After all says it bout right. After all I imagine it went through to get there and after all I been through to get back.

You could have written and told me, she said.

He looked at Athen's ironic face, her mouth sucked in at the corners.

Comin is faster, he said and grinned. Takes two months for a letter.

I guess it is at that. The mail in Mexico is slower than the government, unless they want money from you. She let go his shoulders and raised a shriveled fist to her mouth and coughed into it, a dry cough but one that rattled differently in her chest. She glanced at the two women standing left and right of him. And you've brought two friends with you. Señoritas at that. Qué bueno.

He introduced Athen and Carmen, observing, as he did, the shades of astonishment and confusion cross the señora's face, the hundred questions brimming in her eyes. She'd heard the two names from his first trip, knew of the struggle accompanying them, the decision he'd finally made which kept one and dropped the other and now he stood before her with both as if no decision had been made. That was the muted shock he saw on her face, the perplexity she was throttling that said she would ask him later.

Formalities completed, the señora led them back to the house, her mouth a stream of excited chatter. Of course, they were going to stay a while, she said with maternal directness and, of course, it was a big casa and she had a room for each and, of course, she would feed them and wash their clothes and, of course, there was plenty to keep them busy. In the short time it took to reach the porch their existence and basic needs and life plan were well in place for the foreseeable future, though the inflection in the senora's voice, the look in her eyes, implied permanence.

The dining room was cavernous and with little furniture. In its center was a long table covered with white linen and around the table were throne-like high-backed chairs with scrolled tops. From a vaulted ceiling hung a crystal chandelier, whose lights, he recalled as before, did not burn. The only light came from wall sconces that burned dimly on opposite walls and two tall white candles centering the table. He remembered, too, the assorted pieces of china atop the large sideboard but nothing else, the emptiness of the big room telling the story, of the pomp and grandeur that once was, of an age gone by, an elegance kept alive now only by personality.

With old-fashioned grace the señora directed them to their seats, Jo Shelby at the head facing her, Athen and Carmen along the side facing each other. Something he did not recall was the young Mexican woman who entered the room and began pouring wine into their goblets. She was slender and wore a simple white dress and her long dark hair curtained her face each time she leaned over.

The señora noticed the look of surprise on his face. Jo Shelby, I see you were expecting Maria.

Yessum. She was the one working for you when I was here.

That is true, she said, pausing while she smothered a series of coughs in her table napkin. When she was through she raised her head as though nothing had happened, but raspy vestiges of the hacks crackled in her speech. Now I have a new ama de casa. Her name is Eréndira.

At the sound of her name, the young woman lifted the spout of the pitcher and stopped pouring.

Está bien, Eréndira, the señora said. Les estaba diciendo tu nombre.

The young woman smiled shyly and resumed pouring.

Eréndira does not speak English, the señora said. She did not have the good fortune as I of having a bilingual mother. She has been with me almost six months. She is a little slow at times but she is a good worker and loyal. Maria, Maria is a sad story. She, too, was a good worker, but her loyalty was to her father, which is why she quit, or he made her quit. I fear it was the latter. Perhaps your friends know that story, about Ricardo's assault on you.

Yes ma'am. I told em.

Ricardo is Maria's father, she said, looking left and right to include Athen and Carmen who had been sitting quietly listening. He was fired, of course, following the incident in which—

Mid-sentence her mouth froze, the last word shaping a stupefied grin. She extended her head over the table and squinted her eyes. Jo Shelby, your teeth.

I got em back.

Well, I'll declare, she said, if that doesn't beat all, the old near-forgotten accent, the inflected drawl and jargon of that other world, passed on, breaking forth clear and fresh as though untouched by time or another language or the foreign generations through which it had passed. And he saw Athen's surprised ear cock and catch it, too, the unexpected piece of home in a sound and remembered when it first broke the plane of his hearing and the comfort it brought, the same words and intonation when the señora read the letters he'd brought to her that said they were blood kin.

They look good as new, the señora said.

They'll pay for my funeral, he said, casting a toothy grin left and right.

Athen and Carmen did not smile back.

From what I know of you, you are already living on borrowed time, the señora said, returning his smile. Let us hope that is no time soon,

Eréndira completed filling their glasses and left the room.

A toast, the señora said, standing and raising a silver chalice emblazoned with the heraldic emblems of a family brought down by time and a new age. Here's to Jo Shelby Ferguson and his friends Athen and Carmen and to their safe arrival.

Excuse me, señora, Jo Shelby said, but I'd like to add yourself to that toast and La Hacienda Tierra del Puente.

Claro que sí, she said as they raised their goblets, tiny flames of candle-light caught in them as the rims chimed and resonated over the table then faded into the dim corners of the large room.

The señora sat, signaled the others to do likewise. She coughed again. This time she blinked and shook her head with embarrassment, gestures suggesting the nuisance warranted a comment then, with a flippant wave of her hand before her face, dismissed the episode as though batting away a fly. Now, where was I? she said, fumbling with her napkin and flatware as if searching there for the answer.

You were talking about Jo Shelby's teeth, Athen said.

The incident, Carmen said.

Oh yes, Jo Shelby's teeth. The incident. I guess he told you he was almost hanged.

Athen and Carmen nodded.

I had no choice but to fire Ricardo. Violence is not tolerated here. A week later, Maria quit. Or rather she did not come to work. I sent one of the mozos to look for her and Ricardo threatened him, told him not to come back. So I think her father made her quit. He is a very angry man, one unaccustomed to power. When given a little it goes to his head. He is, I fear, one of my big problems.

You said he left, Jo Shelby said. The only problems you wrote about were the problems with the land and the government trying to take it.

This is true. You said my letter took two months to reach you and much can happen in two months. I have a new administrador, Felipe. He is young, but capable. He is reporting missing cattle and horses. Some machinery has also been stolen. I do not think my people, my workers, would steal these things from me. What use do they have for them. Unlike the conditions at other haciendas, my workers here are cared for, sheltered and fed well. They get medical attention and I pay their medical bills. Of course, Ricardo had all this, too, but he wanted more, felt I owed him more. As I told you, your arrival was a threat to him.

He thought one of your sons sent me, Jo Shelby said.

Oh, yes, she said. My sons. They are, as you are so fond of saying, Jo Shelby, a long story.

Enréndira brought first bowls of chicken noodle soup, setting one before each of them. The señora said a blessing and they began to eat.

I would like to hear about your sons, Carmen said, her voice in earnest.

I would, too, Athen said. I don't know anyplace we're rushing off to tonight. She glanced at Jo Shelby when she said it and he returned a tentative look, his thinking running hours ahead, mulling the señora's comments about Ricardo.

Very well, said the señora. I will try to be brief.

But to tell that story she had to tell the one before it, of the rise and fall of the great Hacienda Tierra del Puenta and its ancestral lineage, so by the time she'd worked her way through Zapata and the revolution and civil wars that followed their soup bowls were empty, the long story of her and her husband and sons yet to come. She seemed to notice how long she was taking and apologized but Jo Shelby told her to go on. She told how, despite the civil war, her mother and father were able to hold the hacienda together. The next twenty years were quieter times in the history of her country and allowed time for many of the haciendas, including Tierra del Puenta, to stabilize and prosper. She told of her mother's death in 1930 and her father's the following year, how she and her brother, Juan, and husband, Gilberto, took over management of the hacienda then Juan was murdered, a crime unsolved to this day.

The telling of her brother's death brought a solemnity to the room and she stopped to absorb the emotion, lightly dabbing the corners of her eyes with her napkin. Eréndira used the pause as an opportunity to remove their soup bowls and replace them with plates of steak bordered with steaming rice and beans and squash.

Gilberto and I had three sons, the señora continued. Juan, Raul and Frederico. Those were good years. We were happy. Then Gilberto died. It was unexpected. The doctor said it was a heart attack. That was 1934, when the problems with the hacienda really began. There was movement again in the country for land reform, for redistribution of the haciendas. Cardenas became president. He believed in the laws. In 1937 he used the constitution of 1917, which said the government had the right to divide the lands of the haciendas in the interest of the public, and broke up the haciendas. Jo Shelby already knows much of this. Most of Tierra del Puenta was taken from us and given to peasants. We were allowed to keep only what was necessary, our homes and barns and farm equipment and two hundred and fifty hectares of land of our choice.

If that happened where I live, Athen said, there'd be a revolution, except it would be the landowners up in arms.

The comment brought a stillness to the room, as though an attendant had interrupted a queen's address. Somewhere, a clock ticked.

Jo Shelby gave Athen a look of disbelief.

Athen, the señora said, lowering her fork carefully to her plate, her face studied. That is your name I believe.

Yes ma'am.

A lovely name, the señora continued. An unusual name, perhaps one from your family's past.

Yes ma'am. It was my great-great-grandmother's name. It's from Athena, the goddess of wisdom. They just dropped the a at the end.

I see, the señora said, pausing, moving her lips as if sampling her next words. Please take no offense, Athen, but your great-great-grandmother and her family, if I understand my history of your country, has already had that revolution. It was called the Civil War.

War between the States, Jo Shelby said, as if in defense of Athen.

Oh yes, the señora said, smiling. You southerners. Well, the comparison is noteworthy, if I may continue. The results were as devastating for us as it was your ancestors, much harder for my sons than for me. My sons were spoiled, she said, her face yielding to a faint apologetic smile, a tone of embarrassment in her voice. Life had been free, easy, given to them. Now they would have to work. Fredrico and Raul found jobs in other places, jobs not as taxing as farm labor. Juan, the oldest, stayed. He wanted to be the boss, as spoiled children will, but he was lazy, as spoiled children are, and there was always conflict with Ricardo, who was the boss and a hard worker. I told Jo Shelby of the fight between them, when I had to get a gun to break it up. Juan left that day and has never returned. When Jo Shelby came, Ricardo thought Juan sent him. Ricardo was always looking over his shoulder. There was hatred between the two. Perhaps there was more between them I did not know. Did not want to know. Perhaps.

She stopped and ate again. The others were almost finished. Eréndira stepped into the room and assessed the situation, saw the señora was still eating and stepped out.

Where are your sons now? Carmen said.

Fredrico was in Puente de Ixtla, a small town south of here. He worked in a bar for a while then moved to Taxco. You know Taxco, she gestured with her fork at Carmen and Carmen nodded. It is one of the more enchanting places in México, then directed her attention next to Athen. It is an artistic center. Tourists go there to buy silver. Fredrico worked in one of the shops, learning how to craft the silver, make jewelry with his hands. He has become successful, has a shop of his own. He and his wife, Yolanda and two children, live in the second floor above the shop. I see him occasionally, usually holidays and special celebrations. He is very happy in Taxco and wants nothing to do with the hacienda. Haciendas are antique replicas that should be turned into museums, he says.

She'd been holding an empty fork as she spoke and paused to lift bites of rice and beans to her mouth and wash them down with a swallow of wine then continued. Raul went to México—

That's the city she's talking about, Jo Shelby said to Athen.

I know, Athen said, annoyed. You told me.

The señora observed briefly the curt exchange then picked up her train of thought. In México he found a job. I refused to give my sons money. He worked in a restaurant waiting tables. That was an unhappy situation so he quit and went to work for the University. I never really understood his job, but it involved the accounting office. He has a very charming personality and was always good in mathematics. He decided to go to college. His work paid part of his way. I helped him with the rest, I thought I should, he was trying to make something of his life. He is, now, the chief accountant for the University. He is married. His wife's name is Plácida. They have three children. They are happy. Raul brings them down here occasionally. The children love the hacienda, all the animals, especially the horses. They are all learning to ride. But Raul cannot even speak of the hacienda without becoming angry. He says I should sell it. The upkeep and taxes are costing me more than the sugar cane we produce. The house is not in good condition and as you could see on your arrival, the walls are deteriorating. I doubt I would get much for it.

What would you do if you sold it? Carmen said.

Raul wants me to move to México, nearer him and his niños, my grandchildren. There is more for me to do and enjoy there, he says. I could go to the concerts at the Belle Artes and spend afternoons in the museums and drink afternoon tea along the shaded boulevards. But I tell him that is not me. I was born on this land. My commitment is here, to live and die here. After that, I do not know what will happen to the hacienda. Eréndira, she called out.

Eréndira cracked the door and peeked in. Sí?

El postre, por favor.

Sí, señora, she said and closed the door.

You said you had three sons, Athen said.

Oh yes, Juan, the oldest. Juan, I am afraid, has done very little with his life. A Methodist mission from your country is building a medical clinic in La Joya, a small puebla north of here, near Jiutepec. He is working, or says he is working, for the mission. He has some skills, he does some carpentry and masonry work. They've let him use a house, really a hovel, next to the mission project. He makes enough to feed his wife and two children. His wife's name is Manuela. She is a homely sort, a little over weight, not very attractive. The children are twelve and ten years old, Gabriel and Victoria. I see them only a few times each year. Always, I have to go there. He never comes to the hacienda. Juan is still very bitter about what happened here. He thinks I favored Ricardo. I was just trying to help my son mature. He was very spoiled. Now he thinks he is maturing, in a hut with a dirt floor. He will mature when he rids himself of his anger. She stopped and, prayer-like, brought her palms together then looked at Carmen who had asked the question. So, that is the story of my sons. It is, of course, a much longer story, but at least you know something about them, and about La Hacienda Tierra del Puerta.

Gracias, Carmen said. Tanta gracias, señora.

Enréndira entered with a tray of plates she placed on the sideboard and began quietly exchanging them, one by one, for their empty dinner plates.

This looks delicious, Athen said.

It is guave with syrup. A traditional Mexican dessert.

Carmen smiled and nodded approval.

In your letter you said you had other problems, Jo Shelby said.

Yes. I do not know which is worse, someone stealing me blind or watching the theft take place before my eyes. There is little an old woman can do about a thief that comes in the night—

We'll see about that, Jo Shelby said.

But if the hacienda could produce a good sugar cane crop, just for one season, that would allow me to pay my taxes. That would feed the government wolves threatening to take my land. That would buy me time, a couple of years, before they started growling again. By then it would probably not matter. She drew her napkin to her mouth and began coughing again.

Your cough, señora Moncada, Athen said. It doesn't sound—

Yes, yes, this horrible cough, the señora said. It is nothing, just a nuisance that comes and goes.

You didn't have it when I was here, Jo Shelby said.

She inclined her head slightly but did not respond; a hint behind her grave expression there was more she was not telling. Eréndira stepped back into the room. With a whisk of her napkin across her plate the señora signaled they were finished and Eréndira began gathering the dishes.

Have you seen a doctor? Carmen said.

Oh, Eréndira, the senora said, ignoring the question. Por favor, traiga cogñac. Or would you rather have coffee? her eyes canvassing the table.

I'd prefer coffee, Athen said.

Café, gracias, Carmen said.

And you, Jo Shelby?

Brandy. That is, if the señora will join me.

My pleasure. Eréndira, trae dos cafés por las senoritas y dos coñacs por mi y el señor.

Eréndira nodded and departed balancing plates in her hands and along her arms.

I got the same question as Carmen, Jo Shelby said.

The señora straightened herself in her chair, pushed back her shoulders. About the doctor, she said.

Yessum.

No I have not seen a doctor. And I will answer your next question. My doctor is in Cuernavaca and for someone my age it has become an ordeal going there. Yautepec and Cuautla are almost as close as Cuernavaca but Dr. Vicario has been my family's doctor all these years and I do not feel I can change, not at this point in my life.

How do you get in and out of here? Athen said. It's two miles back to the road, another five at least to La Joya, the nearest town.

We have two vehicles, both old and American, neither in very good condition. The car, a Ford, just putters. I doubt it could make it to the road.

Spark plugs, Jo Shelby said.

What? she said.

It pro'bly just needs spark plugs.

Yes. Well, I doubt Felipe even knows what they are. Then the pickup will not start.

Battery, Jo Shelby said.

But to buy a battery we would have to go into La Joya or Jiutepec, and one would be heavy and very difficult, I think, to bring back on a horse or burro.

How do you get your food and supplies? Athen said.

We grow our own vegetables. Most of our meat comes from the cattle and pigs on the hacienda. For the rest I send a couple of mozos into La Joya. A small tienda there has all the staples and basics we need. They go once a week. The trip is not long. They go and come in an afternoon.

That's all well and good, Jo Shelby said. But we need to fix the vehicles.

Eréndira returned carrying a wooden tray laden with a porcelain carafe and matching cups and cut glass decanter of brandy and two snifters. Gently, she lowered the tray onto the sideboard. With equal tenderness and care she placed the cups and saucers before Athen and Carmen and poured their coffee, Jo Shelby noting all the while how deliberately and cautiously she moved, as if stirring the air might cause a disturbance, might trip a wire, and he wondered how such care and gentleness could evolve from a history of such terrible and repetitive violence and the answer that came to him was not the one he expected. But it was one he understood. He had seen that same servile caution before, what centuries of fear had done to people of another color in his own country, settling into their bones and sinew, their blood, every movement a foregone conclusion. Eréndira poured the snifters at the sideboard and placed them before the señora and Jo Shelby then departed the room with the same silent vigilance as she had entered, as if her job hung on her every movement. Not because of the señora, who was good to her. But because of her forebears and those before them, the ones who created the fear that was passed on, as though part and parcel of the blood and cells and whatever it was that handed down likeness. Then he thought how long it would take to undo that kind of fear and his thinking would not go that far.

I got a toast, Jo Shelby said, standing and raising his snifter, the light of the candles passing through the swirls of dark liquid like gold vapors infusing the air. Here's to La Hacienda Tierra del Puenta and its cousin to the north and to findin my great-granddaddy's will.

Around the table they saluted each other, their soft echos of his toast a low diminishing murmur blending indiscernibly, trailing off in fragments, as though a rhyme were being chanted, the senora uttering the last refrain.

A will? she said, her old eyes flaring slightly. Testamento?

Jo Shelby was partially standing, not fully seated. Yessum. A will. That's the other reason I came. I would have come anyhow, you understand, but this other just kinda happened in between.

He related to her the sequence of events of the past and current year and the need for finding the will, to prove once and for all that a great expanse of land far to the north should have belonged to his forebears and their progeny, which meant him and anybody else still alive hanging from the branches of that family tree. He didn't stop there but went on, telling her what he planned to do with the land, how the Patricks who owned it now—he glanced at Athen—would keep their fair share but the rest would be parceled out to the Negroes and their families who'd worked the land all those years. He'd keep a portion for himself, he said, then suddenly stopped, remembering the most important part he'd left out. He explained, as best he could, what lawyer Darden back home had explained to him, how the señora, because she never knew of the land much less any cloud on the title to the land, was never put on notice to even stake a claim, probably stood first in line ahead of him.

When he finished she began coughing, a dry cough, one that seemed to come from her face, from behind her eyes.

I'm sorry, he said. I say something wrong?

She recovered from the spasm then paused a moment to get her breath. She drew her napkin across her mouth. I am not upset, she said, her voice weak. Perhaps overwhelmed. I cannot manage what little land I have left here. And you tell me I might possess more, hundreds of miles away? Her mouth was still open as she turned to Athen, but Athen spoke first.

It's my daddy's land, Señora Moncada. She said it almost apologetically, a tone of discomfiture, then looked at Jo Shelby to glimpse his appraisal of what she'd just said but his eyes were fixed on the señora and her reaction.

Carmen looked on and drank her coffee.

A day of surprises, the señora said, lifting her snifter and taking a sip, the same muted perplexity on her face Jo Shelby had seen earlier when he introduced his female companions.

You can say that again, Jo Shelby said, turning his eyes now on Athen who gave a slight nod of agreement.

Athen continued: It was my grandfather who bought the land from a yankee who won it from Jo Shelby's great-great-grandfather in a crap game.

Crap? the señora said.

Dice, Athen said.

Oh yes, of course. Dice. That part of the story I knew. But I did not know—

I didn't tell it all, Jo Shelby said.

The señora cut her eyes at Athen then Carmen and smiled. No, I guess you did not.

Carmen continued drinking her coffee, her eyes concentrating fiercely on the cup, as if trying to divine from its contents her place in the unfolding dialogue, where she might fit in.

And Athen ain't telling it all, Jo Shelby said. Part of her family she's talkin about is down here now.

Oh? the señora said, arching her brows.

It's my brothers, Athen said. We saw them in the square in Cuernavaca. I left home rather abruptly and my mama and daddy probably sent them to find me and bring me home. That's something my mama and daddy would do.

I'd say they're down here looking for something else, Jo Shelby said.

Like maybe their inheritance.

Moonlight had entered the room, a silver slice splitting the table like a presence. There was a muted clammer from the kitchen where Eréndira was stirring and a rooster's crow from somewhere in the walled compound but otherwise quiet in the dimly lit room. For a long while they said nothing, nursed their drinks and watched the moonlight slide across the table, as if it were a separate voice taking up the slack of their own awkward silence.

Then:

This testamento, the señora said, it would be that of Colonel Ferguson, my uncle three generations removed on the American side of the family.

I think that's right, Jo Shelby said. He's my great-great-great-grandfather. I'm not good at bloodlines but I think that would make him your great-great-uncle.

Perhaps so, she said. I have no knowledge of this will. My parents and grandparents never spoke of one. They did speak of the saddlebags of money the colonel brought with him and deposited in a bank.

Which bank? Jo Shelby said, almost cutting across her words.

This I do not know. One in Cuernavaca or Mexico City. I do not recall the place. I just remember the story, the way my grandfather told it, of the colonel dressed in his gold-braided gray uniform and plumed hat striding into a bank, saddlebags hanging from both arms and several ragtag soldiers behind him carrying the same. My parents said it caused quite a commotion. The only foreign soldiers most Mexicans had seen in that time were French, so many thought these armed men desperados from the north, perhaps Texas. Ladies screamed. Bank officers blew whistles to alert the police. Tellers disappeared behind their counters. Customers ran to the doors. Some, in their nice suits and dresses, fell on the floor. She stopped to catch her breath and sip her brandy.

Qué pasó? Carmen said.

What happened? Athen echoed in the companion language.

My grandfather said it was over very quickly, the señora continued. Colonel Ferguson raised his saddlebags into the air and cried out, dinero por su banco. Everyone relaxed, some even laughed. The officers who blew the whistles rushed to him and made many apologies. Of course, they wanted the money.

And you don't know which bank? Jo Shelby said.

No. Why is that so important, the bank?

Cause that's where a will might be, in a safe deposit box.

Oh yes, the will. I understand. I am sorry but I do not know the bank ... or the city.

Your granddaddy said they were ragtag and in uniform, Jo Shelby said.

Yes. That was all in Spanish. Se ven muy estropeados. Those were his words. They looked untidy, unkempt. My English translation may not be exact.

If it's even close, the bank was in Mexico City, when they arrived. They would've looked ragtag. They would've been wearing their uniforms. They probably wouldn't have been wearing them after that.

Why is that? Athen said.

That was part of the deal with the Emperor, or so my great-grandmama Caroline said in her letters. He didn't need another army in Mexico. The United States was friends with Juarez and upset already over a French army south of the border and they were sure to be fightin upset if the Emperor let a Confederate one settle in along side his. So, the Iron Brigade, that's what General Shelby's soldiers were called, had to break up and swap their guns for plows and their uniforms for farming clothes. That's why that bank had to be in Mexico City.

As if her frail vision required a prop, the señora cupped her snifter in both hands and leveled her eyes over the rim at him. Jo Shelby, all of that happened a hundred years ago. There were many banks then in Mexico City. There are more now. Back then I do not know if they even had the deposit boxes of which you speak. I do not discourage you from looking but I think it will be most difficult, to find the bank much less the will. One other thing you must consider. For many people, their wills are not in the banks, in the bank boxes, but with the notario publicos.

I already been told that, he said.

Who told you this? she said.

Mrs King, a lady friend in Cuernavaca. She said I should check with the Notario de Publico in Cuernavaca.

I see. So you have been there.

Yes ma'am.

And what did you learn?

Nada. Nothing on a Calvin T Ferguson in the books. The lady who helped me said the government back then didn't recognize Confederates, that that's the reason the will was probably not in the books, never notarized. It didn't mean there wasn't one, she said. It just might not have been notarized but kept by the family, passed down, in a deposit box or an old Bible or trunk somewhere. She said you might know. That's why I brought it up.

The señora thought, swirled her drink in contemplation before she spoke. My testamento is with my notario, who is an attorney. Often they are kept by attorneys. Of course, I have a copy here at the hacienda. But again, I think you can eliminate notarios. If a notario had a copy or the original, there would be a record in Cuernavaca. About the banks, I do not know. I have a deposit box in a bank in Cuernavaca. Each year I pay a fee to keep the box. If I do not pay the fee, the bank takes the box. If, after time, no one comes forward to claim the box, make my payment, the bank gives the contents to the government.

So, you're sayin the Mexican government might have the will.

I do not know this, Jo Shelby. A hundred years is a long time.

You got any better ideas? The comment drew a sharp look from Athen and Carmen and he realized he'd over-stepped his manners. Sorry, señora. Guess I got a little carried away.

It is nothing, the señora said, putting down her glass and passing a calming palm across the table. I think you are—what is the word?—idealistic. Very determined, but idealistic.

I feel it's something I got to do. If I didn't, I'd spend the rest of my life wondering why I didn't. I'd rather spend the rest of my life satisfied I tried, whether I succeeded or not. He put down his drink and folded his hands, inclined his head across the table. With all due respects, ma'am, I'm wantin to reclaim the same thing you're wantin to keep.

The old gray-haired head flinched slightly and blinked, as if an insect had suddenly swooped close. She recovered her composure and smiled and lifted her snifter. Touché, Jo Shelby. It seems we are chips off the same block. Is that how you say it?

Yes ma'am. My mama would say the apples didn't fall far from the tree.

The señora smiled. I do have other ideas, perhaps not better.

I'd like to hear em, he said.

The señorita at the Registro de Notario in Cuernavaca spoke to you of wills that were not notarized. If there were such a will, it would have been kept in a safe place. When Zapata destroyed the main hacienda near Michapa, there was much that was lost, but not all. I still have some records that miraculously survived and, if I can find them—they are stored somewhere—I will look through them. Of course, there are the ruins of the hacienda. One never knows what might be found digging around in the charred remains of old wealth. There were family rumors the old colonel buried part of his money there. But—she raised an unsteady finger into the air—just rumors. Meanwhile, I will certainly think on this. If better ideas come to me, I will tell you.

The señora pushed back a ruffled sleeve and looked at a small watch on her thin wrist. Mío Dios. It is late, almost nine o'clock. I am usually in bed at this time. Are your rooms satisfactory?

They nodded.

Eréndira will take care of you. There is food in the kitchen if you become hungry, fruit and sopapillas, perhaps some flan. Sorry, no ice cream. There are playing cards in the desk in the salon. A chessboard is on the table but the playing pieces are in one of the desk drawers. I forget which one. I have not played in years. There has been no one to challenge. But perhaps now?

Jo Shelby lifted a finger.

Carmen did likewise.

Athen looked at Jo Shelby. Where did you learn to play chess?

In a Mexican prison.

There is a backgammon board, too, the señora continued, if I could just remember where I put it.

Señora, Jo Shelby, said. The horses you mentioned.

Yes?

The last time I was here they were in a pole corral south of the barn.

Yes. That is where we keep them. Occasionally we let them roam free with the cattle but since the thefts they are kept there. Why do you ask?

I was just figurin me and the senoritas might take a ride this evenin, see if maybe we couldn't scare off whoever's stealing from you.

Athen and Carmen exchanged surprised looks.

Your two friends, I think, have had a long day, the señora said. Perhaps they would like to rest.

He looked at Athen then Carmen. That's fine. I'll go by myself.

No. I'll go with you, Athen said quickly, laying her napkin on the table as a signal of finality.

Muchas gracias, señora, for your concern, Carmen said. The day has been long. But an evening ride would be refreshing. Besides, we are already dressed for one. She smiled and stood and made a pirouette, her poise, her delicate arms and hands a mock pantomime of the model's twirl and Jo Shelby recalled that part of her past, the fame she might have drawn had she stayed in that profession, the misery that would have owned her.

And so you are, the señora said. When you first arrived, I thought you were sisters.

How far does your place go? Jo Shelby said, the property lines.

She sighed and spoke wistfully, a rasp in her voice that another coughing spasm was approaching. Basically, this little valley is all mine, from the road where you entered, extending south between the sierra slopes either side of the hacienda to a narrow gorge left by river which is now barely a small stream and has no name. My workers refer to it as the arroyo because that is what it has become. Of course, my property at one time stretched much further south to the Rio Cuautla and the Sierra de Tetillas. Those were the days of the great La Hacienda Tierra del Puente, before Cardenas and land reform. Before the government divided the large haciendas and redistributed the land among the campesinos. She looked kindly at Jo Shelby. You would have liked him, Jo Shelby. You would have liked Cardenas.

He nodded and said nothing in return, his eyes seeing in hers the trapped balance of pain and justice, her ability to hold the two together, accept their history, somehow find a solution in their counterbalance.

I reckon you got a brand.

Yes. It is the letters T and P bridged at the top by an arch. It has been the brand of the hacienda for many years, over a hundred. Unfortunately, it is one easily reworked with a running iron.

What's a runnin iron? he said.

It is a straight or curved piece of metal that is heated and then the brand is drawn rather than stamped on the animal's hide. One could go to the trouble of making a pre-shaped brand, such as the one we use then stamp it over our brand so the design is changed. But Ricardo would not go to such lengths. He uses his running iron, changes the brand then resells the animal. Where, I do not know.

He'd have to have a truck and trailer to haul them, he said.

Perhaps. I do not know about these things, only that a thief comes in the night and I, an old woman, cannot catch him.

And you're sure it's Ricardo? he said.

No one else would know the location of items that have been stolen. The cattle, perhaps yes. But the equipment, no.

He stolen any horses?

No, not yet. He would like to. Like I said, we keep them in the corral and he has not ventured there. Horse stealing in Mexico is a very bad crime. I do not think he would risk that, coming that close to the house for horses.

We aim to find out if he's a thief, he said.

You should not go unarmed, she said. The hacienda has guns.

Muchas gracias but no gracias, ma'am. Only gun that ever helped me out was one that wouldn't shoot. If it had've, I might not be here now. Ricardo would've used it on me and not waited for a rope.

Very well. Perhaps the señoritas would like to adjourn first to the baño.

Jo Shelby looked at Athen and Carmen who swapped affirming nods and simultaneously began rising. Yessum. I need to go myself, he said, pushing up from his chair.

The señora lifted a hand palm outward. But please, a moment.

As if on command, the three lowered themselves into their seats.

No, no. Not the señoritas. They may go, she said, gesturing with a run-a-long backward flip of the hand still raised. I can tell you, Jo Shelby, about the saddles and blankets, where you will find them.

There had been no time for private conversation since his arrival and he sensed in her look something else, something with no relation to riding equipage.

Athen and Carmen rose again, politely pushed their chairs under the table and left the room.

He sat facing the señora who waited as the booted footsteps reported on the marble-floored hall outside and climbed the spiraled staircase leading from the zaguan to the second floor and faded in soft thuds across the wooden floors overhead then broke the silence she controlled. Would you like to smoke? I may have a cigar.

No'me. I quit.

And the reason?

Athen doesn't like it. She says its not good for you and when I ... well ... she says I taste like the bottom of an ashtray. With all respects, señora, you ought to consider quitting, too.

Yes. She strangled a cough. Perhaps I will some day.

About the saddles and blankets, he said.

They are in the barn. You can find them easily.

He began to rise. In that case—

Un momento, Jo Shelby. I did not ask you to remain to speak of saddles and blankets.

He lowered himself back into his chair.

I am an old woman whose mind is surely frail, my memory as fragile. And perhaps my senses are deceiving me in these late years. But did you not return to your home in Mississippi because your heart was there, not here? And is the señorita named Athen not the one for whom you returned and is not the Mexican señorita, Carmen, the one you left behind and have you not returned to México with both?

Yes ma'am. His brandy was finished and he wished for another but would not ask. Mine might be frailer.

Yours?

My mind.

She smiled faintly, sympathetically. Do not tell me, Jo Shelby, but I am guessing this to be another of your long stories.

He returned her smile. Yessum. I'm aimin to make it shorter.

Considering the present situation, that, I think, would be quite a fascinating, not to mention, challenging strategy. You do have one, I am assuming.

He looked away and thought, then back at her. Not meanin to sound disrespectful, but I'm supposin there's a reason you need to know.

No, you are not being disrespectful. And, yes, there is a reason.

Reason being.

That is my long story.

The movement of feet were heard overhead.

Maybe you could give me a shorter version, he said.

She swirled her brandy thoughtfully and took another sip. There is no shorter version when it comes to matters of the heart, but I will try. Many years ago, before I met Gilberto, my husband, there was another man in my life. His name is of no importance for my story. It is the story that is of importance. She stopped, her gaze assessing his attention. The sound of footsteps above them had stopped momentarily and he could hear a clock ticking somewhere in the big house.

Yessum. Go on.

Gilberto was a man very well known to me. He worked for my father, on La Hacienda Tierra del Puenta. This was at the casa grande as we called it, near Michapa, where I actually grew up. I moved to this hacienda with my mother and father, Carlita and Gabriel, when my grandfather don Fernando divided the hacienda among my two uncles and my mother. That was around the turn of the century. I do not recall the exact year, perhaps nineteen hundred and eight.

So Gilberto worked for your daddy at one hacienda and you moved to another.

Yes. I have even wondered if that was not a motive of my grandfather's for dividing the hacienda. He knew my father was very upset about Gilberto and me, our relationship. Gilberto was tall and handsome, a grand mustache curling across his face like a wing. I thought him someone out of a movie the first time my eyes saw him, riding on a stallion through the hacienda gate into the casa plaza, his dust following him like an entourage. I shall never forget the moment. It was late afternoon. I was sitting on the porch reading before going in to help my mother with the evening meal. He galloped right to the edge of the porch. I thought he might not stop. His eyes were excited and as flaring as the horse's nostrils. He had a message for my father, he said. To this day I do not remember the message. I just remember those dark eyes, so full of energy, of passion.

She sighed and stopped to drink again, tipping the snifter up and draining the brandy.

I was quite smitten, as they say she continued. But I was the hacendado's daughter. A young girl's reputation was very important, much more so then than now, I am afraid. It was considered improper for me to be courting a mozo, a hired-hand. Gilberto was not even a gerente.

What happened next?

There was a dance. It was not here but at the Michapa casa. My father allowed me to go. Gilberto was very bold. There were many young men about me, young men of rank and wealth from the other haciendas. He walked right through them, as though they were stalks of corn he was parting, and asked me to dance.

And you fell in love.

That had already happened, when he rode up to the porch. We would meet, but never with my parents' knowledge. I would find excuses to go to my uncle's hacienda at Michapa. We made secret plans. We would meet in Cuernavaca, Jiutepec, a couple of times in Mexico City. He rode once all day just to spend a few minutes with me in the evening when I could ride my horse and slip away.

You said there was another man.

Yes. That is the reason for my story. There was another man. I met him at this hacienda. It was during the revolution. Much was happening. Buildings were burned. Communications cut off. People crucified and gored in the bull ring. There was terror. We went nowhere. Then when this hombre came I feared the revolution had come to us. He rode through the gate, the same you entered. There were several men with him, no more than six. I was at the fountain getting water. The situation with Gilberto seemed hopeless. I was a young woman then and unmarried. I suppose I was what you would call vulnerable. So, there came this dashing hombre riding in from nowhere. I shall never forget. He was dressed in tight fitting black cashmere pants with silver buttons and a broad charro hat. He wore a fine linen shirt and red scarf around his neck, boots of a single piece, Amozoqueña-style spurs. Carrilleras filled with bullets crossed his chest and there was a pistol at his belt. He had a mustache fuller than Gilberto's and an intense look in his eyes that would fire the air around you. When he spoke to me I could not move. I dropped the pitcher of water I had filled. The other men with him laughed but he did not. He removed his sombrero and gallantly bowed from his horse, dipping his hat before him, so low it almost touched the ground. He wanted to meet the owner of the hacienda. I told him the owner was my father and he was away but my mother was en casa. He said nothing, just nodded. I ran to get my mother. I retreated to the pórtico while my mother walked to the fountain where the hombre and his men were waiting. They had dismounted from their horses and were drinking. They all looked tired and dusty, travel worn. As the hombre spoke with my mother he kept glancing over her shoulder at the pórtico where I stood. He motioned the other men away and spoke a long time with my mother. His face softened and he even smiled. He propped his spurred-boot on the side of the fountain and I thought my mother might do likewise, so comfortable she seemed in his company. If my father had been there, of course, none of this would have happened. When they finished speaking, the hombre looked my direction and waved. He was smiling. I would see him again. Many times. Then never again.

You had a reason, ma'am, for tellin me this story.

Yes. I was miserable in those years. I was seeing two men. I could not make up my mind. Unfortunately, others made up my mind for me. I would feel stronger today, happier with myself, even in these late years if I had made the decision myself.

She paused, composed her hands prayer-like on the table as if arranging her next thoughts accordingly. Jo Shelby, if an angel of the Lord came to your room tonight and said in his right hand he held pain and in his left tension and you had to choose one. Which would you choose?

He thought a long moment. Longer. At first I thought tension, he said. But tension can kill a man. You caint outlive tension, it'll gobble you up. But you can outlive pain. I'm livin proof of that.

Claro qué sí. Absolutamente. Time is God's other name. Time cures, heals all things. Do not ever forget. Now do you understand or is there more of the story I need to tell?

The clock he'd been hearing seemed in his ears. No'me you told it good. Real good. I'm much obliged.

De nada. Now, you know where the barn is.

He nodded. That's where I tangled with Ricardo.

You will find everything you need there. The saddles and blankets are in a side room just inside the bay door. The reins are hanging on the wall above them. Cuidense, she said, her voice deeper, sterner. Be careful.

Yessum. We will. He rose to leave then turned at the door.

There is one more part of that story I'd like to hear.

Yes?

The name of the hombre.

She stared at him with great reluctance, her eyes sad, far away. His name was Emiliano.

So that's why this place is still here.

Her face looked grave as she nodded, graver still when it came back up.

I figure there's more to this story.

There is. Perhaps I will tell you someday.

I'd be much obliged, he said.

Cuidense, she said again and commenced coughing.

Without conversation they strode from the house to the barn, its massive bulk looming less ominous against the sky than the night he stood in its shadows and pulled his defunct firearm on Ricardo and marched him to the house. They found the saddles and blankets and bridle gear and each carried their own to the poled corral where the horses, sensing a burst of freedom, were tossing their heads and whinnying and snuffling the air, colts they looked to be in the dark, their colors indistinct. In silence they stood a short while assaying the small restless pack then chose their rides and saddled them, led them by their reins through the gate and closed it behind them and mounted, still without comment, as though absorbed in the concentrated confidence of a task they knew well, a private ritual that neither required nor desired assistance, one that defied interruption.

They trotted out through the arched rear gate and into the cloudless night, the air dry and cool and filled with the smell of wood smoke from nearby jacales, the moon peaking high overhead, the land phosphorescent between the dark palisades of mountains shaping the sky, a sprinkling of stars above their saw-tooth rims like crumbs of light strewn from the rising lunar wafer. Some dogs came from nowhere out of the dark and barked then fell back as they continued on. They rode south along a crop trail, ribbed chalky fields fanning away either side like petrified waves of another time. Behind the mountains to the east, like a false dawn, glowed the lights of Cuatula and towering over that the pure white cone of Popocatépetl and his supine bride and ahead of them the southern sky depthless in the moon's reflection. They rode aligned at a trot without speaking, as if speaking might disrupt something, their meditative movement atop leather and muscle or their own internal assessment of the triangular situation, the fragile silence defining it.

Then finally:

These horses ride good, don't they? Jo Shelby said, glancing left and right at his sombreroed compañeras, their silver accessories gleaming and flashing in the moonlight, their stylish outfits incongruent for a clash with bandidos, should it come to that.

Something's different, Athen said, not looking at him but straight ahead, her horse's reins loose in her hands.

Carmen rode and said nothing.

How's that? he said.

I don't know. Just different. Like they're more careful.

You're just used to ridin in the Delta where there's nothin between horse and sky but flat ground, a blank check to daylight, to run wide open.

Maybe so, she said.

Mexican horses can ride fast, Carmen said. You will see.

Hope I don't have to, Jo Shelby said.

They rode on through the cooling night.

The fields and the field trail played out and they were riding over terrain cobbled with stones and dotted with yellow lantana near fluorescent in the moonshine and scrub brush and maguey and nopal, until the horses began whinnying and sniffing the air and slowed to a near stop without direction from their riders. It was not long they saw, too, what their horses had sensed, dark clumps of cattle huddled quietly in the gray reflected light then something not-cattle moving among them and what looked to be distant fireflies flickering off and on in the dark until he realized it was moonbeams bouncing off metal.

He brought his horse to a halt and the others did likewise.

They sat, studied the shadowed nocturnal scene.

What is it? Athen said.

It sure ain't a welcomin party, Jo Shelby said.

There are three of them, Carmen said. No four, another to the side.

That's the arroyo, he said. Got to be. They rope the cattle then lead em down into it, then follow it, he pointed west, until they're home.

Is that where Ricardo lives? Athen said.

Prob'ly, he said. The señora said it wadn't far.

Maybe we should scare them, Carmen said.

I think we already done that, he said. Those three riders you pointed to are leaving the herd.

The words were still vapors when the sound, crisp as a slap of leather on leather, cracked the air. Then another.

Get down, he said and they dismounted and coaxed their horses to their knees and spoke in whispers.

That was a gunshot, wasn't it? Athen said.

A rifle, he said.

Perhaps they are just warning us, Carmen said.

Perhaps, he said.

We should've taken the señora's guns, Athen said.

Jo Shelby looked hard at her but said nothing.

Well? she said.

What would we do with them? Carmen said. We cannot see them.

We'd at least shoot back, Athen said. Let them know what they're up against.

Jo Shelby rolled his eyes. Let's go. Vámonos! We'll come back t'morra night.

And with guns, Athen said.

Damn, woman, you wanna get us killed?

The opposite. I want to not get us killed.

You even know how to shoot one? he said.

Yes, I hunted with my brothers all the time.

You never told me.

You never asked.

Huntin animals and people are two different things.

I'm not wanting to hunt *anything*, just keep from being hunted.

I think we should talk no more and do as you said, Jo Shelby, Carmen said, vámonos. They have the guns and we do not.

He nodded.

We'll come back tomorrow night with guns, Athen said.

Maybe, he said as his horse responded to a nudge of his boot toe and rose.

There's no maybe about it, Athen said, rising with her horse. I'm coming back with protection or I'm not coming back.

Let's see if we caint leave without invitin more trouble, he said. Stay low so they caint see you.

They mounted and headed back at a slow trot, their bodies leaning low in the saddles. Not fifty yards in retreat there were two more shots from the arroyo behind them and they put the heels of their boots to their horses. Lying along their necks of their mounts they galloped north toward the hacienda, the hooves thundering in their ears, pounding their moon-shadows into the moon-bleached ground. Hard they rode across the vague terrain to the trail road that lay before them like a silver runner laid down out of the silver night. Nor did they slow there but kept up the charge, knees tight against their horses' necks until they saw the arched gate at the rear of the walled compound and Jo Shelby pulled his horse to a slow walk and Athen and Carmen followed. The same dogs that had barked at them on the way out sallied forth and commenced again their shrill and raucous yapping.

I don't feel good runnin from somethin, he said.

I don't either, Athen said.

Carmen remained silent.

Maybe guns aren't a bad idea after all, he said. Maybe if we had fired back we wouldn't be the ones runnin.

Perhaps we should go a different way next time, Carmen said.

They were walking their horses slowly to the gate.

There aint one, Jo Shelby said. Unless we go down the Valle de Cuernevaca and come in the backside. And that would take all day and part of the night. We'd be wore out fore we got there.

I was thinking of another entrance, Carmen said.

Yeah? he said. He turned in his saddle and looked at her.

The arroyo, she said.

What about it? Athen said. She was behind Carmen and spoke to her back. There was a faint sarcasm in her voice, one that surprised Jo Shelby.

Carmen stopped inside the gate and pivoted in her saddle. The valley lies between the mountains, she said, which means the riachuela, the stream, stops at the mountains or runs beside them.

I don't understand, Athen said, the challenging tone still there.

Jo Shelby sat and listened.

Carmen continued. We could enter the arroyo from the east. We would ride below ground level and not be as visible. We would be coming from a direction they do not suspect. We could shoot first and make them run.

Damn, Jo Shelby said. Wish I'd thought of that.

Carmen cocked her head to one side and smiled a self-congratulatory smile.

Athen turned her horse and headed for the barn.

The mansion was square-shaped around a concentric square courtyard centered by a rose-colored fountain faded from its original hue. At one time water had circulated through the fountain and splashed in its basin but the water in the basin now was dark green and lifeless. Around the fountain was a bright dishabille of tropical plants—oleander and hibiscus, amaryllis and mandavilla—plants once cared for but abandoned to grow wildly over paths of slate stones that led to ceramic benches the color of the fountain, almost hidden beneath the untended foliage. From parallel balconies all around draped vibrant red and purple bougainvillea, hanging so low in places they touched the ground, giving a cloistered ambience to the lower porch.

The house was cool and quiet and smelled old. Upstairs were airy bedrooms with high ceilings and French doors that opened from both sides onto corresponding balconies. He'd gone with the señora to show the girls their rooms. Each had a canopied bed with a mahogany bureau, mahogany night table with a marble top, mahogany valet, an armchair covered in velvet, leftovers from times of great wealth. As if the señora had been expecting visitors, white enamel pitchers and basins on the bureaus were filled with fresh water. In the connecting baños were fresh towels and washcloths, fresh soap and toiletries. On the wall of each room next to a window stood tallcase clocks with Roman numerals, pendulums sweeping behind their casement doors, their hands pointing the correct time. Through the windows the sierras looked like a painting on a wall and breezes from the same mountains billowed the curtains.

He'd seen the expressions on their faces, heard their similar comments, once the shock had settled and they could speak.

A dream, Athen said, a hand laid against her throat.

Maravilloso. Magnifico, Carmen said.

Neither had stayed anywhere nicer they both said.

Perhaps you will not want to leave, the señora said.

La señora es muy tentadora, very tempting, Carmen said, glancing at Athen, a signal the translation was for her benefit.

I could stay here forever, Athen said.

You're not helping this tension out any, he wanted to say but remained silent. He noted the rooms were on the back of the big house, opposite his on the front. There were other rooms but the señora had chosen those for the ladies. He guessed she deemed it proper to separate the sexes but she might have been helping him out after all, giving him some breathing space. Either way it was a mixed blessing. He'd be far enough away to get some sleep and have time to think but they'd be next door neighbors and do what next door neighbors do, gossip and swap notes, he thought as he stood on the balcony fronting his room.

He was staying in Juan's old room, where he'd almost spent the night the year before. She told him then she'd kept everything as it was the day Juan left and Jo Shelby saw nothing had changed since his own brief occupation months before. There was the large mahogany bed with the rods to hold a canopy but still no canopy. He guessed Juan considered a canopy too sissified and the senora had kept it off in case he did return. The shaving stand with cut-glass knobs was in its same place across from the bed and above it the same oval mirror, finely cracked at the edges. The other pieces he recalled took up the room—washstand with ewer and basin and soap dish, bentwood rocker, straight chair, chifferobe, chest-of-drawers, nightstand with a globed lamp. He remembered, too, the top drawer of the dresser was empty and he was told to use it because she wanted him to feel treated like the family he was. A clock he'd not remembered seeing before hung on the wall by the door. I change very little, she'd said then and he wondered if she changed anything in the house at all, if she stayed in a perpetual state of readiness for her sons and their families, for company. Anybody.

He continued standing on the balcony, leaning against its railing, his vision traversing the valley awash with moon shine to the foothills then the sierras higher up where nothing else drew attention but Popocatépetl and the Sleeping Lady, ashen ghost shapes against the purple night and he recalled again the legend, the different ways he kept hearing it. If his own story wasn't enough playing on his mind, the señora had crowded it with hers. He thought of the probable countless others like it in the world, had been since its first dawn, how many of those life-tales had stayed strung-up in strain and tension and how many relieved and broken by pain and how much of the latter was the result of fate or circumstance or somebody else's doings.

He thought of the señora and her lover and how someone else made her decision for her. All he knew of Zapata were fragments others had told to him, which was now not nearly enough. When he'd first heard the name— from Ramón in prison—he knew he'd heard it before. It was the same word in Spanish for shoe, Ramón said, perhaps there. No, somewhere else, he said. He asked Ramon to write it out and when Ramón carved it into the dirt with his finger Jo Shelby recalled where he'd first seen it, on the marquis of the picture show in Drew: ZAPATA. It was a strange name then, not one that made him want to use up a quarter, the sum total of his weekly allowance. It was a strange a name now, but now he craved its life history. Sooner or later he'd learn more of the revolutionary. There would be time.

A cool breeze was blowing down from the mountains and he wished he had a cigarette, wondered if that might help his thinking then reflected on why he quit. It probably didn't matter now. He couldn't remember the last time Athen had kissed him, probably not since Córdoba, before he told her about Carmen. The last time he'd kissed Carmen was at Christmas and she didn't mind his smoking, at least didn't say so. Most likely because nearly all Mexican men smoke and she didn't know the difference. Or she just didn't kiss much. Athen damn well knew the difference, which told a story all its own.

He thought about what the señora had said, about God and time and the angel and the hand he said he'd choose. He thought a long time then decided he wasn't ready to feel the hurt, his and that of another, at least not now then heard a knock on his door and glanced at the clock beside it. Nearly midnight.

He opened the door. Still in the clothes she'd worn all day minus the sombrero stood Carmen, her dark hair hanging long down the sides of her face and over her shoulders. She held something in her hand he could not clearly discern in the shadows. She spoke in a whisper as she moved the object into the light. You asked me to put this in my suitcase, but I thought now you would want to keep it.

He recognized the bolsa that contained the gun and accepted it from her. Muchas gracias.

De nada, she said, and smiled, that smile that folded him in half, brought him to his knees. One that said, won't you invite me in.

If he did, he thought, and Athen found out, whatever happened when they tied up with the rustlers and bandidos would be a mere skirmish compared to the war he'd have started at his own doorstep. I'd ask you in, he said, but I can barely keep my eyes open.

I understand, she said, then leaned over and kissed him on the cheek.

Que duermes bien.

He thanked her again, reciprocated the kiss and told her to sleep well, too, then closed the door.

He laid the bolsa on the bed, as gently as if it might have been a small child he did not want to awaken. He flipped back the flap of the colorful bag and pulled out the holster with the letters CSA burned into the leather. He unsnapped the finnel, slipped the revolver from the holster and laid it on the bed where, against the white spread, its bronze plating shone like old rarified gold. Like a pilgrim viewing a sacred relic he stood there a while beholding the ancient firearm, speculating on its past, its secret history, the hands that had gripped its handle, the fingers that had pulled its trigger, the people who had died from its discharge, those saved from the same. He reached down and picked it up, held it to the overhead light, his eyes taking in once more the long barrel and the revolving cylinder, the brass frame and the name engraved beneath the cylinder: COLT. Pointing the barrel of the gun away from the light and toward him, he looked down its bore and saw nothing but the narrow dark tunnel then suddenly something else he had not seen before. He tilted the barrel up for a clear view and sure enough, etched into the underside of the frame, beneath the beginning of the barrel and up from the trigger frame were five numbers: 70123. They looked hand stenciled, the 1 slightly taller than the other four and the 2 slightly misaligned and closer spaced to the 3. He wondered why they hadn't caught his eye before. He'd looked at the gun every way a person could look at a gun. But he'd never pointed it at himself and looked down the barrel from the victim side. He contemplated the numbers and their meaning and decided they were probably factory numbers, put there when Mr Colt and his crew when they made the gun. He turned it around, spun it once in his finger then reholstered it, fastened the snap and slipped the scabbard back into the bolsa. He stood a moment staring at it, trying to determine what to do with it then decided to place it in the top dresser drawer where it would surely be safe enough.

He unpacked his valise, laid the few items he'd brought with him out on the bed before transferring them in the same orderly inventory to the top dresser drawer, holding back his razor and tooth brush and pajamas. In a bathroom down the hall he filled a large claw-tooth enamel bathtub, surprised he could get hot water. For a long time he lay in warm water all the way to his chin, the closest he'd come all day to relaxing. If a person could just spend his life in a warm bath, he thought, there'd be no tension or pain. The tension and pain would drown in one long, never-ending baptism. The closest he'd even gotten to that was naked in his mama's womb and the closest he'd get to it again was when he breathed his last and his suited body lay in a coffin and not naked in a bath tub. He thought about that a minute, baptism, what it could and couldn't do for a person. It protected you at the front end coming into the world and at the back end after you left but in between brought no guarantees. When he was an infant and the preacher sprinkled his infant head, branded him as one of God's own, there was no magic in the words or water, nothing that sealed him off from tension and pain, those two words suddenly dominating his thinking. The only magic, he was beginning to decipher from the señora's words, was in the word pain, painful coming into the world and painful leaving, but after the pain ...

He finished bathing and returned to his room. In the midst of shaving, lather on his face and a towel tucked around his waist, he heard another knock. By the clock on the wall it was past twelve, almost one.

He went to the door and whispered loudly, Who is it?

A loud whisper came back. It's me, Athen.

Just a minute. I'm not dressed.

He quickly removed his towel and wiped the lather off his face. He had no bathrobe. He pulled on his blue jeans, threw on a shirt he didn't take time to button and opened the door.

Wearing a pink robe and matching slippers she stood in meager light and shadows. Her hair was down and her face was long. In her eyes was a sadness he'd not seen before.

What's wrong? he said. It's almost one in the morning.

I couldn't sleep.

Because of your brothers?

Partly. I won't keep you long.

He stuck his head past the doorframe, looked left and right. Come in, he said.

Mind if I sit down? she said.

In the feigned manner of a stranger lost in a strange setting he looked around then pointed weakly to the rocker. Help yourself.

She wrapped her robe tighter around her and sat, crossed her legs like she was going to stay a while.

He sat in the straight back chair across from her.

What about your brothers?

I'm afraid they'll show up and make a scene.

They didn't see us.

No, but they saw Carmen and talked to her.

So, he said. All they did was ask her the time.

She shot him a look of exasperation. You don't know my brothers.

You think they followed her? he said.

Maybe.

What if they did? Your twenty-one and graduated from college. You're in another country. All they can do is ask you to go home.

But I think you may be right ... about what you said tonight. They're not down here for me—

But where you might lead them.

Yes, she said, her tired voice falling then recovering after a deep breath. Daddy's worried about the judge's ruling. He realizes he sold you short.

So he sent Josh and Jake down here to settle the score. I got more to go on than they got.

I'm not so sure *he* sent them. And I'm not so sure you've got more than they have.

His eyes widened, the sharp turn in conversation taking on the properties of a stimulant. Why do you say that?

There are some things you don't know.

Like what?

Mama went through those letters. She read all of them, then put them back just like she'd found them.

He bolted upright in the chair. Your mama lied to me. She said she didn't disturb the letters. They were at the bottom of the trunk when she opened it and she said she didn't touch em.

I'm sorry.

Nevermind. You caint be sorry for what somebody else did. The question is, did she lie to you, too.

I don't understand.

Did she put them *all* back? I think one's missing, the last one, and she held on to it because she knew, too, there was a cloud on that title and it might've said so in that letter. Who knows what else might be in it. The name of a bank. A safe deposit box number. The name of a notario. Maybe a map.

That's all I know, she said.

He sat and thought. This turns everything around. Maybe we oughtta be following them.

That's not the main reason I came tonight, she said.

What was the other?

What I've got to say doesn't come easily. That's what you said back at the café in Cuernavaca, before we saw my brothers. You never finished.

We haven't had any time together since.

Her voice was soft, a voice different from the one snapping at him all the way from Mexico City to the barn where she'd stalked off to the house in a huff after depositing her saddle and riding gear. She'd said she wouldn't keep him long, but when she mentioned them, he knew better. They'd be there to sunrise and maybe through the next. He put his elbows on his knees and his cheeks in his hands and leaned in towards her, a signal he was dog-tired and waiting for what he hoped would be short.

Her face turned serious. Don't get the wrong idea, she said.

I don't even have one, he said, rubbing an eye with his fist. You blew em all away when you told me what your mama did.

She gave him a long thoughtful look. If she looked at him any longer without saying anything his head was going to slip between his hands and hit his knees.

I didn't come here at one in the morning to sweet-talk and coddle up to you, she said. She paused and looked down, at her hands toying with a button on her robe as though in the fumbling movements she observed her thoughts, then looked back up, her eyes pulling whatever she'd seen into focus. I've just missed being with you. Just you. I guess I needed to know I needed to be here and not somewhere else.

He was trying to think through the sleepy fog about to overtake him. If ... He couldn't complete the thought. If ... He couldn't complete that one either. If you weren't ... That one died too. I'm glad you're here and not somewhere else, he finally managed. I came back from Mexico for you and sure as hell don't need you leaving Mexico cause of me.

It wouldn't be you. It'd be her.

He sat up again. Naw, now. It'd be me, cause you couldn't separate me from her.

Should I?

No. There ain't nothin to separate. I keep telling you, we're just friends. That's all. He'd kept telling himself that was all, like a blind dog in a meat house might keep telling himself.

But I see the way she ... nevermind.

The way she what?

Nevermind.

No, tell me.

Like you don't know.

Know what?

She uncrossed her legs and leaned forward in the rocker. Jo Shelby Ferguson you were in a prison six years of your life and in another in Mexico a few months and missed out on a lot going on in this world but you weren't born yesterday. You're not as innocent as the pure driven snow and as ignorant as the dunce you're trying to make me believe you are. You know good and damn well what I'm talking about. Carmen is head-over-heels in love with you.

He sat up. He studied her, looked at her steadily. What if she is?

She's very pretty. No. She's beautiful.

So are you, he said, a drowsy smile breaking his sleepy face. Beauty ain't got much to do with it. Beauty is as beauty does, my mama used to say, who, by the way, you're beginnin to sound like.

Somebody needs to tell you to open your eyes. She's clever.

That what you traipsed over here at near dawn to tell me, his eyes blinking heavily.

Yes. I just wanted you to be aware.

He stood. I'm aware of more than you think. Besides, I don't think Carmen will stay long. After the independence celebration, she'll go back to Mexico City. She's got a job.

Athen stood. Today's September eighth.

He glanced at the clock on the wall. It's the ninth now, he said.

The ninth then. That's over a week away. She said she had vacation days coming to her.

Then maybe she'll go before then.

She's invited her friends here to help with the hacienda.

Then her and her friends will go back. Who knows, maybe one's a boyfriend.

She crossed her arms and snickered. You're impossible.

He leaned over and grabbed her by the shoulders and kissed her on the lips. I love you. That's what I was going to say at the café. Now go and get some sleep.

Why didn't you say that to begin with?

Cause I'm bout asleep.

At the door she turned and kissed him. I love you, too. Maybe I can sleep now.

I can if I can just make it to the bed, he said and closed the door. He took one look at his half-shaved face in the mirror and decided if he tried to finish whoever found him would think suicide.

The next morning following a sumptuous breakfast they spent assessing the needs of the place. Jo Shelby retrieved pencil and paper from a desk drawer in the salón and, with Athen and Carmen and the señora at his side, made an inventory of needs, starting with the house. First on the list was a thorough cleaning, Athen said, looking at him until he licked his pencil and wrote it down. And waxing of the floors, Carmen insisted, her eyes on him, too, as he wrote. Next came the walls. They had not been painted in over twenty years, the señora said, and the stucco had cracked and peeled so in places the old adobe brick shown through. Several window panes were cracked and needed replacing, something he recorded himself.

Outside, they surveyed the roof and he made an estimate of the number of terra-cotta tiles needed to replace those missing or broken beyond use, as well as those on the four watchtower roofs. The outside walls required painting as well with similar patchwork as those inside. The flower gardens needed to be weeded, more rocks brought in for their borders, bushes around the house trimmed, potted plants on the porch repotted, swing on the veranda re-hung, the patio fountain scoured and its old electrical circuit checked to see it still worked. Damage over the years to the outer walls surrounding the compound was extensive and would require masonry. Carmen said two of her friends coming had experience as bricklayers, which brought a smile to the señora, a blank expression from Athen. Jo Shelby wrote.

In a move that brought an applause from everyone, including the workers on the place and their women and children who lived in the huts within the compound walls and had gathered with great curiosity to watch the operation, as if the word had gone out that a great magician was in town to perform a feat of derring-do, Jo Shelby lowered the hood of the old pickup and got in, turned the key and pressed the accelerator as it roared to life.

How'd you learn to do that? Athen said later as the trio was on their way to Jiutepec to purchase the necessary supplies for repairs and pick up groceries for the señora.

Watched your daddy and mine once when a battery went dead in my daddy's pickup and they transferred one from one of the tractors that had transmission problems. The spark plugs in the senora's old car were bad but the battery had power. It was simple, he said snapping his fingers, leaning forward and grinning at Athen beside him and Carmen by the door.

The two smiled back at him and Athen laid a hand on his thigh.

They rode on.

Jiutepec was a small town which lay in a valley between the foothills of higher mountains and consisted of a string of low-roofed tiendas and cafes and service stations and bars without sidewalks facing a single pot-holed and muddy thoroughfare. There was no square or center or alameda, no park with white-washed trees and benches for people to sit and talk, only the single mercantile stretch, as limited in variety as it was. He recalled the last time he'd been there, how far back in time he felt and the feeling had not changed. The supplies he was buying, and the reason for his purchase of them, went that far back as well. He wondered if the place was simply that recessed in time, locked in another age, of its own stubborn volition, or if it got blindsided and time had just pulled up stakes and left it, or if it knew it was behind and was struggling but just hadn't caught up, or if time didn't have anything to do with it and the place was just an accident of history. Maybe the place and its people didn't know the difference and didn't care and the reason for their retarded state was a combination of all of the above. Either way he cut that thought, moved it around and reshaped it, time probably had nothing at to do with it except the fact that it does move on and some people and places don't and that made him think of the country at large and its pockets of retarded history and of his home and the one it was stuck in.

They stopped at a small government-owned gas station to fill up with gas, the same where he'd been let out after hitching a ride from Cuernavaca on his first trip. There was a tire store on one side and a cocina economica on the other where men sat at tables drinking coffee and several doors down a nightclub. He saw the neon sign of the nightclub still flickered but the last letter had been fixed so it correctly read El Hábito. Hábit or Hábito, either was correct he figured, the place a nightly mecca for those addicted to its pleasures.

He noticed the men at the cocina were the same from whom he'd sought directions before and he thought of the country stores back home and the benches around courthouses and the same men who'd be sitting in those immovable and familiar places of conversation and comfort.

He got out of the truck and Athen and Carmen got out with him. He olaed the men and they olaed back with wide smiles but their eyes were on the two women.

Me recuerdas? Jo Shelby said.

Sí, they said, nodding in unison their remembrance of him.

Encontras la hacienda? one said.

Sí, Jo Shelby said. La encontré.

Y la tía? chimed in another.

He nodded he'd found his aunt, too.

Y mucho más, another said and they laughed, their rotted misaligned teeth congruent with all else about the place that looked soiled and run down and uncared for.

Jo Shelby looked at Athen and Carmen. Carmen was smiling but Athen looked perplexed. He translated for her, that he'd found a lot more, and she forced a smile.

Sí, Jo Shelby said, smiling back at the men. Pero, las aparencias son engañan.

The men laughed again, louder.

What did you say? Athen said.

I said appearances are deceiving.

That might make them think you picked us up at that nightclub, she said nodding in the direction of the low-slung roofed building painted chartreuse with pink neon runners.

Naw, they know better. Hombres, he grinned and shouted at the men. Son mis amigas, no vinieron de El Hàbito.

Sí, sí, the men hollered back again in uniform jocularity and one added loudly, son de un palacio y no encajaron con tigo.

Carmen laughed and shouted back, gracias, gracias.

All right, this isn't much fun, Athen said with irritation. What'd you say and what'd they say.

I told them I didn't pick you up at the nightclub and they said they knew, that you were from a palace and didn't belong with me.

You think you're cute because you know Spanish and I don't, she said and socked him playfully on the arm. If I could find a school I'd join up right now.

Perhaps you would let me teach you, Carmen said.

There you go, Jo Shelby said.

They were still standing around the front of the old pickup, the early afternoon sun reflecting off the windshield.

Athen cupped a hand over her eyes and squinted into the sunlight, first at him, then at Carmen. Thank you. That would be helpful.

A feeling of relief went through him, much as it did when they'd gone shopping together in Cuernvaca and returned talking and laughing with Athen decked out like Carmen. At times they seemed like old chums and at others mortal enemies with looks honed and sharpened to slice the other to bits. What they'd just said to each other was a step forward. An army of three divided wouldn't be much of an army.

The attendant was a young man in his twenties, his enamor of the women much reflected in his sudden burst of hustle and bustle, ogled glances over his shoulder at them as he worked. He filled the tank and cleaned the windshield and was raising the hood when Jo Shelby told him that would be all.

Pero, senor, necesito comprobar su petróleo.

Jo Shelby had forgotten about the oil. The truck had been sitting there no telling how long. The motor had coughed and sputtered and blew a thick cloud of black smoke from the tailpipe when it finally caught. They were probably lucky to get as far as they did. Entonces, está bien, he said.

With a magician's flourish the mozo pulled out the dipstick, wiped it and returned it, pulled it out again like it might have been a sword from a scabbard and held it to the sun. Oh, señor, he shouted, his eyes wide, hay un problema.

Que es? Jo Shelby said.

Tu no tienes petróleo.

To what appeared to be the delight of the mozo Jo Shelby instructed him to fill the truck with oil as well. No need changing it if there was none to begin with. Athen and Carmen sat on the stoop of the station observing and talking in low tones, Athen's first lesson Jo Shelby surmised.

He ambled over to the cocina and engaged the men in conversation. They asked of his travels since they'd seen him last and he spun the tale for them, their faces animated with wonder. They asked why he returned and he told of the señora's plight and the story of the will, what he anticipated doing with the land if he won the legal battle and their faces and eyes stretched even further in awe.

One of the men who looked much older than the rest thumped an ash delicately from the cigarette he was smoking and said, En México la majoría de gente no tiene nada por un testamento.

Jo Shelby shook his head in agreement and said there were many in his country where he lived who possessed nothing to leave to others but that this was a will from another time, when most of the land was owned by a few people who lived in casas grandes.

The man who had spoken took a long drag from his cigarette and looked seriously at Jo Shelby, his old eyes sad beneath the shade of his sombrero, and told him that was the reason people in Mexico had nothing to leave in a will, everything at one time belonged to the haciendas and hacendados, that Zapata tried to make it different but the men after him were corrupt and it was still only the wealthy in México who could even contemplate writing wills, that that was why he and his compadres sat everyday and drank coffee and smoked and talked. There was no work.

Jo Shelby told them there might be work on the hacienda where he was staying, that its owner and recent history were unlike those of old and their eyes lit up. He was not certain, he said, but he would check and get back with them, then asked what they knew of Zapata, the evocation of the name still resonating with him.

Their eyes had not yet relaxed within their sockets from the vigor of the prior hope and at the sound of the name ballooned again and all five burst into excited talk. Zapata this and Zapata that. Zapata, Zapata, Zapata, the torrid repetitiveness of the name interspersing their sudden and raucous chatter like the rat-a-tat-tats of a machine gone wild. Jo Shelby tried to interrupt but they were crowding each other's comments like piglets trying to suck the same teat. From what he could glean from the bits and pieces rapidly flying from the verbal melee, each was trying to trump the other with their story of Zapata.

He looked over at the girls. They were still sitting on the stoop of the small gasolinera engrossed in conversation, unaware it seemed of the disturbance next door. Athen was speaking and looked intent and he recalled his first lesson with Ramon in prison, the concentration required to repeat the words of a new language, shape his mouth to fit those strange sounds. He thought of calling them over but they would only be a distraction.

He looked back at the men. He raised a hand and called out: Hombres, por favor.

As if he might have been Zapata himself, the men silenced and looked at him as though struck dumb.

Yo no puedo intender, he said. De uno en uno, por favor.

The older, who had thrown away his cigarette to talk, raised a finger and went first, the story he told and not his age, giving him top ranking. He had known Zapata personally, he began, rode with him as a young man of twenty in 1910 when El Charro began his local revolution in the state of Morelos. He told how he actually accompanied his representative Pablo Torres Burgos to San Antonio, Texas to meet with Madera and escaped when Burgos, while taking a siesta, was assassinated by los Federales. He told how he made his way back to Morelos and to Zapata, now the leader of *the* Revolution of the South and rode with him on his first attack on the Chinameca Hacienda. He told how the owner, a Spaniard named Carriles was reported to have said that if Zapata were so brave and so much a man, they had thousands of bullets and enough guns waiting to welcome him and his men. He told of Zapata's anger when he heard the challenge, how his eyes flashed with rage and of the terrible slaughter that followed. Then the man stopped and in a high-pitched whiny voice began singing and a couple of the others joined in. It was a song about the terrible Zapata who came with justice and right and how the earth trembled on that day when Zapata entered the hacienda and shouted, Death to Spain and the people shouted back, long live General Zapata, long live his faith and his ideas. The old man stopped and the others ceased their singing and he continued telling how the Zapata's army, as it moved through towns and villages steadily swelled, how the people came because they yearned for freedom and justice, because Zapata gave them rights and they followed him and there the man stopped to drink his coffee and he did not resume, nor did the others attempt to invade the silence, as if they knew some special spirit the silence held.

Qué pasó próximo? Jo Shelby said.

The old man looked up wistfully from his coffee, down then up again as if he did not wish to tell what happened next. He finally spoke and told how he was wounded at the battle for Cuautla, then stood and pointed down and Jo Shelby saw he bore only the stump of a right leg.

Lo siento, Jo Shelby said, expressing his sorrow.

The man sat back down and there was silence a while then the others told their stories. None had ridden with the great revolutionary nor met him personally but they catalogued relatives who had and told their stories and of all the stories there were none second to the others, all of them equally captivating, filled with the cries and shouts of battle, of freedom and justice, Tierra y Libertad, land and liberty, Zapata's signature. And when they had finished, all looked down at their coffees and seemed sad and doleful, that their stories were over and Zapata gone and their state of existence the same.

Jo Shelby glanced next door at the mozo finishing the oil change and the girls intent in their discussion then back at the men silently nursing their coffees. There was something else he needed to know. Qué pasó a Zapata? he said.

The old man looked up and him and spoke: Fue asesinado

Por quien? Jo Shelby said.

He told how Zapata in his last days, because of events of the revolution that took a course of their own, grew more isolated, how his lieutenants one by one, by one way or another, were being killed. He told of the death of Amador Salazar, one of the fighters closest to Zapata, how a stray bullet felled him and the impact it had on the general and of the court-martial sentence of death for Otilo Montaño, his compadre. If that was not enough detail he told how the head of a former co-leader, Domingo Arenas, who betrayed Zapata, was brought to him. Zapata was feeling more and more strangled and isolated, the old man went on, and felt a need to make alliances. He approached all the revolutionary leaders and all without success. His army numbered no more than a few thousand. In August 1918 they lost Tlaltizapán and retreated to their refuge, Tochimilco, at the foot of Popocatépetl. By now, the old man said, Zapata was almost desperate.

Jo Shelby had moved closer and taken a seat at one of the tables. All the men were leaning near the aged speaker, their hats removed as if in reverence, or anticipation of reverence, some sacred words on the verge of evocation. The cook from the cocina came out, drying his hands, as if he, too, had sensed something special occurring on his patio.

The old revolutionary continued: In the year of our Lord nineteen hundred and nineteen, the month of April, tenth day, Zapata went to the Chinameca Hacienda. He had delivered construction supplies there when he was a mule driver, ironically, the scene of his first battle. Colonel Jesús Guajardo orchestrated the deceit. He had repeatedly invited Zapata to lunch and repeatedly Zapata had declined, but one more invitation was given and Zapata finally agreed. Only ten men went with him, the old man said, extending fingers on both hands into the air. Solamente diez, he repeated gravely. The ten followed him to the gate as Zapata ordered while the remainder of his army waited confidently in the shade of the trees, their pistols holstered, their carbines in their sheaths.

Then it happened like this, he said leaning over the table, almost whispering, as though the information he was about to impart was charged with secrecy. Inside the hacienda a squad was lined up. From their formation it appeared they were going to pay Zapata honors. A bugle sounded three times in the salute of honor. One would think nothing else. When the last note faded and dropped away our leader appeared beneath the archway of the gate. What happened next, happened very quickly. The soldiers who had presented arms fired their rifles twice at point-blank range. No one had time even to reach for their pistols. General Zapata, El Charro, fell from his horse.

He was dead then, Jo Shelby risked in the hallowed solemnity of the moment.

The old man looked up at him and the others cast looks as severe, as though he had uttered a sacrilege.

Tal vez, the old man said.

Jo Shelby was in too far now not to press further and asked why, if Zapata was shot point-blank by a whole squad, the old man said perhaps.

The old man told him the corpse was put on display in Cuautla, but many questioned it was the corpse of Zapata. The people know Zapata well. There was no small wart on his face. The birthmark in the shape of a hand was not on his chest. So, it was not the body of Zapata. Some say it was the body of his compadre, Jesús Delgado, who died in Chinameca. He paused momentarily and looked wistfully up into the surrounding mountains, and said, many have seen him at night, mounted on his horse, As de Oros, riding the slopes of these sierras. Then he recited something from memory, a poem.

Jo Shelby asked him to say it again, slower, so he could make clearer the translation and the old man repeated the words and Jo Shelby absorbed the transfigured words of the refrain, probably from a song ...

I will make them return the stolen lands
And I will quiet your pain.
This is an oath, not boasting and bluster,
I give you my word of honor.

... and when he was through removed his hat, as if in apology, and bowed his head to the old man.

Zapata murio? the old man said. No. Zapata vive. En México ... y también en Estados Unidos.

En Estados Unidos? Jo Shelby said. Verdad?

Es verdad, the old man said. Cómo se llama?

Me llama Jo Shelby. Jo Shelby Ferguson.

The old man squinted his eyes at Jo Shelby, as if the eyes became a finger pointing. Tú es también un Zapata.

Muchas gracias, Jo Shelby said, tantas gracias, thanking the man yet again for the honor of associating his name with that of the great revolutionary. He understood, too, why the señora, the night before at dinner, had taken so long telling the story of the revolution before arriving at her own story and that of her family.

The girls were still talking on the gasolinera stoop, oblivious of the drama next door. The mozo had completed filling the truck with oil and was standing nearby, wiping his hands on a dirty cloth and listening. It was time to bring an end to the encounter but there was still one nagging question. How did the old man know so well the story of Zapata's assassination.

The old man looked down at his coffee and waited a long time and for a while Jo Shelby thought he would not answer, that the silence was his answer and that would be the end of it.

Then the old man looked up at him. Porque, fui uno de los diez hombres.

Jo Shelby marveled that he was talking with a man who had ridden with Zapata and was one of the ten men who saw him shot yet still believed he was alive. He wanted to stay and sit all day, ask questions and listen to the old man and his compadres, to their stories of México and its other name, passion, but the sun was moving on and the afternoon shadows growing and there was still much to do. He would return he told them and would enquire of work on the hacienda. The old man said laughingly he was too old to work, but the others gave approval of the idea and seemed hungry and eager. He imagined they had families in casas up the mountain behind them, mouths to feed.

Athen and Carmen were still at it and by the intense look on her face, Athen had already learned enough to pass a grade. Jo Shelby asked the mozo if he sold spark plugs and batteries. The young man, his head down and voice filled with great disappointment, said he did not, but that they could be purchased further down the road and offered to go there and get them. Jo Shelby told him that would not be necessary, that they were going that direction anyway for other supplies but the young mozo persisted. He could ride with them and show them the place. Jo Shelby then asked who would mind his station and he said business was slow, that he would just close it, his eyes on the two women as he spoke. Jo Shelby thanked him anyway, but there was no room in the cab for him and with all they had to buy there would not be room in the back of the truck but that they would return and use his services again. With that the mozo shook his hand and bowed individually to Athen and Carmen. Jo Shelby paid him and they were off.

At an auto parts shop where a huge Bardhal sign served as the door, he bought spark plugs and a battery. At a hardware store next door he orchestrated the purchase of cement, sand, lime, paint, paintbrushes, scrapers and other equipage and supplies while Athen and Carmen crossed the road to buy groceries from a list given to them by the señora. He pitched in and helped the men load the truck, shoulder the heavy bags of cement and lime into the bed forming a corral into which they shoveled sand from a large mound outside the store. Which was one of the reasons there were no sidewalks, he conjectured. At each establishment merchandise and wares were on display in various methods and configurations from the doorways to the roadway. The loading completed he paid the dependiente, as he had paid for everything else to that point, with dollars from his own billfold. The amount didn't total over fifty dollars, the dollar stretching much further in México than the peso, and he figured the señora wouldn't know the difference when he got back and he handed her the change from the pesos she'd given to him he gave to Athen and Carmen for the groceries.

He made a U-turn in the wide thoroughfare and pulled as close as he could to the curb of the small grocery store where Athen and Carmen, surrounded by sacks of groceries, sat waiting for him, wondering as he did how much the girls were able to buy. The place appeared smaller than the country stores to which he was accustomed. His mama and grandmama would enter those diminutive, dollhouse sized depositories of goods and surprise him when they came out carrying everything they'd gone in to get. If he had to bet he'd bet the same. There was one thing he'd discovered in a country less well off than his own. The less they had the smarter they got and he guessed it was like that the world over, the ingenuity of a people rising to meet their shortfalls. That didn't sound right in the chambers of his thinking, but it was right.

He helped the girls load the groceries and they headed back to the hacienda, Athen sitting next to him again, mumbling phrases in Spanish he suspected she'd tried in the tienda and gotten wrong.

Y'all get everything? he said.

No, Carmen said, as Athen continued her mantra.

What'd they not have, he said. Looks like you got everything back there but the kitchen sink.

A Spanish dictionary, Athen spoke up.

You're not going to find any bookstores along here, he said.

We can buy one in Cuernavaca, Carmen said. There is a libería on the plaza.

Too late to go there now, he said.

We can go later, Athen said.

We got work to do later, he said, his thoughts not so much on the time away from work to buy the book but, knowing her, how much she'd accomplish trying to work around a bunch of Mexicans with a Spanish dictionary in her hand.

We won't be working every minute, she said. I'll figure out something.

I will go with you, Carmen said.

Thank you, Carmen. That's nice of you, she said looking straight ahead.

They drove on.

In La Joya at a small cocina cluttered with gas pumps and Coca-Cola signs he stopped.

What're we stopping for, Athen said.

I almost forgot something, he said. Juan, the señora's son, lives up this hill, he said, signaling a thumb over his shoulder. He pulled out his pocket watch and glanced at it. I need to see him. It's almost five. Shouldn't take me more'n half an hour.

Why can't we go with you? Athen said.

Because, somebody needs to stay here and watch the truck. With all it has in it, it'd never make it up that hill. And that'd be a decision that wouldn't trouble us if we left it here by itself. Everything would be stripped when we got back. Besides, that'd be good class time. He was looking at Athen when he said it and winked but Athen didn't wink back.

I hope you're not gone longer than half-an-hour, Athen said.

He tipped the brim of his hat and slapped the window frame with his hand and headed up the hill.

He headed up the same narrow cobbled street, passed the same two-story houses painted different shades of pastels, past the sign that said MISSION JUAN WESLEY and came to the same disheveled hovel and called out, "Señor Juan, hola."

Juan emerged from the same darkened doorway, crossed the dirt yard and they shook hands. In Spanish, Jo Shelby said it was good to see him again and Juan repeated the greeting. They sat beneath the same mimosa tree, around the improvised spool table and on the same Coca Cola crates and sipped on the same brand of beer, Carte Blanca.

Jo Shelby told him of his return visit to his mother's hacienda confirming that she was his aunt and the only family he had left in this world. He related all she'd told him of the three brothers and their families, their separate histories.

Then Juan's face turned solemn, his eyes suspicious. Dijo mi madre algo mas?

His mother did tell him more. She told him of the episode between Ricardo and Juan's departure.

El hombre es un hijo de puta, Juan said, raising an angry voice and rapping the top of the makeshift table with his knuckles.

Jo Shelby nodded in agreement, the nod picked up by Juan as a cue to tell his side of the story. He was surely partly to blame, he began. He was spoiled and hot-headed and easily riled. These were givens he did not reject. But he was not afraid of hard work and worked harder than anyone on the hacienda, harder even than Ricardo. That was where the problem began. It was Ricardo who became jealous of him and not the other way around, as his mother had presented. Ricardo was greedy and had designs. He wanted to be the administrador, the position Juan held. Ricardo would scheme, develop problems then go to the señora and blame them on Juan. Of course, he protested, but the more he protested the more his mother would become indignant, say that he was just behaving as a spoiled child who wanted his way. Then a moment of truth arrived. Juan said he had suspected Ricardo of stealing and had been watching him carefully. One night when he was leaving the house with something in a sack, Juan challenged him. There was a fight and his mother had to fire a pistol into the air to break it up. Once again, she took Ricardo's side. He was not stealing, she said. All he had in the sack was some nopal tunas he had gathered earlier in the day and was taking them home. Juan should grow up and be a man and leave Ricardo to do his job.

Juan spat angrily into the dirt, took a hard swallow from his beer and continued. Looking back he told how it was all a trap of evil design devised by Ricardo. The rest he said, Jo Shelby knew, that he left and has not returned. His mother comes there to visit occasionally, to see her grandchildren, but that was the only contact he had with her. He said it all not in anger but with sadness in his voice, a restrained sadness, one undergirded and braced with pride.

A few moments passed as they indulged their drinks,

Es todo que mi madre le dijo?

That was all, Jo Shelby told him, except what she said about his father. Juan asked what she told him about his father and Jo Shelby told him how tall and handsome she said he was, how dashing he looked riding up to the porch that day where she was sitting and took a message from him, how bold he was to ask her to dance later at her grandfather's hacienda, then bolder still riding many miles for only a handful of minutes with her, of their secret meetings because her parents did not approve of her relationship with a mozo, a hired hand, but that she loved him anyway, married him anyway, and he stopped there.

Slowly Juan turned and looked at him, his eyes still narrowed and fixed and said that his mother did not tell him everything. Jo Shelby asked what else she could have told and Juan shrugged. Solamente más, he said then shrugged his shoulders again as if to say that was all he was going to say.

Jo Shelby looked at his watch and rose. Juan rose with him and asked him to stay and eat but he said he had amigas waiting below and had to move on. He did have one other thing to say before he left, however, and told of the señora's change of heart, that Ricardo had been fired and she suspected him of recent thefts on the hacienda.

Juan looked dumbfounded. De verdad?

De verdad.

Jo Shelby went on to tell him of the planned renovations and repairs and help that would be needed and would Juan consider returning to help, that his mother needed his help and he'd probably get his old job back.

Juan told him he was obligated to the Methodist mission until their project was completed, which might be another year. Jo Shelby told him he was a Methodist and knew the honor and adoration the church gave to mothers that surely the church would allow him time to help his. Juan nodded and said he'd think about it as he walked him to the vined archway. They shook hands and the little man told him to return and visit again and Jo Shelby told him he would if he was in the neighborhood but for Juan to reconsider coming to the hacienda to help, that his mother still loved him then tapped a forefinger on the brim of his hat and bid the man adios.

The girls were jabbering Spanish when he returned to the truck and seemed not to have missed him, almost disappointed he was back, and so soon.

Athen bout to graduate? he said as he opened the door and got in.

No, but I've passed first grade, she said ironically.

She is learning fast, Carmen said.

That's good, he said as he turned the key and the truck cranked and coughed and and finally started.

It was late afternoon and the traffic heavy on the road, workers leaving Jiutepec and Curnevaca and headed to their little casas tucked back into the foothills of the sierras. They passed the last remnants of the pueblo, the road snaking through low hills devoid of any habitation and he felt a cool wind channeling the grassy slopes and whipping through the windows. They made a final turn in the wandering canyon and before them opened up a broad green volcanic plain bordered by folds of hills where mists, untouched by the sun, still gathered in the hollows. There were small farms of terraced land, some climbing the slopes and in places cattle grazed within fenced pastures and they came to the piles of stones that marked the entrance to the hacienda and turned.

That evening during dinner he told the señora about his encounter with the men at the cocina in Jiutepec and of their desire to work and she smiled and welcomed the news. She told him by all means to seek them out. He told her he'd go the morrow, that there should be no problem. They were all in the same spot as he'd left them a year ago and they all laughed. When he began telling of the visit with her son the room grew quiet and a glow spread across the old cheeks as if they had been renewed by the touch of a painter's brush. Choosing his words with great care and diplomacy he represented Juan's side of the story regarding Ricardo. She listened intently and did not eat as he spoke and candlelight flared in her expanding eyes as he told her of Juan's consideration to return and help. When he finished there was a long silence in the room. Athen and Carmen had stopped eating. Eréndira stood motionless by the sideboard.

The señora coughed several times then wiped her mouth with her napkin. She picked up her fork to eat then put it back down as if there was some confusion about what she should do next. Then she spoke: I am very grateful to you, Jo Shelby, for what you have done. Perhaps I have judged Juan wrongly.

Jo Shelby said nothing.

Hopefully he will come, she said. If not I will surely go to him.

Eréndira commenced her quiet movements about the room. Eating resumed and the señora asked many questions—about Juan's appearance, the house, his wife, the size and health of her grandsons. Jo Shelby answered all as best he could and said nothing about the question she did not ask and the one he would not raise, not then, not in the presence of others.

After dinner the señora handed out guns to them, an assortment of lever action carbines she removed from a glass gun case in the salón. Jo Shelby had not noticed the collection before and inquired of them. She told him they'd belonged to her father. They looked older and he hesitated. She said her two sons who came to the hacienda from time to time would take them on horseback rides and shoot rabbits with them, so she knew they functioned. He had no reason to doubt her and recalled the scabbards attached to the saddles. She handed him a small box of shells. He checked the gun chambers to make sure they were full then pocketed the shells in his coat and handed a rifle to Athen and one to Carmen. Athen had hunted with her father and brothers, she'd said. Carmen had said she could shoot. She didn't say where she learned but he suspected an interesting history behind it.

They saddled the horses and rode east across the valley then turned and followed the base of the foothills, as Carmen had suggested. The night was as clear as before, the moon's brightness undiminished. A cool breeze blew down from the sierra, made all the more cooler by their movement against it. They rode half-slouched in their saddles and without conversation, the only conversation that of the horses' silent synonymous intuiting of each other's position and movement. They rode with their reins held low over their pommels, their carbine stocks extended from their scabbards, jostling occasionally against their knees, inches from their hands should they need them. The ride by this route took longer than Jo Shelby had estimated, which meant the same time on the return, which meant they might not get back until early morning, depending upon what they encountered and which way they returned.

The gorge where they entered ran parallel the valley wall and was narrower than expected, the sides steep. The horses stepped nervously and with great caution around scrub oak and cactus, occasional large boulders blown there from volcanoes past. Traprock rattled downward ahead of them and their hooves slipped from time to time, only moonlight guiding the way. Down the floor of the wash they rode, past still inky pools in which moon and stars were mirrored, the dull clatter of unshod hooves through water and gravel and the chink of metal on metal from their riding gear echoing loudly off the walls of the small canyon and Jo Shelby called a halt.

What is it? Athen said.

No need to whisper, he said. Anybody within a mile could hear us breathin.

I did not think of the rocks, Carmen said.

That's okay, he said. We're here now. We'll make the best of it. The herd's a ways away. He looked around at the steep incline, for a place they might exit from the draw. Let's see what happens. If we stay closer to the side and out of the rocks, maybe it won't be so loud.

They moved on up the draw, slowly, single file, the horses walking, treading higher the shoulder of the creek bed, the noise of their hooves muffled in the silt drifts but still audible in the nocturnal silence, their only cover the long shadow in which they moved. It was an ill-conceived plan, Jo Shelby thought, but the only one they had. At least they might scare off the thieves, send a message that trouble lurked here should they decide to return.

Single file they continued along the base of the ravine's slope, in its shadow, where they blended with wild brush and cactus, where they would not be so easily seen should there be company skulking behind the gulch's tilted crevices. They neared the cattle and heard their low bellows and snorts, restless sounds of movement, too much noise coming from a herd near midnight to suit Jo Shelby, or the high-eared horses either who jerked their heads up and commenced nickering and snuffling and he raised a hand for them to halt again and motioned they pull beside him.

What is it now? Athen said, whispering again.

Somethin's not right, Jo Shelby said.

What? Carmen said.

The cattle're makin too much noise and the horses are spooked, he said.

Maybe we should stop, Athen said.

That's just what we did, he said.

I know that, smart aleck, she said frustrated. I meant stop for a while, wait and see.

We might be here till daybreak if we did that, he said. I'll go up and take a look, he said and he dismounted. He handed the reins of his horse to Athen who watched with Carmen as he began climbing the wall of the gulch, attempting stealth, placing one foot before the other with great care, but with each step the traprock cascading loudly beneath his boots. Bushes rustled at his slightest touch, the effects of his movement announcing his coming until he reached the top and looked around, his head barely breaking the chasm's rim when he heard the cricket-like lever-action sound of a shell being ratcheted into a chamber then the voice close behind it as though they were lock and stock of the same action.

Hombre!

Y'all scram! Jo Shelby hollered over his shoulder back down into the shadows. Get the hell out then heard the slap of leather on hide and clamor of hooves on gravel as Athen and Carmen galloped away, the magnified echo of their scramble against the night effecting that of a small rabble.

Hombre! the voice said again, then in English, we meet again.

Jo Shelby pulled himself up over the ledge and stood to face with the voice, the tall lean silhouette of the man behind it. He was wearing a sombrero and not the Western-styled hat Jo Shelby remembered and held a rifle on him, its barrel a slash of reflected moonlight.

I aint got a gun, Jo Shelby said.

We will see, Ricardo said. Muchachos! Le busca!

From a clump of trees stepped three men Jo Shelby had not seen. They all wore sombreros and carried rifles. By the jingle their footsteps made they wore spurs. The only other sound in the night air was the noise Athen and Carmen were kicking up a mile away and he understood why a man had a gun on him and not the other way around.

Two of the three stopped a few yards from him and one continued toward him.

Levante las manos, the man said.

Jo Shelby did as the man said and raised his hands.

The man stepped closer and frisked him inexpertly, moving his hands in a slapdash fashion up and down his sides, then stood up and stepped back. Está bien, Ricardo. No tiene una pistola.

I told you I didn't have one, Jo Shelby said.

Sí señor, Ricardo said, his voice a high sarcastic whine. This is true what you say. But not true before. Comprendes?

Yeah, I understand, he said as he began to understand something else. Ricardo still thought the gun Jo Shelby had pulled on him their first encounter at the hacienda was a real gun and not an impotent relic.

This gun very important to you, no?

It were as though a button had been punched in his brain and he was reliving the scene with the comandante in the Mexican prison when he was trying to negotiate his way out and the beating he received there.

No. The gun is of no importance. What is of importance is that you quit stealing from the señora.

One of the three men stepped forward and Ricardo ordered him back.

This is serious matter, señor. You accuse ... you say we thieves. But we no thieves. We just, how you say in America, we only cowboys.

You're lyin, Jo Shelby said. He could still hear the girls' horses in the distance and worried for them, that they would make it safely to the hacienda.

This time all three men stepped toward him. Ricardo called them off then stepped forward and brought his rifle barrel down across the side of his head.

Jo Shelby grabbed his face with both hands and sank to the ground.

Bad manners, señor, calling Ricardo a liar. He turned to his compadres and said the same thing in Spanish and they howled derisive uniform disapproval.

His ear was still ringing and a sharp pain throbbed across the side of his face up into his skull. He could feel the cut beside his ear and blood running through his fingers. He pulled a bandana from his hip pocket and applied it with pressure to the cut and tried to stand up but Ricardo hit him across the shoulder with the butt of his rifle and he fell back onto the ground. He heard the jingles again and knew what was next. One of the three men stepped up and kicked him in the back then the other two joined in, their boot-toes persistent percussions of pain going in one side of his body and out the other, their infliction so thorough he felt it all over. Except for his mouth, which he kept covered with his hands lest he lose his teeth a second time, his thoughts reliving that other nightmare.

When he came to he was lying on a damp earthen floor in a dark enclosure void of light, his wrists handcuffed in front of him. The air smelled of dirt and mildew and roaches. He hoped not scorpions. His head felt like it had been split open, the halves vised back together. He raised his hands to his head and felt the bandana, the soreness that throbbed beneath it. Someone had tied it tightly around his head so it covered the cut. That must have been the vise he felt. They'd possessed enough forethought for that. At least they didn't want him to die.

He lay there awhile, wondering if his eyes would adjust to light, if there were any for them to adjust to. He could feel a blanket over him. He heard some pigeons cooing and a horse nicker, its hooves champ the ground not far away and he thought of the horse he had ridden and hoped it was being cared for. He thought of the girls and hoped they were safe, wondered if they would try and find him then hoped not. This was a rougher bunch than he'd thought. He'd worked his way out of worse situations before by himself he told himself then couldn't think of a one. There'd always been someone to help him. He'd never expected special treatment over others and knew he wasn't any more special than anyone else in the universe but there sure did seem to be a friend at its heart. He was thinking about that, who the friend might be this time when his eyes began to pick up splinters of light in front of him, then strips overhead stitching the outline of a small square ceiling. A few moments later and he made out the door before him and what appeared to be a corrugated tin roof overhead, light seeping in beneath its warped edges. With time other objects blurred into clarity. Some nearby sacks, probably fertilizer or feed, maybe lime. Leaning against the sacks was an old hand plow. Gathered around it what looked to be buckets. In a corner left of the door were implements stacked in a corner: hoe, shovel, rake, pick ax. Pick ax. Ricardo and amigos weren't very smart, that thought moving him toward the corner when something on the door began to rattle then the sound of a bolt sliding then the door opened and an explosion of light knocked him blinder than he was when he came to.

Ah, hombre, a voice said, Ricardo's.

The shock from the sudden sheet of light faded and he could see the silhouette of the man astride the doorway, his arms outstretched bracing the jamb, a wide jack-o-lantern smile creasing the dark shadow of his face and a big holstered pistol clapping his thigh. The name's Jo Shelby Ferguson, he said.

Ricardo stepped out of the doorway toward him then leaned over Jo Shelby where he lay with the blanket covering him, the sharp nose jutting from the lean face and yellowed rotting teeth and protuberant eyes slamming into Jo Shelby's lingering sun-struck vision like a mask swinging down out of the dark in a haunted carnival house. You name, hombre, es el entruso. Trespasser. Maybe I help you memory. You come to the hacienda. No. You no come, you trespass. The señora, she take pity on you. He spat into the dirt beside Jo Shelby's head. Pity, he said again, louder. The señora is—qué es su frase en ingles?—of the soft heart. Sí, of the soft heart. She have pity on you. Then she terminó me, Ricardo—he rammed a thumb into his chest—her administrador all many years.

Jo Shelby wanted to interrupt but decided to let him play it out, see where his twisted logic was going, would end up. Besides, he didn't want to be kicked again. He'd break like a china doll if he got kicked again. He needed to buy time to heal.

But I think she want me back, Ricardo continued. Maybe soon. He leaned over and cast a sinister grin. She need protection from all the tres-passers. Do you understand this, hombre?

Jo Shelby nodded. The man's logic was a sick form of extortion but he was the one standing up and Jo Shelby the one lying down and a sicker logic would have been a smart remark. Any remark.

So hombre, you want you freedom.

It was not a question. Jo Shelby nodded again, sensing the hook in the statement.

This gun, Ricardo said, the word this said so it rhymed with grease, Jo Shelby thought. This gun you use against me. The one the señora make me give back. The gun make much trouble. The gun make too much trouble, too much trouble for one gun. It very valuable, no?

Jo Shelby shrugged.

Claro qué sí. It very valuable gun. And this gun you bring with you.

No, he said. I don't have the gun.

Ah, hombre. Do not lie to Ricardo, he said stepping closer and kicking Jo Shelby in his legs doubled up under him.

The pain that shot through him touched every cell in his body, a valida-tion Ricardo might as well have kicked his hand or little toe or a stray hair. Every place on his body hurt. How come you know so much? Jo Shelby man-aged through clenched teeth.

Ricardo know. Ricardo have ways.

Somebody had told him about the gun but the only ones who knew were Carmen and Athen and the señora. The only other person who came to mind was … . Naw, he thought. Eréndira was too shy and timid. Besides, she couldn't understand English. He might as well go along, see what this was leading up to. Okay, he said. So I have the gun. So what?

It very valuable gun.

You've done said that once.

Do not be nasty, hombre. Ricardo no want hurt you again.

I'm not bein nasty, just statin fact. Get to the point. What do you want? The gun?

Sí, señor. Now you are being reasonable. Más exactamente, you get me the gun, you have you freedom. It is simple.

And you keep on stealin from the señora, that it?

He kicked him again, this time in the ribs and Jo Shelby thought he heard one crack, if there were any left capable of cracking.

Hombre, Ricardo no es un trespaso. Many years Ricardo work for the señora. Many years he keep out the trespassers, the people from the government who want to take her land, her money. Other hacendados who see her weak and want to take big bites of her tierra. Then one day this trespasser come cayo del cielo who say he relativo of the señora. He come wanting his revanada del pastel, what you gringos call piece of the pie.

Now the idiot was gettin down to the nub of his anger. Sons all gone, want nothing to do with the hacienda. Faithful servant takes over, works hard, expects inheritance. Last minute kin drops cayo del cielo, out of the sky, on the doorstep of opportunity. Sounded almost like a parable from the Bible. Of course, the man was dead wrong but nothing would convince him otherwise. His eyes blazed with false self-righteousness, the worse kind his mama always said. Because it didn't even know the difference between right and wrong.

How can I get the gun locked up here in this dungeon?

Dungeon?

Calabozo.

But you no in jail, hombre. This only temporary home, he grinned sickly again. You have friends. You write message. We take.

He lay there and thought a moment. Writing the message would be easy enough. Trusting Ricardo and his thugs to take a message to the señora and not give it to their informant, who'd steal the gun outright and leave him without a bargaining chip, was something else.

How come I don't know you'd give the message to somebody else?

Now, hombre, why Ricardo want to do that?

So you could hold me under lock and key while you keep biting off the enchilada, he said. He wished he'd bitten his tongue. No need in making a donation, dropping a plan into an otherwise empty head.

Ricardo's eyes widened. His face expanded with an ironic smile. Hombre. You have much intelligence.

It was a donation all right. The man hadn't even thought of it. I'm smart enough to know you caint keep me here forever. My friends will come looking for me.

That is right. You friends. How many friends you have?

Jo Shelby thought. The way the man's eyes rolled in their sockets, he didn't know, had no idea. It was moonlit on the ledge of the ravine, but dark beneath. Athen and Carmen had sounded like cavalry tearing off into the night, the reverberations of their horses' hooves off the walls of the small canyon doubling the effect.

You know what a posse is?

Sí, but—

That's how many friends I got. That's how many were with me last night.

Ricardo blinked. His face drew suddenly downward, his mouth into a thin line. He kicked him again in the ribs. You liar, señor.

Jo Shelby pulled his arms tighter against his chest, prepared for another blow. You got ears. You heard em.

Ricardo lifted a foot to kick him again then lowered it, as if he was generating a thought and couldn't do both at the same time. Sí, hombre, but the night, it is full of tricks. I think maybe two or three riders with you.

We'll see, Jo Shelby said.

And the gun, señor?

Twice now he'd addressed him as señor. Maybe he was gaining some respect, climbing a notch above hombre. I wanna think about it, he said.

Hombre, he said, leaning over once again so his pocked face with its gravely teeth was near Jo Shelby's. You think. He turned toward the door to leave then looked down and saw the pick ax and retrieved it. Sorry, hombre. No escape from the calaboza. Enjoy you stay.

Jo Shelby lay still and watched as the man closed the door behind him and locked it and the small room went dark again. He felt certain he'd called Ricardo's bluff and one of two things would happen. Ricardo would release him after he'd had his fun, exacted his revenge and finally realized he wouldn't get the gun or he would manage an escape or the señora and girls would find a way to free him. It was the latter he felt would happen first.

Ricardo was known in the area. The señora knew where he lived. It was only a matter of time before he'd go free and the small-time thief was put behind bars. All he had to do was bide his time. He and time and calabozas were old friends.

He could only guess how long he'd been there. Whether he ate or not, in prison he was allowed three meals a day. In prison he was at least allowed out of his cell to walk around. In prison there was at least a john. In the two prisons he'd been in in his life there was at least sunrise and sunset, some demarcation between the end of one day and the beginning of the next, some semblance of order to time. At random and unpredictable times someone with a gun brought him food, a mish-mash of tamales and enchiladas and tostados and rice and frijoles and God-only-knew-what, somebody's left-overs all thrown together in a bucket with a wooden spatula for him to spoon the indistinguishable mix in an exercise of guesswork to his mouth so that even the conventional boundaries of eating were reduced to a point of anonymity, of not knowing one substance from the next, everything running together in one gustatory blur to be washed down with water from a glass jar he knew would blow it all out of him at both ends into another bucket he'd located and secured by touch. Because in that dark and meager square footage to which he was confined that was all he knew, what he could decipher with his touch and what came to him through the cracks, vague hieroglyphics of light he resorted to counting each day, then recounting to see if he'd left one out and thought of astronomers who gazed at the heavens counting stars and planets, looking for a new light they could name. But the only new lights he detected were flashes of nails driving his putrid confinement home.

He'd investigated means of escape but there were none. The walls were made of cinder blocks. The only means of ventilation was a small opening the size of a concrete block at the rear beneath the ceiling. It was grated with rebar set in concrete. He was able to get his hands on the shovel and tried digging a hole but it was awkward with his wrists cuffed and the ground was hard and rocky, the cinder blocks set deep. He'd thought at first it was an outback shed for tools and supplies then thought again it may have been intended as an enclosure for a septic tank that whoever had built it had set the blocks in a trench perimeter then after its completion ran out of money for the tank. The door was a solid sheet of iron bolted and padlocked. The more he thought about it, whatever the small blockhouse's original intent or use, some malevolent mind had remodeled it for other purposes and he was not the only unfortunate soul to experience its confinement.

The handcuffs were old and rusty and burned his skin but at least his hands were fastened in front and not behind him so he could feed himself and unzip his pants and urinate and scratch himself where he itched, especially his nose. He could lower his pants and defecate and clean himself with some old newsprint someone threw in after he'd requested toilet paper. He could stand and stretch, something he was constantly doing, brushing himself down for fear a scorpion might have lodged in the folds of his clothing or crawled into his boots. He'd heard the stories, how there were no antidotes for a scorpion sting. No need in going to a hospital. If he got stung by one, adios a el mundo. During the day he sweltered in the smothering furnace and at night shook with chills. His only exercise was walking the few feet the cramped cubicle afforded, enough room to lie down and extend his six-foot frame, but not an inch more. He should be thankful for that, he guessed then tried again estimating the days, years it felt like, he'd been there because something had gone wrong, something bad wrong.

In the long dark and silent hours between bursts of necessary energy, he thought. He thought about his predicament and the one he'd still face when he got out and that getting out of the one he was in might be easier than dealing with the two women waiting for him. One he truly loved and the other he could if given half-a-chance and that was what scared the hell out of him and would tie him in knots so bad he'd need a mythical joe blade swung by a god to cut him loose. The half-a-chance. He'd never thought of himself as weak when it came to women but these two would make a jelly leg out of John Wayne. He just needed to get the señora and her hacienda back in shape then the will he came for and he and Athen could wish Carmen well and say adios and skeedaddle the hell out. If there was a will, that is, and if there was, if Josh and Jake hadn't gotten to it first, and if they had how would he know, and if he knew how he could he get it back, the ifs piling up in his mind like a house of cards set up by an idiot.

When his wheels weren't spinning toward a solution to those problems in his life they were running out of steam how to solve his current predicament. He'd hear firecrackers in the distance from time to time, kids who couldn't wait for the big day to get there and he wondered about his and when it would arrive. He'd exhausted all plans of escape but one, assaulting the woman who brought his food. But he'd never hurt a woman and she was big and evil-eyed and had a gun, a double-barrel sawed-off shotgun with one hammer always cocked and one finger on a trigger. She carried the bucket in her left hand and cradled the gun in her right so it lay across her forearm with the stock against her upper arm. He figured it had been specially sawed off for her and that she probably did the sawing; did it with the same intensity as washing a dinner plate or changing sheets on a bed. A look that said she hated life and where she'd ended up in it. A look about her that she'd been ordained and commissioned to shoot him if he even looked crossways. He could overwhelm Ricardo when he came but Ricardo never returned. Ricardo was letting him sit there and do just what he was doing, waste away in the palpable fetid air and squalid misery and think. Think until there was nothing else to think except ... the gun, which began to link the pieces of a puzzle—incarceration, jail, handcuffs—so they resembled something he'd met before. Mordida. The bite. The word the Mexicans used for bribe.

Ricardo probably belonged to the local police, much in the way sheriffs deputize in the States, Jo Shelby reasoned. Nothing uncommon about that. That was why he had the handcuffs. That was why no one had come to rescue him, Ricardo had protection. Nothing uncommon about that either in Mexico. That was why he was in a private calaboza and all he had to do was pay Ricardo the mordida and go free. From their different perspectives maybe Ricardo and Mrs King were both right. The gun was trouble and needed another home. He thought again about what Ramón had said in the prison in Matamoros, that there was a time a man had to give up sentimental relics to achieve his own freedom, that our salvations are always ahead of us, never behind us.

Señora, he said the next time the woman brought his food. Necesito hablar con señor Ricardo. Over the dark bores of the half-cocked gun her large dark eyes stayed on him as she set the bucket outside the door for him to extend a hand and retrieve, then she nodded and slammed the door, then the bolt and the lock clicked. She'd gotten the message but had that contemptible look in her eyes she might not deliver it.

By the angle and movement of slivers of sunlight filtering through the fissures and crevices of the enclosure he learned to track, though crudely, the passage of time, the only constant in his collapsed and compressed world. So the next time she brought his food he estimated a full twelve hours had lapsed. As always, her ritualistic movements unvarying, she unlocked the padlock and slid back the bolt, then opened the door wide enough only for him to see the bucket she'd set outside the narrow opening. Only this time he didn't take the bucket. Through the aperture he watched her watching him, the sun on her menacing face, the dark gun calibers and dark eyes again aimed at him, both possessive of a quality and capacity to kill without a thought. He waited for her to speak, to tell him she had delivered his message and had a reply. But she spoke not nor did he and they both continued in that stark unblinking attitude he concluded was the next closest to a Mexican standoff he'd ever gotten. The closest hadn't happened yet. The closest would be when he was free and met Ricardo again face to face and Ricardo would be the one to blink first.

Then she finally spoke. No comiste?

No, he told her. He wasn't eating. He wasn't eating until Ricardo came to speak with him. He didn't tell her the rest of the plan that had come to him in the long hours he'd had to think. Or that those who imprison should beware captivity's effects on the mind, on its survival instinct, ratcheting up its creativity so every gear catches and spins and whirs with an accuracy and intensity that, should they see those inner workings, captors would shake in their boots.

Por qué? she said with no emotion.

Por qué, he said and told her he wanted to see Ricardo.

Ricardo no está aquí.

For the first time her eyes moved and he didn't believe her. Dónde está?

She told him she didn't know where he was or when he would return, answering the second question before he asked it.

She was lying. Unlike in his country where dishonesty was a practiced way of commercial life, where a man would look you in the eye and in a voice steady as a judge sell you a car with a cracked manifold, most Mexicans were so damn honest you could tell when one was lying. Their eyes fell and their voice rose. Then he unfolded his plan and told her to tell Ricardo he was sick and thought he had a fever and was not eating until he saw him. If he died, he was of no use to Ricardo and Ricardo would have to explain a death to the authorities, deputy or no deputy, because the señora and Carmen, who knew that world and its people would keep the heat on. The gesture was a bluff, one his mind had considered and reconsidered several times. But it was worth a try. He could always start eating again if it didn't work. The only shortfall was the weight he'd lose and the illness that would surely follow.

The woman said nothing, the gun and her eyes still on him. With a foot she pushed the bucket through the crack and he pushed it back. That seemed to be enough for her and she bolted and locked the door and left.

Another sequence of total dark and splintered light went by and in the next period of dark the door rattled and opened and Ricardo stood in it holding a flashlight in one hand and pistol in the other.

So, hombre. Estás listo. You ready.

A shovel was within reach but that plan deflated as quickly as it bloomed. The flashlight was a small sun directly in his eyes, probably for that disabling purpose, and he was too weak to muster the quickness the act would require. Sí, he said.

Nothing was said as Ricardo handed him a pencil and piece of paper on which he printed in tortured script with a weak hand, BRING THE GUN and signed his name.

That is all, hombre? Ricardo said. No más.

That's it. No más. I figure you'll add the rest. They just need to see my signature.

Sí, hombre. But this gun, they know where it is?

They know, he said. They didn't but they'd find it in the top drawer of his dresser. Women had a knack for that.

Está bien, hombre. You no want you food now?

Sí. But not that pig slop you been bringing me. How about some soup? He knew all Mexican women cooked soup. They wasted nothing. He knew it was safer because they'd boil the water.

No es un problema. He reached out and took the note from Jo Shelby who offered it up with a trembling hand then stepped back and closed the door and locked it.

Within an hour he heard someone approaching, slow large movements, then saw a light bouncing erratically through the cracks. The door opened partially again and this time it was the woman holding the flashlight on him, then on the large wooden bowl on the ground outside the opening. When the light went out of his eyes he saw, too, the gun barrel on him.

La sopa, she said, her voice less harsh than before.

He thanked her in her language and retrieved the steaming bowl.

She closed and locked the door and retreated into the dark with the same shuffling servile gait he had heard her approach. She was probably Ricardo's wife and he thought of Maria, Ricardo's daughter who had worked for the señora and was forced to quit by her father and wondered of her whereabouts, if she might be near, if she approved of her father's behavior. But it probably didn't matter. The women were all as much a prisoner as he in that male dominated world, the only difference being he had a way out and they didn't. Independence Day was just around the corner, if it hadn't already passed, but not for them. They were locked in for life.

With a large wooden spoon he ate the soup, ladled it to his mouth and slurped it in the hurried movements of a man near starving. It was the only decent food he'd had since he'd been there. Ricardo could show a little niceness now. He was getting what he wanted, the gun and the revenge with it. He also didn't want to appear dishonorable and release him sick. Jo Shelby turned up the bowl and drained the last vestiges then, using a sack of sand for a pillow, lay down and slept.

That night he dreamed and in the dream saw himself standing on a golden shore looking across a vast blue sea at a golden shore beyond but no way to get there and a ladder of golden steps and rails suddenly descending from heaven and dropping at his feet then arching forward to form a bridge and on the bridge people of many colors and in many forms of dress waving at him beckoning him to come but when he placed a foot on the bridge there was a loud clattering noise as it raveled back into the heavens from whence it had come and that was the sound to which he awoke.

The lock was rattling again then the door opened and he heard voices in the dark.

Hombre, levántate, Ricardo said. We take you to you friends.

Jo Shelby almost forgot where he was and wished he could fall back into his dream. He wondered how long he'd been asleep for it seemed only minutes the deal had been struck. A rooster crowed and birds chirped away in nearby trees. Whatever time it was, dawn was not far away. Slowly he uncurled his tucked legs and stood. Where to? he said.

Soon you find out, Ricardo said then turned and told one of his compadres to bring the horse.

He ducked and stepped from the hut, looked around for the first time, his eyes scanning for objects, fixations, anything that might betray his location. At first all his eyes could make out were the shadows of small casas, sitting one atop the other it seemed, then they swept downward and caught illuminations far below, random clusters of pebbled lights thinly strung in the long dark valley below like a necklace dropped or thrown against the night and he knew he was on a mountain. The valley was too lit up to be the señora's. Northward a bulging glow behind the mountains had to be Cuernavaca and the strand of intermittent lights extending toward him the main highway south, the larger configurations the small towns on its route, Jiutepec and La Joya among them. With that composition of limited topography of the area he reasoned he was on the small mountain range bordering La Hacienda Tierra del Puerta. But on the other side.

One of the men brought his horse and commanded him to mount. The horse was shaking its head and snuffling nervously but otherwise seemed in good health, as best as he could tell in the dark. You could count on a Mexican to treat a horse as one of his own. He put one foot in a stirrup and with his hands still cuffed grabbed the pommel and propelled himself upward into the saddle. He looked around again for additional points of reference, trying to take in as much as he could before they blindfolded him, which, in Mexican logic and time, they'd eventually get around to doing. Above him the mountain rose several hundred feet and the shadowed houses he'd glimpsed earlier lay skewed against it like building blocks stacked by a child. The distance to the valley looked to be a mile. Immediately below him was nothing but prickly darkness, a sloping field of cactus and far below that scattered lights, another warning of the remoteness of the place. As he raised his head for another reconnaissance of the area, one of the mounted men approached, a folded bandana looped in the cradle of his palm.

Darte la vuelta, the man said.

Jo Shelby did as the man said and when he turned in the saddle he saw, atop an adjacent hilltop, a single blackened cross against the lesser dark of sky. Cómo el cruce? he said as the bandana was being wrapped over his eyes.

Un cementario, the man said.

Cállate, Ricardo shouted angrily at the man.

The bandana was firmly in place over his eyes, tied tightly at the back of his head, but Ricardo's command to the man to close his mouth was a breath too late. Jo Shelby had what he needed, a reference point.

He'd never ridden with someone else holding his reins not to mention blindfolded and the sensation magnified the trust a man should have in a horse. They moved quickly, an indication the riders knew well their way in the dark. The upper reaches of the mountains were sparsely populated and by the distant sound of barking dogs he guessed they were descending this one by back trails, away from houses.

For a long time they continued in descent then leveled out and Ricardo gave the order to gallop. The ride was jarring. With no reins to hold and his hands cuffed, the pommel was a useless anchor so he lay across the horse's neck and held on and trusted. He did not want to give up the gun but he'd pawned it once to get to the next point in his life and he could trade it again for the same. He thought again of all the advice he'd received about letting go of one's past and moving on with the future and what lay ahead of him was a far better sight. He thought those thoughts as they rode hard then they stopped. One of the men said something in rapid Spanish he did not understand then they began a slow descent. The horses moved cautiously downward then were running again. By the sound of their hooves and the water splashing against his legs he knew they were in the arroyo. They rode for another long while then suddenly stopped again and he heard Athen's voice.

We came, just like you asked, she said. We don't have guns. Just the pistol.

We. That meant there was more than one. When the bandana was removed he saw Athen and Carmen. He was glad to see them and knew they were glad to see him but no one was smiling.

Ricardo slackened his reins and moved his horse forward a few paces.

He looked back at Jo Shelby and waved the gun barrel before him. This you posse? he said with a menacing smile, then commenced laughing.

Jo Shelby said nothing.

We work for the señora, Athen said.

Ricardo stopped laughing. His face turned serious. So it take two, no, three trabajadores to replace one Ricardo. And two are women. He turned to Athen. Give me the gun first then Roberto, he glanced back at one of the compañeros, will free you friend.

Eso no es aceptable, Carmen said, speaking in a voice Jo Shelby had never before heard, her face as stern and unyielding, her eyes flashing. Nuestro amigo primero, entonces la pistola.

Ricardo looked down in the dramatic exasperation of one greatly inconvenienced. He removed his sombrero and smoothed his hair as though the gesture were part of the inconvenience. He put the sombrero back on and turned around in his saddle and sneered to his compadres. Muchachos. Los amigos del gringo nececitan aprender una lección.

One of the men moved closer to Jo Shelby. From the corner of his eye he saw the flourish but before he could duck the barrel of the gun cracked against the back of his head and he slumped forward across the neck of the horse.

Okay, Athen shouted. Okay. Don't hit him again. Here's the gun. She reached quickly behind her into a saddlebag and retrieved the colorful bolsa.

Ricardo dismounted and walked towards her, his spurs jingling with the measured crunch of his boot steps on the river rock, his bearing as expressive in its swagger. She held out the bag and he snatched it from her. He looked inside to make sure the gun was there then returned to his horse and mounted. I have guns, he said. You no have guns. I could keep the gun and the prisoner.

Athen glowered at him. We've already notified the police.

Ah, señorita. What police you notify? Jiutepec? Cuernevaca? Cuautla? In this place—he made a sweeping movement with his gun barrel—Ricardo is police.

Jo Shelby's ears were still ringing from the blow but the confirmation of his earlier fears swept into his head like a fire and he groaned. Ricardo may have been bluffing. Then again, maybe not. There were many good things he'd learned about the country and its people, but one not so good. When it came to good ole boys and the good old boy gravity feed of power, the Mexicans truly did have a leg up on the Delta, which was saying something. All you had to do down here was be kin to somebody or know somebody, hand over a few pesos and a badge dropped into your pocket.

But I am not from here, Carmen said, speaking in English this time.

Ricardo's face turned quizzical.

De dónde usted?

México.

Ah, Ricardo said. So you live in the city.

Yes. My father works for Alemán.

Miguel Alemán?

El mismo. El Presidente.

Ricardo's face turned suddenly serious.

She was lying but it was a bluff that might work, Jo Shelby thought as he kept his head down. She was dressed up to beat the band as they'd say back home and she looked and talked like she belonged to that thin upper crust of society from which all power seeped. Jo Shelby couldn't see Ricardo but heard whispers. Carmen had gotten his attention. He wondered if she'd press the issue and demand the gun back.

More silence and whispers.

Then: Quita las esposas, Ricardo said, the grave look still on his face, and the man named Roberto quickly fished a key from a jacket pocket.

Jo Shelby was still slumped over. One of the men pulled him upright while Roberto unlocked the handcuffs and removed them. His wrists were free for the first time in days, how many he was unsure. He felt dazed and his head still rang from the blow. One of the men who'd been holding the reins of his horse led him forward and Athen and Carmen moved simultaneously to accept the transferal. Nothing was said as Carmen took the reins and Athen laid a cool hand on the back of his neck and examined his head.

Remember, hombre, Ricardo shouted, as they were moving away. No molestas Ricardo. And tell la señora Ricardo ready to work, to stop the thieves. He snickered. You tell her, hombre. Está bien?

We will, Carmen shouted back. And my father, too.

Ricardo's lips sneered over his teeth but he did not counter the retort and their horses could be heard departing.

Carmen handed him the reins and the three rode in silence in the violet dawn with the last stars fading, a three-quarter moon lying low on the cusp of the western sierras and ahead of them the first pink blush of light behind the sleeping princess Ixtaccíhuatl and the kneeling warrior Popocatépetl and the scene struck him as an omen as he rode on and felt the morning breeze clean against his face and the water splashing cool along his legs. That the lady was no longer sleeping.

III

The ladder came sliding out of the clouds again gold steps and railing gleaming against the white and bright against the blue and struck the golden beach where he stood with a loud gong as though metal had hit metal in bold announcement then like something thrown made a perfect arc and spanned the body of water to the golden beach on the other side and on the bridge people of many colors and dress waved and called to him and this time the bridge did not move as he stepped upon it and he ran toward the people and among them and the bridge began to tremble and shake with great force and everyone ran each to their own side lest the bridge collapse and when his back foot had cleared and no longer touched the bridge it recoiled like a bent twig sprung straight and was sucked back up into the heavens with a loud whoosh and when he awoke the señora was standing at his window pulling back the drapes.

How long have I been here? he said, trying to raise his head then the pain hit him and he let it fall back on the pillow and felt the pain again, different this time, like a sting.

It is afternoon. Not very long, she said.

His eyes followed her slow movements around the bed to the rocker beside him.

Most of the day, she said, as she lowered herself into the chair. You came this morning.

I remember that. How long was I there?

Three days.

Three days?

Yes. You are surprised? She began rocking slowly.

I thought it was a lot longer. What day is it?

Monday, September twelve.

Silence. A breeze billowed the curtains and the shadow of the land began to climb the eastern mountains. The senora continued rocking and the clock on the wall by the door was ticking, the movement of the two synchronic, lulling, and he fought the heaviness in his eyes.

Somebody told him we were comin, he said.

Who?

I don't know. Somebody from here.

As if the words conveying the stress had stuck and lodged there, she raised a hand to her throat and coughed. Someone from this house? That is not possible.

Your ama de casa maybe.

Eréndira? She stopped rocking and coughed again, this time not a single dry hack but a convulsion of spasms that drew both hands to her mouth and blood into the lilac veins that forked across her forehead and down her temples.

Yeah. If that's her name.

She rocked forward and stopped, leaned in toward him, her voice raspy from the coughing. But how would Eréndira know? She does not understand English.

I don't know. Nobody else heard us talkin about it.

She swung her head back and forth in consternation. I do not know, Jo Shelby. It is of no importance. You are back and except for the knock on your head and being a little weak and undernourished you are alive and otherwise healthy.

He told her why he looked so undernourished, of the plan he'd concocted while held prisoner.

She laughed. The amusement seemed to clear her voice and the strain from her face. Jo Shelby Ferguson, with all the tales you've told, I would never want to be your jailer. How you manage to get yourself into more tight places and out again is an amazement to me.

Even if I look like a ghost escaped from a death camp when I get out.

She smiled. You have lost some weight and are pale, yes.

My mama would say peaked.

Peaked?

Yeah. Don't asked me what it means. You'd think if a person was peaked they'd be in top shape.

You will surely get there, and quickly.

How come I stayed so long? he said.

She told him of Athen and Carmen's efforts to find Ricardo, of their visits to the local authorities, even the police in Cuernavaca but that it was the weekend and with the independence festivities approaching and everyone celebrating no one was interested in helping, which was not unusual especially considering the corruption within the law enforcement in her country. I thought I knew where he lived, but he must move around, she said.

He's one of em, Jo Shelby said.

Yes, Athen and Carmen told me. Carmen also told me what she said to him. It may scare him. I do not know. He must think your gun something of great value.

He knows it's of great value to me, that's all that seems to count.

In his eyes you disgraced him.

He was about to hang me, would've if you hadn't showed up.

The disgrace was not my stopping him from killing you. That, a Mexican man would understand. But my ordering him to return the gun to you, placing you above him, that was the disgrace. At least how he saw it in his eyes. The pride in Mexican men can be an irrational monster. Believe me, she said.

I'll get the gun back. Someday.

The pride in American men, especially southern American men, can be an irrational monster as well.

She did not smile nor did he and silence followed.

The señora commenced rocking.

Where are Athen and Carmen? he said.

They are working, she said, shifting her posture and bringing the palms of her hands together so the tips of her fingers touched her chin beneath a broad smile. Everyone is working. I cannot tell you how splendid everything is looking.

I cannot tell you ... the words and the southern accent with them broke through again in the excited, happy voice and he might as well have been at home in his own land in his own bed.

She went on to tell of the arrival of Carmen's four friends two days prior, three women and a man and how they, along with her hacienda workers, had almost finished painting the house while Athen and Carmen were searching for him.

If I can get out of this bed, that'd be one more hand.

For now you stay. You are weak and need nourishment and rest. Tomorrow you can work.

And go into Jiutepec and hire those men.

Oh yes, I had almost forgotten, she said.

That'd be four more. Five if Juan would come ... did I tell you he's a brick layer?

No. Only that he is working with the mission.

If he'd come, that outside wall could be fixed in no time, he said.

But do not expect him to come. I am afraid there is another wall he cannot repair. He is still very bitter.

I think he's lightening up.

Lightening up? she questioned.

Puttin it behind him. When I told him what Ricardo was doing he said, *Entonces ya no culpable.*

I never thought him guilty, she said. Just selfish and spoiled. But maybe I was wrong. Perhaps I missed something. Sometimes mothers are too close to their own to see all the good.

Her eyes were sad when she said it and in them he saw something not close, but far away, the same dark depth he'd glimpsed in Juan's eyes when he said, *my mother did not tell you everything.* Her face saying it, too: I have not told you everything. He wanted to ask the question but it was not the time or the place and he wondered if there ever would be. If it was just one of those questions that need not be asked. As his granddaddy used to say, let sleeping dogs lie. So all he said was, Yessum, then changed the topic. Soon as we get through here I need to go into Cuernavaca and check with the banks, see if I can come up with anything on the will. Athen told me something about her brothers that leads me to think they might know where it is.

This I did not know, she said.

Athen's mama read the letters my great-grandmama left. One of them, the last one, which I never got, might have some information about the title on the land as well as the will.

Then you should not be helping me. You should be finding them.

No'me. I need to be helping you, he said.

You can do both.

Maybe.

I located my family papers, she said, and searched them carefully, more than once. There was nothing dating back to your side of the family. I looked in Bibles, albums, scrapbooks, as you call them. Nada. The oldest document was a copy, I think a copy, of the certificate of matrimony of Fernando Edgardo Cruz Linares to Caroline Ferguson, my grandmother.

That'd be the colonel's only daughter.

Yes. Unfortunately, we have no knowledge of the sons, Taylor and Jonathan. I looked for information on them as well.

You'd think there'd be something about them, he said. That was their sister.

I understand. But they have vanished. Perhaps they were imprudent and tried to fight the zapatistas when the hacienda was destroyed. Perhaps they ran like others, to Cuba, Brazil, Honduras.

It just don't make sense, he said.

There was not much that did in those days, she continued. I think you can eliminate the notarios publicos. If the Registrar de Notaria had nothing, then they will not. You can, of course, check the banks for a trace of this will, if your great-grandfather had a safe deposit box and the remains somehow were transferred to someone else or turned over to the government. When you go to Jiutepec to hire the men, you can go to Cuernevaca and enquire at the banks. I would recommend you investigate first with Banamex. It has been there a long time, since the late eighteen hundreds. It is doubtful you will find anything, but one never knows. After all, you found me.

He smiled.

She rose and stepped next to the bed, laid an old cool palm over his forehead then withdrew it.

You have no fever.

He raised up. He thought of telling her hand was too cold to detect one then thought against it. Good, then I can get up.

Gently, she pushed his head back onto the pillow. Not yet. You are still weak. Eréndira will bring you dinner. Athen and Carmen will want to see you. You can meet Carmen's friends. They are all very nice. I am a very grateful old woman to have so many young people helping me. She held his hand a moment, squeezed it then departed the room.

When the door opened next he was hoping it would be Athen but it was Eréndira carrying a tray of steaming chicken broth and baked bread and hot tea.

He sat up and greeted her. She nodded and smiled shyly but said nothing as she laid the tray across his lap. He tried to make eye contact as she leaned over but she would not look at him.

De dónde usted? he said.

Cuernavaca, she said.

Why would anybody leave beautiful Cuernavaca to come here? he wondered. Cómo vino aquí?

Porque, vino con mis padres.

He asked where her parents lived and she told him Tetécalita, which was down the valley. He asked if she lived with them and she said she did when she was not at the hacienda working. He asked how often and she said not often. She was standing by the bed rolling her thumbs and looking at the door but he pressed the dialogue, asking harmless questions, making small talk. She seemed to relax as she spoke of her family and her pets and how much she enjoyed working for the señora. He thanked her for her brief company. As she opened the door, he spoke to her in English and asked her to ask the señora if he could have a glass of milk and some bread to dip in the soup and she said, Sí, and smiled and left.

He was almost through eating the soup when she returned with the milk and bread and set the glass and small loaf on the tray.

Muchas gracias, señorita, he said as she was leaving. You can get my tray in a few minutes.

She nodded and closed the door and within a short time returned and retrieved the tray.

Outside dark purple clouds had gathered, their glowing undersurface fired orange and pink by the setting sun then the colors were gone and there was only the dark. The wind picked up and blew freshly through the room and a soft rain began falling. The only light was the glow of a small shaded lamp on the bed stand. He reached over and turned it off. He could always hear rain better in the dark. In the dark he felt closer to time, as though the blackness was time. Of late he'd also learned to think better without the distraction of light, interpret his life better and there was much he had to think about and share with Athen when she came. But lying there waiting, absorbing the steady rhythm of the rain, gazing sleepily into the mirror across from him at the lighter shades of dark outside, a different dark ambushed his eyes, shutting out the rest.

The señora said you and Carmen were coming to check on me last night, he said, as he shifted the gears on the truck and tried to throttle the hurt he sensed oozing from his face like a bad leak.

We did and you were out like a light, Athen said.

You could've waked me up.

You needed the sleep.

I needed to see you.

You've got me. We've got the whole day in Cuernavaca by our lonesome, she said cockily with an air of triumph.

How'd you manage that?

I just did, she said, winking with a smirk.

Did your brothers ever show up while I was gone? he said unsmiling.

No. I'd almost forgotten about them.

I hadn't. I see em in my dreams.

They're not that terrible.

They didn't tie your hands behind you and put a croaker sack over your head and dump you in a cotton field in the middle of the night.

She looked out the window away from him. Maybe they gave up and went home. Or got sick and went home. Or both.

They didn't do either one.

I don't know why not. They're spoiled and there's nobody down here to take care of them.

He changed gears with the rise in the road and gave her a hard look on the downshift. That's exactly the reason they ain't left.

What's that?

They're spoiled. If you knew the silver spoon that'd fed you all your life and was supposed to all the way to the grave might be taken away and you were where you could stop it, would you leave?

She raised an indignant brow. But I'm not spoiled. So I can't answer that question.

He smiled and drove. The road from the hacienda to La Joya was sparsely traveled, mostly by old men on mules pulling carts filled with fire wood bundles and young men on horseback riding to work, aimless children riding wobbly bicycles and wide-bodied women waddling along carrying empty bolsas that would be full of vegetables on the return trip. The eroded pot-holed macadam threaded a narrow curving pass leading from the valley into La Joya where it intersected the main road south and there he pulled over and stopped.

What are you stopping for? she said.

Ricardo's somewhere down that road, toward Tetécalita and Zacatepec.

How do you know?

Cause I was on the west side of the mountain and—he pointed toward the road south—that road follows it. Somewhere down there is a mountain with a cross on top where there's a cemetery and this side of the cemetery is where I was locked up. That may not be where Ricardo lives, because he wadn't around much, but that's where he had somebody looking after me.

He drove on and told her what he hadn't had time to tell her before, about the hut where he was held, of its construction and dimensions and the mental activities he'd invent to maintain his sanity. Of the woman who brought him food each day, though at irregular intervals. Of the hope he held he'd be found.

Carmen and I tried, she said. We went to the—

I know. It wadn't your fault. If he hadn't been afraid I might die on him before he got something out of me, I'd pro'bly still be there.

They passed the gas station and café in La Joya and waved at his friend the cocinero sweeping off the front and he waved back.

If somebody at the hacienda hadn't told him we were comin, I wouldn't have been there in the first place.

What?

Somebody tipped him off.

But who?

The maid. I can't ever say her name right.

Eréndira. But she can't speak English.

Might not can speak it, he said, but she can sure nough understand it. He told her of Eréndira's visit to his room, how he lulled her into conversation in Spanish then caught her off guard with English. She understood every bit of it.

You need to tell the señora about this.

She knows I suspect her. After I get that gun back I aim to. Meantime, the little señorita might just come in handy.

She turned in her seat and glared at him. Jo Shelby Ferguson, you're crazy, you know that. Slap dab, genuine, bona fide, certified crazy. That gun, like the flag it fought for, belongs in a museum.

If it does, it'll be one I build.

They pushed their way through heavy glass doors, as if the effort were a foreshadowing, and stood in a spacious marble-floored, marble-columned area, conspicuous in their blue jeans and T-shirts and everything else about them that said American except the sombreros, which highlighted them even more, he thought, as he removed his and elbow punched Athen to do the same. To their left was a row of tellers stationed behind low windows and on their right parallel rows of desks occupied by professionally dressed women and all of them looked up when they entered.

They're lookin at us like we're a couple of bandidos, he said.

Like Bonnie and Clyde maybe, she said.

It aint funny.

I wasn't trying to be funny. That's how they're looking at us, like we're here to rob the place.

Por favor, en que puedo servirle? A lady at one of the front desks stood and said to them.

He stepped up to the desk and Athen followed. Hablas ingles? he said.

Un poco, the lady said.

He introduced Athen then himself and told her briefly why he was there.

Momentito, she said, raising a finger. She turned and walked the length of the bank to a door at the rear, next to what appeared to be the gated entrance of a vault, and knocked. A man wearing a white shirt and tie came to the door. They talked a while then the man shook his head and followed her back to her desk.

Permiteme presentar señor Paredes, el presidente del banco.

Mucho gusto, the man said shaking Jo Shelby's hand and bowing slightly to Athen. Perhaps I can help you.

The woman sat down and Jo Shelby thought they might be invited to an office but the man kept standing, as if he sensed a speedy dismissal.

I got one question that might save us some time, Jo Shelby said.

Yes? señor Paredes said.

How long this bank been here?

This bank, Banamex, exist since the year 1884, but before that it merge with Banco Nacional and Banco Mercantil Mexicano.

Which was this bank, the one we're in? Jo Shelby said, pointing at the floor, aware every eye in the bank was glued to them.

Banco Nacional.

When was it founded?

In the year 1882.

That's the year my great-great-great granddaddy died.

Cómo?

Jo Shelby told him the story a century removed of the Confederados journey into Mexico and the rise and fall of Carlota and his great-grandfather's escape and eventual settlement on the Hacienda Michopa south of Cuernavaca, of his death there and the marriage there of his daughter Caroline to Fernando Alfonso Cruz Linares, the son of the renown hacendado Roderigo Fernando Cruz Edgardo.

His fingers propping his chin, señor Paredes listened intently, nodding rhythmically as one might whose heard a story before.

Omitting the legal details, Jo Shelby expressed his belief the colonel left a will and that the will might have been left in a safe deposit box in a bank, which was why he and his friend were there.

I understand, señor Paredes said. But it is not possible. Much has happened over the years, Mr—

Ferguson. Jo Shelby Ferguson. And this is Athen Patrick.

The man's eyes twitched as though something had flown into them. Yes, yes, of course. As I was saying, Mr. Ferguson, Miss Patrick, much has happened over the years. There was the revolution and after that many changes in the banking industry. Besides, even if your relative of long ago had left something in a safe deposit box, by now it would have been drilled open and the contents turned over to the government. And as you probably know, in my government, most unfortunately, there is much corruption. Then there is the country's history of political instability.

I know all that, Jo Shelby said. But I thought his daughter might have put it in one and kept up the rent, then possibly one of their children.

Señor Paredes continued. During part of the time of which you speak, these Confederados were not welcome by our government. President Juarez issued warrants for their arrest. Then in 1876 Porfirio Díaz became the president and he showed more favor to foreigners. I tell you this because your grandfather, he may try to secure a safe box before his death and before Díaz, in which case you may wish to consider foreign banks. Some of these banks were in existence before Maximillian, before your civil war.

He did stop in Mexico City and put money in a bank there, Jo Shelby said. At least that's the story that's come down.

Athen chimed in. The senora also said some of it might be buried on the hacienda.

But he could have put some of it in a bank here, Jo Shelby continued, one he'd be closer to. You got any foreign banks in Cuernavaca, like maybe branches of the ones in Mexico City?

No señor. They are in México.

Maybe you got a name or two, Jo Shelby said. That would help.

Sí. There is the Banco de Londres y México and the Deutsche Bank. There is also a French bank, BNP Banque Paribas, but I am unsure of its history, if it was in existence that many years ago. There are others, but these banks are very old. You can go to them, señor, but I do not encourage your success. Any safe boxes with unpaid fees would be confiscated.

I understand, Jo Shelby said. But you don't ever know.

Sí, señor, this is true.

Then, you wouldn't mind lookin in your records for me, just to make sure. If the box had been confiscated, I'm sure somebody would have written it down. Y'all do keep records like that, maybe back there in your vault. Banks don't throw anything away.

Sí, señor. We keep records. If that happen we would have a record. But this name, I have already investigated. And there is nothing.

Already investigated?

Sí. These men come to the bank, two of them. They ask many questions, same as you. It is coincidence, no? He laughed nervously. Their apellido the same as your friend. Patrick.

Jo Shelby looked at Athen whose face looked as stretched in surprise as his felt. Well I'll be damn, he said.

I am sorry, señor Ferguson, señor Parades said.

Nothin to be sorry about, Jo Shelby said. You were just doing your job.

When did they come? Athen said. They are my brothers.

Ah, I see, señor Paredes said, his face animating with the connection.

Several days ago, I think. Maybe a week.

You tell them the same thing? Jo Shelby said.

Sí. Exactemente.

About the foreign banks?

Claro.

They were still standing at the lady's front desk and every eye was still upon them, as if the strange drama being played out were one already partially known, the next installment forthcoming as soon as they departed the building and the gossip began to spread.

Guess that's that. Muchas gracias, Jo Shelby said shaking hands with the bank president and nodding a thanks to the lady behind the desk.

Muchas gracias, Athen said, extending a hand as well to him, then one to the lady.

It was the first time Jo Shelby had heard her use the language and he recalled his first plunge into its foreign sounds and the swelling of pride feeling it evoked.

They walked back through the heavy glass doors and into the sunlight and put their sombreros back on.

The haystack just got bigger, he said.

I guess now we go to Mexico City, she said.

I guess not.

Why?

You heard what the man said. He told your brothers everything he told us. Which means they're one step ahead of us, when it comes to banks anyway. If the bank president is right, and I got a good hunch he is, there ain't nothin there and if there was, there ain't now.

How are we going to know? she said.

Next time we see em.

And if we don't see them again.

Then no need to bark up that tree any longer.

She put her arm around him. I'm proud of you for trying.

It ain't over yet, ain't over till the fat lady sings. My daddy used to say that. Don't know where it came from but it meant the last page hadn't been turned.

It's from the opera, she said. The last song is usually sung by a fat lady.

The comment brought to mind something Miss Floy, his surrogate mama back home, had told him about an opera and he thought of Carmen back at the hacienda and how Athen pulled off the separation.

You didn't tell me how Carmen got left this morning.

It was simple. She didn't know we were going.

You didn't tell her.

Nope. I mean, yes, I didn't tell her. She was painting in one of the back rooms with her friends.

So you just skedaddled.

Yep.

He put his arm around her shoulder and they walked to the truck.

At a bookstore on the Plaza de Armes he bought her a paperback pocket Spanish/English dictionary. He told her she was one up on him, that he'd never had one and she told him he'd never needed one, that he was one of them.

At the Cocina Economica in Jiutepec they stopped and picked up four of the men looking for work, leaving behind, to Jo Shelby's disappointment, the old man who rode with Zapata. He was too old, he said, even to ride in the rear of a truck and his children, with whom he lived, would miss him. Besides, someone needed to remain behind to tell where the others had gone.

It was almost noon and Jo Shelby said he'd return the workers before dark but the old man waved it off. He was staying put. He'd ridden with Zapata, fought fierce battles, seen blood and death and torture. No further excuses necessary. In his mind his honor was achieved in this world and nothing more was needed. Not another journey. Not another step.

The men in the truck bed huddled forward against the cab to shield their cigarettes from the wind, their animated voices jubilant with the prospects of work, so unlike those of others back home in his country, Jo Shelby thought, whose jubilation erupted when they could quit. The Mexicans sure enough had one up on Americans when it came to work. And if they ever some day crossed the border looking for it, heaven help the slackers and goldbrickers and ne'er-do-wells on the other side. They wouldn't know what hit em and would never catch up to find out.

At La Joya past the cocina and gasolinera he turned right and shifted into low gear as the truck began a steep ascent. The sudden turn threw the men in the back into a commotion and they commenced waving their arms and shouting that he was going the wrong way that there was no hacienda up the mountain. He leaned his head out the window and shouted back that he was going to pick up another worker and they regrouped against the cab and continued smoking.

You think he'll go with us? Athen said.

I don't know. Thought it was worth a try. He knows the señora's had a change of heart. He works with concrete, knows how to lay bricks.

The truck groaned low against the incline then vaulted an octave when he turned left at the fork up a slant steeper than the one he'd just ascended and he wondered if the gear would sustain them to the top, the truck now sputtering, its wheels barely turning. He looked back into the bed but the men were a thought ahead of him and already bailing out, one shouting they'd wait at the bottom at the cocina as the old truck regained momentum.

They reached the small plaza at the top with its white-washed trees and home-made vendor stalls and handful of small shops and she remarked with fascination of the stirring commerce, that it was like another world unto it-self tucked back in the mountains.

It's the only one they know, he said. Some of em hadn't even been down the mountain.

Almost reminds you of home, she said.

How's that? There ain't no mountains back home.

The Negroes that have never set foot off a plantation, looking across that flat land as far as their eyes can see, where it hits the sky, and wondering if that's all they're ever going to see. That's a mountain to them.

They were midway across the small plaza and he stopped the truck and looked quizzically at her.

What? she said.

He kept looking at her with that same bemused stare. Nothin, he said.

There must be something. You wouldn't stop and look at me that way.

I just don't expect you to make so much sense sometimes. Kinda slips up on me.

Thanks a lot. I'll remind you the next time you make sense. But don't hold your breath.

I meant it as a compliment, he said.

That's something you might work on.

He muttered something inaudible about women then shifted gears and continued on across the small plaza and down the rock-strewn road that veered off the other side into the bajada. They passed the same naked children he'd seen days before swimming in the fifty-gallon drums and among them the small girl with one lock of black hair dangling like a tassel from her bald head and burn scars of twisted skin covering her body extending outward from that point as though the tassel were a grip, an insignia of salvation.

Look at those kids, Athen said. There's not a one of them over eight or nine. They could drown in those drums. And look where they live.

He slowed as they approached the cinder block house with the tarpaulin roof anchored at the corners by large stones and bricks.

Look at them, Jo Shelby, they're so cute. There's a little girl that's been burned. Oh, we must stop.

He stopped the truck in front of the swept dirt yard where the children were playing and let the engine idle. What are you going to do? he said.

I'm going to get out and talk to them, she said. You can turn off the engine and save some gas.

He killed the motor. You need me to help?

Let me try. I've been practicing.

Remember we got workers waiting at the bottom and one more to try and retrieve up ahead and daylight burning.

She didn't respond and opened the door and got out. Hola! she called to the children.

Hola! they called back in unison with bright smiles creasing their brown faces.

She approached the small girl with the single lock of hair and burned skin. Cómo se llama?

Pati, the girl said. She was sitting beneath a lemon tree braiding the hair of a small child seated before her.

Pati?

Sí, Pati.

Es ella su hermana? Athen said, pointing to the little girl in front of her.

The girl named Pati nodded shyly it was her sister.

The others climbed dripping wet from the drums and walked uncertainly up to Athen. There were four all together and a fifth hiding sheepishly behind another tree.

Y son ellos su hermanos—

She looked back at the truck. What's also in Spanish?

También.

Y son ellos su hermanos tambien?

Sí, she giggled.

Cómo te llamas? Athen said waving her hand inclusively across the siblings and they began calling their names back to her in polite and deferential sequence.

Santiago.

Luis.

Jesus.

Angela.

Y tú? she said, pointing to the small boy peering from behind the tree, only half his face visible.

Miguel, he said, the name almost inaudible in the small reluctant voice.

Y todos viven aquí? she said, nodding at the diminutive hovel, the black tarpaulin sagging inward from its corners.

Sí, they said in unison.

Me llamo Athen.

They all shaped their mouths and tried out the new word, their faces beaming as though a god had dropped some new and wonderful discovery into their world.

Y mi amigo se llama Jo Shelby, she said pointing to the truck.

This one was harder and not quite accomplished, too many words and syllables for their small mouths, their nascent vocal muscles.

Let's see, Athen said to herself. How about José? Se llama José.

José they all shouted proudly, like a cheer, flushing the birds from the nearby trees.

How am I doing? she called back to him.

Aside from a couple of plurals you missed, you're doing better than I did when I started out.

She smiled and turned back to the children.

She was doing better than better, he thought, as he observed a part of her he had never before seen, a part of her capturing a part of his heart he didn't even know was there, a part touching him where she'd never touched him before, as if something new had clicked between them and the something new was ... children. He watched her interaction with them, all of them, leaving none out, her calming voice reeling in the frightful child behind the tree, drawing him smiling into the group. With proud awe he observed how gently and with such delicate care she touched the burned child, how her eyes held all theirs and her voice all their attention, then marveled at a different magic unfolding before him when she exhausted her Spanish and continued in English and their rapt faces beheld her as though they did not know the difference, as though she were a famous story teller suddenly come to town whose magnificent gestures and expressions, not her language, told the tale and they missed not a beat. She could have been speaking in Chinese and they would have understood her, followed her ... anywhere. As she patted each on the head and bid them adios and returned to the truck he swallowed the lump in his throat for he had been privileged to watch the greatest teacher on earth in action. He swallowed something else, too, in those precise moments of new knowledge.

As she got in the truck and closed the door he leaned over and kissed her.

From the small circle where she'd left them standing, the children cheered.

I love you, he said.

I love you, too, she said.

They passed the small pavilion with the white cross on top that was the church and stopped above it in the area where the boys had been playing ball.

She left the truck and followed him up the narrow trail and into the shaded dirt yard. Scrawny chickens scampered from their steps and the dog roused from beneath the mimosa and commenced barking. She stood beside him this time as he faced the misshapened shack and holaed.

A short lean figure materialized in the dark doorway.

Hola, Juan said. Cómo está?

Bien, Jo Shelby said. Permite presentar mi amiga. Se llama Athen.

Mucho gusto, Juan said.

Mucho gusto, Athen said.

A lady appeared beside Juan and he said, mi esposa, Clotilde and gestured toward her with an upturned palm.

Mucho gusto, Jo Shelby said, tapping his hat brim with his finger.

Mucho gusto, Athen said.

Clotilde nodded guardedly but said nothing.

Por favor, pase, Juan said, the same upturned palm inviting them to enter.

Jo Shelby glanced at Athen whose look said why not.

Following Juan and his wife they stepped over the threshold onto the dirt floor of what appeared to be the kitchen. A table made from unplaned scrap lumber occupied the center and along one wall was a sink and short counter, a cast-iron stove and refrigerator. Crude shelving of canned goods and pots and pans and assorted crockery surrounded the room permitting only enough space for one person to maneuver.

Clotilde stepped aside to allow them passage. Jo Shelby let Athen go before him and as she passed in their eyes they read each other's concerns. Juan stepped up into another room and waved for them to follow. It was a small room with uneven walls, cracks between the boards and tin sheathing where thin spears of sunlight penetrated, displaying astral configurations in the gloomy dark and Jo Shelby recalled the shed where he'd been held and the patterns of meager light he'd seen there. On the floor were pallets for sleeping and separating them narrow woodworn paths wide enough only for one person to walk. Centering a sidewall was a chest of drawers covered with family photos in cheap, garish frames and extending either side of the chest of drawers homemade shelving filled with the accumulation of their life's belongings. Shoes and folded garments and various clothing accessories. A radio. A few books and pieces of pottery and more family pictures. An antique jewelry box made of rosewood with burnished inlaid silver. A guitar dangled from a crooked nail jutting from a two-by-four stud. On the opposite wall, on a rod suspended by ceiling wires, hung an assortment of clothes. Except for the calculated paths along which they moved, there was no space unused.

Juan pointed to a plank across two concrete blocks, the only feature resembling a place to sit, and Jo Shelby and Athen sat down.

Clotilde sat Indian-style on one of the pallets and Juan joined her, apologizing as he did for a stray fly that had found its way around the loose edge of a leather skin covering the only window.

For long seconds no one spoke. Jo Shelby was working on his approach, feeling his way along. Donde están sus niños?

En la escuela, Juan said.

Naturalmente, Jo Shelby said. They had passed a building on their way up the mountain that looked to be a school but seen no children or signs of children. El mismo que pasamos abajo?

Sí. El mismo, Juan said matter-of-factly.

Time for the small talk to end and get down to business, Jo Shelby thought. Juan and his esposa had the same look in their eyes: you and your friend didn't come all the way up here to discuss our children and where they went to school so quit beating around the bush. No trabajaste hoy? Jo Shelby said.

Yes, he was not working, Juan said. He was waiting for supplies from Cuernavaca.

Jo Shelby knew the answer to the next question, but he asked it anyway. Cuándo van a llegar estos materiales.

No se. Posible mañana.

Pero mañana es eterna, Jo Shelby said manufacturing a laugh.

Juan returned the laugh and Clotilde smiled. The ice was breaking.

Entonces, tengo una proposición para ti, Jo Shelby said.

Qué?

Jo Shelby had given considerable deliberation to his presentation and had the thoughts lined up in his head marking time, their logical sequence just waiting to be released. He began first with what he'd told Juan on his previous visit, about the señora's termination of Ricardo and her suspicion of theft on his part then moved on to the validation of the latter nodding at the witness beside him. He told of his capture and ordeal with Ricardo, describing in great detail his incarceration and the punishment inflicted, the number of days that passed and the bargain struck.

Para una pistola? Clotilde said, speaking for the first time, her eyes wide with amazement. Por qué solo una pistola?

Es una historia larga, Jo Shelby said.

Pero no estoy trabajando, Juan said. Tengo tiempo.

He might not be working and have time, Jo Shelby said, but there were workers waiting for them down the mountain.

Entonces, Juan said, qué es su proposicion?

The next regiment of thoughts was ready to march. He had a vague idea of Ricardo's location, Jo Shelby told him and needed his help in finding him and bringing him to justice, that he would pay for his help.

A broad mischievous smile broke Juan's face, his decayed upper teeth hanging in his face like those of a rabid animal eager to bite. No es un problema, señor, he said, pushing himself up and standing. Estoy listo. Pero no estoy aceptar su dinero.

Jo Shelby shook his hand on the deal and thanked him for his readiness, said they would talk about the money later then mentioned casually one other item of business that needed more immediate attention. Juan asked what could be more immediate than putting the thief behind bars and Jo Shelby told him again about the workers waiting below, how he was driving them to the hacienda to help his mother and how desperately she needed a mason to assist in repairing the walls. Once the walls were repaired he and Juan would go after Ricardo. His mother would pay him for his labor.

Juan looked down at Clotilde, as if he needed some confirmation. Not on the first decision, which he'd already made, but on the second and its related history. One shared over the years by husband and wife, beaten to death by both and both now suddenly leery of any resurrection.

Clotilde shrugged, signaling it was his decision but also embedded in the gesture, behind the eyes, the clear message, should it arise again not to bring the problem back home.

Juan looked back at Jo Shelby. From across the bajada in the distance came the cry of the tamalara. Okay, he said with a tentative half-smile, as if to say, it can't hurt.

By one o'clock they arrived back at the hacienda, a sight to behold they must be, he thought, the rickety truck bouncing down the crude road of stones, the heads of the Mexicans popping up and down in the rear like a carnival toy. As they passed beneath the arched portal gate he saw the señora and Carmen standing on the porch, their faces expressionless as though trying to interpret the composite of phaeton and wild riders hurtling their direction then the señora threw her hands to her cheeks and bolted toward them.

He veered right the large fountain centering the yard and was going to bring the truck to a stop beside the west patio but the señora was already upon them, running beside the truck, one hand waving and one hand on the fender calling out, Juan, gracias a Dios, Juan, gracias a Dios, over and over, coughing and crying at the same time. Before Jo Shelby could bring the vehicle to a halt, Juan, to prevent his mother falling beneath the wheels, lept from the bed and pulled her back and embraced her, the other Mexicans looking on unsure of the event they were witnessing, if it were someone long-lost and presumed dead, a prodigal returned from a far country or a hero from an unknown war or some of both or neither. Whatever it was had no boundaries of emotion and they got caught up in it and began clapping and huzzahing. The only person not caught up in the hoopla was Carmen. She was still standing on the porch, her arms folded across her chest, her dark and elegant eyes burning empty space.

The emotional reunion between mother and son continued inside the house for another half-hour. The others stood around on the porch and in the yard by the fountain waiting for it to end, as if to do otherwise would be impolite and disrespectful, an affront to a resurrection, like not waiting for Lazarus to get all his hugs and kisses in. Carmen introduced her friends to Jo Shelby, names that flew by him in the wake of the excitement. Except the lone male of the foursome, Edgardo, the only one to greet him in English. The three girls were all tall and shapely and very attractive and and Jo Shelby guessed they might be models from Carmen's once-upon-a-time career. The thought struck him, too, that in a bevy like that, Edgardo just might have something in common with him. The introductions behind them and the Mexicans still waiting under the hot sun in the rear of the truck, Jo Shelby excused himself. There was work to do.

He drove down to one of the out-sheds by the barn to supervise the loading of supplies to be driven back and deposited along the wall where the work would begin, his mind still riveted to what he had seen, emotions still riding high. In his mind's eye he envisioned the day in his own life that should've been but wasn't, his homecoming from prison and his mama bursting from the doorway of their home like he saw the señora come off the porch and kick up dust in her wake. He thought of how long he'd dreamed that dream and the infinite nights its incompletion had awakened him and the interminable struggles to return and recapture the elusive conclusion but the sleep he reentered was a blank screen. He thought of the millions of separations all over the world and their separate pains and the pain the Lord must feel looking on and wondered if He might not have had second thoughts, that ultimate Power that chose not-power so people could be free to hurt and heal and know the difference and in the difference know what living was all about. Then he recalled God's rejoicing in heaven over the one lost sheep and thought not. It takes a pretty powerful person to deny his power so he can hurt and heal with you. But that's what God was like. He wanted to be that close. And He was rejoicing now.

The truck loaded he drove the Mexicans to the wall where they deposited the supplies at various points then they joined the others in front of the house. Juan eventually appeared on the porch, his mother behind him. The women had divided their chores between painting and weeding the gardens and Jo Shelby directed the men to stations along the wall where the tools and supplies had been placed. The señora bypassed her usual afternoon siesta and sat on the porch rocking, the beam on her face and the rate of the rocking an indication her old heart had not calmed. Occasionally they could hear her coughs across the hacienda grounds, intermittent hacks resembling weak barks of an aging dog, and Jo Shelby thought again of her need for a doctor. She had not heeded him. Perhaps she would listen to Juan.

Jo Shelby initiated conversation with Edgardo, happy there was another body in his motley crew who spoke some English. They were working side-by-side rotating clockwise around mounds of dark sand and concrete and lime, spading the mixture, turning it over and over with their shovels. Edgardo was tall with distinct pleasant features, neatly groomed black hair, and lighter skinned than most Mexicans. If Jo Shelby were a girl he might, at first sight, think handsome. He and the three girls were all from Cuernavaca and on break from their jobs because of the holidays, Edgardo said. The girls were secretaries and he was an abogado. Jo Shelby told him he looked too young to be an attorney then Edgardo told him he was thirty-three and had been practicing already several years, not solo but with a firm whose main office was in Mexico City.

What kind of practice you got? Jo Shelby said. Civil or criminal?

Civil only, Edgardo said. And you work, what it is you do?

Jo Shelby thought. He kept spading the mixture. What was his job? What the hell did he do? Nothing in particular, he finally said. For the time being I'm just helping señora Moncada.

Then you rich americano, Edgardo said.

Nope. I'm one of the poor ones.

That is not possible, Edgardo said.

Why not?

All americanos are rich.

Jo Shelby told him to the contrary, there were many poor Americans, many who lived in poverty much in the way the rurales and campesinos of Edgardo's own country lived, without any political power, without a right to vote and that most of them were of the black race.

They had stopped shoveling and Edgardo was listening intently. Only the color is the difference, he said.

Jo Shelby agreed and they commenced spading the mixture again.

How'd y'all get here? Jo Shelby said. Besides that old truck and car down by the barn, I didn't see any other vehicles.

We took a taxi.

From Cuernavaca?

Yes. There were four of us and we divided the cost. It was the best way. The bus goes only as far as La Joya.

You're a lawyer. Don't you have a car?

Señor Jo Shelby, in México, only the rich have cars. In America, do you own a car?

Nope. Never owned one. My parents either.

The black people?

Nope. Most don't. Not in the South anyways.

Edgardo paused at his work. Señor Jo Shelby?

Yes?

I make apology to you.

Why's that?

You are no rich americano.

Thanks. I aint even close. You're closer to being a rich Mexican than I am just breaking even with poor.

After a few minutes—How you know the señora? Edgardo said.

Jo Shelby told him the story, breaking it down, jumping light years, trying not to bore himself with the retelling of the tale, trying to keep it from getting any longer, as retold tales tend to get.

When he finished Edgardo's hands were propped on the handle of his shovel, his eyes glaring stupefied above his knuckles. Cuántos años tienes usted?

Jo Shelby had to stop again and think. He'd almost lost track of his age. He'd had six birthdays in an American penitentiary and his last in a Mexican prison. All were uncelebrated so he hadn't been counting. The last time he was asked his age was several months back in Sunflower County when he went to get his driver's licensed renewed. He hadn't had a birthday since so he was still twenty-five. Veinte cinco, he said.

Veinte cinco? Edgardo said disbelieving.

Sí.

With that story, Edgar told him he should be a hundred and Jo Shelby told him he left some of it out.

Mío Dios, Edgardo said. It is incredible.

They resumed working.

Opining there might be more to his relationship with Carmen than appeared on the surface, Jo Shelby inquired the reason Edgardo and the other three would drop everything and come, just like that, just on one phone call. Edgardo told him they came because Carmen asked them and because they were friends, that no other reason was needed then inquired of Jo Shelby if he would not do the same for a friend.

Jo Shelby thought. He'd been in prison since he was eighteen, just out of high school. The friends he'd had to that point in his life were no longer friends. They were still there and they were something, but not something he could put a word on. They wouldn't even call. There was Mr. Bo and Miss Floy. He'd go if they called, but they were like family. No one else north of the Rio Grand came to mind, except Athen, and she was other than friend. In Mexico were Ramon and his wife, Rosario. They were not the kind to impose, but he would go if they called. The señora was not a friend but family and she did not call but wrote. And he came. Then there was Carmen. Yes, he would go he finally said and wished he hadn't asked.

They continued rhythmically scooping and turning the materials until the mix was a thorough ashen gray texture, without trace of color or streaks. As though he'd performed the function often, Edgardo took the blade of his shovel and carved a moat around the conical heap then began pouring water on it from a bucket, carefully assaying the amount poured, waiting a few minutes then pouring more, until the mass was a melted amalgam. As the water began seeping and running from the beneath the edges he shouted, Mezclalo! and they commenced mixing again, working their shovels in and out of the gray swirls of congealing aggregate, repeating the process over and over until Edgardo was satisfied with the consistency and tested its adhesion by smacking a trowel-full against the wall where it stuck in a wide even spread, then stepped back and said, Perfecto.

It was a fascinating procedure, Jo Shelby observed, everything done on the ground, without a mechanical mixer or wheelbarrow. Then the smooth wet mix was shoveled into discarded gallon syrup cans with jerry-rigged handles made by nailing two-by-two wood strips inside the lip of the opening, using bottle caps as reinforcers. Mexicans wasted nothing, not even the crooked rusty nails scavenged from around the premise and beaten straight with hammers.

Jo Shelby stood back and watched the scene along the wall, the Mexicans bending and scooping the concrete, mud, or lodo as they called it in Spanish, onto their trowels and throwing it with precision onto the cavities in the wall, their movement rhythmic and fluid, the backward swing and forward motion of their arms as focused and graceful as a martial arts move.

He thought he'd give it a try and grabbed a trowel. His first effort sailed over the wall and he laughed with the others laughing at him. He tried again and hit the ground and there was another burst of laughter as everyone by now had stopped working, their eyes on the rookie. Edgardo stepped in to assist but Jo Shelby waved him back. He wanted to try one more time by himself. This time the gray mass flew from the trowel and splattered the wall creating a pattern not unlike a round of birdshot fired at long range.

Por lo menos, impactas la pared, one of the Mexicans shouted and everyone laughed.

He had done that. He'd at least hit the wall but he was ready for help.

Standing behind him, Edgardo guided his arm and the load delivered with some measure of success, half of it crumbling, the other half peeling and falling to the ground.

El movimiento es cómo zurrando un niño, one of the other Mexicans shouted, then pantomimed a demonstration.

Jo Shelby shouted he'd never spanked a child and Edgardo asked if he'd ever played tennis.

I've tried a time or two.

It is the same principle, everything in the wrist.

After several more tries, Jo Shelby was beginning to get the knack and by mid afternoon was slinging mud like a one-man machine, Edgardo and the other Mexicans cheering him on, occasionally stopping to come over and check his work with exaggerated and playful inspection. But the big success of the day was his emerging newfound friendship with Edgardo and another problem it might solve.

The American señorita, Edgardo said, she is most beautiful.

She's every bit that, Jo Shelby said, bending down to fill his trowel.

Her name is Athen.

Yep.

I would like to meet her.

Splat! The mud flew from Jo Shelby's trowel and smacked the wall.

I thought you already met her. Y'all been here a few days.

Sí, this is true, but Athen and Carmen have been very busy looking for you. So I just have very quick introduction.

So what you really mean is you want to get to know her.

Yes, to know her.

Both quit scooping and throwing and stood facing each other over their pallets of cement.

How come you wanna get to know Athen when you got three of your own, four counting Carmen?

Oh, but señor Jo Shelby. That is not possible.

Why not?

Because the three señoritas, they all have novios. Two are engaged to marry.

And Carmen? What about her?

Carmen is ... she is my friend and she ... she likes you, he said smiling nervously, pointing his trowel at him.

I like her, too, Jo Shelby said. But we're just friends.

But señor Jo Shelby, Carmen does not look upon you as her friend, but something much more. I think she is in love with you. I think this.

He wasn't sure what to do with that. It came out of nowhere and had the dull flat ring of a pock of mud hitting the wall. He stopped and looked at Edgardo. I think ... you wanna know what I think? he said, pointing his trowel back at him.

Sí. Yes.

I think she oughtta be in love with you. You're a handsome feller, muy guapo. Successful. Got a good job. Ready to settle down and raise a family. He was jabbing his trowel at him with each point. You no have a novia back in Cuernavaca?

Edgardo grinned. Ooooh, mas o menos, he said, seesawing an open hand teasingly in the air. But no, no novia. No one special.

Don't you think Carmen's special?

Yes, but—

Well, here's your chance.

But I do not think she would be very receiving, is that the word?

Receptive.

Yes, receptive. Because her heart is in another place.

Jo Shelby wanted to tell him to just give her a few more days but then he might go right back and tell her everything he'd said and he didn't need to dish up any more trouble on a plate already full he was trying to unload. You might want to give it some time, he said. You never know with time. It can work wonders. It can make that heart you were talking about change places.

I see, Edgardo said, appearing bemused, as though he'd heard the comment first with his eyes before it reached his ears and achieved any circuitry of thought and Jo Shelby sensed he detected in the immediacy of the look, before it had a chance to acquire logic, a glint of wishful desire, as though he'd planted a seed there that just might grow.

As for Athen, Jo Shelby said.

Yes?

Her heart idn't likely to change places.

What place is it?

Jo Shelby patted his right hand over his chest and said, right here.

Edgardo attempted a smile that melted quickly.

That's why I'd bet my cards on Carmen, Jo Shelby said, and smiled and pointed his trowel toward the pallets of concrete on the ground. Now I'm not a professor of adobe but I'd think we better get this stuff up and onto this wall before it hardens.

Sí, sí, Edgardo said, snapping back from his distraction, and they commenced scooping and throwing again.

Moments later:

Señor Jo Shelby?

Yep.

This thing you say about time.

Yep.

I still want to know Athen, Edgardo said. He was grinning but above the mischievous white gleam, in the eyes, Jo Shelby saw something more intentional.

They continued working.

You said you were an attorney?

Claro.

I bet, just bet, you win lots of cases.

This is true.

I got one for you.

Yes?

He told him of his search for the will and the history behind the search. They had the afternoon and had become brothers in labor so he took his time and left nothing out, as though he were sitting in an office with a clock ticking and he'd have to cough up money when it was over.

Edgardo listened intently, stopping his work every now and then to absorb the veering twists and turns of the tale, his eyes steady and balanced, as though he were missing nothing and weighing impartially every detail. When Jo Shelby was through and he'd told of the impasse at which he'd arrived the sun was low and they were standing in the shadows of the mountains, Edgardo rigid as though fixed by a hex.

Increíble, he said, his eyes wide with astonishment. And her brothers, they are still here, in México?

Don't know.

Yes. If your great relative—

The colonel.

Sí. If the colonel did use a safe deposit box, there would be nothing there, not that many years ago. The contents would be, as you say in America, gone with the wind.

That's what the bank president said. But I'm wondering if he even used a safe deposit box in the first place.

Why do you say this?

I've been thinking. He was at the Hacienda Michopa, near Michapa.

Yes, I know Michapa.

The only banks that would do business with a confederado were foreign. They were in Mexico City. Michapa's another hundred miles south of here, almost to Taxco, which would put him two hundred miles from a bank where his money would be and he could do business.

But you said he left money in a bank in Mexico City.

That was a hearsay tale. He might have and he might not have. The señora said she wasn't sure. She just remembered the story, not the place. She said it could have been a bank in Cuernavaca. It was a bank. I just thought it was in Mexico City because they were ragtag. They were on the run. If they were on the run and they knew where they were going, wouldn't the colonel want to put his money closer to where he was going?

Yes. Or perhaps closer.

That's my point. If the story is even half-true there's another part half as true.

I do not understand this half-true, señor Jo Shelby.

If he did leave money in a bank, he wouldn't have left all of it. That's the other half of the story, that he buried part of it at the hacienda, close to him. The señora had heard that other half, too. He wouldn't want to have to trek a hundred miles into Cuernavaca every time he needed to transact business and get his money. Besides, at the time there weren't any foreign banks in Cuernavaca and when they learned he was a confederado they might have turned him down. The Juaristas were all over the place, breathing down their necks.

So he would not use a safe deposit box, Edgardo said.

He'd use one all right. It just wouldn't be in a bank.

And if the Registro Notario has no record you are thinking—

The same thing you're thinking.

That it's at the hacienda.

Claro. Exactemente. Somewhere there.

Do you think her brothers know this? Edgardo said.

They ain't smart enough. I'm hoping they hit the banks and the Registro and hauled hinney home.

Hauled hinney?

It's an expression. They got the hell out.

Edgardo laughed. You Americans. So what you do next?

Next I find the Hacienda Michopa, or what's left of it. It's in ruins somewhere near Michapa. The señora will know.

Buena suerta.

I'm going to need more than good luck. I could use your help.

Me?

That's right. You and maybe that truckload of your countrymen over there slinging mud. The more shovels the better. Besides, this way you'll get to know Athen, he winked.

Ah, señor Jo Shelby. He stood erect as though at attention and smiled. Señor Edgardo at your service.

Before dusk the men began shutting down along the wall, cleaning their tools and washing the wooden pallets, leaving everything where they left off and would return the next morning. Jo Shelby began walking toward the barn to get the truck. He did not see the figure in the cab until he was almost upon it and could not discern the identity until he opened the door.

Carmen?

I will ride with you, she said, to take the men back to La Joya and Jiutepec. She was wearing shorts and a widow's blouse pulled down around her shoulders, a pair of low-heeled sandals. She had not just come from work.

Where's Athen? he said.

She is still working, helping the señora. I do not know exactly.

He turned the key. The motor turned over grudgingly then caught and he hoped his thinking would as well. Edgardo was between him and the wall walking toward the house and he pulled the truck up beside him and idled the engine.

Come go with us, Jo Shelby said.

Edgardo studied the situation. He looked at the house then back at the two of them in the cab then back at the house.

Come on, Jo Shelby said. The more the merrier.

Carmen frowned but he pretended not to notice.

Edgardo stepped up to the truck and ducked his head in the window. How long this will take?

Not long, Jo Shelby said. He kept looking for Athen, thinking she might emerge from the house. To La Joya and back. Less than an hour. His back was to Carmen and he could only imagine the silent message she was sending to Edgardo.

Edgardo pulled back. Muchas gracias. But I think I stay here. Rest and wash for dinner.

Go get the others, Jo Shelby said. Some of them might wanna go.

It is getting late, Carmen said. We should go.

Nevermind, he waved to Edgardo, let the clutch out and the truck lurched forward.

Juan and the Mexicans were waiting for him at the archway and one by one jumped in the rear as he slowed down and passed through.

There was silence in the cab on the rough cobbled track from the hacienda to the road and silence still as the tires whined over the narrow macadam to La Joya. Mountains rose from foothills either side of them, twilight advancing quicker in the converging shadows overtaking the lone strip of byway threading the valley and he turned on the headlights of the aging vehicle, hoping they'd work and they did. A single evening star shone brightly over one peak and the quarter moon hung nearby and against the shifting and changing colors of the dying sky they might have been the emblems of some faraway undulant streamer, signs in which a stargazer of old might divine wisdom, foretell the future and in that moment what he would give to be that prophet. For it would be dark when they returned and darker still if Athen did not believe him.

Carmen looked straight ahead and said nothing. It was not her style or manner to to be forward or pushy. She had too much class for that but she had sure enough ratcheted the tension up a notch, somehow managing to out-Athen Athen. He figured Carmen knew she was the magnet she was, that all she needed was time and space and no competition occupying the space and the object of her desire would be drawn to her. That was what the silence was saying. The silence along with the hooped earrings dangling along her cheeks and dark hair flowing around her bare shoulders; the cleavage of breasts no eye, male or female, could help glimpsing and the long bronze legs, first features of her beauty that caught his attention and the last that would be forgotten.

For distraction he tried whistling but his lips were too dry. The men in the back were smoking and jabbering away. Through the rush of wind he caught occasional scraps of their talk, fragments about wives and children and of their hopes for the evening. But nothing else came his way that resembled conversation. She just sat there, looking ahead, as if that was all she felt she needed to do, be a presence in the rarified vaccum.

What all'd y'all get done today, he finally said, speaking straight ahead, talking over the steering wheel.

Some of them worked outside in the gardens but I painted inside.

And you got through before they did?

Yes.

He drove.

Later.

That Edgardo's quite a feller, he said.

She looked at him for the first time. Yes. He is.

How'd y'all meet?

His father and my father are good friends. They both taught at the University in Mexico City. I have known Edgardo since we were both children. When my parents moved to Monterrey, I saw less of him but we have kept in contact with each other.

So, y'all kind of grew up together like Athen and me?

As though she sensed the direction of his thinking, she did not answer immediately. Perhaps there is a similarity.

Well, y'all grew up together, were close friends and now here you are back together.

A nod from her but nothing more.

How come he lives in Cuernavaca and not Mexico City?

He is an attorney.

I know that.

A law firm in Mexico City needed additional staff for an office in Cuernavaca. Edgardo was single and had no family attachments. The money was good. He has fallen in love with Cuernavaca. I think he will marry someday and live there.

You like Cuernavaca?

It is all right, okay as you Americans say. I love Mexico City. She scooted nearer him and laid an arm across the seatback, her hand near his neck. But I could be happy living anywhere, if it were with the right person.

That Edgardo's certainly got a lot to offer. He's handsome, smart, got a good job. A lady could do worse than latch on to him.

Yes, this is very true, she said. She was drumming her fingers nervously on the seatback and and he couldn't distinguish between that galloping sound and his heart running away in his ears.

They rode.

I can't remember if I thanked you or not for taking care of the gun, he said, going to Cuernavaca and getting it and all. I'm very grateful to you for your trouble.

You are most welcome. It was really nothing. I called Edgardo. He picked up the gun at the pawnshop for me and brought it to Mexico City. I paid him back with the money you wired. It was no trouble for anyone. But Jo Shelby, she laid a hand on his shoulder.

Yes?

For you, I would go to much trouble.

His hands squeezed the steering wheel and he swallowed hard. Her hand was still on his shoulder, the heat of all her body funneled there, it seemed. He could no longer hear the men talking and wondered if they were looking, getting their eyes full. He figured she figured this might be her last chance so she was pulling out all the stops. The combination gasolinera-cocina came into view and he brought the truck to a stop. Juan jumped out and thanked him.

Por la mañana, a las siete, Jo Shelby said.

A las siete, Juan said. He came around to Jo Shelby's window. Muchas gracias, señor. Muchas gracias.

De nada, Jo Shelby said and tipped his hat with his finger.

They drove on to the next and final stop down the road, the Cocina Economica in Jiutepec. The men jumped out and shouted muchas gracias.

Por la mañana, a las siete, Jo Shelby said.

A las siete, they called out in unison as they headed up the mountain road.

Her hand was still on his shoulder and she had scooted closer, her long legs almost flush his as he steered a U-turn in the wide road and headed back. Her perfume rose upward through his nostrils and into his head like the vapors of an intoxicant and the excitement triggered a warm rising further below. He'd heard the stories before of what men did with women in their pickups but not the other way around. There was no other traffic on the road except lights of a car some distance behind him and the night almost accomplished, the shapes of the mountains rising ominously from the valley floor like dark parallel walls closing in, the dim headlights somehow scoping passage between them.

There was only one way to deal with the situation, he decided, and that was head on. I'm not sure how to say this, he said.

It does not matter, she said, tapping a confident fingernail on his shoulder. Just say it.

I really like you, Carmen. But—

She placed a finger on his lips. Do not say more just now. We have not had much time to talk, to share our feelings. Allow me, please, to say some things.

Her finger was still on his lips then she took it away. Okay, he said.

When I first met you, you remember, in front of my house in Mexico City?

I remember.

At first, I was not impressed with you. But, very quickly, you captured my heart.

I wadn't tryin to.

I know. That was the beauty of the feeling, it was so innocent. You were not like the other men in my life, trying to possess me, to take me in ways I did not want. But I—this I must say is very difficult for me, because I know you have other feelings—but I cannot deny my feelings for you.

Her voice was losing strength and beginning to quaver. In the dark of the cab he glimpsed only the shadow of her face, but even those quick glances, stolen from the cone of light and road ahead, detected the intensity of her eyes and furrowed brow and fragile mouth and chin quivering with the struggle of her message. He removed one hand from the wheel and placed in on her thigh and she began to weep.

I am sorry, she said, trying to regain composure. This is not like me.

That's okay, he said, patting her thigh. That's okay. He pulled the truck off the road onto the shoulder and slipped the gear into neutral and turned so they were facing each other.

The car that had been behind him slowed down then passed them and drove on.

When you came to my house and I showed you the city that night—

Yes. I remember that.

And you told me then of Athen ... . She paused to sniffle and wipe her eyes.

Go on.

Do you remember, I said even if you were not her novia, she was still yours.

I do. And I told you that Mexican ladies didn't beat around the bush.

She smiled weakly, regaining her composure. Yes. And you said that was not like your novia, or something to that effect, then you said many nice things about her, compliments, that she was in college, made good grades, could ride horses, etcetera, etcetera, all of it somewhat confusing to me, as though you could not make up your mind.

I wadn't sure there was anything to make up, not after all I'd been through.

I know this. Perhaps that is why I saw something you didn't see.

What was that?

That for all you had been through and endured, for that tragic tale of your life, I saw the loneliness inside of you. I saw, in the pain of your loss, the pain of my own. I thought God was smiling on me, that he had dropped you into my world for a purpose and, Jo Shelby ... she placed a hand over his that remained on her thigh ... I fell in love with you. She squeezed his hand then leaned over and kissed him on the cheek.

The words entered him as though they'd bypassed his ears and shot, instead, through every pore in his skin and made a beeline for blood and bone, so thoroughly they distressed him, so quickly from the inside out that he could not speak. Did she know what she'd just done, he wondered, driven her words into him, touching him where he was weakest? Did she know how long his life had hung in the balance and how for once he thought he had it steadied and all worked out and now she was about to throw it out of kilter again. Did she know how close she was to driving him absolutely crazy? Did she know he needed help, because the words he needed to say he couldn't, because that was his weakest part, the fear of hurting someone else? He opened his mouth, an attempt to say something, the word sorry figuring somewhere in the jumble of might-be-words and she placed her finger over his lips again.

You returned from Cuernavaca, she continued, and stayed with me during Christmas. Two weeks. I thought that might be enough time to hold you.

If she only knew, he thought, how close she was to having him then, how he almost never left Mexico.

I found you a temporary job. We celebrated the city every night as though it were ours. We laughed. We had fun. I thought it would never end. When you left to go home, I thought I would never see you again. Those months following my heart was still very full of you, but my life empty. She sighed, stroked his neck briefly with her hand then withdrew it. Time went by and I readjusted to the old life, became somewhat comfortable again in my old routine. Then the letter came from you about getting the gun. Of course, I would do anything for you. I called Edgardo and the rest of that story you know. When you appeared at my door that night, with Athen, I was shocked beyond belief. My heart lept, then quickly sank. The novia you had told me about was, indeed, your novia.

But—

I am almost finished, please. Then you told me the story about the land and its history and the will, this court case and Athen's parents on the other side and I ask myself, how this can be? How this woman can love this man who wants to take the land of her father? How can these two worlds meet? This is madness. This is loco. Something is not right. So ... she paused, I decide ... no ... love is not something decided, but something that just takes you. But I decided to see *where* it would take me. And this is the reason I am with you tonight, alone, to tell you I question this situation with Athen, that it will work. That I love you enough to tell you this. Love you enough to wish you much happiness if it does work. And love you enough to wait for you if it does not. That is all. She leaned over and kissed him again. Now, you may speak.

The only words that came to him were no match for hers but they were all he could think to say. You Mexican women sure nough don't beat around the bush.

She smiled faintly.

I'm much obliged for your honesty ... and for takin a burden off my back. I don't like hurtin' anybody, and you, of all people. Next to Athen, you're the best friend I got. In fact, she just happened to come first in my life or I would've stayed Christmas and never left. For what it's worth, and probably not much, I wouldn't have made it home without you. I wouldn't be where I am now. As for the two different worlds and all, I been told that before. We may have come from two different worlds but our minds aren't different. We see alike. One thing sure nough, though.

Yes?

She's really jealous of you.

She should not be, unless she leaves you.

I don't reckon that's likely.

Perhaps not.

I don't know what else to say except I do love you, just in a different way.

I understand, she said. There is nothing more you need to say.

He pressed his foot on the clutch and shifted into low and pulled the truck back onto the road.

The hacienda was dark when they arrived, the only light visible a muted glow from the dining room. Eréndira was probably setting the table, preparing for supper. He'd yet to eat with the entire group and was looking forward to getting to know the rest of the crew, which brought Athen to mind and he hoped she wasn't upset with him for leaving without her.

They passed beneath the archway and drove on past the house toward the barn, neither aware nor suspecting of a lone figure skulking in the shadows of the long porch. He pulled alongside the barn and into the spot where the truck was kept, beside the '48 Ford sedan and killed the engine. He reached for the key in the ignition and she grabbed his arm. He was worn down emotionally and had no resistance for what happened next, her other arm encircling his neck and pulling him toward her, her body and legs against his then the desperate pressure of her mouth, her tongue hungry, the contact drawn out like the last clutch of a last goodbye and when she was through whispering in his ear, I love you, Jo Shelby and he whispering back. I know.

He walked behind her toward the house, allowing her to gain distance ahead of him, conscious he was watching her as she walked, the slow lanky movements, the elegant rhythm, the stunning passion of a lifetime moving away from him as his mind shifted to the one that counted and what he would tell her: Carmen was already in the truck when he got in. The men were anxious to get back to their families for supper and he'd waited on her as long as he could. He didn't count on it being dark when he got back. He wouldn't tell her what he didn't count on happening next in the dark.

He encountered no one as he stepped through the front door into the mansion, quiet but for the faint rattle and clink of sounds from the kitchen. He crossed the marble-floored hall, his heels loud against its polished gleem, and looked in the dining room and saw no one. He walked down the long hall to the kitchen in hopes he'd see the senora but there was only Eréndira and he had no desire to speak with her. He walked back to the front zaguan and crossed it to the side doors that opened onto the patio but it was empty and he decided everyone was in their room and he'd have to wait until dinner. He climbed the spiral staircase. He flipped on the light in his room and glanced at his watch. The senora served dinner at seven. He had fifteen minutes. It had been a long day and he wanted to lie down but knew his eyes would hammer shut if he did. He went to the lavatory to wash his hands and almost panicked at what he saw in the mirror. He grabbed a washcloth, quickly wet it and began rubbing at the red smear across his mouth. His brain would get a rest if Athen saw that. He wouldn't have to think what to say. Satisfied he'd erased that evidence, he checked his shirt and collar but saw nothing else incriminating. He was dashing water on his face when he heard the sound of an engine chugging, then the roar when it caught. He stopped and listened, thought. Who'd be driving this time of evening with supper almost ready? Probably one of the hired hands. The señora let them do that every now and then, she'd told him. He continued washing his face as the roar diminished, then faded.

The señora was seated in her place at the head of the table, the others around it when he entered. They greeted him in unison and he nodded and said buenas noches back, immediately noting Athen's absence, then Edgardo's as he seated himself and his eyes surveyed the table. They were probably just running late, he thought then the señora asked them to bow their heads for prayer. As with all her blessings, it was a long and rambling list of graciases, her intense memory scanning the loaves and fishes of her life. As though she feared any omission might diminish her gratitude to the Almighty, that she might be held accountable. As though all future blessings depended upon a thanksgiving that exhaustive.

He heard her voice but not the words it carried; his thoughts distracted with Athen's absence, surely coincidental with Edgardo's, and why he heard a car motor and why the prayer did not wait. The señora always waited for everyone.

... y gracias por todo, Señor. En el nombre del Señor Jesucristo, amen, the señora said then nodded to Eréndira to continue serving.

He waited, thinking some explanation would be forthcoming. A nervous energy seemed to pervade the room. Everyone was quiet, too quiet. Carmen's three friends kept their eyes on the table, where Eréndira was placing their bowls of soup. Carmen looked once at him. When he looked back she quickly averted her eyes. The candles even seemed to flicker more, as though their tapered lights, too, were infused with the jitterness of the room.

I guess everybody else here knows something I don't. Where's Athen?

All heads turned toward the end of the table at the señora. She looked up, her face a mask of serenity. She has gone to La Joya, possibly Jiutepec, she said, her voice low and steady. It is for an errand. You were not here and she asked Edgardo to drive her.

But I was here. I just heard em leave.

I think she did not know you were here, the señora said. Anyway, it is no problem. They will go and come back.

They go in the truck?

Yes.

But I still have the key.

I keep two keys for everything, she said, ladling a spoonful of soup to her mouth, nodding at the others they do likewise.

They couldn't wait till after supper? he said, his voice rising.

The errand is one of some urgency, she said.

What urgency? He noticed the others squirming.

Jo Shelby, the señora said bluntly, blushing. It is a matter most delicate, one that does not need discussion.

He felt blood rush to his own face and began spooning soup to his mouth mechanically, his appetite gone. The room grew quiet again, only the soft slurping sounds coming off the raised spoons disturbing the silence. He glanced at the three attractive new faces around the table and tried to recall their names but could not. The introductions had gone so quickly in the excitement of Juan's return. He apologized for his lapse of memory and reintroduced himself and they did likewise, one by one calling out their names—Delores, Carla, Carolina. He inquired of each their place of origin in the country and how they came to know Carmen and so the meal progressed, each in turn telling her story. When the last had finished, they requested the same from him but he pulled out his pocketwatch to check the time and demurred. It was getting late and his story much too long he told them and politely rose and excused himself.

No postre? the señora said, as if she sensed his troubled depths and was attempting levity.

No gracias.

And no cogñac?

No'me. If you don't mind Athen outta be back soon. I thought I'd sit on the porch and wait for her.

She should've already been back, he thought, as he climbed the stairs to his room to get his jacket. If they left just before seven and it took an hour coming and going, give or take the time to find a store that had Kotex, which he'd finally figured was the delicate matter, they should've been back before nine and it was past that.

He opened the door to his room and turned on the overhead light. He walked past the bed toward the lavatory and thought at first the object on the bedspread to be a small bath cloth Eréndira had laid out for him, as she did each night with a towel, except there was no towel. Upon closer inspection he saw it was a single piece of paper folded once and he wondered why he didn't see it before. He picked it up and opened it and saw the pencil scrawl, slanted forward, her handwriting, and his breathing stopped.

Dear Jo Shelby,

This will be brief and to the point. Details are not necessary. The big picture is all that counts. When I saw what I saw tonight I knew I could no longer remain in this situation. It was not, however, a mistake that I came. I learned what I need to do next with my life and where it can, and should, go from here. I have refused to believe others when they said our lives together would never work, that there was too much attached to us that does not fit. Now I believe. I just wish you had been up front with me. I left the way I did because otherwise there would have been a scene and no one needed that.

Don't worry about me. I can take care of myself. Ironically, thanks to your friend Carmen, I know enough Spanish to get me back across the border without your help. Do not come after me. I've made up my mind and, besides, I don't want to see you.

Athen

He sat on the bed, his insides a voided crater where a bomb had exploded. What did she see? It was pitch dark. He reread the note. It read like another he'd received from her before, after he'd told her about his search for the will. But then the problem was land. This time it was another woman. This time it had the ring of permanence to it. He sat staring at the words, as though they might somehow rearrange themselves and tell him it wasn't so.

He quickly descended the stairs to the dining room and motioned the señora away from the table into the hall.

Yes? she said. Is there something wrong?

He gave her the note.

She read it and looked back up at him. She was very upset, she said, but I thought it was because of her sanitary need. That is all I know. What did she see?

He pointed to the zaguan and she followed him into the entrance hall where they couldn't be overheard.

I don't know, he said. Carmen went with me to take the Mexicans home. It was just the two of us. We had this talk. It was dark when we got back. I don't know what she could've seen.

What she *could* have seen? she said. She was looking at him with those pale blue maternal eyes that knew more than they saw, the same omniscient hint carried in the tone of the voice.

He told her what Carmen had said on the way back and what happened when he parked the truck.

Then she does not know the truth of this matter, the señora said seriously.

No'me. But she said not to come after her.

That is her anger speaking. Do you love her?

Yessum. A lot.

Then you must go for her. She will work through her anger. Women do, you know. She said it with depthless eyes projecting the same wisdom that had flushed out the truth.

No'me. I don't.

Well, they do. She handed the note back to him. Edgardo has not returned. You may use the car but you should wait for him. He will have some knowledge of her, where he left her for the evening.

I might be waitin a while.

Why do you say this?

He's all wrapped up in that knowledge you mentioned. He's sweet on her.

Sweet on her? Oh, yes. But she is not on him.

You don't understand. He's a lawyer.

So.

They don't never give up. They'll talk the horns off a billygoat.

She smiled faintly. I know someone as stubborn. Follow me.

He followed her into the sala. She crossed the antique-filled room to the large Spanish desk encrusted in pure silver with a family crest. She pulled out a small drawer and lifted from it a ring with two keys. She removed one and handed the other to him. I haven't driven that car in years. No one has. I cannot assure you it will run. You replaced the spark plugs, though.

He nodded.

And the battery you exchanged for the truck?

Yes ma'am. I knew to do that.

Yes, you would.

Señora Moncada?

Yes?

You got any advice, what I can say to her?

Just tell her the truth.

What if she won't believe me?

Give her time.

But I don't have much time.

She commenced coughing then quickly brought the spasm under control. You really have no choice. You must allow time to work. If she loves you, in time, she will want to believe you. If she wants to believe you, in time, she will grow to believe you.

Mañana and no problema.

Cómo?

Nothing, he said. Just a couple of expressions I've picked up from you Mexicans. This is everyday life for y'all.

What is that?

Waitin.

Perhaps so. Waiting can be very difficult. But if one does not tell the truth and live with honesty, there is nothing to wait for.

I'll do my best.

Be careful, she said and gave him a hug.

His left foot steady on the clutch, he kept turning the key and pumping the accelerator and all the engine would do was chug over and over like it was in the last throes of dry heaves. He got out and raised the hood and in the palpable darkness that smelled of gas and oil he groped with his hands over the greasy cords and cylinders and attachments but found nothing that seemed loose or out of joint. He lowered the hood and slammed it shut, the noise echoing through the valley like a cannon boom. In his nervous haste he decided he'd flooded the carburetor, which meant more waiting.

Back and forth he paced beside the car, hoping for some blessing in the waiting, that Edgardo would return with news of her whereabouts or the wilder more improbable hope. That she'd simmered down and appear in the truck with him. He gazed upward at the domed purple night, cloudless and besequined, a broach of cicle moon pinned against it, a wizard's sky he thought, hoped, then saw the confirming squirt of light. Then another and another, as though sprayed from a fountain, and he recalled the shooting stars they'd once wished upon beneath a similar star-crowded heaven, the wish he'd made that had held true till now and the new one just hurled at the gauzy spangled tapestry of magic.

He got back in the car. First turn of the key a spark caught and the engine sputtered then started. He eased his foot off the clutch and the car lurched forward, hesitant at first as the old nuts and bolts, the ancient parts shook and shuddered, like some ancient mechanical memory trying to kick in. The undercarriage rode low, scraping occasionally over the bumpy cobbled road and in places he had to creep lest he lose the universal joint. The señora was probably right. He probably should have waited. But he kept thinking he'd pass Edgardo and be a leg up on time and distance when he did.

At the blacktop he revved the engine hoping to clear out the lines and feel a hum of power on the open road but all he felt were the erratic vibrations of missing valves, of an auto probably never tuned since the day it was bought. The panel was dimly lit and the dust filmed dials barely visible in circular pools of faint yellow light but he could make out the one most important. A quarter of tank of gas would get him into Cuernavaca. Whether it would get him back or not was a hazzard conjecture at best. On top of that no telling how long the gas had been sitting in the corroding tank. No telling when a flake of rust might hit the carburetor and stop him dead in the middle of the night. If that happened, he did have a last resort. Sooner or later, Edgardo had to come back that way.

The accelerator was on the floor but the most he could pull from the engine was thirty miles per hour. He couldn't see his watch in the dark of the car's interior but by the moon's elevation he guessed the time near nine. At the rate he was going he might make Cuernavaca by ten. If Edgardo didn't take her on into Mexico City, which was doubtful. Edgardo was too smart for that. The truck wouldn't make it that far and back. He'd drop her off somewhere in the centro near the bus station, which was her only way out. At one of the hotels around the Plaza de Armes. Maybe the only one she knew. The Buena Vista. That would be the most logical place for Edgardo to leave her. Nowhere else seemed as logical. Except. Naw, she wouldn't do that, he thought. Edgardo'd invite her, but she wouldn't go.

In weak beams the headlights cast, the unmarked road spooled beneath him with maddening slowness and he thought, framing in his mind what he would say when he found her. He thought of enlisting Carmen's aid, getting her to write a note backing him up, then thought not. He'd be hiding behind a woman and that was the worse kind of coward. No need dragging in an alibi. Was that the word? No, alibi was an excuse to be somewhere else, what he needed six years ago on a Saturday night in downtown Drew when he was not guilty and done nothing to defend. Only this time he'd done something, or had it done to him, went along with it because it happened too fast for will to act, for thought to put into motion a hand pushing her back. If not being able to think faster than a woman's quick passionate hand on your neck and her mouth on yours made him guilty then he ought to be the first in line to be so judged and condemned. That was one thought that came to him, that he considered good enough to keep repeating over and over to himself, stamping it into memory. Because it was the truth and if the truth couldn't stand on its own, it wasn't worth standing at all. Like the señora said, there'd be nothing left to wait for. For her or for him. For them. The only other good thought he could conjure up; at least he was moving forward.

He passed through La Joya like it was a one-horse town speedtrap. Locals congregated around the handful of small cocinas as though it was Saturday night and they'd just been paid. In Jiutepec the neon lights of the bars began to appear and traffic picked up. By the time he reached the boulevarded outskirts of Cuernavaca people in various conveyances were honking at him like he was a blight to progress. He'd almost forgotten. In Mexico cities didn't come alive till ten o'clock at night and didn't shut down till early dawn, more energy circulating their cobbled streets and around their plazas than if it was high noon. With independence celebration three days away the effect was doubled, which meant a crowd in the centro.

On Avinida Morelos several blocks from the bus station he squeezed into a parking place between two late-model cars and began walking. The depot was a place he had been before and, as expected, was noisy and busy. He stood at the entrance, his eyes sweeping the moiling scene, people milling around with their families, venders hawking souviners and food, vagrants loitering around the edges like vultures. No sign of Athen among the teeming crowd or those standing in line at the counters. His eyes raked the benches that were nearly full but no sign of her there either. Arrivals and departures blared over a raspy speaker. He walked through the sally port to the parking lot and checked the benches outside then turned to the buses were lined up for departure. A sign in the window of one said Ciudad de México. The driver, a small mustached man who swaggered with imaginary authority, held out his arm and requested Jo Shelby's ticket. He said he was just looking for someone. The driver said he was about to leave. Jo Shelby said it was urgent and the driver lowered his arm and allowed him up the narrow steps into the crowded carriage that smelled of body odor and dust and exhaust. Slowly he moved down the narrow aisle of seats, his eyes cutting left and right, scrutinizing the passengers. He thanked the driver and looked to see if there were other buses destined to Mexico City but there were none.

He returned inside and inquired at a ticket booth about buses to Mexico City. The next one departed eleven o'clock, the woman behind the dirty glass said indifferently. He glanced at the clock on the wall over the sally port. Nine forty-five. He'd made better time getting there than he thought. He enquired of the next bus and she told him, as if annoyed, there was no next bus to Mexico City that evening. The next bus after eleven left at six in the morning. He tipped his hat and thanked her.

From the depot he continued up Avinida Morelos. At the Hotel Borda he turned right onto Hidalgo and made his way to the Plaza de Armes and the heart of the city. The sidewalks were crowded and he began second-guessing his decision, that perhaps he should have waited for Edgardo. But the night was advancing and if he was to catch up with her before she left Cuernavaca, he needed to do something and needed to do it quickly. Once she got to Mexico City she'd get a taxi to the airport and fly home. She'd flown before. She'd traveled the world over with her rich parents—Europe, Hawaii ... South America. She could take care of herself. He needed to catch her before her thinking got that far.

He was sure he had not passed the pickup on the highway. It was possible he missed it once he entered the city and its irregular maze of streets. There was no telephone service to the hacienda to see if Edgardo had returned, so that was out. If she was still in Cuernavaca she'd either be with Edgardo or at a hotel. She would not stay with Edgardo, his reasoning of this emphatic. He wondered if she was still with him and whether he should look for one or both of them then decided spotting either would be a relief in the teeming stream of strange brown faces. In the loneliness he felt tightening around him.

The Plaza de Armes was lit up like a carnival and swarming with people, the air thick with tobacco fumes and women's cheap perfume and oven smoke from the street vendors. Red and white and green banners hung from the building facades and strands of colored lights spoked outward from the bandstand and latticed the streets encircling and radiating outward from the centro and he thought of how the spectral and chromatic mesh might appear to God looking down from the sky, a city trapped in the merriment of independence beneath its own giant self-strung netting of celebration, and one

Jo Shelby walking right into the middle of the glittering and festooned, contradicted web. And what he heard as garish and dissonant as what he saw. Mariachi bands and vendors competing with each other for attention and table talk from open-air restaurants and cantinas and bars spilling over onto the sidewalks and streets and mixing with the low rumbling roar of passersby and in the cacophonous din of sound and light he discerned nothing intelligible, nothing that would tell him where to position himself, what to do next and he wondered if the people around him, most of them poor, felt the same, that theirs was a paper mache independence and not a real one.

A boy dashed up to him hawking jewelry. Brazaletes y colares, he was shouting in his little adult voice, adding they were made of genuine Mexican silver. His arms were strung with bracelets and necklaces looped around his neck and he carried a small black box. He had a cute brown face and couldn't be a day over eight, ten at the most. Jo Shelby figured his parents had one of the many stalls set up around the city and he'd been sent to forage among the crowd, a practice common to the country. Everybody worked.

Tienes un anillo, Jo Shelby said.

Sí, the little face lit up. With an entrepreneurial flair he opened the black box displaying several rows of silver rings slotted in tiny slits of coarse material.

He'd just go ahead and propose to her, he thought, as his eyes scanned the rings, get this over once and for all. He didn't know her size so he'd have to guess, at least pick one big enough to go over her knuckle.

He reached down and plucked one he liked. Es para mi novia, he said to the boy.

Ah, qué bueno, his eyes wide and bright as though Jo Shelby was his first customer of the night.

He held the ring up into the artificial streetlight. On its outer surface was a a zig-zag pattern, delicately engraved. Y qué tal si no le queda bien?

The boy pointed and explained his parents had a booth in the market behind the Palacio del Cortes, that he could bring his novia mañana and have it sized correctly.

Jo Shelby explained to him there might be no mañana.

The boy gave him a puzzled look and said there was always a mañana then asked why he was buying the ring.

The ring looked too small and he placed it back into the slot. I been tryin to figure that one out myself, he mumbled to himself.

Cómo?

He apologized and translated for the boy in Spanish that his girlfriend was mad at him and had left him. He was trying to find her and when he did he was going to propose to her.

Qué romántico, the boy said, rolling his eyes in an exaggerated swoon, his face turning suddenly serious. Tu novia, señor?

Sí?

Americana?

Sí.

Cómo es?

She is very pretty, Jo Shelby said, hermosa, muy guapa.

Más específico, the boy said, bracelets jangling along his arms, some excitement building in his movements.

He wasn't sure where this was going and was becoming anxious about the time but Jo Shelby quickly described Athen to the boy, her height, length and color of her hair, what she was probably wearing.

The more he said the wider the boy's eyes grew until he finally blurted out, he visto esta señorita.

Cuándo?

Esta noche.

She was there then, somewhere. A qué hora?

The boy told him he saw her in the plaza about thirty minutes ago, that he tried to sell her a bracelet but she was in a hurry. Jo Shelby asked where in the plaza and the boy pointed in the direction of the bandstand and said near the carousel. Jo Shelby asked which direction she was going but the boy shook his head wistfully and said he did not know. The boy seemed anxious to move on and make more of his night but Jo Shelby had one more question.

Estaba ella solo o con otra persona, posible un hombre?

Solo.

He thanked the boy profusely then knelt so he was on eye level with the small round face and said he wanted to look again at the rings. He picked one that looked large enough. It just needed to go on her finger. The meaning in the action was what counted, not how well the ring fit. He asked the price and the boy told him ten American dollars. Jo Shelby thought about dickering with him but based upon the wealth of knowledge he'd just received, the boy should be the one dickering, doubling the price. The boy took the ring and wrapped it in single sheet of white tissue he pulled from a side vest pocket then dropped it into a small turquoise cloth pouch he pulled from another pocket then pulled the draw string on the pouch and handed it to Jo Shelby, the small operation accomplished with great adroitness and aplomb, as if the boy had done it many times and Jo Shelby thought he would go far in life.

He paid the boy fifteen dollars, explaining he should probably pay him more for the information he rendered. The boy told him, de nada, that he was glad to be of help. Jo Shelby told him if he saw the señorita again to tell her that her novio was looking for her and had something to give her.

The boy smiled grandly and acknowledged then demonstrated once again an enterprising skill far beyond his years and told Jo Shelby he would bring her to him.

The boy was a step ahead of him. He looked around and pointed to a bar where he might be or if not there, around the plaza or at the bus depot. The boy thanked him and drifted back into the crowd peddling his wares in his shrill clarion voice.

Jo Shelby put the ring in his shirt pocket and buttoned it. He walked over to the bar he'd pointed out to the boy and ordered a beer. The bar faced the plaza, a good place where he could sit and watch. And think.

On the carousel near the bandstand painted wooden horses on whorled tubes pistoned grandly in slow circulation and above them revolved panels of pictures, on one two lovers reclining by a lake at sunset wrapped in each others arms and every time it came around he whispered to himself, Athen where are you ... where are you?

He felt his head bobbing and shook himself out of the trance-like state to which he felt his tired mind slowly surrendering. He pulled out his pocket watch and checked the time again. Almost ten, already the longest day of his life and long from over. He'd return to the bus depot before eleven and check there again. If she were not on a bus to Mexico City she'd still be in Cuernavaca. If she weren't at the bus station at eleven, she'd be at a hotel. There were hundreds in the city, but only a handful of good ones around the centro. He knew. He'd tried them all once himself looking for a place to stay. There was time to check out a few before returning to the depot. If the boy did happen to find her, he'd bring her to him. That logic based not only upon the relative smallness of the centro but on the boy's persuasive ingenuity.

He downed his beer and paid the bartender.

He doubted she'd stay at the Bella Vista where she'd cross paths with Mrs King and get hit with questions from a friend of the enemy, but he'd start there anyway and work his way back toward the centro.

Ella no ha estado aquí, the clerk at the front desk said.

He asked him how long he'd been on duty and the clerk told him since six. He asked if Mrs King was in and the clerk told him she was on the patio with guests. That meant meeting people and answering questions, which meant wasting time valuable as life itself so he thanked the clerk and continued on. Between the Bella Vista and plaza were a number of nice, mid-range hotels she would have possibly noted previously but her name appeared on no register and none of the clerks, who had been on duty since early evening, had seen her.

Keeping a close eye on the time, he circled back to the depot. He positioned himself at the sally gate where he could keep one eye on the all the doors and one on the only bus destined for Mexico City. He stood and waited. And waited.

Eleven o'clock came and went and no sign of her. No sign of anyone of a nationality other than Mexican. He made his way back to the zocalo and continued his reconnaissance. He walked up Juarez through the street peddlers and pimps and down Humboldt. He saw men drunk wobbling past children with tin cans held out for money and whores tugged at his sleeves but he kept on. He walked along streets with names he remembered— Gutenberg, Salazar, No Refleccion, Independencia—beneath high mysterious walls draped with bougainvillea and hedges intertwined with hibiscus and oleander and beneath flowered trees where birds cried raucously in the upper branches as though it was broad daylight, as though they knew his plight. One hotel after another he checked and at none was she registered and no one had seen her.

At Calle Victoria he stopped. She wouldn't have gone that far and he turned and headed back. On Avinida Galeana halfway to the zocalo he passed Calle Lerdo de Tejapa and recalled the street and hotel where he'd stayed, Hotel Mercado was the name, and wondered how he'd missed it in his careful reconnoitering of the area.

The clerk at the desk was the same. Yes, he remembered him and, no, he'd seen no senorita of that description, he said then asked if he wanted a room. Jo Shelby thought about it then said he might. He'd have to get back with him.

He passed a noisy bar and heard someone shout, Señor, above the din, a voice faintly familiar but he kept walking. It came once more, louder, a waiter calling after a customer who had not paid his bill he thought, that tone of frantic urgency in the voice and he continued walking, past the open-air entry of the place and its rowdy clamor and the voice came yet again, clearly and unmistakably: Señor Ferguson.

He stopped so abruptly he teetered like a drunk whose feet were suddenly stuck to the sidewalk. He wheeled and saw, exiting the bar and weaving through the sidewalk tables, stumbling in his excitement, the old pawn dealer who'd kept his gun.

Señor Ferguson, he cried out again, one arm raised in the air as if signaling some rare find in the night traffic of the busy city, a long-lost relative unseen in years. He had white hair and a white mustache, contrasting black eyebrows as though that part of his face forgot to grow old, his animated eyes as youthful.

Señor Montilla, he said, the two greeting each other with a prolonged and energetic handshake.

Cómo está? Señor Montilla said, smiling broadly, his eyes glassy and face florid with spirits of the evening.

Bien. Y tú?

Muy bien. Porque estás aquí, en Cuernavaca?

Jo Shelby told him he was on an errand of much importance, the story too long to tell and attempted politely to move on but the man stayed at his elbow. He asked if he had received his gun and Jo Shelby told him he had. With a voice of great concern, as if from the devotee of a sacred relic, he enquired of the condition of the gun, if all was in order and Jo Shelby assured him it was, picking up his pace, hoping the man would get the message, that he was in a big hurry and had to move on. The man asked if he had the gun with him or if it was with the young man who collected it and Jo Shelby told him the gun had been stolen but he knew the thief and would eventually get it back.

Qué lástima, the man said, letting out a startled gasp then asked Jo Shelby if he knew about the piece of paper in the gun?

Jo Shelby stopped walking and the man stopped with him. Qué papel?

Senor Montilla told him it happened when he was breaking the gun down to clean it. Backing the screws out from the handle he found one that had been sawed off and lodged behind it was a small scroll of paper tightly rolled.

Sólo papel? Jo Shelby said.

Sí, pero con escritura.

Escritura?

Sí.

Qué tipo de escritura? Jo Shelby said.

Los números.

Cuantos números?

Cinco, the man said, flashing five fingers, the barred and caged effect of his dancing spirit-driven eyes behind them causing Jo Shelby to pause and assess the burst of new knowledge, if it was born of alcohol or some other artificial means, if he should trust or reject it, then the man's hand came down and he saw the heartfelt earnestness registered full force on his face and he believed what he was telling him to be true. He ask if that was all of the writing, just numbers, and the old gunsmith shook his head and said there were words. What words Jo Shelby asked and señor Montilla said he did not know, he did not speak English. They stood there on the sidewalk, people scurrying around them, his mind momentarily overwhelmed.

Estás bien? The old gunsmith said, looking up with great concern into Jo Shelby's face as though he observed there, moving in his eyes, the passage of some inexplicable and unknown wonder.

He was all right he told the man, just a little shocked at what he'd heard. Señor Montilla asked why and Jo Shelby told him that was a longer story than the reason he was in a hurry. He asked señor Montilla what he did with the paper, if he still had it, and he told him he thought the numbers to be of some importance and put the wad of paper back behind the screw when he finished cleaning the gun.

Bueno, Jo Shelby sighed, and patted him on the shoulder. Muy bueno, Señor Montilla. Muchas gracias. Now all he had to do was get the gun back, decipher the meaning of the numbers and he might be in luck, luck hanging out there now close to miracle. He was mumbling to himself, the old gunsmith's eyes steady on his lips, trying to detect some enlightened scrap of intelligence from the otherwise mysterious puzzle of which he'd become a piece.

Muchas gracias, tantas gracias, he said to the man again then told him the news he'd just received made his mission of the evening all the more urgent and he had to move on. The old man's veined hand held to Jo Shelby's as they shook. He asked him to come to his shop and see him and Jo Shelby said he would then bid him adios, that God go with him. The old man shouted the same to him, his voice echoing down the narrow cobblestone corridor, dying in the cloistered din.

Back at the Plaza de Armes he checked his watch again. The time was past midnight but nothing around him suggesting the evening was winding down. If anything, the festive tumult in the zocalo had picked up. A band played in the gazebo and in places couples were dancing in the street. He looked around for the boy who sold him the ring. Children were every where, a few loaded down with merchandise, their shrill high-pitched voices working the crowd but none resembling his little reconnoiterer. He wished he'd gotten his name so he could shout for him but the boy wouldn't have heard him above the hubbub. She probably wouldn't have come with the boy anyway, as mad as she was. But at least he'd know where she was, if only temporarily. He'd know she was still in the city.

Americans were easier to see in the moiling mass of brown faces and he caught glimpses of a few scattered here and there, most of them sitting at tables beneath the café awnings watching the passing crowds with passive curiosity. He knew a number of retired Americans lived in Cuernavaca, along the barranca where the generals of old had built mansions and behind high walls in the gated and secluded dead end callas. But the Americans he saw were dressed like tourists, snapped their fingers at waiters like American tourists, talked loud like American tourists. Athen would not be among them and he gave his eyes a despairing rest.

He headed across the plaza, toward the bar where he'd earlier drunk a beer, and caught a glimpse of something on his left, two sombreoed figures rising from an outdoor table beneath the awning of the Café Universal. They were some distance away and in the halflight he was unsure why they even drew his attention except something about the flat-brimmed hats snagged his memory and sent a chill through him. He stopped and watched as they paid the waiter then began walking through the rows of tables toward the street. In the shade of their hat brims he could still not see their faces. Quick-stepping he recrossed the plaza and headed toward the intersection where they would step down from the restaurant to cross to the gazebo and carousel, where he could get a better look but when he got there they had turned instead and disappeared into a heavy flow of revelers streaming along a colonnaded sidewalk away from the plaza. Keeping to the less crowded street he began running along the curb of the arcade, his eyes scanning the moving throng between its columns. They couldn't be that far ahead of him, a block at the most. He ran on.

After three blocks and no sighting of the hats among the mass of bobbing heads he stopped. Maybe he out ran them, he thought. They didn't cross the street. He would've seen them. The stores bordering the sidewalk were closed. But the market beneath street level was not. He'd forgotten about the market, that teeming nether world of barter and commerce, and the narrow stairways off the arcade leading down to it. He'd never find them in that jam-packed swarming maze. If they were her brothers, and he could not be certain, he was thankful Athen was not with them. At least for now.

If they were her brothers, she soon would be. In that tight small foreign world it was bound to happen. Unless he got to her first.

He returned to the Café Universal and inquired there about the duo, possibly Americans, wearing western-style sombreros but the waiters said they had been busy and did not notice, that there were many men in their restaurant wearing hats of that style, mejicanos and americanos. He crossed the plaza again to the bar where he'd begun the evening and ordered a beer. He sat once more where he could pan the zocalo and its undiminished commotion. He sat wondering why he was sitting. It was almost one o'clock in the morning and wherever she was she'd be in bed. He believed still she would not be at Edgardo's. The boy had said she was alone. Odds were she was at a hotel somewhere. He just didn't find the right one. He thought about that, the odds. The odds of seeing the brothers when they arrived, the odds he might have seen them again tonight, the odds they were still hanging around after having come up short, as he had, at the banks and registro. The odds running into the boy vendor who'd seen Athen and the odds he might see him again bearing some news of her whereabouts. The odds of his running into the old gunsmith. The odds of the gunsmith finding the note. The odds. The numbers. The words with them, whatever they were. The odds they might connect with the will. What plan to devise to get the gun back. Sooner or later he was going back for it but hadn't planned on it being sooner. And so his tired thinking drifted with the beer and the long night, with the restless rambling crowd and the aimless cars circling the plaza and the carousel turning round and round, the repetitive panel of lovers wheeling into view. The odds he would get her back.

The sounds of people talking drifted in and out and he felt something hard against his ear and the side of his head. He opened his eyes to a vertical blur of moving shapes and color scissoring past him then blinked and saw the scissors were legs and he shot up from the bench and remembered where he was. The first bus for Mexico City left at six he'd been told and the clock over the sally gate said five-thirty. He gave a sigh of relief and looked around. The place was not as crowded as earlier but people were filing in through the double front doors and the echo of commotion in the high-ceilinged terminal was growing louder and amid it all he saw no Athen.

He grabbed his hat and headed for the sally gate and found the bus designated for Mexico City aligned with others awaiting departure. The door was open and he climbed up into the cab. An elderly lady sat in the first seat knitting but no one else was on the bus. He stepped down and took a seat on a bench opposite the bus. This was the best vantage point, he decided. Besides, the cool morning air and a brisk breeze blowing through the open colonnaded area would keep him awake.

He waited, rehearsing in his mind what he was going to say first, then next, if he got that far. All he needed to do was tell the truth. That shouldn't take long but he checked his pocket watch and time was closing in on how much truth he'd have time to tell, twenty minutes if she showed now. His mama once told him if you told too much truth it might not sound like the truth so maybe time was helping him out as he watched the minutes tick by, paring his story down accordingly.

At a quarter to six, dressed in a white shirt and black tie and black conductor's cap, the driver emerged from the depot and stood by the open door of the bus. There was something familiar looking about him. He was short and squat with broad shoulders. His eyes were deep set and close together and a bushy mustache hooked around the corners of his mouth. He kept shifing his weight from one foot to the other, his ticket puncher from hand to hand and shot quick nervous glances at Jo Shelby. As if he didn't want his eyes to get caught looking. As if he, too, was watching a clock, one he needed to speed up.

Jo Shelby studied the man, raked him through his memory then recalled where he'd seen him. The odds again, he thought, that he was looking at the same driver who stole twenty dollars from him only months before and the driver acting like he knew Jo Shelby knew it, too, and all Jo Shelby could do was sit there and fire bullets at him with his eyes. There were no police around that time of morning. If he made a scene that would only create confusion and distraction and he wasn't going to miss Athens over twenty dollars. He scrutinized the driver thoroughly, collected mental images, memorized the number of the bus. They would meet again.

A mother and father holding the hands of two small children came out of the terminal and approached the driver. He punched their tickets and they climbed up into the bus. An elderly man and woman in clothes they might wear to church shuffled behind them. A loudspeaker squawked departure times, ten minutes for buses departing to Mexico City, Puebla, Vera Cruz, Acapulco, Oaxaca, Taxco. More people entered the bus bay from the terminal, only a few ticketed aboard the bus holding his attention.

She had five minutes now and he felt his heart racing. Buses left every hour on the hour to the capital and he would stay there all day if he had to but if she were in that big a hurry to get the hell out he'd be seeing her come through the sally gate any second, that thought not even completing its circuit and the second struck.

She was struggling with her purse over one shoulder, the other tilted by the weight of her duffel bag. She did not see him at first as she entered the bay. When she turned toward the bus and saw him standing beside it she dropped the duffel bag.

Where've you been? he said, holding his hat with both hands. I've gone to every hotel in town looking for you.

Next door, at the Jardin Borda, she said.

He hadn't thought to check there, where only the rich stayed. They'd been living hand to mouth and he'd forgotten she had money. He approached to help with the duffel bag.

I can get it, she said, and bent down and grabbed its corded handles. I told you not to come after me.

I had to. I had to tell you the truth.

I saw the truth.

Whatever you saw wasn't the truth.

Seeing is believing.

Naw, not always. I waited for you to ride with us.

Not very long.

As long as I could, he said, his voice rising in pitch. The men were waiting. They had to get home to supper, to their families.

That wasn't the truth I saw anyway, she said. She had not moved and was still standing holding the duffel bag.

He stepped closer. Here, let me hold that for you.

I've got it.

Why not put it down? He was holding his hat again in his hands, rotating the brim nervously through his fingers, wondering if he should bring the ring out now.

Because I'm getting on that bus. She moved past him to the driver who took the bag from her and slung it into the railed bin on top.

You can at least hear me out, he said, crowding her elbow.

She handed her ticket to the driver and he punched it, holding a wary eye on Jo Shelby.

I guess you're going to tell me it was her idea to drive down by the barn.

The bus driver was getting antsy and about to board the bus.

No. That's where the truck stays parked. But it was her idea to do what she did. We'd had this talk and I told her she was just a friend, that I loved you and that was that. He knew time was running out and he was talking fast. He reached in his pocket and fumbled for the drawstring and pulled out the turquoise bag. Then I drove down there to park the truck and she just pulled me over to her. It was dark. How'd you see?

I saw you come in and drive down there. I followed, not to snoop but to greet you, tell you dinner was almost ready. Then I saw.

Don't you believe me?

Vámanos, the driver said.

No, she said. You stayed with her last Christmas. She took care of that blessed gun for you. I don't belong here. It's not too late to get my teaching job back.

But I love you. I don't love her. Here. He held out the turquoise bag. If your hell bent on going, at least take this.

What is it?

Just take it.

He was standing with his hand extended, holding the small drawstring sack

She looked at him, sad eyes drawing up in her sockets. Her mouth quivered. No. I cannot say I don't love you, Jo Shelby. But right now it's not enough to stay down here and go through all this hell and torment with her.

He decided to change directions. We're almost through at the señora's. I have new information about the will. It'll be just another day or two then we can leave. Together.

A day or two too long, she said.

The bus driver told her she had to get on the bus or stay, that he had to leave and he climbed up into his seat and started the motor.

She leaned over and kissed him on the cheek. You take care of yourself, Jo Shelby.

I love you, he said then shoved the small bag into her hand.

She climbed up into the cab of the bus and looked back at him, her long dark hair sweeping her shoulders, one hand clutching the turquoise bag. She said nothing but he saw the tear streaming down her cheek.

He thought of one more ploy that might change her mind. Your brothers are still here, he hollered as the driver was closing the door and he saw her eyes widen, the alarmed look taking over the tear and the rest of her face then the driver pulled the door shut and the bus backed up and rolled away, the driver who stole his money pulling out with the love of his life. The odds.

IV

The morning was still early as he left the outskirts of the city, the sun not yet visable above the eastern sierras but the sky behind them glowing orange with the promise of its approach, when its first bright beam would crest the peaks and sere the layered mists in the valleys and throw a clean sheet of bronze across the land and the long daybreak mountain shade would stop and begin withdrawing. Between intermittent trees and buildings he glimpsed Popocatépetl, the shuttered visual effect of the conical stack and its horizontal stream of vapor that of a trail of smoke dragged across the sky by a train, the Sleeping Lady in tow. He thought again of the legend of the tragic lovers, how closely it mirrored his life, how some tales may be carved in stone for a reason. One glimmer of hope, even if born of wishful thinking, he did glean and decipher from the mythical tableau. The train was going his way.

Heavy traffic approached him but there was almost none on his side of the two-lane boulevard lined with white-washed laurel trunks, as though he were going the wrong way on a one-way street of life, his life that voided and lonely and heavy, the vehicle in which he rode that out-dated and crippled. But for the shopkeepers raising their corrugated cortinas and sweeping off their store fronts and vendors firing their street ovens and children walking to school in their blue and white uniforms, he would have thought he was driving into an old dawn and not a new one. He didn't want to leave the spot where he'd left her. He stood there at the terminal a long time waiting, hoping the last terrified look he saw in her face would take over her thinking and she'd pull the cord and the driver would stop and let her off and she'd walk back to him. But once he decided the bus wasn't stopping and she wasn't coming back he wanted to get as far away as fast as he could.

A cool wind whipped through the car, the kind that made a man want a smoke, made him think it might calm his nerves, somehow dampen his hurt but he'd thrown away his cigarettes, for her, and didn't want to stop to buy any. He pulled out his pocketwatch and checked the time. It was almost seven. In his frantic scramble to find her he'd almost forgotten about Juan and the workers he was supposed to pickup. At least something was going right in his life. After Jiutepec La Joya was next. He was running late but Mexicans waited. He glanced over his shoulder and guessed they could all fit, three in the back and two in the front.

In Jiutepec he passed sights of increasing familiarity to him. The auto parts tienda with its huge Bardahl door and hardware store next door and grocery across the street. Other tiendas along the way, each, however gaudy and garish, offering their own unique mercantile display, bearing their own mark of identification. He passed people whose faces he recognized and waved at them and they waved back as though they recognized him, too. He wasn't sure if the feeling moving through him was one born of sudden need or if something else was going on down deeper inside of him, growing on him, a settling-in feeling to a new place because he couldn't go back to the old one and its old memories and old pain. A feeling that will or no will, whether one even existed or not, if worse came to worse, if it was possible to get any worse, there was a life for him here, in a land where his other fathers died, among a people steadily becoming his own, a place where he could stay and call home.

The needle on the car's gas gauge had been on empty since Cuernavaca and he pulled up to the pumps in front of the gasolinera. At the adjacent cocina the workers were sitting around the tables smoking and drinking coffee. They all waved and shouted holas to him. He waved but did not hola back. The mozo came out with his ready smile for business. Jo Shelby asked him to fill up the tank and check his oil. He added it needed a tune up then wished he hadn't. The mozo jumped on that and it took another five minutes returning his focus to gas and oil. When he was through the mozo asked again if Jo Shelby didn't want the tune up. Again he told him not for now but if he had to make another trip into Cuernavaca he might need a major overhaul. The mozo laughed and nodded he understood but Jo Shelby knew the boy thought the reference was to the car. No one could understand all that was broken inside of him.

The men finished off their coffee in quick gulps and stubbed their cigarettes into jar lids spread haphazardly around the tables. They began walking toward the car. He invited one to sit up front with him but they preferred piling into the back seat. He guessed they knew he had one more passenger to pickup. They had to remove their sombreros to make the fit.

In La Joya Juan was standing in front of the small cocina. Jo Shelby stopped and Juan opened the passenger door and got in, removing his sombrero like the others. He wore a white sleeveless T-shirt and blue jeans belted with a hemp rope knotted in front and sandles with no socks and radiated a ready-to-work look. In his right hand he carried a trowel, one much larger than those at the hacienda, and in the other a level.

Tu paleta es más grande, Jo Shelby said.

Sí, Es mío. También éste nivel. Son mejor.

Jo Shelby thought of carpenters he'd seen come to work back home, bringing their own hammers and levels, probably taking them off a wall where they hung alongside others, like a hunter might a particular rifle from a rack for a particular game.

He put the car in gear, looked both ways and pulled into the road.

Juan sat quietly looking straight ahead, the men in the back equally quiet. In the silence Jo Shelby reflected again on the gun and what the old gunsmith had found. The numbers could belong to a bank deposit box but he'd already run that logic as far as he thought it would go. He ran it again to see if he ended up at the same dead end and he did. They could be the combination of a safe. They could be some other secret code. They could be nothing. Heaven only knew. More intriguing than the message was how it got into the gun in the first place, who put it there. He needed to look at the numbers and the words, whatever they were, and see for himself.

The men in the backseat were jabbering among themselves. Clutched in their arms their sombreros looked like strange malformations rising from their laps.

He turned to his passenger and spoke in a low voice: Juan?

Sí?

Quieres viver una aventura?

Juan looked at him and smiled. Claro. Dónde?

Aquí. En Morelos.

Dónde en Morelos?

Ahora no sé. Qué es parte de la aventura.

Qué tipo de la adventura?

Peligroso.

At the word dangerous Juan's grin flattened and his brow furrowed. Cómo peligroso?

Es tan peligroso como caballgara con Zapata, Jo Shelby said, curious the reaction the name might stir.

Juan's eyes had that same distant look Jo Shelby had seen before, as though focused on something far away. Seconds lapsed and he did not respond, his face in that same severe fixation, frozen by the same severe thought or image or recollection or whatever it was Jo Shelby evoked by the mere utterance of the name, then finally he turned, dragging the deep longing look with him, and spoke. Eso es peligroso, muy peligroso, a dark flash in his eyes when he said it.

Sensing the emotion he'd created, Jo Shelby said perhaps it was not that dangerous, that Zapata was killed and Juan shot up straight in the seat and turned and glared at Jo Shelby. Pero Zapata no murió, he said. Zapata vive, then went on to say how, on nights when the moon was full and the sky clear, he would see El Charro riding along the mountain trails on his white stallion.

Jo Shelby canted a thumb over his shoulder to the men behind them and said they'd said the same. The men didn't hear and kept up their private discourse.

Es verdad, Juan said emphatically.

Jo Shelby told him one of the men had been with Zapata when he was killed then caught his error. When he was shot, he said.

Overcome with sudden excitement Juan asked which one and Jo Shelby told him it was not one of the men in the car with them, but the old man of the bunch at the cocina where he'd picked them up. He knew the old man but did not know he had ridden with Zapata. Mío dios, mío dios Juan kept muttering to himself.

Jo Shelby asked Juan if he still wanted to help and Juan, his face still animated, affirmed he did then asked to know more of the dangerous adventure. Jo Shelby told him the story behind the mission, which he now called it, of his encounter the previous year with Ricardo, the loss and recovery of his gun, the señora's dismissal of the administrador and his subsequent acts of revenge, the latter of which Juan already knew and he nodded. To make a long story short, Jo Shelby said, Ricardo had the gun again and he needed to get it back, which was where the peligroso came in. Juan looked at him as though he were loco and asked, in a voice as astonished as the look, why he would risk his life for a pistola. Jo Shelby told him that was another long story and Juan told him if he was going to risk his life for another man's story he was going to know the story, long or short.

Jo Shelby noted where they were on the road, over halfway to the hacienda. If he talked fast, he had enough time. The men in the back were smoking and talking, telling their own stories, which was how most Mexicans survived, he guessed, on the honor and valour and strength of their stories. Then he began his.

The hacienda looked sleepy and quiet as the car crested the treeless rim where the land bowled downward. The sky was clear and blue, the air cool and crisp, a slight breeze blowing down from the mountains. Woodsmoke rose white and ragged from the workers' huts inside the wall but nothing else moved in the enclosed compound. Too still he thought, as the car bumped slowly over the rutted stone road. At that time of morning the handful of trabajadoras who lived on the place would've been feeding the horses in the corral or harvesting sugar cane in the fields or gearing up to ride out and check on the cattle, feed them.

He stopped inside the arched gateway for Juan and the workers to get out and head to their workstations along the wall, where they'd left off the day before, then he drove on down to the barn and parked the car beside the pickup, which meant Edgardo had made it back. He slammed the cardoor. It didn't catch so he slammed it again, harder, thinking that might rouse attention, at least announce he was back.

He walked up to the house to change into his work clothes. He was tired. His eyes were dragging the ground. He needed to sleep but there was too much to do.

The señora met him on the porch. She was in her housecoat, clutching it tightly around her as though she was cold. Her iron-gray hair was uncombed, her eyes faded and washed out, as though she'd had a sleepless night as well.

Did you find her? she said, looking up at him in tired expectation, her voice thin and wheezy, as though it was speaking for the first time in the new day.

I found her all right, he said, removing his hat.

Edgardo said he tried to talk her into returning, she said.

That must've been a long talk, a lot longer than mine.

I do not know, she said. He did not say.

Guess he wanted her back, too. but not as bad as me.

What? she said, her voice weak, on the verge of a cough.

Nothing. I did what you said, though. I told her the truth.

She opened her mouth to speak then covered it with her hands and shut her eyes and began coughing. Her face turned red and tears squeezed out of her eyes. Jo Shelby reached over and patted her on the back. At last she stopped. She removed a clot of tissue from the pocket of her housecoat and dabbed her eyes and blew her nose.

Señora Moncada, ma'am, you need to let us get you to a doctor.

She waved the tissue fussily in front of her face, as though batting at a fly. Nonsense, she said, her pale blue eyes flaring. The doctors around here cannot help me. She wiped her eyes again. So you told her the truth. That is good.

There's nothing good about it I can see. He looked around as if, by the gesture, to prove his point.

The truth is always good. Your heart is clean. You must give her time.

He looked down into the crown of his hat then back up at her. I think I'm giving her more than time.

What do you mean?

She left. She got on the bus for Mexico City. She'll pro'bly fly home. To Memphis, then Atlanta where she's got a teaching job. I won't ever see her again.

She reached out a frail hand and laid it on his arm, her old flesh cool like a cream just applied. Jo Shelby, if she loves you, you will see her again.

Only way that will happen will be if I go after her.

No, I think not.

You didn't go to yours when you had the chance.

She blinked hard and removed her hand. That was different. Different culture. Different circumstances. She looked hard at him. I wanted to go. Many times I wished I had. Then it did not matter. Fate took my decision from me.

They killed him.

She blinked hard again and looked away, across the big yard, toward the workers gathering along the wall, her son among them.

I guess that's the time you were talking about, the one that heals everything.

She looked back at him, the hardness of seconds before suddenly softened, first in her eyes then spreading outward across her face. Yes, it does, she said. But there are always scars. I am tired. You look tired. May we sit. There was an edge to her voice, as though he'd pushed her too close to something that pricked her and needed to back away.

All right, he said.

She sat in one of the rockers on the porch and he pulled another in closer, hooked his hat on the back and sat beside her. Sunlight played on her face through the bougainvillea draping from the eaves and he figured the same broken pattern covered his.

Where is everybody? he said. The place is quiet as a graveyard.

Tomorrow is a holiday. She began rocking slowly, looking again at the men preparing their first batch of cement. In the distance they looked like characters atop a music box, the synchronized piston-like movements of their arms and shovels turning the mix, rotating clockwise round and round. We celebrate our independence. I gave my workers the day off, Saturday as well. This way they will have four days to themselves. They work hard. They deserve a little independence of their own.

Don't we all, he said. You think we should give them the day off, too? he said, nodding in the direction of Juan and the other workers from La Joya. A couple of sparrows swept up under the overhead rafters, flitted playfully among the beams then were gone in an eyeblink.

If you wish. I had not thought of them, perhaps for selfish reasons. I wanted to see Juan again. Have him here again working, where he belongs. See him come through the door again into the kitchen, watch him wash his hands at the sink and feed him again. That is a special feeling, a mother having her own back into her world.

Yessum, I guess so. He was sure his mother had had the same feelings when he was in prison. He knew he'd had them, too, longed to get back to her kitchen and wash his hands at her sink and eat her steaming home-cooked black-eyed peas and butterbeans and okra and greens and cornbread and drink her chilled sweet milk and cool iced tea and on and on and on, in his daydreams and nightdreams the tastes and images would keep coming. Then she was killed and that warm kitchen, that world of tastes, gone forever. He considered, momentarily, sharing those thoughts but held them to himself.

Maybe they've had so much time off that this is like independence for them.

Who is this?

The men yonder. They hadn't worked in a while. They can feed their families now.

Oh, yes. Then let them work.

They rocked.

What about Edgardo and the girls? he said.

They are all sleeping. They all stayed up late, waiting. Carmen, I do not think, slept at all. She has been most upset.

She oughtta be.

I know the story.

How?

She told me. I cannot fault her. She did what I should have done years ago and did not. She attempted discretion. She did not want to cause problems, to hurt you. She is very much in love with you and, I think, very much distraught with what has happened.

I understand. Given this time you keep talkin about, I might in time be in love with her. But right now, in this time, I'm not and this is the time that counts, not what's dead and what's not born but what's livin 'n breathin right now.

I do not dispute, Jo Shelby, what you say. Perhaps each of us, in our own way, must pursue the one we love. But there are times when the pursuit is in the waiting. Do you understand?

Not really.

Do you know the Book of Ecclesiastes, in the Holy Bible.

I've heard of it. My mama used to read to me from it.

Perhaps you know it speaks of time, that for every thing there is a time and a time to every purpose under the heaven. A time to build and a time to tear down. A time to plant and a time to reap. A time to cry and a time to mourn. You have heard this before.

Yes ma'am.

You have heard, then, the scripture that says there is a time to get and a time to lose, a time to keep and a time to cast away.

He nodded.

For you, Jo Shelby, this is a time to lose and cast away. It is, of course, a paradox, a seeming contradiction. By losing and casting away, or in your case, not pursuing, you might gain. That is your best and wisest choice.

By letting her go I might get her back.

Yes. The essence of all love is the ability to let go. But I think the key word is wait. Like Popo on the mountain, waiting for his lady to awaken. He never stops. That is the strength of his love. That is the strength of Mexico, waiting for its real independence, never giving up.

Mañana y no problema.

Claro.

He sat there and thought a moment, considered the flaw in her philosophy. But Popo'll be sittin there till the cows come home. Mañana comes and goes and el problema no es resuelve. You gotta do more than just wait. Otherwise nothing would happen.

I use Popo metaphorically, symbolically. I did not say there is no action. I said it is all in the timing, a time to every purpose.

They continued rocking.

The shadows in the front yard were growing shorter as the sun rose and he could hear one of the big clocks inside ticking counterpoint to their rockers across the wooden planks, a sound he was beginning to think might be his own sound, one that discordant. He was growing too tired to keep going but her last comment roused a thought. He stood and lifted his hat from the chair back. In that case it's time for me to pay Ricardo a visit.

Her mouth fell open but before she could say anything he was already inside and on his way up the stairs to his room.

When he awoke it was past noon. The mansion was quiet as early morning. The señora was sitting at her desk in the salon writing something when he found her.

I overslept, he said.

You have not slept enough.

I need to stay up. If I slept any more I'd have my nights and days more mixed up than they are already. Where are the girls?

I told them they could take the car, now that it has proven itself, into Cuernavaca to shop. Juan and the workers have already eaten and returned to their work. Edgardo is with them. Eréndira can make you a sandwich if you wish.

I could use something to eat.

Very well. Eréndira is in the kitchen.

He turned at the door. Why don't you come with me, he said, his thinking taking a sudden creative leap forward.

She put her pen down and swiveled in the chair so she was facing him, her small blue eyes static and stupified behind the lingering gaze, as though they might cross.

I got somethin I want to tell you, he said.

She raised her brows and folded whatever she was writing in, a leather notebook of some type, a diary maybe, and pushed herself up from the chair, the summation of expression and movement signifying inconvenience.

Eréndira was peeling potatoes over the sink, her back to the door when they entered and she let out a slight yelp then quickly collected herself.

Perdón me Eréndira, pero señor Jo Shelby querría un sandwich.

Qué tipo? Eréndira said matter-of-factly, drying her hands on a towel.

Jamón, he said. Si posible, con la lechuga y tomates.

No es un problema. La mayonesa?

Sí, gracias.

Eréndira crossed the big square kitchen to the refrigerator. She opened the door and began setting out the ingredients on a large table similar in appearance to the butcher block he recalled seeing in the meat section of Piggly Wiggly back home.

The señora stood watching, the same enigmatic, baffled look on her face.

Señora? he said.

Yes. Her arms were folded across her chest in that stern manner his mother would fold hers when she was growing impatient with him.

Just wondered if there's been anymore rustling and stealing, if you've missed anything else lately.

No. Nothing has been reported. I think what Carmen said to Ricardo, about her father and Alemán, probably scared him.

He laughed. That Carmen. She's something else. Alemán doesn't even know her daddy, wouldn't recognize him if he bumped into him on the street. That was all a bluff, he said, an eye on Eréndira's canted head as she sliced tomatoes, wondering if she'd nick herself in the skewed focus.

The señora relaxed her arms. I see. Well, it seems to have worked. Let's hope so, anyway.

It's working so good we're going to let the horses out of the corral, run them in with the herd.

But—

Just for tonight. Let em get some exercise.

You think this is wise.

Trust me, he said and winked, hoping she'd catch the intended signal. It'll be okay. They caint go nowhere, not with the natural boundaries of the place. Besides, they know where their trough is. They'll come back. He knew little to none about her horses, but she'd said they'd let them out before and hoped she'd catch the hint and play along with him.

Without looking, as though her eyes and ears worked the same circuit, Eréndira reached for the head of lettuce and tore off a green sheet.

The señora's brow wrinkled. She raised a closed hand to her mouth and cleared her throat as though she would cough then brought her hand down. Very well. Is that all you wanted to tell me?

That's it.

Nothing more.

Nome.

You brought me all the way down here just to tell me that.

Yessum. I was hungry, wanted Eréndira to get started on that sandwich.

Very well. Then I will return to the salon.

Señora?

She stopped in the doorway and looked back.

Doesn't Eréndira get some holiday time off?

Eréndira did not flinch at the sound of her name, gave no natural indication she'd heard it.

Yes. She asked to work part of the day then she will join her family.

Where does her family live?

I do not know exactly. Near La Joya. Not far from here.

Eréndira still said nothing, her eyes focused on the sandwich taking shape.

I'd be glad to take her in the truck.

The señora conveyed the offer to Eréndira in Spanish but Eréndira shook her head and said she'd rather walk to the road where a brother was picking her up at two o'clock.

All right, Jo Shelby said. Thought I could be of help.

The señora continued down the hallway to the salon.

Eréndira finished his sandwich and and put it on a white china plate then poured him a glass of sweet milk. She pointed to a stool he could pull up to the island but Eréndira was beginning to give him the willies so he went to the front porch and sat in one of the rockers and ate there, pleased with himself at the two curves he'd just thrown Ricardo.

After he ate he took his dishes back to the kitchen and gave them to Eréndira who took them unsmiling and put them in the sink. He went to his room and changed into his work clothes. He retrieved the last two of his great-grandmother's letters from the dresser drawer and reread them, made sure he'd remembered right, and he had, confirming more than ever his belief there'd been a final letter bearing the meaning of the numbers and the letter had been destroyed. So now all that remained was five digits, the same as the number on the gun, if that coincidence was of any consequence, the odds playing with him again, and the gun was with Ricardo in a triangular area somewhere between the hacienda and a mountaintop graveyard and La Joya. He returned the letters to the dresser drawer and closed it and headed back down the stairs to join the men working the wall.

They all holaed him when they saw him coming. Edgardo had a sheepish look on his face as one who might be charged with a crime but unsure of the crime. Jo Shelby picked up a trowel and took a station beside him and began throwing mud at a place in the wall so badly deteriorated they must have spent most of the day tearing out the rotted debris and re-bricking the cavity.

Hotter out here today, Edgardo, idn't it?

Yes. I am sorry about Athen. I tried to talk—

I know. The señora told me already. It wadn't your fault.

She was very angry. She would not talk even to me.

You dropped her off at the Hotel Borda.

Yes, this is true.

I looked all over and couldn't find her. I didn't think of the Borda. I thought she might've gone home with you, figured you'd invite her. He threw a trowelful at the wall then their eyes met.

Yes, I must tell you the truth, I did. That made her even more angry. I was glad, quite frankly, to get rid of her.

But you were late getting back. I looked for you on the highway.

I did go to my place, after I took her to the Borda. Then I drove by to see my parents. It is not often I have transportation. I did not think to get back quickly and report. Again, I am sorry.

Don't mention it. I finally found her.

Oh, yes! His arm stopped on the back swing then followed through, a loud splat rising into the air. Where did you find her?

At the bus station. This morning.

She was still angry? Edgardo said.

Yep. Madder 'n a wet hen.

What is this?

It's an American expression. She was profoundly pissed off and in so many words, not very many, let me know I was in caca profundo.

Edgardo let out a chuckle then tried to smother it with his free hand. Sorry, señor Jo Shelby. It is not funny.

Naw, it ain't. And quit callin me señor. Jo Shelby'll do fine.

Sí, señor, I mean Jo Shelby.

Besides, if you feel so bad about it and want to make it up to me, I might have a job for you along with the rest of these zapatistas, he motioned toward the other workers along the wall. That is, if I can trust you.

Oh, Jo Shelby. You can trust me with your life.

Yeah, as long as it's not my wife, he mumbled beneath his breath.

What is that?

Nada. Just a thought. Not a good one, at that.

They worked, bending, scooping and throwing wet concrete, scraping off excess and reapplying, smoothening. Then after a while:

This job, Jo Shelby.

Yeah?

What it is?

What is it? you mean.

Sí.

Jo Shelby scooped and threw, drew the sleeve of his arm across his brow. You say you are licensed to practice law down here?

Yes.

Not some shade tree lawyer but the real thing.

I do not understand shade tree.

Falso.

No, no. No Falso. Certificado.

That's good. That means if I hire you, then what I tell you goes nowhere. Confidential.

Es verdad, Edgardo said. He had stopped and was standing in a full shower of afternoon sun, sweat running in streams down his spattered face and neck and beneath his spattered T-shirt so he looked like some gray bespeckled breed of another race.

Wonder if I look as bad as you, Jo Shelby said.

How do I look?

Jo Shelby stood and scrutinized him closer. Like you got the small pox, only they aint small.

Edgardo feigned a frown. You wonder right, amigo.

How's that?

Then he grinned. You look as bad.

They laughed then started slinging mud again.

So why you need my help?

I got to steal something back that was stolen from me.

That does not sound good.

It doesn't get any better. You know what happened to me? Ricardo kept me locked up in a dark hole for three days then demanded my gun for ransom.

Some of this I know. The señoritas, they tell me. But why the gun? Why not dinero. Why not American money?

That's a long story.

Edgardo stopped and stood akimbo with his hands on his hips. He looked first at the sky. Then at the wall. Then back at Jo Shelby. Mi amigo.

He pointed his trowel at the sky. The sun is yet high. Then at the wall. The wall is long. Hay mucho tiempo.

All right, Jo Shelby said and commenced telling of his first visit to the hacienda the year prior and Ricardo's refusal to admit him to the señora with the papers he was carrying proving his kinship to her. Of his return that night with the defunct firearm and his confrontation with Ricardo in the barn, how Ricardo's men jumped him and almost hanged him, had the rope ready, the noose dangling over his head when the señora appeared in the window above the scene and stopped it cold, in the nick of time. He told him about the ongoing feud between Ricardo and Juan, the constant jockeying for power, how Ricardo suckered Juan into a fight and Juan stalked off and hadn't been back until now. He didn't tell him the other reason Juan might have left.

And he want your gun because of this, Edgardo said.

That idn't all. He took the gun and the señora made him give it back. That's what tore his shirt.

Tore his shirt?

Upset his applecart, cooked his goose, got his goat. Whatever the hell you Mexicans say down here when something royally pisses you off.

I understand. He was humiliated.

If that's what it was.

I think so. So he wanted the gun, as you Americans say, to even the score.

Edgardo, I think you just might be on to something, he said ironically. And now the gun, I come to find out from the gunsmith who kept it while I was back home in America, who popped out of a bar last night like some geni out of a bottle while I was lookin for Athen, tells me it contains possible information related to the will I been tellin you about.

His eyes widened. Information in the gun?

Yep.

His eyes grew wider. Inside the gun?

You got it.

Increible!

Do I need to say more?

No, mi amigo. This story is most interesting.

They worked a while in silence.

Then Edgardo said, but how can I help you?

You're a lawyer.

He nodded.

I want you to go with me, be a witness to a crime.

What crime?

A theft.

What theft?

Rustlin.

Stealing cattle.

You got it.

But how does that help get back your gun?

We catch Ricardo in the act. We agree not to prosecute, if he gives us the gun. He doesn't agree, we prosecute. But that's a last option. Ricardo is the law, or says he is, some kind of constable or something.

This is a problem in my country.

Yeah, I know. The mordida.

Yes. I think you would have a big problem prosecuting him. And I am no prosecutor.

Yeah. But Ricardo doesn't know that. So we're gonna out-mordida him. I just want to get the damn thing back and be gone.

I do not know, amigo. This is risky thing you ask of me, an attorney who is supposed to uphold the law.

Which is what you'd be doin.

You know where this Ricardo live?

I got a vague idea. It's up a mountain. I remember some landmarks. He pointed west with his trowel. See those hills yonder?

Yes.

Ricardo's somewhere on the other side of em. Think I could find my way back to him. May not have to, though.

What do you mean?

I'm bettin Ricardo'll come to me.

When?

Tonight.

Tonight?

Tonight.

Edgardo bent down and scooped another trowel-full of cement and raised up. I do not know, amigo.

You'd just be along for the ride.

The ride?

Yeah, ride. We'll use horses. Señora's got enough for the seven of us.

You mean the workers from La Joya, too?

Correcto. Couple of em might have to ride bareback. Not sure how many saddles she's got.

Amigo. Edgardo dropped his loaded trowel into the cement box and threw up his hands. This is not just you and me going to get your gun. This is a posse.

Just for support. Juan and I'll go in and make the transaction. Like I told you, he's got an old score to settle. The rest of y'all will hang back for reinforcement, as a bluff. Ricardo's only got three men working for him.

When do we do this? Edgardo said. Oh, do not tell me. He rolled his eyes and sighed ironically. Tonight.

Yep. After we shut down. The girls are still in Cuernavaca shopping. No tellin when they'll get back. We can grab a bite to eat in the senora's kitchen. Then off we go, he said and twirled his trowel in the air.

But it is a holiday.

That's why we're doin it tonight. I'm thinkin Ricardo's thinkin the same thing. It's a holiday. Everybody's celebratin. Nobody's minding the store. Cept he'll find a surprise.

How do you know this?

I know. Just trust me. He thought of the time, almost two, and how long it would take Eréndira to get to the road and how quickly a message traveled among Mexican kin. Quicker than wildfire.

Edgardo picked his trowel back up and pointed it down the wall where the others were working. And you have already asked the men to go with you?

Nope.

And you think they will go?

Yep.

Why you think this?

Cause I'll tell em it'll be like the days of old, like ridin with Zapata.

Edgardo rolled his eyes. Zapata is of another time.

Maybe to you young city slickers. But not to folks livin in these hills.

Single filed, horses and riders passed beneath the south portal arch then one-by-one fell into a line and rode, seven abreast, pushing their mounts to a lope past green fields of brown tassled sugar cane, commencing full gallop once they hit the broad open valley plain, the air cool with the smells of horse manure and cactus and dirt, the western sun coppering their faces, the wind lifting the brims of their sombreros, the only sounds those of their hooves drumming the hard ground. They wore gunbelts with assorted holstered pistols and carrilleras criss-crossing their chests and leather scabbards with long-barreled irons hung from their saddles. The assorted collection comprised every firearm the señora could muster from her odd dusty collection—single shot rifles and repeating rifles and carbines and shot guns and six-shooters and one over-and-under double barrel derringer—muttering and coughing as she rummaged and handed them over that they were all loco, Jo Shelby chief among them, going after Ricardo with a small army, an untrained one at that. He needed a doctor worse than she, she said, twirling a finger at her gray temple.

She might be right, he thought as he rode, assessing the disheveled un-shaven retinue flanking either side of him, their cement-splattered workshirts and baggy trousers flapping like flags in a storm, pockets bulging with cartridges, the brims of their sombreros flat against a wind they rode hard against, leaned into as though it held them up. So spurless and motley a band. So untrained and ill-equipped. Toting guns unfired in years, maybe decades. Maybe never. Hell bent for leather. That was the phrase he'd heard all his life and wondered where it came from. Now he was seeing it. Feeling it. They knew what they were getting into, he reasoned with himself. Juan and Edgardo came aboard right away. The workers from La Joya he was not sure about, always anxious to quit on time, get back to their families, a cerveza or two and dinner on the table. He watered nothing down, pulled no punches. It could be dangerous he told them in their language, they might get shot at. They looked at him with empty faces. They might get hit, their faces still blank. They could die. Nothing, as though their decision had been made before he began. It might be like riding with Zapata, the name barely clearing his tongue and they commenced hootin and hollerin, like an amen corner in church when the evangelist cries out all who want to be saved shout amen.

He glanced over at Edgardo, leaning over his pommel and grinning like he was on a carnival ride. Then to Juan on his right, erect in his saddle, his long dark mustache, the dark brows and intense focus of his eyes beneath them. He thought of all the improbabilities in this world, what he might have been doing if he hadn't been standing in the wrong place at the wrong time on a Saturday night in Drew, Mississippi and landed in the state prison for a crime he didn't commit. If his parents hadn't been killed while he was in. If he hadn't opened a trunk when he got out and found a stack of letters a hundred years old and a revolver as aged. If none of that had happened he'd have gone to college and gotten a degree and come back home to do God only knew what, practice law or drive a tractor or supervise field teams. Instead he was in Mexico leading a vigilante posse hell bent for leather and the son of the most famous revolutionary in Mexican history riding at his side like something off the silver screen.

The latter was conjecture, derived more from what he hadn't been told, the protected spaces, than what he had. But what he saw with his own eyes wasn't speculation or supposition or anything based upon the imaginary. He'd seen pictures of Zapata. They hung over mirrors behind bars throughout Morelos. On the walls of restaurants. In the lobbies of hotels. They were glued and enameled onto the curios and souvenirs the street peddlers hawked to tourists. The señora had a small, framed one on the desk in her salón. He'd not given resemblance a second thought. Not until Juan put his foot in a stirrup and swung himself up into the saddle and glared down at him with that full lower lip and dark flare in his eyes beneath the broad brim of his sombrero then jerked the reins of the horse, gigged a heel in his flank and said Vámonos.

Down the broad valley between the mountains they rode, the sierras to the west dark in deep evening shade, a line of bright copper edging upward the slopes of the eastern foothills and higher against the gathering dusk Popocatépetl and the Sleeping Lady radiant pink in the sun's last light. Overhead puffs of clouds glowed like remnants of a great fire that had come and gone and those further west streaked the twilight red and yellow and orange, the last flaming vapors following the fire. It had been that kind of day for him, a fire that had moved on. So much burned off, consumed, laid waste. A day across whose ruins he now rode. Hell bent.

They rode on.

The sun slipped out of sight. The sky began closing down over the mountains and the ground darkening. A bright evening star, like a hole suddenly punched into the firmament, appeared over Popocatépetl and the Sleeping Lady. The wind blew fresh and sharp against his face, an analgesic filling his lungs. He remembered again, as he felt the muscled power beneath him ripple and piston against his legs, what his father had said about horses, how the outside of one made the inside of a man feel good. He recalled those Saturday matinees, how he felt stepping from them into the sudden glaring sunshine, dreaming someday he'd ride like Tom Mix or Hopalong Cassidy. But never in his wildest, as he rode with his hand on the stock of a Winchester in his gun sheath. He thought of Zapata and how he must have felt, hundreds riding either side of him, behind him, the excitement, the power that must've boiled in his blood. He wondered, too, of the passion the revolutionary had stirred within the peasants of his day and how the mere sound of his name, Zapata, did it once again, a half century later. The sound the name made, like something electrical ripping the air, like lightning striking. He thought of General J O Shelby and the Iron Brigade, how they must have felt riding into battle against the Juaristas and the French and the passion that drove them. He thought longer as he rode, back through the layers of his own history, the stories he'd been told and grew up with and the names began to come, like stars punched into the heavens—Gettysburg, Shiloh, Chickamauga, Bull Run, Antietam. And he understood.

By nightfall they reached the herd, dark clumps strung out against the lesser dark of land and sky. Jo Shelby pulled his horse to a stop and the others halted with him. From a coat pocket he retrieved one of the two flashlights with working batteries the señora could find, turned it on and threw a weak beam of light in front of them.

The arroyo's on the other side of the cows, he said. It makes a U and runs along side the valley walls. It was a river once. It's mostly dried up now.

We know an arroyo, amigo, Edgardo said smiling. But you forget, I am the only one who speaks English.

Oh yeah. He repeated what he'd said in Spanish, omitting the lecture on the arroyo. He told them how Ricardo and his men would come down the gulch, how they snuck in and snuck out and everyone uttered aha in unison, a strange chorus against the lowing cattle.

So we wait in the arroyo, Edgardo said, turning on the other flashlight, the beam equally weak. He shined it at a huddle of cows nearby, their double-barrel eyes red and bleary in their turned curious heads.

I'm thinkin, Jo Shelby said. While I'm thinkin we oughtta turn off the flashlights, save the batteries. They're already weak.

The others looked absently at one another then the lights went out and they understood what was said.

One hand on his pommel and the other on the rear lip of his saddle Jo Shelby twisted his body left then right, surveyed the situation. He thought. He rode through the cattle to the rim of the arroyo, turned on his flashlight. He looked left, no evidence of a trail up, then right, the same. He rode a short distance west along the edge, shined the faint light again. This time he saw a track. It had two switchbacks and by its width and impression had seen frequent use, though not recently. No fresh hoof prints. He rode back to the group, their horses nickering and snuffling impatiently, as though anxious for action.

He dismounted and requested the men do likewise and they made a circle and honkered down for a powwow. He drew aimlessly in the dust, something that had no relation to what he was going to tell them. He told them of the recent rustling and his suspicions regarding the senora's maid and the ruse he'd planted and they all aha'd again and the cows nearby, as though picking up a cue, mooed louder and they laughed at the spontaneous comedy sprung amid them. When the amusement subsided, Jo Shelby presented a plan that met approval then they took their positions and waited.

And waited.

Hours passed, the only sounds the nervous high-pitched intonations of the cattle and horses, their instinctive clairvoyance of something imminent in the air; the off and on again whir of the cicadas and crickets and a Pygmy owl's throaty poip ... poip ... poip somewhere in the distance. A bright three-quarter moon had risen out of the east and by its height Jo Shelby guessed the time near midnight. There was a halo around the moon. A halo around the moon meant rain his mother had told him but the sky was clear to the east and only high thin clouds over the western mountains, which didn't mean much. Storms could blow down out of the mountains in a flash. If one was coming, he hoped they weren't in the arroyo when it hit. They might end up somewhere further south, washed up in a pasture in Puebla or a gulch in Guerrero.

He was getting stiff but should probably stay put. He assessed again their positions, the strategy. He lay on the ground behind a large cactus near the arroyo, where he'd calculated Ricardo and his men would ride up and he'd be at their rear when they did. Fifty yards ahead of him, scattered among the cattle and using them as a screen, were Edgardo and Juan and the four workers. In between were the horses, standing together in a cluster. They were the bait but he questioned if he'd done the right thing by leaving the saddles on. Ricardo wouldn't see the saddles in the dark but he hadn't factored in a spotlight moon and the tiny blisters of light it reflected off the leather, sparks of its luminance he could see blinking on the harness rings and buckles each time the animals turned or moved. He'd devised no signals for communicating with the others, no whistles, no calls imitating the wild. He hadn't thought that far ahead, didn't think they'd be there that long, the night now moving into morning. They'd just have to stay put. Sure as he got up to make a round and tell them they needed to get the saddles off, Ricardo would come riding up. The odds again. He felt his hands shaking and leveled one out before his eyes, observed it aquiver and blanched in the moonlight, like the pale tremors of a death rigor, then put it down. He'd stay put and keep waiting. And thinking.

Athen would've made it to Memphis by now and caught a bus home. Or called her mama and daddy, if they'd even drive up and get her, traitor she was to the family. Or she flew straight to Atlanta so she could march through the front door of a schoolhouse and announce her presence, ready to teach, the one bridge she didn't burn, held as security. As if she'd kept one thought in reserve all along, never let it go, that they were just too different and Carmen just an excuse for the difference. But they never started out different. They played in the same sandbox together and swung on the same swing set, chased lightening bugs and made clover chains together and together sold lemonade by the roadside beneath the vaulted gate that spelled her family name in wrought-iron. They rode horses together across fields of cotton as young and fresh as their years and bounced atop the white gold in trailers on their way to the gin and and stood and watched as a big silver pipe sucked it up and and miraculously slid it down a ramp in a neat packaged form and shape their eyes could not believe. They laughed together when either did something funny and cried together when either was hurt, as though their feelings knew no boundaries or demarcations, no difference.

So where did the different begin? Where did their lives get sucked up like fresh picked cotton and run through a compress and repackaged so when they came out they were different, different as daylight and dark his mama once said? Was it when Athen started looking different, dressing different, wearing makeup and skirts and high-heeled shoes? When she turned sixteen and made her debut at junior cotillion and got her first car, a blue Corvette convertible, and he'd catch glimpses from his father's pickup of her goings and comings in her new grown up world? Not then surely. They still rode horses together on pretty days after school and helped each other with their homework. They went to the Saturday matinee in Clarksdale and held hands and sent each other valentines on Valentine's Day. They were still together, but they weren't. Something was different. Maybe his mama, now that he thought about it, saw something he didn't, daylight and dark, as he watched the bitten moon cross the sky and recalled the evenings he'd hear the cars pull into the long drive and stop in front of the columned mansion, a car door close then quiet then voices and two more doors slamming close together and he knew there were others she saw at night, their lives divided by the earth's rotation and rituals and traditions set in place generations before, conventions and practices that belonged with the land, who owned it and who didn't.

He looked back at the horses, becoming restless, snorting and whinnying, shuffling about, bumping each other. Lightning flashed behind the western mountains like bombs discharging far away. He canted his head to one side to open his ear more to the night and listened for the thunder but what he heard in the distance didn't sound like thunder. He leaned over and placed an ear to the ground and listened, drew back and listened again. He waited a few seconds, let the sound clear from his head then tried again. This time when he raised up he still heard the sound. Distant, faint. He pulled out his pistol, a Colt of later model dispensed by the señora. He checked the chamber in the inadequate light to make sure it was full then returned it to its belted holster and thought how far the gun had come in a hundred years, from lever action to automatic, and where it might go from there. Not much further, he hoped. Killing a man was easy enough as it was now. He picked up his rifle and shucked a round into the chamber, the single cricket click echoing and multiplying in the night air as the others heard him and did likewise, the conspiratorial silence creating its own signal. He pushed the safety latch off and held out his hand again to see if it shook and it did not. He wondered why and decided there were times when the nerves in a person simply got used up and a backup took over. He guessed that was courage.

He waited.

Like the birth of a landslide, first trickle of rock, the sound came, thin and sibilant in the distant dark, growing louder and louder, clatter upon louder clatter until the avalanche of noise was upon him and riders and horses exploded upward out of the blackened gorge into air bleached with moonlight and stopped, stark against the luminance and he gripped tighter the rifle, and waited. They were so close he could smell their horses, hear their chatter. One voice was surprised the horses were there and another that it would be easy, they were all together, then a voice Jo Shelby would know in his sleep, Ricardo's, counting them. Then he stopped counting and Jo Shelby heard the word *sillas*. They'd seen the saddles. He couldn't make his move now. They had to catch them in the act. He lay still, tried to throttle his breathing. His heart thudded against the ground. They still hadn't moved, only yards away. If they heard him he could cast his worries of breathing aside.

Ricardo spoke again, something about mejicanos estúpidos, letting their horses get away with their saddles. Another joined in that the stupidity meant more dineros for them. A third agreed and the four commenced laughing loudly, poking fun at their own countrymen then the laughing subsided and Ricardo said, Vámanos, and they moved toward the horses.

Jo Shelby's crew knew to wait until the act was in process, the horses were being led away. That was the plan. Then Ricardo saw something he didn't like and raised a hand for his men to stop and they stopped.

Jo Shelby caught his breath, held it. What was wrong? What if Ricardo turned back? He'd lose his leverage. Ricardo'd say they were just out taking a midnight ride and were bushwhacked by a gringo and posse of mejicanos. Or that he, as constable or whatever the hell he was, was on a routine jaunt with his deputies or whatever the hell they were, protecting his beat. Some crap like that, Jo Shelby thought, then decided he might better quit thinking and take action.

Then, Mira! Ricardo said loudly. He was pointing at the horses, jabbering something about the reins hanging loose. He didn't like the looks of it, five saddled and two bare, the riders probably nearby. One of his men questioned if they were nearby, in the bright moonlight they would have seen them. Another surmised the horses had been spooked at the hacienda and run off. In that case, somebody would come looking for them, opined a third and so they babbled back and forth, aimlessly, laughing at their conclusions as though the exercise was a necessary prelude to theft then Ricardo finally brought it to a close. Whatever the reason, there were seven horses, five with saddles and no owners around to claim them and they got out their ropes.

It didn't take them long and they were headed back toward him, the horses in tow. Jo Shelby waited. When they were a few yards he rose from behind the cactus, the rifle stock against his shoulder, aimed. Hombres, he shouted, levántese sus manos.

The horses neighed and snorted and rared up and when their hooves came down the men sat stunned in their saddles.

Immediatamente, Jo Shelby shouted and cocked the rifle.

Their hands finally went up.

What is this you do, hombre? Ricardo said.

He saw the others sneaking up quietly from their rear and needed to keep Ricardo talking longer. He raised his cheek from the rifle butt but kept it firmly against his shoulder and aimed. It's what you're doing, Ricardo. Horse stealin's a crime in Mexico.

Ricardo grinned treacherously. Oh, but hombre, we no steal the horses, he said, casting slant eyed looks left and right at his men, his hands still up. These horses lost, no have riders. We take them for care, for protection. Amigos, he looked left and right again, this is truth, no?

The men nodded agreement but said nothing.

Sorry, Ricardo. That dog won't hunt.

Dog? Hunt?

You're lyin.

Ricardo's smile disintegrated and his face turned grave, his eyes splintered and sucked back up under his brows. He lowered his hands.

Get your hands back up, Jo Shelby said, motioning with the rifle.

Ricardo's hands went up again. This is serious charge you make, hombre, that Ricardo no tell the truth, that he lie.

We all heard you.

We? Ricardo cackled and pointed an elevated finger mockingly at Jo Shelby.

I see your rithmetic aint improved much from last year when you had your three buddies here, I recognize em now, and I had a six shooter and you said if I shot you I'd have to shoot them. My math then figured four men and six bullets and now it figures seven riders take away one leaves six and if you care to turn around, that's the *we* who heard you and your boys here plottin your crime.

Ricardo and his men turned in their saddles and saw six men spread in a line, their guns on them.

Believe it's called intent. That right, Edgardo?

Sí, señor Jo Shelby, Edgardo said. He was standing in the middle of the line, Juan beside him.

Edgardo's a lawyer, abogado, Jo Shelby said. Believe you know Juan there, too, Ricardo.

Juan raised a hand, tipped a finger on the rim of his sombrero and cast a taunting smile. Cómo está, Ricardo?

Ricardo spun back around. He was breathing heavily and his eyes bulged and ballooned in the moon-shade of his sombrero like cue balls warped from heat and near explosion. He hands were still up. He thumbed his sombrero back and it dropped and hung down his back by a cord from his neck and his black hair lay in wet curls, like hooks, across his brow. So, hombre, what it is you want?

First off, I want you to throw your guns on the ground and tell your men to do likewise. Slowly.

Ricardo said something to his men in rapid Spanish and slowly they pulled their guns from their holsters and sheaths, leaned low in their saddles and dropped them on the ground.

Juan shouted something at the Mexican workers and two of them scrambled forward and collected the guns then backpedaled vigilantly.

Jo Shelby lowered the rifle's position to waist-high, the barrel tilted up at Ricardo. You can put your hands down now.

Their hands came slowly down.

I Just want two things, Ricardo. I figure you can count that high.

Ricardo rocked back in his saddle and took a deep, indignant breath but did not reply.

Jo Shelby waited then spoke again. Horse stealin's the charge, not to mention the saddles and equipage, and there's seven witnesses and one of em's an attorney at law. You or your men as much as set foot on the señora's property again and she and her son, Juan, are filin charges. Edgardo, her abogado back there's going to help them. We got friends in high places.

A wicked smile creased Ricardo's face. Ah, but amigo, also we have friends. They say no, this not true.

You got one friend, or relative, whatever the hell she is. Eréndira, the señora's casa de ama, who after tonight's going to be looking for a new job. He went on to tell him of his suspicions and how he planted the false information, Ricardo's eyes rolling in disbelief, his face screwing up and twisting like a man being strangled.

You say two things you need, amigo, Ricardo said.

The gun's the other. And quit callin me amigo.

The gun?

I want the gun back.

Oh, yes. The gun. It is very valuable gun, no? It is made of gold? Silver? What?

None of that. It's just important to me and I want it back.

This can be arranged, Ricardo said.

I want it back tonight.

Tonight? I do not think—

Tonight! and he lifted the rifle again to his shoulder and aimed. You're going with me and Juan to get the gun. Your men will stay here. When Juan and I get back here with the gun, you and your men are free to go.

Then we get our guns back.

No way, José.

But, hombre, now your matemáticas no is correct. You get one gun, we get no guns.

It's correct all right. It's called evening out. That's the way it's going to be. Either that or the señora and Juan file charges. He nodded at Juan.

Juan heard his name and saw the nod and tipped a finger again to his sombrero as though he'd caught a cue, and, again, gave a menacing smile.

Or we blow you and your compadres to bits now and claim self-defense against horse thieves, Jo Shelby said. He cocked the trigger of his gun.

Ricardo turned in his saddle and assessed again the men behind him, glared at them, then turned back around. Hombre, you tough gringo, tough customer.

Nothin tough about it. It's called the law. It's gettin late. We gonna shoot or ride? Which will it be?

Ricardo spoke again to his three companions, an approximate translation what Jo Shelby could pick up of the rapid-fire transaction but he wasn't satisfied.

What'd he say, Edgardo?

It is much similar, Jo Shelby. But he did not tell them about their guns.

Tell him to tell em.

Edgardo stepped forward and stood beside Jo Shelby and said, Dinos sobre las armas.

Ricardo spoke again to his men and they commenced grumbling among themselves, shaking their heads.

He got it right this time, Jo Shelby said.

Sí, Edgardo said. They are very unhappy.

Tough shit.

Tough customer, tough shit, Edgardo said. Caga profundo.

They laughed.

Keep an eye on em while Juan and I saddle up, Jo Shelby said.

He motioned to Juan and they walked over to the horses that were roped and strung out behind Ricardo and his men. Jo Shelby pulled out a pocket-knife to cut one of the ropes and Juan stopped him. Quedarte para Ricardo, he said.

Jo Shelby nodded and slipped the knife back into his pocket. They un-did the ropes from around the horses and recoiled them in loops around their arms then walked over to Ricardo. Jo Shelby told him to put his hands behind his back and Juan stopped him again. Cómo éste, he said and began demonstrating, manipulating the rope with his fingers and making, what looked to be in the light of the moon, a small loop at one end.

Jo Shelby pulled out his flashlight. Quieres una linterna?

No! Juan said, flipping his hand sharply into the air, as though annoyed at the intrusion on his focus.

Everyone watched. Jo Shelby's men standing, their guns still drawn and aimed. Ricardo's men in their saddles. Ricardo with glum surrender. Poip, poip, poip came the call again of the Pigmy owl, closer this time it seemed, and further down the valley the plaintive howl of a coyote. A faint breeze stirred nearby brush and bramble and audible, too, in that midnight silence, the whisper of a lizard scurrying nearby through dry grass. The loop com-pleted, Juan tightened and tested it, then began threading the opposite end of the rope through it.

Qué vas a hacer con un lazo? Jo Shelby said, a concern coming to mind Juan had something else in mind other than tying Ricardo's hands. The possibility unnerving Ricardo, too, rocking him in his saddle.

Juan remained silent in deep concentration then motioned with a raised finger that signaled, you will see. Rapidly he drew the rope through the small loop then stopped, fed some of it back out slowly until the larger loop was the size he wanted then stopped again. He extended the coiled hoop from him in his right hand, jiggled it slightly in his open palm, delicately, as if testing for balance, closed his grip and raised his arm, whirled the loop round and round over his head—whop, whop, whop—then opened his hand and the oval of rope sailed fluid-like through the air collaring Ricardo, a look of despairing incredulity on his face.

Jo Shelby had seen the act performed many times before, at the Saturday matinee by Hopalong and Roy and Gene, Tom Mix and The Cisco Kid and Pancho, and it all unspooled before him now with a similar sense of unreality, that it wasn't really happening, that it was all somehow a dream spun from dream pictures the air carried like it carried gravity and electricity. That he wasn't really standing there with his own self-organized posse, holding a gun on a Mexican bandit and his muchachas. That Juan wasn't really who he probably was and didn't ride like he was born in a saddle or throw a lasso like it had eyes. That Athen hadn't really left and would somehow materialize out of the same magical air from which everything else seemed to be coming, along with a Navy Colt gun and a will and a fast ticket home.

He blinked and it was real. Juan moved quickly, drawing the loop tightly against Ricardo's chest, encircling his horse several times so the rope coiled around his chest and arms then lashed his hands to his pommel, all of it accomplished with unbroken rhythm as though it was a task for which he'd trained many years and Jo Shelby marveled at this new person he was suddenly observing, how only days before he'd stood anxious in the shadows of his own doorway and was now taking charge, giving orders and he pondered the cause of such transformation, if riding the horse, the thrill of the chase, had brought it about or being again at the hacienda where he was accustomed to giving orders and it was growing on him. Or perhaps something else not on the surface but deep inside the man, a part of him released from some bondage unavailable to human scrutiny and examination, one that ran that deep. The more he thought the more he thought the latter. Like father, like son.

They went back and mounted their horses then walked them back to Ricardo. With the left-over rope and Juan still choreographing every step of the procedure, they strung a line from Ricardo's harness and lashed it to Juan's saddle horn then looped another through the corded spirals around Ricardo's torso, attaching it in similar fashion to Jo Shelby's pommel so horses and riders were bound and bonded together like links in a chain, whatever happened to one, happened to all.

That's so you don't get any bright ideas about gallopin off, Jo Shelby said to Ricardo then thought again if he did he'd have to run over Juan. He turned to Edgardo. You the boss man, the head jefe now. Tell our men if any of them bandidos try to run to shoot low, at their legs. Tell em we got shot guns. We don't want to kill anybody but we'll shoot if we have to. Say it now before we leave.

Edgardo called out the directive and the workers nodded their understanding. Ricardo's men grumbled again, louder.

You will pay for this, hombre, Ricardo growled with contempt.

I'm payin now. You just don't appreciate the pay off.

Pay off?

No jail. No noose, like the one you were gonna use to string me up. Or have you forgotten. All you gotta do is march us over to your casa. Give me my gun. You go free and everybody's hunkydory happy. Comprendes?

Ricardo just looked at him and glowered.

Now let's move, Jo Shelby said. If I recall, we got a ways.

The vertical moon above beamed brightly, splinters of light breaking off their rifle barrels, the rings and buckles of their bridles and reins, winking on their pistol-holsters. All around them, as far as the vast valley stretched the land lay luminant, as though dusted with a silver film, the arroyo a silver gash across the darker earth, the steep trail leading downward into it an iridescent Z their tethered horses carefully, slowly executed. At the bottom they broke into a trot. Juan leading the way and Jo Shelby pulling up the rear, Ricardo joggling up and down in his saddle between them, his sombrero bouncing on his back. They rode without speaking, anything they might have said drowned out by the roar of hooves over the gravel wash reverberating off the canyon walls.

They rode for a long while, following the channel wash across the wide valley. They came to a place where the arroyo veered south and Ricardo shouted something and they slowed the horses and stopped. A spur of the sierras towered darkly before them and lower among its purple foothills random lights glowed faintly like glitter scattered on velvet and behind it all white sheets of lightning flashed.

Aquí, Ricardo called out to Juan. Vamos arriba aquí, and nodded right with his head. Juan reined his horse in the direction and saw the trail and led them scrabbling up the rocky hairpin bends out of the arroyo and onto the valley plateau where all around them there was nothing but low scrub and brush and cactus. Soon they were on a dirt road and climbing. The air felt heavier instead of lighter and lost some of its chill. The lightning flashes behind the peaks seemed closer and he could hear the thunder now, miles away by his count between the bright bursts and rumbles, but coming their way and coming fast. Jo Shelby called out to Ricardo how much further and Ricardo said poco, not much.

Up through low hills they rode, past random low houses of concrete blocks and mud-brick, jacales of brushwood and mud with broken-thatched roofs that gleamed in the moonlight. Houses where sleeping families with little to their name but the brush roofs over their heads and the ragged clothes they slept in and the left over food they begged for would soon arise and celebrate their country's independence, as though it held meaning for them. They roused sleeping dogs that sallied out and barked, snapped at their stirrups and kept barking till they were past, setting off a chorus of aimless yaps and howls and cock-a-doodle-doos across the hillsides, of dogs and roosters barking and crowing at nothing but their own barking and crowing, as though from some instinctive tribal obligation or duty and the triggered clamor fired a warning thought between Jo Shelby's ears.

Ricardo! he whispered loudly to his captive riding ahead of him.

Ricardo turned his head but did not respond.

Don't get any ideas.

Cómo? he said, not whispering.

Keep your mouth shut. Quédate su boca cerrada. No llames por ayuda. Don't call for help. Intiendes?

Ricardo shook his head he understood and faced forward.

Dissatisfied with the lack of response, Juan stopped and turned around in his saddle and said the same to Ricardo, that he would shoot him if he cried out for help.

Not to worry, Ricardo said. I will not die for a stupid gun, for a loco gringo.

Watch it, Jo Shelby growled.

They rode on.

Higher up they came to a small tin-roofed village of decrepit adobe and plywood huts the dirt road passed through and Jo Shelby was hoping Juan was thinking what he was thinking then felt relieved when Juan motioned with his hand to leave the road and go around it. From what he'd been told of the country Jo Shelby knew of its turbulent political history, of the hundreds of political parties and how the verbal and physical battles between them spun an unsolvable tangle at all levels, down to the smallest puebla, like the one they were skirting, and how the turbulence overflowed the formal boundaries of legislatures and spilled into the local bars and casinos and brothels, that the dominant figures were usually the generals. But not always. He knew there were the governors who were warlords and the feudal caciques, the local political bosses, chiefs, who had the ear of the governors and harbored visions of becoming governors themselves some day, eventually Máximo Jefe, El Presidente. He knew Ricardo was one of the caciques and they were riding now through his beat or district or territory or whatever it was, legally or illegally he and his pistoleros controlled, through a part of the country, México bronco, Mexico untamed, land of the gun that had not caught up with the rest of the country and that that was why they were riding clear of the village, of a bushwhacking in the making.

A short distance past the village the road branched and they stopped.

Derecho, Ricardo called out.

They turned right and the dirt road quickly became a mule trail angling sharply across the side of the mountain they'd been steadily climbing. The path was rocky across the stoney hillside and badly eroded and the horses moved more slowly, cautiously, a hoof slipping uncertainly here and there. Wild goose chase crossed Jo Shelby's mind and he figured Juan was thinking the same, the way he kept looking back and shrugging, his palms upturned in the air. But Ricardo was the one with the most to lose. His math was deficient, but it wasn't bankrupt. He was not the cacique of this backside of near nowhere for nothing.

The clouds had increased and were moving faster, the combination of their fleeting passage over the moon and sheets of lightning further west a shutter effect of light and shadow, Jo Shelby's vision catching what it could in the illumined gaps. A plateau where low tin-roofed shacks tiered drunkenly against the side of the mountain. A field of cactus immediately below. Further down darkness and scattered lights and further below a string of them running north to south. The Jiutepec highway. Another long cloud passed blocking the moon and when the moon came back he glimpsed on an adjacent hilltop, notching blackly the sky, a solitary cross. This was the place.

As they grew nearer he saw more crosses, of different sizes and shapes, leaning and jutting at different angles from the top of the hill, a grove of strange dark cacti. A cemetery, all the way up here, he thought. There were more shacks, too, suggesting a small village thrown haphazardly together. He'd heard if a Mexican could build a structure, however crude, over a plot of public land and hold it for twenty-four hours, house and plot became his. Like a latter-day Robin Hood, Ricardo, the mestizo, must have gathered a merry band of Indians around him and carved out his own little Sherwood here on top of the mountain, his own little kingdom, fiefdom ... thiefdom.

A dog began barking then a rooster joined in. Ricardo called out something to Juan Jo Shelby couldn't hear and Juan stopped. Ricardo muttered something else in rapid Spanish and Juan angled left, toward a two-story cinder block house set apart from the other dwellings, like the castle from the village, only on a smaller scale.

It was unlit and dark. Around the roof edges strands of rebar protruded into the intermittent half-moonlight like the frayed loose ends of something burned in a fire. Across the front was a pole and brush ramada. From one corner ran a wire to a nearby jerry-rigged utility pole. Jo Shelby traced it in the darkness, down the mountain and out of sight. Ricardo was a thief of more than cattle and guns. He was stealing electricity. Somebody was collecting a mordida not to turn him in and that somebody in turn paying somebody else not to tell on them and so the intertwined symbiotic chain of theft and obligation and indebtedness went, from the lowest of the lowly, to the most powerful of the powerful, all the way up the political gravity feed to Máximo Jefe, El Presidente. All the more reason they needed to act quickly. The chain reaction. What went up the mordida loaded column came down. Ricardo's silence was unreliable. He had his own bunch of hooligans, thugs and ruffians who'd spit on an affadavit. Getting the gun and hightailing before Ricardo could make it back and shoot a message up the grapevine was one thing, Jo Shelby thought. Finding the will as quickly, by tomorrow if possible, then catching the first bus north to Matamoros was something else. Timing was on his side. He at least had mañana. Ricardo could fire a message across the chain but the chain would be temporarily broken. Mañana was Independence Day. Every Mexican would be in a plaza, somewhere, celebrating.

They pulled their horses to the front of the house and stopped and Juan and Jo Shelby dismounted. Jo Shelby unholstered his Colt and held it on Ricardo while Juan unwound the rope coiling his chest but left his hands tied then ordered him to dismount. They threw their reins across the horizontal railing of the ramada and stood in its entryway, beneath the eave.

Anybody inside? Jo Shelby said in a low voice above a whisper.

Mi esposa, Ricardo said.

Anybody else besides your wife?

Nadie.

Maria, your daughter, she's not there? Jo Shelby said.

She live in Jiutepec.

Eréndira?

Ricardo screwed up an indifferent face and shrugged his shoulders, as if to say how the hell should I know, but said nothing.

Disturbed by the intrusion of horses and voices, cattle nearby began mooing and bellowing. Jo Shelby took out his flashlight and pointed it uphill in the direction of the sounds and caught, in the sweep of the weak light, a small pole corral full of livestock. He turned off the light.

Those yours? Jo Shelby said to Ricardo.

Sí.

In that case, they'll have your brand.

Ricardo shrugged again, contorted his mouth defiantly as if to say, piss on you, but again remained mute.

Juan said something to Jo Shelby in Spanish he didn't catch and Jo Shelby ask him to repeat it. Juan said the cattle might belong to his mother and Jo Shelby told him great minds thought alike and Juan smiled.

Vámonos, Juan said to Ricardo and pushed him in the direction of the corral.

Jo Shelby switched on his flashlight again to guide the way over the stoney ground and saw immediately the tracks. He ran the light along the parallel ruts and they led straight to the corral. He wondered how a truck and trailer could get up the mountain then turned around and followed the tracks as far as the dim cone of light would reach, where they curved out of sight and down the mountain.

Ricardo? Jo Shelby called out in a loud whisper. He didn't want to wake the neighbors or spook the cattle mooing louder and moving restlessly about in the flimsy constructed enclosure. If they bolted and scattered it'd be a night's work and part of the next day rounding them up.

Sí, Ricardo called back, louder, his intent clear. Wake up the mountain. The rooster was still crowing and another dog had joined in. It wouldn't take much more.

Jo Shelby opened his mouth to tell him to keep it down but Juan beat him to it and rammed the rifle stock into his back. Ricardo groaned loudly and Juan hit him again and he fell silent.

There a road going down this mountain? Jo Shelby said.

Ricardo kept walking as though he didn't hear him.

Respondelo, Juan said and punched him again, this time across his shoulders.

Sí, Ricardo said, a high-pitched whisper of pain and anger.

That's what I thought, Jo Shelby said. The road veered down the other side toward to the main Jiutepec road. Nobody would see the cattle rustled up the eastern slope facing the valley. When Ricardo took them down the western slope one at a time to sell them at the market in Cuernavaca, in that measured fashion, he'd look like any other farmer taking a cow or two to market. No one would scratch their head and ask how they got up there in the first place because nobody ever ventured that high up the mountain, which was why Ricardo had chosen the place. Which was why the cemetery was there, Jo Shelby guessed. Protection from grave robbers. They wouldn't put forth the effort. Ricardo probably charged a fee for protecting them anyway.

They came to the corral and Jo Shelby saw it was more crudely put together than he'd imagined, slender unpeeled poles lashed loosely together by rope, gate stobs held by a single loop of hemp twine. He aimed the flashlight through the poles onto the haunches of the milling cattle turning their heads and regarding the inconvenient beam with detached suspicion. The señora was right.

Juan saw them, too. Éstos son mis madres. Mida, la marca de ella, he said pointing to one of the brands. Pero ha estado cambiada.

They'd been changed all right. Ricardo had used a running iron. The arch connecting the T and P and the lower loop on the P had been burned off and straight parallel lines singed across the top and bottom so the design now resembled a Roman numeral II. Jo Shelby estimated about fifteen, not counting the calves he couldn't see. They looked lean and underfed, ribs protruding on some. No telling how many Ricardo had stolen and sold. The señora didn't keep good records. At least these could be saved. The problem was getting them back down the mountain.

Juan was pondering the same solution. Mucho ganado por dos hombres, he said.

Jo Shelby nodded in agreement but said they could do it, they'd just have to take their time.

Juan pointed toward the cloud-covered moonless sky. Then west at the lightning quivering over the mountains. No tenemos mucho tiempo.

Sí, Jo Shelby said. Pero suficiente.

Cuantos ganados? Juan said.

About fifteen, Jo Shelby said to him in his language, give or take a few but they needed to get the gun first.

You no will get away with this, Ricardo said gruffly.

Juan spun him around roughly and headed him back down the slope toward the house.

Just go in quietly, Jo Shelby said. If your esposa wakes up, tell her you came back to get something. Don't tell her anything else. Tell her not to turn on a light. If she turns on a light ... on second thought maybe I better go with you.

He pointed the Colt at Ricardo and pushed the mestizo under the ramada ahead of him. He followed him through the door and told him he'd blow his head off if he made one false move, his wife's too. He couldn't believe he said what he said, especially about his wife. But he couldn't believe either he'd already done what he'd done and was where he was doing what he was doing. He couldn't believe he was stealing back a gun that was stolen from him and that he and Juan, Zapata junior, were getting ready to ride herd on a small flock of twice-stolen gaunt and emaciated cattle and that it was all taking place somewhere in the high sierras and all he had to do was get them down a mountain and through a deep arroyo with lightning and thunder and a wall of rain breathing down their neck. As if disbelief and unbelief had merged, become one and the same, and in the confusion somehow conferred a fantasy justification to his thoughts and that that was why he said he'd shoot Ricardo and his wife. In the disbelief and unbelief he was beginning to believe he just might. He just hoped Ricardo believed it too.

The air inside was stale and damp and smelled of mildew and woodsmoke and something sharper, something possibly burned for supper and the trapped odor still lingered. In the dark Jo Shelby made out the shape of a couch and table, a cabinet and sink and refrigerator against a wall, a doorway in a back wall.

Ricardo moved slowly toward the doorway.

Where's the gun? Jo Shelby leaned in close to his neck and whispered.

Ricardo pointed ahead at the doorway.

They moved on in the dark. The horses outside whinnied and stamped the ground. Another rooster chimed in and more dogs were barking and a mule somewhere near the huts began baying loudly. They were waking up the whole damn world it sounded. The Colt weighed heavier in his hand. He'd never shot a man and began wondering now if he could. He wouldn't shoot to kill. He'd shoot low, like he'd told the others guarding Ricardo's men. He wouldn't shoot his wife. He wouldn't shoot a woman. He didn't want to shoot anybody. That would sure nough wake up the world.

Ricardo passed through the doorway and Jo Shelby followed him. They were in a utility or junk room of some sort, one where anything without a place was thrown and that's where his gun was. He pulled his flashlight from his hippocket and turned it on and saw the bolsa in a corner on top of a five-gallon can and jiggled the beam of light for Ricardo to hurry. He could hear his wife snoring in the next room.

Qué es? Ricardo's wife suddenly called out.

Jo Shelby poked the gun barrel in his back. Tell her nada, he whispered.

Nada, Ricardo called back.

Tell her to go back to sleep, that you've got to tend to the cows.

Vuelve dormirse, he said. Hay problemas con los ganados.

She mumbled something unintelligible and resumed snoring, as though she'd never awakened, the interruption part of a dream sequence. Ricardo grabbed the bolsa and handed it to him and they made their way back through the dark and out the front door where Juan stood waiting with a cocked rifle.

Juan held the rifle on Ricardo while Jo Shelby reholstered his pistol and walked to his horse. He unbuckled the straps of his saddlebag and tucked the bolsa with the gun inside then pulled the straps tight and renotched them. He remounted and unholstered his pistol and pointed it at Ricardo and told him to mount and kept the pistol on him while Juan retied him and lashed again his hands to his pommel but recoiled the tether rope so the three were no longer in tandem.

They trotted their horses back up the hill to the corral. Jo Shelby had what he came for and could ride on but he owed it to the señora to retrieve her cattle. The question was how.

Hell, I guess we just let em out and drive em ahead of us, he said, mumbling to himself. And keep Ricardo out front.

Juan asked him what he said and Jo Shelby told him and Juan said he couldn't think of anything better, then told Ricardo he'd shoot him if he got out of his sight.

Ricardo sat still in his saddle and grumbled something again about gringos and dying.

Jo Shelby leaned over and unlooped the twine around the gate stobs and swung open the flimsy gate. He guided his horse inside the enclosure and moved along the fence and began hitting the cattle with a coiled rope like he'd seen cowboys riding herd do in the movies. The animals commenced churning and mooing loudly, bumping wildly against each other as they spilled in confusion through the opening and down the hill, Juan along one flank shouting at Ricardo to stay in front of him and Jo Shelby pulling up the rear, the small herd and three riders moving down the dark mountainside like a bottle of ink turned over.

The lightning was striking closer, the time between flashes and thunder shorter and shorter. He could hear the rain coming, like enormous breathing from the mountains. The moon was completely gone and all about was dark but he could glimpse, in the lightning bursts, the mule trail they'd traversed coming up and figured the cattle could see it too because they were following its downward track as though they smelled home. He could see Ricardo, an armless rider he looked jostling stiffly ahead of the cattle where he'd been told to stay and Juan close by, his rifle angled across his pommel. But he saw nothing else in the flickers of luminance and hoped Juan could see the dirt road when they came to it then he felt a cool fresh wind, the kind one feels before a storm breaks, then the rain came.

It fell slashing down the mountain, large single drops at first hammering the ground then, like something out of a myth, the deluge. Blades of lightning quivered through its needled curtain long enough to forge shapes out of the dark and thunder pealed along its flanks like an assault barrage and he felt the ground beneath him become suddenly soft, the hard beat of hooves turn to slosh as they slopped down the mountain, the trail turning mush that fast, as though the earth was melting. All he could do was tuck his arms in and hunch over his pommel. His hat brim rendered some protection then it saturated and water began coming through the crown and he might as well have been wearing a wet mop someone was squeezing. He was afraid to put his head down. Afraid he'd miss something when the lightning flashed again. Afraid he might not see Ricardo, which would pose a whole nother problem. Then the lightning forked again and the sky lit up and he glimpsed him with Juan close behind and the dirt road just ahead.

They veered left at a downhill run onto the dirt road-turned-river-of-mud, the splash of hooves louder than the hard splash of rain against the earth, the combined sound, he imagined, that of riding beneath a waterfall and he could feel the mud spattering against his legs. When the lightning went on again he saw the tin-roofed village they'd skirted coming up but saw no way they'd go around it again. The drenched road was channeling the small herd like a stream. At least the downpour would shield them. Nobody would come out in it, not even the dogs. And they did not as riders and cattle slushed through the narrow street of the small puebla, nor did any lights come on nor any sign of life present itself in the shuttered wet dark of the place. On they scuttled down the mountain, the drove rushing along as though they knew, better than their escorts, the way down the mountain, back past the scattered low houses and sleeping families surely awakened now by the mutual roar of storm and stampede, the yelping dogs silenced by the same.

The herd hit the valley plateau without letting up and the rain poured ceaselessly down. Jo Shelby shouted to Juan in Spanish to steer them away from the arroyo and stay on the plain but it was too late. When the lightning lit up again Ricardo and Juan and part of the herd had dipped out of sight and he had no other choice but to follow.

The arroyo had become a small river, water up to the horses' knees he guessed by its sound and sluggish drag on his mount then the sky lit up again and he saw he guessed right. The rise was enough to slow the herd down but if it got too much higher they'd be swimming. If that happened he didn't know what they'd do then thought again and knew. Just swim along and hope the rain stopped. Nothing else they could do. Nothing else a body can do in a flood.

The rain was unrelenting, driving its needles into his face and through his clothing. He was wet through and through and getting wetter and wondered how much wetter he had to get before his body started giving it back. His hat lay heavy and soggy on his head. He thought of taking it off and tossing it aside into the drink he was splashing through then thought of all it had been through, too, that you didn't throw things away that had been through that much with you. He reached back and patted the saddlebag carrying the gun, to make sure he still had it. Little wonder the way the leather pouch bounced and flapped behind him coming down the mountain. He needed to keep the gun dry. What was written on the paper inside of it was probably written in ink. He felt of the flap again to make sure it was buckled tight then reined his horse nearer the shoulder of the wash where the ground was higher.

Through the rain and the dark they rode on. In the bursts of lightning he could still see Ricardo and Juan up front, the cattle sluicing along behind them, but little else. His big concern had been keeping the animals together, getting the herd home intact. For that he could thank the rain and the arroyo. In storms everybody follows a leader and he guessed the cows had their own. His was Juan. This was his land. He'd know the trail leading out. If he didn't, the cows would. The scent of their own herd, the closer they got to them, would take them home.

The storm moved on, the lightning playing across the plateau and range of mountains ahead of him, the sky cracking and recracking over and over as if one more fissure would send it crashing to the ground with nothing behind it. He thought again of the life behind him and the one ahead, of all that was broken on both sides of the now and wondered what kept him going and why he hadn't crashed. His daddy once told him all he had to do to make life work when the going got rough was to simply do the next thing, then the next thing after that, one step at a time. The next thing he had to do was get out of the arroyo with the herd he was following, surely not leading, and the next thing after that was make it back to the hacienda in one piece then after that examine the gun, then after that ... piece by piece in his mind, as he rode, he connected the next things, all the way through the morrow and into the day after that and the next time the lightning broke he saw Juan and Ricardo ascending the switchback trail, the cows charging up behind them.

They rode up out of the gulch and the cattle rushed to join the herd from which they'd been abducted months before, the animals shaking off rainwater and mooing and bellowing their greetings like the halloing of long-lost relatives at a family reunion. Beneath the only tree around Edgardo and his crew crouched huddled with their guns on Ricardo's men. The horses stood smoking in the filtered moonlight that had returned, the fast moving storm assaulting now the eastern sierras ahead of them.

Juan dismounted and began unraveling the complicated configuration of rope that bound Ricardo to his saddle. When he was through Ricardo stretched his arms and rubbed his wrists and hands in relief then said, Now, hombre, you have you cows and you gun. Give us our guns and we go.

Nothing doin, hombre, Jo Shelby said. That wadn't the deal. Ride on and don't come back. Remember, we got witnesses. We also have evidence.

Evidence? What evidence? You have only what people they say.

Those cows over there we brought back. The brands you tried to change. Is that not evidence, Edgardo, mister lawyer?

Edgardo stepped out from under the tree and motioned to his three captives to mount their horses. Sí, amigo. Evidencia sólido.

And what's the punishment in México for stealing cows? Jo Shelby said.

Many years in the prison, Edgardo said. Maybe death.

You will pay for this, hombre, Ricardo growled. Yeah, you've said that already, Jo Shelby said. You're a broken record. People quit listening to broken records. You as much as set one foot back on the señora's property and Juan here is reporting to our attorney friend, Edgardo, over there and you're not gonna be here or there—he pointed back toward the ridges from which they'd come—but in the caboosa in Cuernevaca. Comprendes?

Ricardo snapped his reins and jerked the head of his horse around. Vámanos muchachos, he said and his three compodres yanked the reins of their horses and followed him down the trail, the rattle of their hooves over the sliprock fading into the night.

You think he will be back? Edgardo said.

Not for a while, Jo Shelby said. You understand now why I wanted you along.

Yes. It was like in the movies.

It almost wadn't.

Why is this?

Ask Juan. I'm tired of even thinkin about it. We got to mount up and git back, let everybody get some sleep before we head out again.

Again? But you have your gun back.

That was just the next thing before the next thing I gotta do.

And this next thing, what is it?

Don't know. Gotta get back to the hacienda and find out. Might have to take a longer ride.

Tomorrow?

Yep.

But it is our celebration for independence.

That's all the more reason. Juan's in. You with us?

Edgardo thought a moment. I think so. Being in the movies, it is most exciting.

That might be stretchin it a bit, Edgardo. I think the movie part just ended.

The pistol was damp and glistened with moisture from the humidity in the air but untouched by the rain. He dried it off then laid it, its bronze casing gleaming in the overhead light, on a white towel on the bedspread. He thought of the burden of its long history and how many times it had been fired and thrown and knocked about and dropped, how many screws replaced. He was only interested in one as he picked the gun back up and slipped the head of the screwdriver he retrieved from the truck into the grip screw and began turning, backing out the bolt until it fell onto the towel and he peered closely and saw packed in the back of the hole, just as the old gunsmith had said, a small white wad of paper. The head of the screwdriver was too large to penetrate the opening and he looked about the room for an idea. A pin was all he needed. Pins were usually everywhere. He could go downstairs and look for one in the salón but it was almost four in the morning and he didn't want to wake the señora. He opened the drawer to the nightstand, the dresser drawers. Nothing. He sat on the edge of the bed and thought. The goal of his long journey centimeters away and he couldn't get it out. There had to be a way. It just hadn't hit him. He got up and walked around the room, examined the drapes for a hook but they were on loops. He stepped onto the balcony. A splinter or piece of straw might do but the planking was swept clean. He walked back inside, stood in the front of the mirror and his eyes struck his belt buckle. It had saved his life once before. He removed his belt and sat back onto the bed and with the buckle tine probed the hollow space, slowly working the wad out and onto the towel. With great care and meticulousness he unfurled the tightly curled roll deftly with his fingers and held it up to the light. At first he could not see the faded inscription, then sat up and moved his eyes closer and it burned into his vision like something from holy writ:

safe code

11942

He thought, too, he detected marks above and below the numbers but could not be sure. They could just be smudges or defects from the passage of time, the way the paper had been rolled and compressed. Recalling a magnifying glass he'd seen on the señora's desk in the salón, he descended the stairs and retrieved it, ran back up and steadied the oval curvature of lens over the paper in front of the light and there they were, rising to meet his eyes as though blown upward by some breath from the parchment, small dots, above and below the numbers in alternating sequence. For the longest he held the faint message on the fragile paper, thin and worn, translucent in the glare beneath the magnifying glass near the overhead globe, his eyes straining for anything else they might decipher until his arm grew tired and he brought them down and placed them onto the towel beside the gun, the paper looming larger than life beneath the glass.

The words were clear enough: *safe code*. But the numbers, he was unsure what to make of them, the strange marks above and below them. Had he not known what he knew, they could belong to a safe deposit box. But that door, he was convinced, was closed. More than likely they were the combination to a safe, the dots possible indicators of turn sequence on a dial, the best his thinking could accomplish at nearly four in the morning. The message could not have been written by the old colonel, he was in Mexico. Unless he wrote it before he went to Mexico and hid it in the gun, but that made no sense. If he did that, he would have taken the gun with him, not left it behind. Unless the message was not for him, but someone else, Foster. He may have told Foster to write it down and hide it in a safe place. Foster had every reason to keep the will secret, its very existence much less its location, hide it but not destroy it in case he needed it later. Or he hid it for someone else coming along later that might need it to prove a point. Any or all of which raised a huge missing piece of the puzzle: how did Foster know? There was only one way. By mail. There had to be a missing letter, the one he could not find when he first read the chronologically ordered stack because the last one he read didn't read like a last one.

He crossed the room and opened the top drawer of the dresser and took out the two letters he'd brought with him. He unfolded the last dated 2 June 1866 and shuffled to the last page and ran his eyes down to the final paragraph. *This may be my last communication with you for some time,* his great-grandmother Caroline had written. Then the next sentence: *As soon as possible, I will write again.* Two sentences after that: *Wait for word. We pray to God it will be soon so I can write to you again …* Those were her last words, at least on this letter. But there had to have been another, one the Patricks had read and squirreled away, possibly others. The family had known about the will all along but said nothing. Let a sleeping dog lie. Why else would Josh and Jacob be down here? They knew about a safe code and the numbers but they didn't know what kind of safe. That's why they went on the same wild goose chase he did with all the banks. They had the same information he had and were at the same disadvantage. Or were they? They may have more to go on because they've had one or more missing letters.

He looked at the clock on the wall. Half past four. The senora got up at five o'clock each morning. She wouldn't mind if he woke her a half-hour early. She'd understand.

She came to the door pale and bleary, her long gray hair loose down her back and a small blue-veined fist clutching her robe at her neck. Yes. What ... is there a problem?

Sorry to wake you up, señora, but I got your cows back.

She nodded and smiled faintly. That is good. She glanced at the wall clock in her room. You woke me now to tell me that.

Nome.

Well, don't just stand there. Come in.

I'd be much obliged, ma'am, if you'd kindly step down to my room. There's something I need to show you.

She raised her brows and sighed. Very well. I trust this is important.

It is.

She shuffled behind him around the upper story quadrangle and down the long hall to his room and entered before him while he held the door then shut it behind them. He showed her the gun and the message and pointed to where the message had been in the gun, summarizing for her how he got the gun back and the cows with it.

She raised an unsteady hand to an astonished mouth. My, My. I had no idea he'd still have them.

Yessum. We didn't either. We just lucked up on em. The brands had been changed. Like you said, with a runnin iron.

He should be put in jail, she said.

He will be if he sets foot on your property again, he said then told her about the threat and the force behind it. With all due respects senora, ma'am, I'd strongly recommend you fire Eréndira. She's his spy, was passing everything along to him.

That's why you had me go to the kitchen with you.

Yessum.

I see. Well, I can take care of that well enough. Jo Shelby, why am I standing down here before the break of dawn looking at a gun and piece of paper?

He handed her the magnifying glass. Take a look at what's on the paper.

She took the glass from him and leaned over the bed where the fragment lay, peered a long time at it through the thick lens. He observed her as she did, the tiny stooped frame, frozen in that attitude of inspection and long iron gray hair she rolled each morning into a bun the size of a dinner roll streaming nearly to the floor. She did not look well and he felt guilty for waking her up.

Then she raised up and looked at him.

What do you think it is? he said.

A code of some sort.

That's what I think, too.

And you needed me for that. Her voice had an edge and she seemed irritated and began coughing, the coughing carrying the sound of something in it, something that needed to be spit up but she swallowed it instead.

He waited till she finished. I'm sorry, señora. I shouldn't have waked you up. Please forgive me.

No, no. Nonsense. I'm agreeing with you about the paper. I'm just not sure how I can be of more help to you.

He invited her to sit down and she back-pedaled to the rocker behind her and lowered herself carefully into it. He sat on the side of the bed facing her and told her of his theory, that there was one or more letters from his great grandmother to their son Foster and that this letter or letters contained the same code and possible additional information about the will and other possessions and that the letter or letters were confiscated or destroyed or both and that there was probably a safe somewhere and the dots were part of the combination. She rocked gently and listened quietly, then stopped rocking when he finished.

Who would do that?

Do what?

Destroy the letters.

The Patricks.

This would be Athen's parents?

Yes ma'am.

The son, Foster, may have done it, for good measure.

If he'd a done that he'd have done it to some of the others, too. The more I think about it I think it was probably just one letter. It would've been on the end of the stack and got their attention right off.

I would not worry myself about the letter. I think you are correct about the numbers. They are probably a safe combination. They probably do not belong to a bank deposit box.

Yessum. We already been down that road.

But the gun came from your country. The safe could be there.

I've done thought about that. If it came from my country, Athen's brothers wouldn't be down here. They'd have known about it and any will would've already been found and destroyed.

She moved to get up.

He said, I figure the only safe would've been at the hacienda at Michapa, the one where the colonel and his family stayed when they left Carlota and the one Zapata destroyed.

She sat back down. Finding this safe might be most difficult, she said. The ruins of the old mansion are still there I am told but the government owns the rest of the land. It is now a park for the people, a place they can go for recreation.

I was told that.

Yes? Who told you this?

An old administrador at a ranch north of Miacatlan. He told me the same story you did, about your great-great-grandfather, Roderigo Ariosto, and how he split up his land before the government did it for him.

And the government still prevailed, she sighed, at least on that section.

But they never cleared off the old house, just left it.

That is our government. Probably they did not want to waste the time or money. Maybe they wanted to leave it as a replica of the past, a reminder. I do not know. I have been told it is now an empty shell taken over by weeds and rats.

We're goin over there today, that is if we can borrow the truck.

Please. It needs to be driven. It has been idle all these years. Hopefully, it will bring you back.

I'll be careful with it.

The truck is not my main concern. The house and its grounds were quite large. The safe could be buried anywhere.

I'm takin help.

Who is going?

Juan and Edgardo and the workers from La Joya.

She nodded approvingly. There are shovels and pickaxes in the tool shed. Anything else you need.

The guns might come in handy. You never know.

Yes, of course. But you must be careful. You will be on land now owned by the government. I did not even ask. Did you have to use them tonight?

We used em but didn't have to shoot em.

You were most forceful then.

Not me, Juan. He took charge.

She pushed herself up out of the rocker and stood. There was a gleam in her eye, a look that carried with it a touch of foreknowledge, one that needed no subject and verb to finish it off. I am going to bed now, she said. You get some rest. I will take care of Eréndira. You are not taking the girls with you?

Hadn't planned on it.

They were late getting back from Cuernavaca and are sleeping but the more you have helping in this the better. We have enough shovels.

I'll think about it.

She turned and left the room.

He returned the screw to the gun grip and cleared the bed and lay down, asleep before his head hit the pillow.

He'd been to Michapa before, by way of bus from Cuernavaca through Taxco. This time they took the state road south to the small village of Tetécalita where they crossed the Valle de Cuernavaca to Xochitepec and the federal highway to Miacatlan, a road he'd hitchhiked once before going the opposite direction. He drove while Juan gave directions. Edgardo sat in the back with the workers. They'd left after breakfast with the girls still asleep and stopped in La Joya to pick up Juan and the four workers. Seven was was a good number, he'd decided. The women might just get in the way, especially when one was trouble.

One village after another they passed, clusters of life too small for a whistle stop but they had signs with names and he recalled them along with the same scenes from his earlier journey. At Apuyeca the temperature gauge was running hot and he pulled over at the gas station where he'd slept on the floor months before. He holaed to the young attendant who holaed in return and asked the mozo if he remembered him. The boy grinned and said he did then made a remark about Jo Shelby driving and not walking this time. Jo Shelby laughed and pointed to the truck and workers and said he'd struck silver in the hills and was now a jefe with a crew. The mozo looked at the truck and said he'd struck something but it was not silver and they laughed.

Pressing his palm over a rag looped through his belt the mozo carefully unscrewed the radiator cap, talking to himself as he did, then filled the coils from a rusticated five-gallon can. The gas gauge showed half empty and Jo Shelby requested a fillup which the mozo efficiently executed then held out his oily hand. Jo Shelby gave him a fifty peso note and the mozo grinned and said this time he had more than thirteen pesos and six cigarettes. Jo Shelby congratulated the boy on his memory then told him he was being a smart ass. Edgardo overheard and laughed.

Qué es smart ass? the boy said.

Nada. Es una expresión americana de afecto, Jo Shelby said and slapped him on the shoulder and laughed. The boy laughed back and waved as they drove off and far down the road through the rearview mirror Jo Shelby could still see him waving. The truck vibrated and shook and sputtered along, fifty miles per hour the most the engine would give. With a good tune-up they'd probably already be there.

By noon they'd made Michapa and were at the plaza drinking Coca-Colas and eating steamed corn and natillas, then on their way again on a potholed and eroded road leading northward out of the town. They passed mud brick houses as badly eroded as the road and small tiendas the size of school bus shelters back home and the further they went into the desolate hills the less they saw of anything resembling life, human or animal. Jo Shelby inquired if perhaps they had taken the wrong road. Juan said it had been several years since he'd been to the old hacienda but his mother had re-freshed his memory and he was certain of his directions.

They drove on.

After a series of hills and valleys they crested a ridge and below, at the end of a long dirt road among a grove of trees, Juan pointed to a group of buildings. La Hacienda Tierra del Puente, he said.

It was not a sight Jo Shelby had expected. Land that had once bloomed with corn and wheat, cotton brought by the colonel and other Confedera-dos, now barren and uncultivated, the surrounding hills lifeless. They'd passed no sign indicating government property, no evidence of any area set apart for recreation, nothing suggesting a national park, that it was owned by anyone. He thought of old tumbledown houses and shacks in Mississippi in the midst of vacant fields. He asked and Juan told him the park was miles ahead in the state of México and accessed normally from San Guspar. They were still in the state of Morelos, he said then went on to tell him what his mother had told him, that this part of the great ranch, along with the house, had been abandoned by the government, not of the country but the state. Then it all began to make sense. One jurisdiction ended, another picked up. There was not enough of the old estate in the state of Moreles to justify spending money. So it was left to wither and decay and he saw how badly as they neared the house and its out buildings.

As had been described to him, the outer wall had crumbled entirely, the roofs all fallen. There was nothing remaining of the mansion but twin chim-neys front and back and walls black-streaked where flames had once licked, where torches had been thrown he imagined as that dark ephemeral scene of history floated through the daylight like a mirage spilling over the top of his brain, Zapata leading the charge of shooting and shouting horsemen as they encircled the buildings, galloped across the grounds and along the porches hurling their lighted flares through windows and onto rooftops and people inside screaming and running for their lives, his own possibly among them, then he blinked and it was gone.

They drove through the derelict gate, where the archway once was, and the scene that slammed against his eyes caused Jo Shelby to slam on the breaks. Well I'll be damn, he said.

Mío dios, Juan said.

Edgardo and the men in the back saw it too and began chattering loudly.

Jo Shelby and Juan got out and the others bailed over the sides.

What the hell? Jo Shelby said.

Someone already has been here digging, Edgardo said.

Yeah. Somebody, Jo Shelby said. He looked around. The entire ground within the walls and around the house had been dug up. Looks like somebody plowed it with a tractor, but I don't see any around. He turned and translated for Juan and the others.

Quién? Juan said.

No se exactemente.

Look around, Jo Shelby said to Edgardo. See if you see any place where it looks like somebody took something out of the ground. They know why we're here? He nodded at the workers.

I do not know, Edgardo said. You did not tell them?

Naw. Didn't wanna scare em off. But we need to tell em. Tell em it's a big metal box, but that's all. If we don't find it today, I don't want half of La Joya out here tomorrow on a gold rush.

Yes, boss, Edgardo said, grinning and casting a mock salute.

The men shook their heads up and down as Edgardo spoke and when he was finished they began spreading out across the grounds.

The air was dry and warm and clouds floated overhead shuttering off and on with intermittent shade. Jo Shelby stepped up onto a brick foundation, all that was left of the front porch and crossed the threshold into what would have been the entryway. Huge charred timbers and planking, remains of the roof and flooring, had been pulled aside and stacked along the sides of the walls and the ground beneath, where the wooden floor had been, thoroughly spaded up to the pilings. Whoever did it, he thought, had, literally, left no stone unturned. And they'd done it recently, the aroma of the place that of freshly turned soil. He walked from room to room, crunching clods of dirt beneath his boots, and saw the same, the same when he peered through the gutted windows, then the thought hit him. They didn't find what they were looking for. If they had, they'd have stopped when they found it. From the back of the ruined mansion he called to Edgardo and

Juan who were further out in what looked to have once been gardens and they hurried back.Somebody helped us out, he said to Edgardo. They've done our digging for us and didn't find anything. That means we gotta look somewhere else, then translated for Juan who shook his head in agreement at the conclusion.

Pero donde? Juan said.

Jo Shelby looked around. There was no ceiling. No floor, which meant no trap doors leading to a secret compartment or basement. If there had been it would've already been dug up leaving a crater or cavity and he saw no evidence of one. The outer walls were two feet thick and made of brick and mortar and the main interior walls and those around the rectangular court-yard a foot in width and made of cinder blocks smoothened over with cement and painted white. Nothing would be in the outer walls. They looked too solid. He'd heard of Mexicans who built their homes with con-crete blocks and left intentional gaps they'd use for windows and ledges, cubbyholes. He sounded the idea out with Edgardo and Juan and both agreed. Juan had done it in his home and Edgardo confirmed his relatives had as well. It was a long shot. No other options came to him. They couldn't come all that distance and turn around without doing something.

Jo Shelby walked back to the truck, cranked it and pulled it closer to the house, up to the porch. The workers from La Joya retrieved seven shovels and five pickaxes from the bed.

What about the guns? Edgardo said to Jo Shelby. You think it is danger-ous?

Jo Shelby scanned the surrounding countryside. They were in a small valley surrounded by nearby low hills, a few trees on hills further away. Noth-ing back down the only road toward the main highway. Flat as a pancake. He saw no other way in or out. I'd say leave the guns in the truck but take two rifles. There ain't but five picks so somebody can stand guard. We might be here a while.

Mid-afternoon they'd whacked through two walls and found nothing and Jo Shelby called for a break. They hunkered down in what he guessed was probably a dining room, a larger room adjacent it on the back of the kitchen.

This is gonna take longer than I thought, he said in Spanish and the men validated his thought and shared their own about the length of time it would take, probably into the night they all agreed, their heads bobbing unanimously.

They had four flashlights now, he told them, with fresh batteries the señora had supplied so they could work on in the dark and the bobbing heads stopped. He saw immediately the displeasure on their faces. Pero no mucho, he said, and the men grinned and their heads began nodding again.

They returned to chopping at the walls while two of the men from La Joya stood guard with the rifles, one at the front and one at the rear. They worked on till the sun began setting and the men began grumbling they were hungry. Jo Shelby hadn't thought about food in so long he'd forgotten what hungry was. Edgardo and Juan weren't complaining but if the others weren't happy they'd slow down and eventually quit.

He sent one of the men to the truck to retrieved the sandwiches the señora had prepared for them along with some bottle drinks they'd purchased at a tienda in Michapa. The two men who'd rotated on as sentinels propped their rifles against a front wall and they all sat around the hearth of one of the fireplaces, in the deepening shadows of a large front room that had probably been the mansion's salón. As he ate Jo Shelby's eyes took in the ruined room, the rosey shifting hues the rays of the setting sun tinted its walls yet to be demolished and he contemplated all that remained of the elegance and splendor once sheltered there, the polished mahogony and cherry and walnut furniture, brocaded couches and chairs, crystal candelabras and silver fixtures and carved chests and ceramic vases filled with colorful flowers, oriental rugs draping the walls, people sitting amid it all drinking tea or coffee and talking about their good life. And he thought of another land in another time and all its elegance and splendor and another civil war and a movie he saw at the picture show in Drew called *Gone with the Wind* and he thought how worlds could come and go, vanish that violently and quickly when a people's lands were threatened or taken from them, that it was land that spun the world on its axis and the other word for the spinning was ... revolution. In that detached attitude of reflection he was eating and thinking and set his Coca-Cola bottle, that had been on the ground, down on the hearth in front of the fireplace opening and the hollow *thunk* that echoed off the blighted walls stopped every masticating mouth and raised every head. All eyes fixed on him. He lifted the bottle and set it down again and again the dull vacant sound resonated in the dusky air.

If that aint somethin, Jo Shelby said.

He removed the bottle and got up. Wordless, the others rose with him and in concert, as if a common unspeakable wisdom suddenly permeated the place, placed their hands alongside his beneath the edges of the large slate slab. Stuck hard in its old cement the piece, at first, would not budge. The men grunted and groaned and and heaved hard and eventually the entablature broke free and began slowly rising until it was perpendicular the hearth and they were gaping into a dark rhomboid hole, breathing in a dank and fetid stench.

Liberate, Jo Shelby said.

They let go the slab and it fell backward onto the hearth shattering in smaller pieces.

Es posible una tumba, Juan said.

Posible, Jo Shelby said. Vaya por una linterna.

Edgardo ran quickly to the truck and back with a flashlight and gave it to Jo Shelby. He flipped on the switch and shined the beam into the hole and its narrow cone of light scoped out the top of a large square object about two feet in dimension embedded as many feet down in damp mud and silt.

What is it? Edgardo said.

Dunno, Jo Shelby said. We gotta tear this hearth up to get to it. He looked back over his shoulder and told the men to get the pickaxes. Five could not work at one time around the small space so Jo Shelby and Juan hammered away, cracking and breaking and throwing aside slabs of slate until they were down to ground level and able to let the others get in with shovels.

It was almost dark now and they were working by flashlights, rotating them to save the batteries. Jo Shelby stood by and watched as spadeful by spadeful of dirt came flying out and the shape of the bulk more and more revealed then one of the shovels hit something that made a pinging sound and Jo Shelby shouted they stop. He climbed down into the hole and felt where the contact was made, scraped away the stagnated dirt with his hands and in a beam of light uncovered a dial then uttered in a loud whisper, it's a safe, una caja de cuadales.

Una caja de cuadales, the men passed the word along in their mummured excitement and he pulled himself out of the hole and they kept digging. Anticipation rose inside of him and he grew anxious just standing and waiting. More of the hearth had to be pulled up and torn away for them to shovel behind the safe and it took almost an hour of excavation before four of them could lift it out and onto the ground.

Jo Shelby reached into his jeans pocket and pulled out a piece of paper he'd transferred the numbers to and asked Edgardo to shine the light on him. Everyone stood and watched. Time would only tell if this was just another abandoned safe or if it was *the* safe. Using the dots as forward and backward indicators he deftly turned the rusty dial, first one way then another, stopping at the numbers on the sheet, working the sequence down to the last then pushing down on the steel handle and nothing happened. He'd guessed a dot over a number meant a right turn and one on the bottom a left but he figured he'd guessed wrong and reversed the logic and this time he heard the click behind the dial and the safe popped open when he pushed the handle.

Bueno, Juan whispered, a wide grin on his face in the dim light.

Fantastico, Edgardo said.

Jo Shelby was speechless. He felt as he did months before standing over his family trunk before he unloaded it piece by piece and found the letters that brought him to where he was, his heart pounding, a feeling rushing through him that he was in the presence of something sacred, something that when opened could hurt him or heal him or both and he needed to know which, even if it hurt.

The heavy door squawked on its ancient hinges as he pulled it open. A handful of silver coins spilled out and a gasp went up from the men leaning over and looking in, the bulge of their eyes glistening in the reflected light. Jo Shelby took a flashlight from Edgardo and shined it inside. Taking up the bottom of the old cubicle were stacks of frayed papers curled and browned along their edges and on top of them bundles of money tied with string and on top of those sacks of coins that had split over time, their contents shaken out and scattered with the jostling of the safe as it was moved. He picked up one of the coins and shined a light on it and saw what he did not want to see, a Spanish inscription. He reached in and picked up one of the bales of money, a brighter sight hitting his eyes.

Hot damn, he said loudly, the shout echoing off the walls still standing and resonating up the chimney flue.

What is it? Edgardo said.

Confederate hun'red-dollar bills. They couldn't get rid of em so they stashed em, thinking they might use them later. A Mexican wouldn't save em.

Quickly, he unloaded the bags and money bales and worked his way down to the papers hoping most would be in English but the first was in Spanish, a small square white sheet that looked to be of little value. He was about to lay it aside as inconsequential but something caught his eye and he drew the light closer. There was a bank's name at the top, Banco de Londres de México, and a column of numbers along the right margin side totaling $500,000 at the bottom. The date was 6 junio 1910. It was a withdrawal receipt, in pesos. He didn't know the amount then in American dollars but at the current exchange rate it would be about fifty thousand. It could have been withdrawn by a Mexican but he remembered what he'd been told about Confederados having problems with Mexican banks and a scenario began to take shape in his thinking. In 1910 the colonel had long been dead but his daughter had married don Roderigo's son and his three sons, who would also have still been alive, would have been allowed to remain on the hacienda, as other Americans he'd read about in the university library on his first visit to the country. They'd reportedly fled to the four corners and what he was looking at was what they couldn't take with them, probably stashed in the safe along with the Confederate bank notes they couldn't spend then but might return and recover later and all of it in a safe probably hidden hours before they heard Zapata was headed their way. That would have been about the time he was on his tear. He handed the paper to Juan and shared his conjecture.

Juan turned the flashlight he was holding onto the note and examined it. Es possible, he said, his expression grim. Es muy possible, and he passed the slip of paper on to Edgardo who looked at it and nodded agreement.

Jo Shelby continued sifting through the papers, removing them one by one, drawing the light close to each and to each rendering the same meticulous scrutiny before setting them aside in that same sequential order beneath the curious and inquisitive faces hovering over him. To his disappointment all the documents were in Spanish and of no significance—Sales receipts, promissory notes, stock and bond certificates, family letters but no names he recognized. He came across some old deeds and titles and proof of sales he examined carefully but they all pertained to land in that country and not another, not his own. Midway down the stack he uncovered some birth and marriage certificates, one of the latter that froze his hand mid air: Fernando Alonzo Cruze Linares y Carolina Suzanna Ferguson se casaban el 9 de Junio, 1870. The next almost caused him to drop the light he was holding, the old colonel's death certificate, establishing without question his passing on April 2, 1882, just like it said on his tombstone.

Son of a gun, he said.

What is it? Edgardo said.

The colonel's death certificate. He died in 1882. His daughter married the don's son in 1870. By 1910 they would have had kids, may have even been grandparents by then. They were prob'ly living here then, her brothers, too, when Zapata came through. He looked up at Juan when he said the name and Juan looked away.

He continued rummaging, his hopes buoyed by these discoveries. He was not disappointed. As though the marriage certificate of his great-great-grandmother were some property line of demarcation, everything else he touched was in English, including two old letters from Foster, one dated 28 August 1866, in response to his great-grandmama Caroline's last letter. His hand still shaking with the discovery and in unsteady light provided by others who leaned in close, as though they had a stake in it, too, he read it, his eyes confirming what before he'd only previously speculated. There *was* a missing letter regarding the will and its location. As if they'd grown too heavy in his hands, he lowered the pages and laid them on the top of the safe and tried to collect his thoughts.

Qué pasó, Juan said.

Las cartas son muy antinguas ... de mi familia.

How old? Edgardo said.

Jo Shelby handed him the first page of one and pointed at the date.

That is very old, Edgardo said.

They been in this safe long before it was tucked away.

Tucked away?

Hidden, he said and reached in and pulled out a leather pouch wrapped tightly and tied with a single leather cord. He set the light down beside the letters and began working the knot with his fingers. He picked one side loose with fingers that still trembled in the light then pulled the straps free their entanglement. He flipped the flap back and reached a hand inside the packet and pulled out three sets of paper, all neatly folded along even lines. He opened the first set and had to look twice at what he saw, at the top of the page in large handwritten script, THE LAST WILL AND TESTAMENT OF TAYLOR FERGUSON. Not bothering to read further he quickly opened the second creased collection: THE LAST WILL AND TESTAMENT OF JONATHAN FERGUSON. Different name, different handwriting. His heart was beating in his hands as he opened the last and the words, like a gift of grace rising from an altar, met his eyes and he saw the similar official phraseology, written not in a time of youth or early manhood but much further along in years, the leaning script awkward and tortured and near illegible but the name, in the same painful and afflicted style, as unmistakable as the clear beam of light upon it: CALVIN TYSON FERGUSON.

For a moment his breathing stopped and his eyes locked, unable to move further down the page. Then he breathed again and whispered, this is it, and again, louder, this is it. Then he stood up and lifted the paper into the air and shouted, hotdamnamighty, THIS IS *IT*. The men around him cheered, all but Edgardo and Juan unsure why, just that there was a celebration and they should join in. He calmed himself down to read the contents, but when he put the light back on the pages a voice called out from the dark behind.

Believe you got something there, Jo Boy, that belongs to us.

He knew the voice and turned in hopes it was one hallucinated from the ecstasy and rapture of discovery but there, standing inside the entrance holding pistols stood Josh and Jake and someone else in the shadows behind them he could not make out until Juan and Edgar threw light on them and he saw who it was.

Athen? What the hell?

To borrow a phrase, Jo Shelby, it's a long story.

One we don't have time for her to tell, Jake said, then he took a step forward and pushed his pistol further in front of him. A pair of binoculars hanging around his neck told a story. They were the ones who dug up the place and had been perched on a hill nearby just waiting.

All we want is that paper you got in your hand there, Josh said and stepped even with his brother.

Jo Shelby looked down at the papers he was holding then back at the two brothers. He looked around to see where the guns were and spotted the two rifles against the wall behind the three visitors. Y'all were the ones who plowed this place up, he said.

We aint sayin we did and aint saying we didn't, Jake said.

He wasn't getting anywhere with them. Athen, I can't believe you'd join up with them. Why?

That's the long story she aint got time to tell, Jo Boy, Jake said.

How'd you even know we were here? Jo Shelby said.

We've had our eye on you, now hand over them documents, Josh said and both stepped closer. Edgardo's and Juan's flashlight beams moved with them leaving Athen further back in the shadows and almost invisible.

You won't get away with this, Jo Shelby said. Six witnesses. Count em.

Six Mexican witnesses, Josh said. Who do you think'll believe a wetback witness north of the Rio Grand?

Seven, countin Athen, Jo Shelby said.

Nice try, Jake said, but blood runs thicker than water.

Athen was visible again behind them in the dim periphery of light. She was holding one of the Mexican's rifles and said in a sharp voice that cracked the air: Drop your guns Josh and Jake and don't turn around.

Jake moved to turn and she fired a shot into the ground at his feet and a clod exploded around his legs. You've forgotten I could kill more doves than the two of you put together.

The Mexicans were statues with marble eyes bulging out and Edgardo and Juan had automatically raised their hands. Jo Shelby didn't know what to say or do and an inner voice told him to keep his mouth shut and do nothing.

You wouldn't kill us, Sis, Josh said.

Your right. I wouldn't kill you. I'd just make sure you limped the rest of your life. On second thought, don't drop your guns, toss them gently toward Jo Shelby.

They stood, the guns still in their hands.

She fired again, this time at Josh, so close to his heel he began hopping.

The guns arced through the air and clunked on the ground in front of Jo Shelby. He walked forward and picked them up then back-peddaled to the safe and the group huddled around it. He handed one to Juan and steadied the other he was holding on the brothers.

The rifle perpendicular her waist and sidestepping one foot over the other, Athen moved slowly around her brothers until she was in front of them and beside Jo Shelby.

You lied to us, Sis, Jake cried out, his voice strained, whiny.

All I said was I was going with you, that I had a stake in it, too. And I did. She smiled at Jo Shelby but he didn't smile back. He still wasn't sure which way the wind was blowing, it was changing so fast then he saw the ring on her finger.

What're you gonna do with us? Josh said.

I know what I'd like to do with them, Jo Shelby said, recalling the night they hooded and tied him and dumped him in a Delta cotton field. Edgardo here, he's an attorney, Jo Shelby said thumbing over his shoulder. Maybe he's got an idea.

A look of surprised ignorance flew from Edgardo to Jo Shelby. I do not know about this situation, he said. Perhaps you tie them up, we take them to Cuernavaca to the police.

What's the charge? Josh said.

Highway robbery, Jo Shelby said, just like it was back home.

Attempted robbery, Edgardo said.

That's bullshit, Jake said. Y'all were the ones stealin.

Athen stood and watched, her gun barrel still on her brothers.

The name on this, Jo Shelby said, holding the will up with one hand, is Calvin Tyson Ferguson, my great-great-great-granddaddy. It belongs to me and my family and not to any other. It was in that safe—he pointed with the hand still holding the paper—that belonged to his daughter-in-laws and their offspring which are my blood kin. This land and this house are owned by somebody's government, doesn't matter which. They been sittin here idle and neglected for almost fifty years and there's something in our country called eminent domain which boils down to, if nobody else wants it, I can have it, especially if it's got my family name on it. How am I doin, Edgardo? and looked back at his friend.

Perfecto.

So, you got two options, Jo Shelby continued. You can get the hell out of here and never come back, cause if you do we'll prosecute. We got witnesses a Mexican judge and jury will believe, an American judge and jury would as well. Or you can sit down and let us tie you up and haul your butts into Cuernavaca. Take your pick.

The two men looked at each other. At Jo Shelby. At Athen. One turned then the other and they began walking toward the collapsed entryway.

We'll tell daddy about this, Josh turned and said then turned back around and continued walking.

Don't leave this out, Jo Shelby shouted, waving the will in his hand, but they had already melted into the dark.

The señora was waiting for them on the front porch. Seated in a rocker with her legs crossed and a robe clutched against her neck, she was barely visible in the shadows of first light and resembled a light blur an artist might have forgotten to paint over in the dark quadrant of a painting then she rose and ambled to the edge of the porch, her white robe tremulus, luminant in the silver dawn, as the truck pulled up to the fountain and everyone got out.

Thank God you are all safe, she said, her voice thin and raspy in the cool morning air.

Yessum, Jo Shelby said. We dropped the workers off in La Joya. Juan came back to take care of you. I gave them the day off tomorrow.

That is good, she said. Everyone needs to rest. She commenced coughing as Juan stepped up onto the porch. He put his arms around her and mumbled something inaudible to her. Her eyes flared and resisted but Jo Shelby heard the word doctor. He'd already tried and lost and wouldn't enter that fray. He hoped Juan won. The old woman was as stubborn as her pernicious cough but the cough was taking over. His only medical knowledge was the homespun lore handed down to him and the fragments he'd gotten from his Weekly Reader in school. He'd never heard the sounds of pneumonia but what he heard sounded like it came from deep in her chest, a heavy congestion she couldn't cough up and spit out, one that was beating her up when she tried, whipping her more than the congestion. He thought of the two of them standing there holding each other, of their divergent histories now reunited, the common bond they shared and how proud she would be of her son had she seen him in action, minus the charo clothes and silver buttons and silk scarf and Amozoqueña spurs but classic in every other sense of daring and bravery and honor ushered up by the remembrance of the name. He would not tell her, at least not now. He'd let Juan tell his own story, in his own way, the way his mother might tell it, brief strokes without all the bravado.

Their embrace completed the señora stepped again to the porch's edge and peered out, her eyes blinking rapidly, unbelieving. Is that Athen?

Yes ma'am, it is, Athen said.

Goodness gracious, girl, what happened to you? We've been worried sick.

Out of the blue dawn it came, as he'd heard it before, the old peculiar character of accent and idiom and dialect, surprised into sound once more as if shock of sight overrides speech and the new habit gives way to the old and original voice. *Goodness gracious … worried sick.* How many times had he heard his mother utter those phrases? How many times Athen's mother? How many times, Sissy, their maid? How many times the women of the South he'd grown up in? How many times he couldn't count and the reason he couldn't count them was the reason he still heard them, traces of that old world so embedded and a part of it that neither time nor generations nor culture nor geography nor foreign language could wipe them out.

We can tell you later, he said. Right now we all need to get some rest.

Edgardo, who'd been standing by quietly and listening, excused himself and headed for the front door.

Jo Shelby and Athen approached the señora and he showed her the will. We left the safe, he said, but we brought everything that was in it. There's some old money and silver coins and family papers in the truck. You can have the silver. The Confederate money is useless and probably only good for souvenirs. You'd be interested in the papers, though. I'll bring it all to you in the morning. Your eyes look like they might bite anything they were trying to read.

The señora chuckled. I do not know how to thank you, Jo Shelby. I say that not just for myself but for Juan, too.

Upon hearing his name Juan's head, which had been nodding sleepily over his mother's shoulder, jerked up. The señora apologized and translated for him and in his language he offered thanks to Jo Shelby. For his hard work and effort in helping his mother repair her hacienda and keep her land. For bringing them together so he could, once again, become the hacendado and take care of her health in her old age. For opening a door that would allow him to move his family soon from La Joya to the hacienda. For finally ridding them of Ricardo and allowing him to ride with Jo Shelby like a warrior of old and bring honor to his name though the name of the warrior was unspoken.

Jo Shelby listened and when he was through they embraced.

Tu eres mi amigo por la vida, Juan said and Jo Shelby responded, confirming the friendship for life.

The sky they faced was brilliant red and orange, Popocatépetl and the Sleeping Lady silhouetted dark against it. The moon was long gone, a washed-out beacon descending the opposite heaven. A cool breeze blew down from the sierras, one stirred by a rising sun yet to show itself. He'd pulled two chairs from his room onto the balcony and they sat side-by-side, finally alone, waiting for the other to speak.

Then he said, why did you come back?

The same reason the lady went to sleep, she said without emotion, looking not at him but straight ahead at the mountainscape. The same reason

Popo came back to wait for her. She raised her hand and as she did, as if orchestrated by the movement, the sun bulged brightly from behind the mountains, its first rays firing the thin silver band around a pale delicate finger. And this.

It wadn't just the ring.

No. But it helped. When you told me Josh and Jake were still there I couldn't leave.

Where'd you find them?

The centro in Cuernavaca is a small world, as you know. I began checking the restaurants, the bars. They were in the Bella Vista, of all places. I told them what had happened, that I'd broken off with you, which I had, thought I had. I was still angry at the time. They believed me. Part of me believed me. They'd been drinking a lot and began running off at the mouth. They'd rented a jeep and told me how'd they'd followed Carmen the day they saw her in the plaza, traced her along with us to the hacienda. They watched us with binoculars.

At the hacienda? he said.

Yes. Then they began tailing you, even followed the two of us at one point. They were behind you and Carmen that night.

He recalled the slow passing lights when they pulled over. But how did they know about the hacienda at Michapa? No one went there.

They knew about the will. You were not the first to read the letters.

There was at least one I never read.

Yes. I learned that, too. They thought at first, like you, the numbers were to a safe deposit box. The letter was partially destroyed and unclear. Your great-grandmother just said their family papers, in case something happened to them, were there and gave the numbers. She asked Foster to write them down and put them where he would remember, then destroy the letter.

But he didn't destroy the letter.

Apparently not. They were drunk and running their mouths, telling me everything. Mother found it along with the others. When she read it she handed it to my father who did destroy it after copying what he hoped he'd never need.

Foster wrote in the return letter, one in the safe I read, that he put the numbers in the gun because the gun had five serial numbers on it which would help him remember.

She reached over and laid a hand on his and sighed. That gun.

Yep. Good thing I hung on to it.

Good thing Carmen got it back for you, which strangely, was another reason I came back.

He looked at her but said nothing, safety in silence on that terrain where a simple Why? might blow up in his face.

After I cooled down I thought about why I reacted the way I did. I was threatened by her. She's a gorgeous lady. She looked at him. But she's not the lady for you, Jo Shelby. She could not leave her land and go home with you. She squeezed his hand. And I will, because it's our land.

He remembered another time on the balcony the year before, when he'd thought about why he had come and what he had found and what he'd left behind and if it was worth it all and he'd listened to the wind and murmur of the land that moonlit night and the voices of his ancestors that blew across the purple plain and the voices of others after him reminding him of the family he must seek first and what he must discard to find it, that a man of vision, a true romantic, cannot hold to his past. He remembered what he'd given up then, the family he'd traveled so far to find, so he could return to the one awaiting him back home which wasn't there when he got there, then was, then wasn't because of the land, now was again sitting beside him. He thought then about the land in Mexico and the one back home, that without families both were heartless deserts, that that was what life was all about, finding one's heart. And he lifted his eyes again to the mountains, from which his hope would come, as the scripture his mother had taught him said it would, and saw in the princess and her warrior lover against the bloodred sky the story he'd been told before, of strife and conflict, family against family, blood against blood and he knew then what it was he must give up. He got up from his chair and entered the bedroom. He retrieved the will from where it lay on the bed and returned to his chair and sat down and handed it to her.

What's this? she said.

The will, he said. I'm turnin it over to you.

She took it from him and kissed him and when he looked back at the mountains the lady was no longer sleeping but rising with the new born sun.

The End

EPILOGUE

Granddaddy, tell us how you and grandmama met. The twelve-year-old boy and his sister two years younger were sitting on the rug in front of the fireplace sifting through some old photographs they'd found in the attic. They had round brown faces and black hair and dark black eyes.

Jo Shelby grunted and pushed himself up from the large leather chair where he'd been napping. His wife sat next to him in a chair of similar size and design. She was reading and looked up at the question and they both winked at each other. He crossed the large room to a window and looked out, at the land prostrate and and depthless, at the cotton running white and gauzy all the way to the horizon like an inverted sky with the clouds on bottom.

We met out there, Calvin, he said.

Here? the girl said.

That's right, Caroline, her grandmother said.

When was it? Caroline said.

Athen laid her book on her lap and thought. I can't think of a time. We just grew up together.

Gosh, Calvin said. Mama and daddy sure didn't grow up together. Daddy met her in Mexico on a church trip.

Athen smiled. It was a mission trip from our church, she said. Your granddaddy paid for it. He'd been there before and knew a man who worked there.

That's when you went to Mexico, granddaddy, wasn't it?

Jo Shelby turned from the window and nodded. Hanging on the wall beside him, encased in a shadow box, was a pistol.

And that gun, granddaddy, tell us about the gun, his grandson said, his dark eyes flashing.

Her grandmother picked up her book again and glanced at him over the top. That's a long story, Calvin. Longer than this book I'm reading. Longer than any book you'll ever read.

That's pretty long, he said.

I know she said. It's that long, and she looked up and smiled at Jo Shelby still standing in front of the window and he looked at her and smiled back.

ACKNOWLEDGEMENTS

Michael Hartnett, dear friend and best-selling fellow author (*Generation Dementia, The Blue Rat, The Blue Gowanus, Windmill Bluff,* etc.) who painstakingly, and amid his own writing, read and edited the first manuscript and several versions that followed. A mainstream publisher would do well to hire him. His talent is worth gold ... no ... platinum. But there is another touch to this story. Perhaps another reason for his intense focus. He, and his wife, Amy, were married in Cuernevaca.

Josefina Rayburn, my Spanish teacher, who reviewed the final manuscript for corrections of Spanish, and read and edited the final revisions. She was also most helpful in assisting my navigation of the complex genealogical issues on both the American and Mexican sides of the families.

Brian Hargett of the Lee County Library, reference librarian *extraordinaire,* continued, with great efficiency, to respond to every request.

Reagan and Winna Rothe and their Black Rose Writing staff for their continued support and willingness to take on the series project and their assistance in editing, cover design and promotion.

Jan Cobb, prominent artist and my map maker, for artistically producing another map better than the first one in the first 2002 edition. Thanks again, Jan, for providing maps for other books—*The Lost Page, The Lost Gospel* and the future publication of *The Lost Years.*

Sandi Morris, for applying again her former English teaching editorial skills and providing daily encouragement.

And thanks to my indispensable readers:

George Dent, Peggy Webb, Francis Sheffield, W. O. "Bill" Rutledge III and those who are deceased: Phyllis Harper, David Sparks, David White, Gerald Walton, Beth and Henry Brevard, Bruce Smith, Betty

Harrington, Martha Francis Allen, Francis Patterson, Bowen Burt, Cliff and Berylyn Davis, Larry Brown and Barry Hannah.

Lastly, to my late mother, Joan F. Morris, a strong and proud Ferguson; and my late father, William Edward Morris, good and unpretentious man from whom I continue to drew inspiration for the character of Jo Shelby Ferguson and the heroes in other novels. Thank you, Dad.

ABOUT THE AUTHOR

Joe Edd Morris is the author of novels that include *Land Where My Fathers Died, Inherit the Land, The Prison, Torched: Summer of '64, The Lost Page and The Lost Gospel. Land Where My Fathers Died* and *The Prison*, were awarded Best Fiction of 2002 and 2020 respectively by the Mississippi Library Association. Joe Edd's non-fiction include *Ten Things I Wish Jesus Hadn't Said.* His short fiction has appeared in multiple literary journals with a nomination for the Pushcart Prize. Joe Edd is a psychologist and retired United Methodist minister. He and his wife, Sandi, live in Tupelo, MS where he has a psychology practice and enjoys, besides writing, gardening, playing the piano and traveling to places where the road ends.

OTHER TITLES BY JOE EDD MORRIS

FICTION

Land Where My Fathers Died

Inherit the Land

The Prison

Torched: Summer of '64

The Lost Page

The Lost Gospel

The Devil Walks at Midnight

NON-FICTION

Ten Things I Wish Jesus Hadn't Said

Old Testament Stories: What Do They Say Today?

New Testament Stories: What Do They Say Today?

Revival of the Gnostic Heresy: Fundamentalism

The Christian Right: Neither Christian Nor Right

Jury Selection in Mississippi: A Systematic Approach

NOTE FROM JOE EDD MORRIS

Word-of-mouth is crucial for any author to succeed. If you enjoyed *The Will*, please leave a review online—anywhere you are able. Even if it's just a sentence or two. It would make all the difference and would be very much appreciated.

Thanks!
Joe Edd Morris